Happy Birthday Fellow Bookworm —
Katie Lynne
love from
Tutu

Kirtland

Kirtland

A Novel of Courage and Romance

SUSAN EVANS McCLOUD

BOOKCRAFT

SALT LAKE CITY, UTAH

To my beloved daughter
Jennie Sandstrom
Her faith and courage
are a light in my life

Apart from historical figures who appear briefly
and with whom the author has taken the
literary license customary in a work of fiction,
all characters in this book are fictitious,
and any resemblance to actual persons,
living or dead, is purely coincidental.

Library of Congress Cataloging-in-Publication Data

McCloud, Susan Evans.
  Kirtland / Susan Evans McCloud.
    p. cm.
  ISBN 1-57345-850-3
    1. Mormon women—Fiction. I. Title.

PS3563.A26176 K57 2000
813'.54—dc21

00-044493

Printed in the United States of America   42316-6741

10   9   8   7   6   5   4   3   2

Characters

Esther Parke Thorn

Husband:	Eugene Thorn
Brother:	Jonathan
Sister:	Josephine, called Josie, married to Randolph Swift
Daughter:	Lavinia
Son:	Nathaniel, named for Jonathan's twin, who died at birth

Georgeanna "Georgie" Sexton Hopkins

Husband:	Nathan Hopkins
Daughter:	Emmeline, died in infancy
Twins:	Josephine and Lucy
Brother:	Jack, courts Aurelia then Emmeline

Theodora "Tillie" Swift Whittier

Husband:	Gerard Whittier
Brothers:	Randolph (Josie's husband)
	Peter
Sister:	Latisha
Son:	Edward Lawrence, called Laurie
Daughter:	May

Phoebe Sumsion Turner

Husband:	Simon Turner
Stepdaughter:	Esther
Son:	Simon Jonah

Chapter One

Another May Day. I find myself in a new place, where everything is changed and different; even myself. Earlier this morning the day appeared promising, with nothing more than a cool breeze blowing in from the lake. Now the wind has risen. The grasses bend to it, and the high arms of the giant horse chestnut trees flail against the cold blast shuddering through them. I shudder, too, in anticipation and perhaps with a small sensation of fear.

Not hesitation, but more like a sense of awkwardness and wonder. I am twenty-five years old, I have a two-year-old daughter, and I have left home and family and everything I ever loved since I can remember so that in a few moments I might wade down into the chilly waters of the Chagrin River to be baptized. Immersed. I was not immersed as a child or a baby; I have never experienced anything like this in my life. I look to find Eugene, standing near enough to the edge that the water laps over his feet. Georgie smiles and hugs her arms to her body the way we did when we were young. Suddenly I am back in Palmyra, and we girls, all five of us, are dressed in the shimmering linen-soft gowns of Phoebe's creation. Because of Phoebe we know that we are the best-dressed girls there. The boys glance at us in open admiration. Tillie giggles and Josephine preens. Phoebe and I turn sideways and pretend not to notice, but our faces are shining. And the Maypole waits—almost seems to shimmer in anticipation—its long streamers flowing in splashes of color as brilliant as new spring blossoms.

"Esther—"

With a start I come back to reality, to the small group huddled beneath the wide chestnut tree. I return Georgie's smile, but I know that my mouth is trembling. Peter and Jack are here. They, too, belong to those May days when all was gaiety and nonsense and high, bright hopes. I recall the hopes with which Peter and his brother went forth

1

to work on the canal; the unknowing, untutored excitement and eagerness . . .

I see Bishop Whitney. He is dressed in white, for he is to perform the baptisms. He approaches Eugene and places a hand on his arm. Sister Whitney stands with a small knot of ladies, Brother Joseph's mother, Lucy Smith, among them. Both women turn and smile at me; gentle smiles of kindness and encouragement. The trembling inside me increases, and I realize that I want to do this more than I have ever wanted to do anything—even marry Eugene, even give birth to my daughter. This knowledge thrills through me with a sudden warmth and amazes me anew.

I walk with steady purpose toward the water's edge. Although the chill air reaches under my shift and the simple dress I am wearing, I no longer mind. I feel solemn, almost regal. I walk with my head up, and when my eyes meet Eugene's they are swimming with tears.

❧

2

Eugene goes first. He reaches for my hand, and our fingers entwine automatically, for no more than the space of a heartbeat, before he moves on. I wonder what my husband is thinking as Brother Whitney raises his arm above his head and speaks with quiet authority.

I think, *A year ago I would never have dreamed that this moment could happen.* Why, it has been little more than six months since I returned from my visit to Georgie in this place and discovered that my husband—who had forbidden me to touch it—had read Joseph Smith's Book of Mormon from cover to cover and was in his heart converted. This I had never expected. He had shown no previous interest, while I had. Perhaps if Georgeanna had not been so enthusiastically devoted to the new cause, if she had not virtually glowed when she spoke of that book—perhaps if I had not experienced that night outside my parents' house when Joseph Smith prayed for my young brother, and felt the gentleness and power of the young prophet's spirit for myself—

Who can say? Who can unravel the many interwoven threads that make up the tapestry of our desires, perceptions, and decisions? Was it somehow inevitable that I find myself here on the rich frontier lands of Ohio starting a new life, doing something brave, perhaps even extraordinary?

When it is my turn to step down into the water I catch my breath with the sharp coldness sweeping over and through me. My dress is sucked close to my body and becomes at once sodden and encumbering.

"Sister Esther Parke Thorn, having been commissioned of Jesus Christ . . ."

The words calm me. I feel alone with the words, with what is happening to me. I close my eyes and bend my knees and let the water close over me, encase me, cleanse me. As I emerge and gasp for air I see the blue of the sky far above, and the sky seems to go on forever. Alma's beautiful words come clearly to my remembrance: *And now behold, I say unto you, my brethren, if ye have experienced a change of heart, and if ye have felt to sing the song of redeeming love, I would ask, can ye feel so now?*

I feel that redeeming love like a song in my heart, like a prayer that touches all about me with a reverence and beauty, and I know, as surely as I breathe, that the heavens have opened—opened to me this day, and embraced and blessed me.

Someone drapes a warm dry blanket about my shoulders. Eugene wraps his arms around me. Four other people are baptized beside ourselves. There is a spirit of rejoicing among our little group and a reluctance to move, to break up the proceedings. Someone suggests a hymn, and so we sing. Beside the gentle curve of the river we raise our voices to God.

> Glory to God on high!
> Let heav'n and earth reply.
> Praise ye his name.
> His love and grace adore, . . .

I feel as if I have come home. The faces that smile upon me are faces that I can trust. This is a different sort of community; a community of men and women who are spiritually united, who share a commitment which ennobles and alters them . . .

> Let all the hosts above
> Join in one song of love, . . .

3

I am here, heaven help me. I am truly one of the Saints now. I have accepted the restored gospel of Jesus Christ, and I sense with some heaviness what this acceptance might mean. Lavinia reaches for me, and I take her from Georgie's arms. This will be the only life my daughter will ever know or remember. She will grow up learning the truth and being blessed by it.

After the hymn is finished the brethren place their hands on our heads, one by one, and confer the gift of the Holy Ghost upon us, confirming our baptism and our entrance into the kingdom. *Kingdom*. This is a word the Mormons take quite literally. We are part of a kingdom on earth, preparing ourselves for a higher kingdom of glory to come. We are acknowledging our true nature as sons and daughters of God.

As we disperse and begin to move away I notice something—someone—moving cautiously just at the edge of the clearing, well concealed by the dense scraggle of bushes just beginning to green and leaf out. *Who is spying on us?* The muscles of my stomach contract, and all my senses tense into an alertness that is almost painful. I can remember too well the scenes I witnessed back in Palmyra: the mob gathered outside Grandin Press, their faces pinched and ugly with the brutal emotions that were impelling them; cruel, angry men riding to the Smith home, hunting young Joseph through the dark, silent woods with nothing less than murder cankering their hearts and dulling their eyes. Even Georgie, sitting so placidly beside me, watched her house burn down around her head, her own father having a hand in the destructive mischief. This was all real. And there have been more than rumblings of the same kind of nightmare here.

So I keep glancing behind me as I walk toward the horses and wagons, but all that I see is a flash of blue calico, like a bit of sky turned upside down, a smudge against the nearly colorless bushes. And yellow hair, long yellow hair; I am sure of it. Nothing more. I take Eugene's hand and step into the wagon. I say nothing. Why say anything? What is there to say? Anyone could be watching us, for any number of reasons. I put the moment out of my mind and push back the damping fears it gave rise to. Fear has no place in a day like today. Faith is above fear, and so is the joy I have experienced. This realization strengthens me as I sit down beside my husband and reach for his hand.

4

❦

Kirtland swells daily, and there is no room for all the newcomers. But Georgie has found us a house; a double house, really. She and Nathan occupy a small room above one side; we occupy an identical room above the other. There is a very small connecting parlor in front and an equally small kitchen in back, which we share. The arrangement has worked out nicely, with surprisingly few upsets or adjustments. We have been here but a few weeks, though, and I am still struggling to establish some pattern that will fit this new life into which we have entered, trying to remember that, truly, we have been lucky thus far.

Eugene, though a writer and newspaper man by vocation, was well-trained in his father's blacksmith shop, and he has found work with Brother Frey, steady work, though not necessarily what he had wanted. And I have a garden to plant! On this afternoon, Eugene had gone back to the smithy and would not join us again until evening. And Nathan had returned to his school. Georgie and I sat on the narrow porch, with the baby at our feet, mending shirts and stockings, grateful to be out-of-doors, only hours away from the extraordinary events of the morning.

"As long as Esther can work every day with her hands in the soil, then nothing can make her unhappy." Georgie has always said that, even when we were girls. And, of course, she was right. I had completed my first sowing of peas and the most essential herbs, but now that the ground was softening I must begin in true earnest.

"We shall have food to eat at last!" Georgie chirped. For she is no good at growing things; she cannot even keep houseplants alive. "Esther will grow it, and I shall cook it up nicely."

A welcome arrangement. "You can grow cats," I reminded her. Looking about me I saw four full-grown felines, and how many kittens of various sizes and stages? At least thirteen. "We must discover homes for these as quickly as possible," I said. I found the number a bit overwhelming. Georgie only laughed.

"How many would you like to lay claim to?"

I grimaced a bit theatrically. "One for Lavinia—"

"And one for yourself."

"No, Eugene does not like cats the way we do." I leaned back into a patch of sunlight that had found its way through the heavy gray ceiling above us. I remembered the kitten my sister, Josephine, and I brought home for our baby brother, Jonathan. I remembered my mother's horrified reaction, her unreasonable fears concerning this precious child.

"I know you miss him, Esther, probably more than the others."

"How are you able to read my thoughts, Georgie?"

"Perhaps because I have known you since I was that size—" She nodded toward Lavinia, who was busy chasing a gray-striped kitten.

"Oh, Georgeanna," I sighed. "Twenty-five cents for postage is half a day's wages. I dare not write letters the way I wish to. But Phoebe's baby is due before the month's out. And how are we to know how she fares, and if the child is a boy, as she hopes it to be."

"We are *not* to know, dear." Georgie reached out to touch my arm lightly. "That is one of the changes, one of the conditions you must accept now."

I sighed.

"Are you sorry, Esther? Even a little?"

"Not sorry, no. I would not do differently if I had all the choices before me again. Only, it is more difficult than I had imagined—"

"Yes, for you it will be." Georgie's voice was low with the rich resonance of sympathy that so characterizes her. "Esther, you fuss and fret too much; you know what a mother hen you've always been." She leaned close and placed her hand over mine. "It is not up to you to make everything right for everybody—what a burden for you to take upon your shoulders, my dear."

My expression melted into one of reluctant acquiescence; we had had this discussion before. I rose. Lavinia had strayed too far in pursuit of her kitten, and I thought I would fetch her, then perhaps go in and start supper. So I was the first to see the child, thin and waiflike, approach from the side of the house.

Her hair, which should've been tidily braided, was a wild uncombed scraggle, like the mixed and woven shades of corn silk: dull gold, pale yellow, and matted brown. Her frock was blue—a faded, much mended blue calico.

I knew suddenly that it was she, this wisp of a girl, who had secreted herself to watch our proceedings down at the river's edge. I glanced toward Georgie for a cue. To me the girl was a stranger; but at the sight of her Georgeanna's kindly face broke into a smile.

"Emmeline, greetings! Has your mother said you may take home a kitten then?"

The way Georgie said *Emmeline* made the hairs on my arms rise. Emmeline was Georgie's daughter, dead as an infant, buried wide-eyed and speechless, a bud frozen before it had time to open. *Has this quiet, pale-eyed girl, digging her bare toes into the wet earth, in some odd manner replaced the lost child?*

"Not yet." Emmeline answered. "She's a hard 'un to crack."

Emmeline's voice was as thin and insubstantial as the rest of her, airless and colorless.

"Georgie—" I prompted.

Georgie's smile, as natural and unassuming as sunlight, enveloped both of us. "Emmy, this is my dear friend, my best friend, Esther. We have been friends since before we were your age."

Emmeline turned her large, cautious eyes in my direction. She neither blinked nor spoke, and I saw no expression at all.

"Esther, this is Miss Emmeline Lee, lately of Lynn, Massachusetts, but now a Kirtlander along with the rest of us."

I nodded and tried to speak brightly, for my friend's sake.

"Hello, and welcome. Have you and Georgie been long acquainted?"

I asked a question on purpose, that she might be forced to reply. She inclined her head, looking both reluctant and uncomfortable. And, before she could make her mind up, Georgie came to her rescue.

"Her family was here when I first arrived, Esther. But she and I met quite by accident, just a few weeks before you came."

Georgie surprised me; she is a teacher and knows better. *Why is she mollycoddling this youngster?*

Emmeline squirmed and of a sudden glanced over her shoulder. "He's coming!" she hissed. I had seen or heard nothing, but the child was obviously trembling and pale.

"Go round the back way, dear. I'll keep him here a few moments while—"

"You won't tell him I came?"

7

"No, of course not." Georgie's face had gone ashen, her lips a tight line. I seldom see her that way. I bit my own lip to keep from asking questions. And during the space of those few tense seconds the child was gone, dissolved into thin air as though she had never existed. And the tall man approaching us came closer and closer, his long face with a sagging horse jaw fixed in a scowl that made my insides cold. As he turned into the yard, I scooped up Lavinia into my arms and held her, squirming, against me.

"Has that weasel of a girl o' mine been wastin' her time here again, missus? I'll take a strap to 'er this time. Only thing that gets 'er attention." The man's voice, belying his loose-faced appearance, was as tight as a rope. When Georgie did not answer, he spat a jetty of tobacco juice at her feet, followed by a stream of oaths as foul as the brown, nasty liquid.

"I've new-made bread inside." Georgie smiled as though the man who confronted her was pleasant and congenial, and she enjoying herself!

I seethed as I watched her snatch one of the two loaves we had scrimped enough flour to put together, wrap it in a clean white cloth, and hand it over to the thin, loathsome man.

In his turn he said nothing, not a word or gesture of thanks or gratitude—no indication of friendliness. As he shuffled away I raised a quizzical eyebrow to Georgie, but she did not respond. Rather, she sank onto a low stair, buried her pretty face in her hands, and began to weep—quietly; Georgie was not one for a show of emotions. But her tears stung me like nettles.

I let go of the baby and sat down by her side. "Georgie, sweetie. I'm sorry, so sorry." I put my arm round her shoulders and smoothed back her dark hair.

"Her father *will* beat her, Esther. And I can do nothing about it."

A shudder passed over her body. I though of Peter and how harshly our Tillie's husband had dealt with him.

"Dearie," I crooned again. "I hate to watch you suffer this way."

She leaned her weight against my body as the tears quavered through her. My brave, uncomplaining Georgie, who has suffered untold trials on her own account—even to the destruction of her home, the rejection of her father, the loss of her only child. Prosaic Georgie, who can always view things from the larger, long-term perspective, and therefore take heart—this same Georgie who sat now, unraveled to the point of distraction by a little girl's pain—unable for the first time to reconcile herself to the cruel inequities of life.

Chapter Two

Kirtland: May 1833

A few days following my baptism I walked with the baby to Brother Whitney's. We live on Joseph Street, perhaps a mile and a half distant from the inns and stores that mark the center of town. The windows in our tiny house are so small and the glass so thin and of such a poor quality that upon looking out, I deemed the morning to be churlish and cloudy; I could not have been more wrong. The sun was a weak spring sun, but it shone merrily, with a delicious warmth that made me push Lavinia's cap back from her round cheeks and dawdle like a school girl beside the clear stream, which is no more than a trickling tributary of the Chagrin. We watched the miniature fish dart to and fro and dipped our hands into the cool liquid that seemed to be affording them such delight. We laughed at the butterflies that etched erratic patterns above our heads, dipping down like swallows to test the sweetness of the newly greening clover with the starry violets peeping through. I wondered if my mother had ever behaved this way with me, her first child. Surely she had not always been cautious, reticent, and immune to simple wonders and pleasures.

Brother Whitney's store was the first general store established in Kirtland, and it is a spot of particular enchantment. I half-closed my eyes as I entered the big warm room and drew in the smells of onion and potato, fresh cheeses, freshly canned preserves, licorice root, jars of spices, and a dozen or more odd herbs hanging in bunches from the rafters above—all blending in a manner most satisfactory. For a moment I let myself imagine what it would be like to select a bit of this and a bit of that, choose one of every item that caught my fancy, so that a delivery wagon would be needed to haul it all home!

Distracted by such reveries I nearly missed the tall man who crossed the room in a few long strides. But he paused and turned back to smile at me.

"Esther Parke, is it not?"

"Yes." The Prophet had recognized me, remembered me! "Though I am married and a mother now."

His smile relaxed into a tenderness I could feel. "A Palmyra boy?"

"Eugene Thorn. His father is in the—"

"Blacksmith trade. I know him." Joseph nodded, as though remembering something, perhaps many things. "And you were both baptized Wednesday last."

I nodded. He was moving toward me, stretching out his arm. "Welcome, Sister Thorn. I am glad your convictions have brought you here to be one of us."

His handshake was firm, but not smothering. The sincerity of his voice, the warmth of his presence seemed to vibrate the very air about him.

"I visited Alvin's grave before leaving and placed some flowers there." *Why had I said that?*

"Thank you, Esther," Brother Joseph replied simply. "Your little brother is buried nearby, isn't he?"

I nodded again.

"But it was most kind of you to remember Alvin one last time."

One last time. The words seemed like a death knell. But what else had he said? *I am glad your convictions have brought you here to be one of us.*

He was touching his hat to me when another gentleman spied him and drew him away. Joseph and Emma live in the rooms above the store. And, of course, everyone knows him, and everyone desires a word from him: counsel, advice, some little kindness, even a blessing, perhaps. He had blessed my brother; Joseph had saved the sick child's life with his prayer.

With reluctance I brought my attentions back to the immediate, the mundane. I turned to the counter to ask after thread and needles and a bunch of pennyroyal to sprinkle between the sheets against fleas.

11

❧

I found her walking home, though I wished it would have been Georgie. Georgie would have known what to say and just how much to do. She was sitting hunch-shouldered, with her knees drawn up to her chin, her head buried in her thin arms. She had been crying and was sniffling still.

"Emmeline—"

She looked up at the sound of my voice but shrank visibly when she saw that it was I, not her friend. I crouched down beside her, resisting the temptation to reach out and touch her. I am one who communicates at awkward times more easily with touch than with the spoken word.

"Let me help you," I said. "There must be something I can do to help."

Lavinia squirmed, so I gave her a bit of licorice bark to suck on and attempted to hold her on my bent knees. "Come," I said, willing my voice to be both patient and gentle. "You can tell me."

No response.

"Georgie would want you to tell me."

That was the truth. But the girl's eyes grew wide and her face contorted. "Would not! She'll never want to see *me* again!"

"You are wrong there," I replied with conviction. "Where our Georgie loves, she is fiercely devoted and loyal."

At my words the girl burst once more into tears, bitter tears that shook her slight body pathetically.

"Emmeline, tell me," I said, this time adopting a tone of distinct authority. And though she did not look up, she began to speak in gulps and jerks and frightened mutters.

"Threw it into the fire, he did."

Something about her tone, more than her statement, made me go cold inside. "Your father?"

"Caught me reading, you see. I thought it was safe—" Her voice rose to an unhappy wail. "I did all my chores and rocked the baby to sleep and even blacked his boots for him. But he didn't care. He knew it was her book, and he hates her, and he thinks she looks down on him, and—"

She could not go on. "So he snatched the book and threw it into the fire," I supplied, "just to let you know who is boss." I was trembling myself by now; injustice always undoes me. This time I reached out my arm and drew her close, so that Lavinia dribbled licorice-flavored saliva over both of us. It was the way the child had said *she* that disarmed me. I realized that to her Georgie was on a level above other humans: a champion who fought back the dragons of ugliness, shame, and fear; an enchantress who revealed beauties and wonders and possibilities this girl had never dreamt existed, and who held out them all—in her warm, ample arms—to her.

"She'll never trust me again, and I don't blame her! She won't want me near her—she'll never trust me, she'll hate me, the way I—"

"Hush, Emmeline!" I placed my finger against her lips. "You are speaking nonsense because you are afraid and miserable. But I can vouch for Georgie." I lowered my voice and my head so my lips were nearly touching her hair. "She will but love you all the more, child. Believe me, she understands."

Emmeline was too amazed to give way to tears again. She gazed up in stark wonder. She could not help but believe me, but she could not begin to imagine or understand.

"I will explain to Georgie," I assured her. "As precious as books are, they can be replaced. And we must find a way to get more to you."

The girl's head, her whole body, drooped. "Isn't possible. He'll see to that."

I laughed aloud, without meaning to. "He is not as clever as we are, child. For all his brusqueness, he's no match for us."

She did not know what to make of me. But I had surprised her out of her misery and allayed the terrible guilt and fear that had gripped her. "Give me a day," I said. I was thinking out loud a bit. "Emmeline, where do you live?"

She pointed. "In that meadow below the bluff, just beyond Sutter Road."

No more than half a mile from us. "What is the easiest time of the day or evening, child, for you to slip away?"

She shrugged her shoulders, the bones sticking out at odd angles,

13

the gesture as tired and hopeless as that of an old woman, worn and unraveled by life. "No time's good. And each day would be different, anyhow."

"Give me a day or two," I repeated. "Meet me, let us say, Friday evening, an hour or so after dark—at that little copse of elms, just past the road—"

I, too, pointed, and she nodded eagerly. "I know them," she said. "My father goes drinking Friday nights, so I ought to be able to get away."

"Good." I gave her shoulders a hug. I moved to rise and lifted myself and the baby up awkwardly. But Emmeline rose to her feet with the easy grace of a young fawn.

"Don't let your folks see that you have been crying," I cautioned.

"I'll cool my cheeks with the creek water."

She was moving away from me. "Do not forget Friday."

"I won't forget, ma'am." Even as she spoke she skittered away from me, like a frisky colt, like a young, frightened hare. Watching after her I realized that she had not in any way thanked me, as I had expected her to do in that impulsive way of children. Nor had she smiled. *No one has taught her polite manners,* I realized, *and no one has taught her joy.*

I waited until after the evening meal. The four of us ate together most nights, finding it much easier that way and much more provident. The men, having their own work to do, drifted out into the cool night. Georgie sat with a lapful of mending, and I tackled the unpleasant task of rubbing my brassware clean with a mixture of salt and vinegar. But I was grateful to have my hands busy when I broached this delicate and volatile subject.

As I had guessed, my description of the afternoon's scene distressed Georgeanna. She put her hand to her mouth, and the frustration of her suffering darkened her eyes. "It isn't right for such people to have children, tender, impressionable daughters when—" She stopped herself.

"I know, dear. I have already thought of it myself, you know, dozens of times."

Georgie turned large eyes upon me, childlike in their sincerity. "It is a cruel turn of fate that this girl has the same—the same name—as—"

"As your own Emmeline," I helped her.

"Yes." She was still holding her breath, her narrow chest rising and falling with the effort. "I would have cared for her anyway, you know. I believe I would have been drawn to her without this uncanny connection—"

"I believe you would have, Georgie," I agreed. And I spoke honestly. "I know your heart. And you are a teacher. You have been helping and encouraging youngsters for as long as I remember. And what is more, you found yourself by and large alone here, with precious little to practice your good services upon."

My words made her smile. Her eyes said, *What would I do without you, Esther?* And there was no need of words.

"We must turn our attentions and our energies to action," I encouraged her. Then I proceeded to outline my plan. She chewed on her thumb, her sewing idle in her lap, then shook her head slowly.

"That will not work, Esther, though it is so like you, romantic and impulsive."

"But we could hide books and other favors in that hollow trunk; that's why I thought the spot would be good. Surely the cavity is deep and protected enough—there is little chance others would happen upon them—"

Her fine brow puckered into a scowl. "*He* would find out, and it is not harm to the books that concerns me."

Another thought, a bold alternative was forming slowly at the back of my mind. "Brother Frey's wife has been ill these past weeks, and she has a new babe and half a dozen other children—"

"Three of them daughters in their teens capable of helping out."

"One would think so. But I know that Eden works at Bertha Walker's millinery for wages. And Eugene tells me that Elinor is ill, which means that Edith, being the youngest, has her hands full."

Georgie was listening; more than that, I could see that she was thinking hard.

"Emmeline's a good worker, did you not say so?"

"She looks frail as a willow wand, Esther, but her kind often has a

15

terrible endurance. Hard work would be pleasure if it came unmixed with cruelty."

I could feel my pulse quickening. Hope, to which I am so vulnerable, began its enticing flutterings. "They are a good, gentle people, the Freys. I believe we could appeal to them, could—"

Georgie was on her feet beside me. "It would be an answer to prayer, Esther!"

"Yes, dearie, I know." I looked into her pale, drawn face and smiled in encouragement. But there was time for no more, for we heard a shuffling at the door and the sound of laughter, loud and ringing.

"What are those men of ours up to?" I asked Georgie. But it was not Eugene and Nathan who stomped impatiently into our quiet chamber but Georgie's brother, Jack, and Tillie's brother, Peter, with something altogether different and unexpected on their young eager minds.

"We've come hat in hand," Jack began.

"Heart in throat, rather," Peter teased.

"The answer is yes, of course," Georgie replied, and they all laughed at my apparent confusion.

"Jack is going courting," Peter explained, "and you know we two share a hovel at the top of Brother Lamb's attic. Thus the lad needs some place, any place where he can sit and spoon with his sweetheart."

"We wouldn't impose," Jack stammered, "or make a nuisance of ourselves." His discomfort was all the more touching because it was so rare. "Saturday nights and Sunday afternoons would be more than sufficient—"

"I greatly doubt that," I said, with a wink. "But I am willing to do my part if Georgie is."

"By all means." Georgie's smile was a touching mixture of pride and relief. "I like this young woman of Jack's very much."

"She is not Jack's young woman, not yet!" Peter was enjoying himself too much to give quarter.

"Tell me about her," I said to Jack, and Peter moaned dramatically. Jack colored a little, but stoutly ignored his friend, unable to resist the temptation to talk about the lovely creature of whom he was enamored.

"Her folks both died when she was a child, and she was raised by two maiden aunts. She lives with them still."

"She?"

"Aurelia. Aurelia Martin."

"Ah! A musical name," I replied. "A favorite of mine."

"She is quite beautiful—"

"Of course."

"No, really!"

"She is that," Peter conceded. "A tiny bit of a thing with black hair and fair skin."

"Petite and ladylike," I mused.

"And an excellent seamstress. Sister Walker praises her work constantly."

"Can she cook? Has she a temper? Surely her nose must be too big, or her eyes too small."

Jack shrugged his shoulders, and a bit of the old gleam flickered in his eyes. "You could fault her in nothing, Esther. Nor will you, when you know her as well as I!"

I felt a sudden desire to sweep him into my arms and hug him fiercely. These boys were like my own brothers. I had watched them be born, fumble through the awkward years of childhood, and grow up. I had watched Peter stick out the hard life on the canal, then the hard life with his father, and endure the persecutions of his haughty, hypocritical brother-in-law. I had watched Jack's quick spirit separate truth from error, commit himself, and risk all, even life itself, for the sake of friendship and loyalty.

"I want to meet Miss Aurelia Martin," I said.

So it was arranged. The Sabbath was approaching. We would invite the girl to take supper with us, then discreetly leave the parlor to the two of them.

"We shall have our hands full," Georgie remarked after Jack and Peter had shuffled off again.

"Yes, I know. You shall want the place cleaned spic and span. So do I. And something extra special baked to impress Aurelia's dainty sensibilities."

She shook her head at me. "That, too," she conceded. "But I was thinking about—the other—"

"Emmeline. Yes, I'll speak to Eugene tonight and Brother Frey in the morning. So sleep well, will you, Georgie?"

17

"I shall try!"

The hour had crept beyond half past seven, but not by much. Georgie and I knelt together, with Lavinia at our feet. It was our hour of prayer, when we knew that, back home in Palmyra, Phoebe would be kneeling, too. So we were together, our spirits united in a very real way for these few moments as we raised our prayers and our longings to heaven, as we thought about one another, pleaded for one another, and shared even the small pleasures and events of the day. As well as actually praying, we talked to Phoebe almost as if she could hear us; and this night we told her all about Emmeline and our bold plan.

"We're making ready to meet Jack's sweetheart," I said. "But are you nourishing a new son at your breast, Phoebe, and are you well content?"

Georgeanna and I prayed that she was, that God would have mercy upon her because of her patient and guileless heart.

When I spoke to Eugene he was sympathetic enough, though he did not feel our same urgency. *That is part of the difference between men and women,* I remarked to myself. *Emotions, matters of the heart, do not press deep enough to disarm them. Except, perhaps, during courtship . . .*

"Esther, you stop this at once!" Eugene, who had been watching me, drew me into his arms. "You need diverting, lass, and I am just the fellow to do it." He kissed me once, then another time. I still go soft inside at the touch of him. "It is not your place to straighten out the whole world, Esther. Must I keep reminding you and reminding you of that?"

"Yes, I suppose you must," I sighed. "After all, it is good to do what we can for others, to lessen the burdens of life whenever we have opportunity."

"By all means." He pressed his warm lips against my forehead. "But to search for them, as for a needle in a haystack—that is quite another matter, my girl."

He was part teasing, part in earnest. But there was nothing harsh or truly critical in his manner.

"Sometimes," he whispered a bit fiercely with his lips against my throat, "I want you all to myself, Esther. Is that wrong?"

"It can't be!" I replied, with a shudder of pleasure. "I'll not take issue with it. Not now, not ever." There was a lump forming in my throat, and I thought with a sense of amazement, *The more my husband wants me, the happier I am. His desire, his admiration makes me feel whole.*

Perhaps I was wrong about men. Perhaps they *feel,* but merely express those feelings very differently. I should have to do some thinking on that.

Chapter Three

"It's the good wife whose go-ahead you'll need," Andrew Frey had told us two weeks ago. But the blacksmith's wife had not been difficult to win over.

"I've three daughters already," she had said. "But we can find room for one more, if Andrew believes it to be the right thing."

And this evening after meeting Emmeline at the copse of elms, Georgie and I had accompanied her to the cozy rooms above the smithy where the Frey family live: three daughters, two little boys, an infant, Sister Frey, and her bear of a husband, as large in bulk and statue, I'll warrant, as any three men. *How could there be room for Emmeline?*

When I said as much to Georgie she replied, "'Twill be better than the one room the child has been used to—one room with no furniture to speak of, and filthy as a pigsty, smelling of unwashed bodies and stale alcohol."

"You have seen it?" I asked.

"On one or two unhappy occasions." Georgie shuddered. But she was beaming now as she led Emmy by the hand into this family circle, which did not seem to consider one more mouth to feed an encumbrance.

"There's money in the trade," Eugene had assured me. "Brother Frey does quite well."

He *had* offered modest wages as well as room and board, but when Janet Frey had heard that the girl's father insisted the money be paid over directly to him, she bristled with indignation. "You make the wage as low as you dare and keep your respectable name, Andrew, and then we'll give Emmeline a small sum monthly for her own use."

And so it had been arranged. Now we were settling her in and bidding a fond farewell. She had two new aprons Georgie had made for her, as well as pen and paper with which to practice her numbers and letters and a book to read for pleasure when both her duties and her lessons were done.

"She'll never get to it," I predicted. "They won't mean to take advantage, Georgie, but I believe there is simply enough work here of a day to keep half a dozen extra hands busy."

"We shall see." Georgie was a bit smug. "The child enjoys learning, and she does not wish to disappoint me."

I held my peace, actually hoping that Georgie would prove right. But I believed the girl had her work cut out for her, especially since her father insisted that she return home every week's end. And I could not see the man relenting and letting her catch her breath, not even on the Sabbath.

"We shall have to wait and see how it all turns out." Georgie reached over and patted my hand. "Let it go for the present, Esther. We've done all that we can."

We walked home in companionable silence, and when we arrived, Nathan was waiting. He had picked up the post, and there was a letter from Josephine waiting for me.

21

❦

I read aloud to Georgie, savoring the thought that I could share it all again with Eugene when he came home from the School of Prophets meeting he was attending. There were surprises in the letter, and probably much more information than Phoebe would have thought to include.

> Phoebe has her son. All went well, and she is pleased as punch. I wish you could see him, Esther. He has straight dark hair and eyes as solemn as a preacher's. They are naming him Simon Jonah, and he shall go by Jonah. Is Simon content with his new son? For the first time since Emily died he is all smiles.

I glanced at Georgie with tears in my eyes. At least some of our prayers had been answered.

> You should be here, Esther, to rejoice with her, to fuss over her a little. Her folk are certainly not the fussing type, and Tillie refuses to see her—will not even speak when they pass on the street. It is nothing

but nonsense. I told Randolph he must do something with her, since she is his sister. "That is wishful thinking," he reminded me. "She is a married woman and has gone her own way, and I have no influence over her." More's the pity, I say. Oh, Randolph sends his love to you. He misses you dreadfully, Esther. Nearly as much as I. With no exaggeration I can truthfully say that not a day passes but what he is talking of you: dredging up old memories and wondering how you are doing, and if those Mormons are treating you right—

Georgie and I laughed. "Josie will never change," I sighed. "She still does not understand—refuses to understand that I, too, am one of those Mormons, and by my own choice."

"You might as well have been bewitched here, for all she cares to see! Yet you do miss Randolph, I know."

"I am as fond of him as I am of anyone," I admitted. "And I cannot help but worry, knowing my sister the way I do. He loves her, strange as it seems, and we can do nothing about that. But can she make him happy?"

"*Will* she?" Georgie squinted at me as she posed the hard question.

"He deserves to be happy. He deserves so much."

"What has that to do with the price of beans?" Georgie quipped, but not unkindly. I picked up the letter again. There followed a long, glowing catalog of the progress and accomplishments of "Josie's Boys," as we called the homeless lads who had worked the canals under rough, coarse conditions and now had found refuge and hope for the future with her.

We have four apprenticed out, three we are teaching here, and two who are preparing to continue their education in the city. Can you imagine that? We have tried to persuade Danny to leave us, but he will not. Which is good, since we need him. By now he does some of the teaching, since good teachers for causes such as ours are not easy to find!

"Will that indirect reference to teachers be her only word to me?" Georgie wondered aloud, her brow darkening a little. Not so long ago it had been all of us—no distinctions or separations, no petty grudges, no withholding of our affections. I know we both felt it more painfully than we cared to admit.

Mother and Father do well. They received your last letter safely. She never mentions your name, I fear. You know how Mother would rather forget and ignore anything that distresses her. But Father speaks of you often and wonders about the baby and how she must be changing and growing. Esther, it is not fair! You bring pain to everyone, and for no conceivable reason. You ought to see how Jonathan moons about for missing you. Why cannot you admit that you have made a mistake, and come home?

I did not look up and meet Georgie's eyes; I dared not, but bent my head and read on, gripping the paper so tightly that it creased under the pressure of my fingers.

I have saved the best until last, hoping this will move you, Esther. I am with child! It must have been there, growing within me, when you left us. As soon as we knew for certain, Randolph whooped with joy and raced about the room like a wild Indian. And now he is careful with me, and oh so tender. What have I done to deserve him? Nothing, I know you would say. But I love him to distraction. And he does not seem to tire of me. We act like children together, and any little pleasure can make us laugh with delight. This child grows well, and because it is his it must come full term and be born right. That is why you must be here, Esther! There is still time. You must come! You must see how much I need you! . . .

I groaned out loud and buried my head in my hands. Georgie moved quickly to drop down beside me. "I am so sorry, Esther. This is not fair of Josie—"

"Fair! Josie does not know what the word means. She never has." Her silence was loud assent. "I could not go if I wanted to. There is no money with which to travel, and I would not hazard the river during the hot summer months with Lavinia, nor would I leave her again behind—"

I felt Georgie tense. "Was it terrible when you left her . . . the other time . . ."

I lifted my head and looked straight into her dark troubled eyes. "No, it was not. Looking back, I can see that Heavenly Father must have helped me. I had no fear, neither for my daughter and my

23

husband, nor for myself. I *wanted* to be here, and I was somehow at peace within myself."

Georgie leaned her head against my knee. "We *have* been blessed, Esther."

"Yes, dearie, I know."

"And you are more dear to me than—"

"Yes." Somehow I did not want her to say it, to speak aloud of the schisms that life had cruelly driven between the five of us.

"I feel guilty, thinking about it, that I had you when I needed you, and Josie, for all her failings, shall not."

"She does not need me, not really." I spoke the words slowly, for they were painful to utter. "She has our mother, and Mother will see to her every need; Father, too, for that matter. She has her passel of boys, who will be delighted to do their part in helping her." I drew in my breath. "And she has Randolph, a good, devoted husband."

"You mean, she ought to be counting her blessings?"

"Yes. Yes! Why can Josephine never rejoice and be grateful? Why must her grasping soul desire to possess everything and everyone before she can be content?"

We sat silently together. There were no answers, only the pain we shared and our understanding of it and our terrible helplessness. And our conviction that nothing could be different, that we would never choose differently than we had chosen if we had it all to do over and over again.

I had been excited at the prospect of reading my letter to Eugene; now I held back. But he spied it on the bureau and was, naturally, eager for me to open it. I sat in his arms, on the one chair that we had moved into our bedroom for privacy. Lavinia slept in her trundle, and I was glad that at last we two were alone.

I had not meant to cry, but before I made it through the last part I was weeping, so he had to finish the rest for himself. He did so silently, then let the papers slide from his open hand to the floor.

"Esther, my sweet," he murmured, "cry if it helps you. But I hate to see your tears."

I buried my head against his shoulder, ashamed, trying to gulp back the burning in my throat and the swimming in my head. I could not have said precisely why I was crying, could not have untangled the dozen interweaving threads that wove the fabric of my misery. But Eugene was concerned only about one thing, and one thing alone.

"Do you wish it were different? Do you wish we had never opened a Book of Mormon, Esther?"

"No, Eugene. No, I do not."

"I feel I have brought you nothing but hardships since I married you, and that is not how I intended our marriage to be."

I smiled through my tears. His love was so real that I could nearly reach out and touch it, as I could touch his hand, his face, the long silken hairs of the mustache he was growing. That love, like the sun on ice, broke up the frozen blocks of fear and unhappiness within me.

"I am happy with you, Eugene," I said, and the very words worked further to loosen and dissolve my misery. "I do not regret any decision we have made together. I do not wish anything different—" I held my breath for a moment. "Do you?"

His face grew thoughtful and he did not answer at once. "Life here is not easy," he began, "but when I look back and remember how things were before, I realize how wonderful it is to have a purpose to every- thing and to work with men who care about the same things you care about and who care about you."

"I know what you mean!" I smiled as I wiped the last of my tears away, but his thoughts were sober still.

"Are you frightened, Esther, by the uncertainty and the persecu- tion?" I shook my head. "I worry for you, Esther, for us." He glanced at the sleeping infant. "I worry about providing for Lavinia, for keeping her safe."

"That is natural for a man," I soothed, "especially for a good man, whose devotions go deep."

He turned moist, grateful eyes on me. "But you do without so much, Esther—living like this! We have nothing compared to a year ago. I've dragged you out here, to the edge of civilization, to heaven knows—"

I pressed my finger against his lips to stop him. "Have you heard me complain?"

"You, complain?" I wanted to kiss him for the compassion and

25

regard behind those words. "Just because you are good and noble doesn't make all of this right."

"We know what we are doing, and we know why we are doing it." He was beginning to distress me. "Do not even say such things out loud. What would we be without the gospel? And what would we be without each other?"

His face softened at last. *Men are different; different things are important to them,* I thought. *A man considers that he must provide well for his family in order to feel good about himself.*

"You had the heart to recognize the truth, and the courage to follow it," I reminded him. "That makes you extraordinary, as far as I am concerned. You have given me something beyond price, Eugene. You have given me your love and your tenderness, and you have given me truth. All the other things can be added on—whenever." I waved my hand as if to dismiss them, and he caught up that hand and kissed it. Then he rose and carried me to the bed.

"I hope Lavinia is sleeping soundly," he whispered as he bent over me and gathered me gently into his arms.

❦

Nathan was wound up as tight and dark as a storm cloud as he burst into the house. "What's this?" he growled, and Nathan never growls. "Where's my tobacco, then, Georgie? Where have you hidden it?"

He grumbled as he made his way into the kitchen, opening drawers and lids, looking behind and underneath everything. Georgie threw me a quick, panicked look. "We're clean out, Nathan."

"I know that. I told you to buy more today when you went into town."

"Well, I did not."

"You forgot? How could you, Georgeanna! My one comfort!"

Georgie drew a deep breath for courage. "I didn't forget."

"Didn't forget? What is going on here, Georgie?" He lowered himself, still stiff as a board with anger, into the nearest chair.

"Tobacco's expensive; you know that, Nathan. And, it's not only the money. Remember what the Prophet said, what he has asked us to do."

Nathan blinked in disbelief. I felt my sympathy quicken; this would not be easy for him.

"The revelation they call the Word of Wisdom. The Lord is quite clear about the consumption and use of certain things, tobacco among them."

If truth be known, I enjoyed the smell of Nathan's pipe of an evening. I liked to watch him tap out the old tobacco and pack in the new, then see the fragrant smoke rising lazily into curls and wisps above his head. I believe it gives me a homey sense of peace and contentment.

"I understand the problems Brother Joseph has been having at the school of prophets, Georgie. But I don't chew and spit. What harm does it do to have a pleasant puffing on my pipe after a hard day? Can you tell me that, Georgie?"

He could not help defending himself. There were so many changes, so many challenges thrust at us daily and, in truth, I felt sorrier for the men. Many of them had had their very livelihoods snatched from them and were at loose ends here, unable to find sufficient work to support their families properly, and few doing work they knew or truly enjoyed. I knew it was hard for Nathan to teach part-time for a pittance, then spend the rest of his day doing field work. And Eugene, though he would not say so, itched for pen and paper and inked blocks of type, not the feel of a blacksmith's tools in his hands.

"'Tis not my saying or doing," Georgie answered gently. "You're as good a scholar as the best of them, Nathan. Read the revelation for yourself, then make up your mind about it."

Nathan gave his wife one long hard look, then rose with a sigh. "I'll do that, this minute. Do not hold supper for me." He walked wearily out of the room, bent with the new burden that had been placed on his shoulders.

"He'll rise to the occasion," I said.

Georgie was not so confident. "By and large he loves the doctrine, Esther, but he hates being told what to do."

I could not help smiling. "You have just described every man I have ever known," I said. And she could not help laughing a bit with me.

When Nathan returned after a couple of hours he said nothing about where he had been, what he might have learned, what he might

27

be thinking. Perhaps he would confide later to Georgie when they were alone.

We had saved a plate for him and offered good conversation to go along with it while he gulped down his food. Then he and Eugene went to see if the cow had broken out of her shed again. We share a cow with the Cutlers, who live down the road from us. But the arrangement has not been easy, for on the days they are contracted to care for her, the vital task is often neglected or poorly done. Yet on their milking days they are Johnny-on-the-spot, as the saying goes, and keep to themselves every last drop of the milk. And it is not uncommon for Patience or one of her sons to come a-borrowing or a-begging just a cup or two when it is our day. Nothing much we can do about it, but it can prove terribly irksome!

❧

The following morning we tackled another problem, one that was reaching crisis proportions: we had to find homes for Georgie's passel of kittens!

"Summer is nearly upon us," I reminded her. "In June you can scarcely give kittens away—by July you cannot *pay* people to take them."

Georgie laughed with her usual aplomb. "Not my kittens!" she said.

We put Georgie's boast to the test and set out, each with a basket over one arm, bright and cheerful as tinkers wandering with pleasure the long dusty roads. Widow Godfrey, who keeps a small herd of dairy cows and sells her fine, clean milk to a goodly number of satisfied customers, decided to take two.

"I've cream and plenty to direct a few squirts in their direction," she laughed, her plump face red and friendly. "And they'll keep the mice down."

Brother Barrett, who never married and has lived alone these fifty years or more, still makes the smartest, most fashionable shoes with the least leather of any shoemaker I've ever known. He took my favorite little female and was tickled to death at the prospect.

"You are a conniver by nature," I scolded Georgeanna. "Why, you make these poor folk feel as if you are doing them a favor to let them have one of your mischievous kittens, which will take over their lives, turn their households topsy-turvy, and eat them out of house and home."

"I am doing them a favor."

I laughed. "They believe it because you believe it!"

Before we were through we had lightened the weight of the baskets considerably and had but two kittens left.

"Let us drop in and see how Emmeline is doing before we go home," Georgie suggested.

I acquiesced, curious myself, for we had seen the girl only once since we had established her in the smithy's house.

It was late afternoon, and the sun was beginning to slant so that warm, lazy shadows formed across field and road. Emmeline herself opened the door and ushered us in as primly and properly as if she had been lady of the house. She then offered us chairs in a nearly spotless kitchen that had fresh curtains at the window, a scrubbed gleaming table, crocks of flour, sugar, rice, and beans neatly lined up and labeled, *and* at the moment smelled of fresh ginger cake.

29

"Emmeline does all the baking now," Janet Frey told us proudly. She sat propped by pillows on a daybed in the corner, with a basket of mending beside her. "There is nothing this child can't do," she continued. "And what she does, she does well."

I was astonished and tried to keep it from showing, but Georgie was clearly delighted and jumped up to hug the somewhat startled child to her. "I told you it would be a lucky day for you, Sister Frey, if you showed favor to this young one," she cried.

Everyone was delighted then, and we sat and ate slices of ginger cake and heard of each adventure, each triumph. And it was the most pleasant experience I had had in a good long while!

"She's organized the lot of us," Janet explained. "She and Edith rise first, care for the baby, and dress and feed the small boys. Not until then is Elinor roused, and the extra hours of sleep have been good for her; she is getting better at last. They pamper me shamelessly," she added. The expression on her face was beautiful to look upon. "Each day they divide the tasks according to their own tastes and preferences, spelling one another with the care of the children and the heavier work."

"What about Eden?" I could not resist asking.

"Eden works in town, you know. She has become one of Sister Walker's most skilled and valued seamstresses."

Why is it most women dote so shamelessly upon their eldest, be it son or daughter? I wondered, feeling a little stab of concern lest I might turn out like that. I dearly hoped not. Josephine was *my* mother's eldest, and I knew too well what it felt like to be second place, offered hand-me-downs, not only in clothing, but in matters of more account.

"I shall return Saturday to check over your lessons and assign you new ones," Georgie promised as we rose to leave.

"We've nearly finished the book, reading aloud."

I looked round to see a lean-faced and tidy Edith enter the room.

"Splendid!" Georgie crowed. "You need some sort of reward for your efforts." She spun about and fixed her gaze on me. "Did we leave those baskets on the porch, Esther? Do you suppose our darlings have run off and gotten themselves lost?"

"I suppose no such thing!"

Georgie ignored the touch of sarcasm in my tone and hurried out in search of her kittens. By the time I caught up with her, the decision making had become so anguished that Georgie was saying, with an air of kindly concession, "Keep both then! You can try them out for a day or two and discover your favorite, then give the other to your little friend Edith. What say you to that?"

All were content. We hugged Emmeline, backed away, waving three or four times, and returned home in the gentle shadows with our empty baskets swinging and our spirits well pleased.

"Just think how many people we have made happy this afternoon," Georgie chirped.

"Yes," I agreed, too reconciled to argue, even for the sake of pretense. "And the happiest among them Eugene and Nathan—at least until the next, inevitable batches start coming!"

Georgeanna grinned, and for a moment she looked like the girl she used to be, her dark eyes shining. And there was nothing in our lives more pressing, more important than to see her newest litter of kittens and fuss over the soft, furry bundles of pleasure—content to give our all to the moment and take all it had to offer. I should've liked to remember how to live in such simple wisdom again.

Chapter Four

Beginning this day, our lives have changed very suddenly and unexpectedly.

On Saturday, the 13th of the month, Brigham Young returned from his Canadian mission in company with some twenty or thirty Saints he had converted or worked with while there. Brother Brigham seems excited to be back in the city of Kirtland, back in the bosom of the Saints, enjoying the daily company of the Prophet. But there is very little work available in the city, and his converts are having difficulty finding ways in which to sustain themselves. Some have already gone on to Cleveland and Willoughby, non-Mormon towns. But Brigham, himself, refuses to join them, which is so like the man!

"I am not going anywhere to build up the Gentiles," he responded boldly, "but will stay here and seek the things that pertain to the kingdom of God."

I know this because I have been told it first person.

Today is the third Sunday that Jack has come to court his Aurelia in our front sitting room. Although we find it some inconvenience to be denied the use of the room for ourselves, the weather has been generally fine, and we four, with Lavinia hoisted on her father's broad shoulders, have walked for a while in the mild air before retiring to our small, private rooms. We harbor no concern for the welfare and propriety of the lovers, for Aurelia has come both times escorted by her proper and most serious aunts. Dorothy wears fine knitted shawls trimmed in lace and a lacy day cap over her graying curls. Helen is more austere; perhaps her spectacles add to that impression. Where Dorothy comes laden with knitting or tatting, Helen brings books and settles herself to read, with her spectacles pushed far down on her nose.

At first we had laughed at the uncomfortable prospect the two young people must face.

"If their love wins out after this," Eugene had maintained, "they will have well earned one another's company and companionship."

We all agreed. And they have taken it in good form. But what can a man say to his sweetheart when two pairs of curious ears are constantly tuned his way? Why, even we have had little opportunity to come to know the girl, for her protectors whisk her off as soon as the allotted hours are ended. She is certainly a pretty thing, as pretty as the two lads had claimed. I like the set of her head, the way in which she carries herself—not proud, but somehow noble and decided, self-assured. Yet she has a gentle, modest aspect that speaks of womanly qualities, those that would make her a good wife.

This particular afternoon we were determined to find some way to draw out the two aunts, but we were given no chance. Within minutes after the foursome had established itself, there came a bold knock on the door. Georgie and I were still in the kitchen, finishing up the last of the supper dishes. We called out for Nathan to answer it. A few moments later he came into the room, his face a study in perplexity and reluctance.

"What are we to do now, Esther?" Strangely, he turned to me with his question. Not so strangely after I learned its nature, for his countenance reminded me of those dark days when I had come to Kirtland to help him care for Georgie after the loss of their daughter, to coax her reluctant spirit and body back to life and health.

"Whatever is it, Nathan?" We pulled out a chair for him, but he would not sit down.

"A man and wife are at our door, in the front room this minute. They have come to ask our good offices, as they put it in their Canadian accents—"

His words, coupled with his actions, made an uncomfortable sensation creep over me.

"They are seeking our brotherly compassion—"

"For what, why?" Georgie was growing impatient. "What is it they require of us?"

"They require a place to live. There is hardly a thing available in the city, as well you know, and nothing they can afford. They wish to stay here, to follow Brother Brigham's example. And, until the man can find work—only a few weeks, it is hoped—they desire to live in our parlor, and perhaps even share the cooking facilities with us."

Nathan's face had gone pale by the end of his terse delivery. He licked his dry lips with his tongue but still remained standing. Georgie placed her hands on her hips, looked about the small kitchen, and laughed. "Why us? What made them choose us?"

Nathan shrugged his shoulders. "I have no idea at all."

"Where is Eugene? Has he met them? Is he out there?"

"He's in your room with Lavinia, I believe."

"What's to be done?" I looked at Georgie, and she looked at me. "It could not possibly work out," I stammered. "We're already crowded, already sharing—"

We stood in miserable silence for a few moments until we heard something like a scratching along the doorframe. "Georgie!" It was Jack, speaking in a hoarse whisper, even after he had pushed open the door and stepped in. "Will you go out and deal with these people? They have settled themselves in our chairs, while the aunts have the others, and they look as though nothing short of a tornado will dislodge them."

Despite myself, I grinned. His words had conjured a thought that tickled me. "One of us will be out directly. Why don't you take Aurelia by the hand, excuse yourselves politely, and step out of doors? There is a lovely walk if you turn south and go along that bank of willows and flowering honeysuckle."

He stared blankly for a moment until my meaning sank in. Then he planted a kiss on my cheek and disappeared even more quickly than he had come. We went back to staring disconcertedly at one another.

"Surely we can refuse them? Surely they will not expect us—" Georgie stopped herself mid-sentence and sank into a chair with a moan. "I am so selfish! If we are Saints, we must behave as such. It will be but a little while."

"Put on a brave face and go out to meet them, then?"

She nodded, but her teeth were clenched, and her eyes bright with a sort of panic, which I well understood.

"You slip back and let Eugene know what is going on," I told Nathan. "Georgie and I will go out."

I linked my arm through hers and drew a deep breath as we pushed open the kitchen door.

❦

Garrison and Gertrude Woods were not what my mind had been picturing during those first panicked moments. He was a man in his forties, she perhaps ten years younger; both as thin as rail posts; Brother Woods with no hair at all, and a pate so shiny one might have used it for a looking glass. But Gertrude had a wealth of brown hair twisted into huge, elaborate sausage rolls that seemed almost too heavy for her small head to bear. I expected her shoulders to sag and her thin neck to wobble every time she turned her head to talk or answer a question.

"Yes, we came with Brother Brigham," she beamed. "And we aim to follow him still, the way we've been doing since we heard him preach by the old stump at the fairgrounds. We've grown accustomed to it by now."

She probably thought herself clever and meant no harm. I smiled wanly. "Who sent you to us?" I asked bluntly and was taken aback by her reply.

"Why, the good smithy and his wife. They speak so highly of you! She said she knew of no women as Christian and caring as you two, and she knew you would understand and be moved by our plight."

I felt stunned, but Georgeanna burst out laughing. "It is our own faults," she cried, startling our visitors with her vivacity. "What a fine pickle our imaginations have gotten us into this time."

During the next half hour arrangements were made, arrangements as satisfactory as anything so entirely unsatisfactory can be! For the time being, our front parlor would become the Woods' bedroom; their sole habitation, save Sister Woods' invasion of—no, assistance in—our kitchen. She would bake bread if we wanted; no one made bread as light as Gertie's back home. She would help us on washing day, and Brother Woods would chop kindling and milk the cow for us of a morning before he went off looking for work. "A few weeks only!" was repeated so many times that I grew uncomfortable. I watched Eugene as much as I dared, trying to figure out what he was thinking of all this, but it was not easy to tell. When at last the two departed, pleased to the point of excitement and assuring us that they would be back first thing the following morning with their belongings and household effects, we were still not left to ourselves. The aunts, who had taken in the whole scene, sat blinking at us.

"The Lord will bless you," Helen said, as though she were pronouncing a sentence. I shuddered and, for the moment, avoided my husband's eyes.

"Our youngsters will not be pleased with this new arrangement," Dorothy cooed, wrapping up the sweater she was knitting and sticking it into her bag.

"Won't hurt them a bit. Denial is good for the soul," Helen assured us all.

"We will find some other way," I soothed. "Surely they deserve these few hours together each week."

"Deserve?" The eyeglasses went forward on the nose again as Helen peered sharply at me.

"Yes," I maintained stoutly. "There is little enough of joy in this mortal sojourn, you'll grant. And besides, the more truly they know one another the better when it comes to making the most important decision they will make in their lives."

I found myself close to tears at the end of this outburst. But Helen said nothing, and Dorothy Willis patted my arm. "Such a wise young woman," she muttered, "such wisdom in a girl of your age, my dear."

When she had shuffled out, Helen marching along beside her, we closed the door firmly. Nathan took a ladder-back chair and wedged it securely against the frame and the door jam, and at the gesture we burst into laughter, we were all so exhausted and relieved.

But it was with many misgivings that we looked forward to the morrow when our new tenants would descend and, well-intentioned though they were, turn our house topsy-turvy and rob us of the one precious commodity we had clung to through poverty and trials: our privacy.

Chapter Five

Kirtland: July 1833

I have always used my garden as a means of escape, but never before have I felt the need for it as I do now! It is not that Gertrude Woods is harsh, unkind, unfair, or difficult to deal with. She is simply next to impossible to be around!

She is so happy, so bubbling with energy and enthusiasm that half an hour in her company wears me out and sets my nerves on end. She is warm and sympathetic when she has time for it. But mostly she is a paragon of organization: she works with the steam of a canal boat, forever puffing, puffing, pressing forward. I believe she does not know how to hold still.

They have been unable to have children, so nothing has invaded this absolute order and control she wields over her domain. And now not only our parlor but our entire household has become that domain!

Georgie handles it better than I. "You are too much like her," she tells me, "and that is why you clash with her."

I am not flattered by the comparison. In truth, there is nothing Gertie leaves for us to do. And, in truth, once I am out from under the sight and sound of her, I find I do not mind it a bit.

I have never before had so much time to spend with Lavinia. We play some mornings for hours on end, not watching the clock for fear the bread is rising, the butter needs churning, the clothes wet down and folded for ironing—the dozen or more household tasks that pile up and around one another in such a pattern that they leave no time free at all. This is bliss! An unlooked-for advantage. And how my gardens do grow! My tomatoes are half a foot taller than anyone else's, with the hard balls of fruit already forming. Nathan and Eugene see to the potatoes, corn, and squash planted in the big field, but I have already had three crops of peas. I have beans of several varieties growing, lettuces, cabbages, onions. Close beyond what I call my kitchen garden I have my herbs—all my old favorites and half a dozen new ones: basil, angelica, chamomile, dill and fennel. Also parsley, sage, and rosemary, mint and lemon balm, tansy, and sweet cecily. The list goes on and on. Then further still, in their own patch of sunny soil where the houses give way to uncultivated prairie lands, I have an assortment of melons, rhubarb running as wild as it wants to, blackberries, blueberries, and grapes trained along a low stretch of rock wall. These days I find I have time to care for each plant almost to the point of fussing, and most mornings Lavinia accompanies me, both of us wetting our aprons halfway to our waists from the abundant dews that yet linger. We may not always have bread or meat in the house, but we shall eat in rich abundance once my fruit and vegetables really mature.

There is even a magnificent old apple tree at the end of our lane which I am making an effort at saving: paring away the crossed branches, pulling out the root suckers, and mulching the topsoil all the way out to the drip line. I must ask Eugene to make up some tar for me to fill the large rotten cavity that still weeps with shavings and insects and debris, like an open sore.

Evenings are the hard times. The men come home hot and tired, eager for our quiet company, a little relaxation and peace. To our horror Gertrude attempts to arrange parlor games for the six of us—an activity both men abhor. Nathan takes refuge behind his books, and Eugene escapes to the shed that serves as a barn, with a vague, mumbled explanation about some tool he needs to mend. But that keeps us apart from one another during those few hours which before were so jealously, deliciously ours! When I can stand it no longer I have the baby as an excuse, but Georgie's cats do not serve so well. I *am* one for privacy. I need my daily dose of scriptures, with a peppering of poetry thrown in for spice, and I need to jot and scribble in my journal now and again; my thoughts virtually itch to be recorded if I ignore them too long.

Gertrude is ever-present. And Garrison, when he comes home, unleashes a line of talk as endless and muddled as a fisherman's tackle box. There was never a town gossip born who could put anything over on him! We tire easily of such conversation. Only last night, as I sat unbraiding my hair and combing out the snarls, I asked Eugene if he did not think we four a bit snobbish in our attitudes and opinions. He laughed at me; he often laughs at me in his quiet, affectionate way.

"I do not know if I would describe us in that way, Esther. We have our likes and dislikes, our definite opinions and tastes. Always have."

"Yet, the four of us get along most famously."

"That is because three of us were raised in the same spot, in by and large the same way. And Nathan, the one outsider, shares several of our most passionate interests—not to mention the fact that he is in love with one of us."

"Sometimes I want my house back," I confided one evening.

"Sometimes! I don't even feel comfortable alone in our room anymore!"

⁂

Even our evening prayer ritual, which we share long-distance with Phoebe, has become difficult to effect. Always it seems, when that time comes round, Gertrude suggests something for us to do.

"If you'll hold this yarn for me, I'll roll it into balls this evening and get that out of the way." Or, "I told Sister Edwards to expect us at seven to help her get the quilt finished that the sisters started last week." And, "I've that buttermilk that will spoil before long. Would you like to fry up some donuts for those hungry men of ours?"

Gertrude's list of suggestions went on and on. Finally, when we had, through weak capitulation, missed two evenings of prayer in a row, I found myself speaking out without meaning to.

"Georgie and I have a set time every evening," I said, "when we offer a special prayer—for a certain friend of ours—" Once started I was not certain how to finish without telling more than I desired.

"Well, I never!" Gertrude fairly bristled, and her thick coif of hair seemed to rock back and forth as she shook her head at us. "God doesn't care what time you pray; it's the intent of the heart that matters."

I bit my lip against the retort that pressed to be spoken. Georgie saw my distress and stepped in.

"It's a special matter, difficult to explain," she began. Gertie stood unblinking and waiting. "There are five of us girls grew up in Palmyra together—"

"Palmyra! Where the Prophet Joseph went into the grove and prayed? Where the gospel came forth?"

"The very same," I replied. *Do you wish to hear our story or not?* I wanted very badly to say.

"You see—" Georgie was losing patience as well. "You see, we left one or two of the girls in troubled conditions, and we made a pact—"

Lavinia had toddled into the room, and Gertrude turned her back to us to lift the child into her arms and hold a bit of sweet maple candy up to her lips. *Enough is enough!* "Suffice it to say," I blurted in rather a loud voice, "we are not available, not for anything whatsoever, any evening of the week at the hour of seven-thirty, and that is that."

I felt like a spoiled child who had just said her piece a bit pertly and stamped her foot to emphasize it. Gertrude turned wide, innocent eyes on us.

"Do as you like. I am not one to intrude on other people's routines or pleasures. It seems a silly notion to me."

Half a dozen retorts trembled on my lips, but I did not trust myself to answer her. With as much calm as I could muster I took my daughter from her arms, turned, and walked through kitchen and parlor and to my own little room. Five minutes later Georgie followed. We knelt by the bed together and attempted to pray. But we felt miserable, irksome, out of tune altogether. Georgie suggested a hymn. We sang "Guide Us O Thou Great Jehovah" then "How Firm a Foundation." The words made a difference. I began to feel calm and softened, but not ashamed. When at last we were able to approach Deity with our requests, our feelings and longings, we found we could pray for Gertrude and Garrison Woods, too. We could feel compassion for them and be reconciled to their weaknesses, as we were to our own.

"You have not been alone with Jack these three weeks!" I said with dismay.

"And more! The aunts will not allow it."

"He is forbidden to come to your house?"

"Absolutely."

"According to what reasoning? Have they something against the lad?"

Aurelia sighed. Her eyes were dull and lusterless and beginning to fill with tears. "I believe they are afraid of losing me."

Ah, I thought. *Then we have something serious and rather delicate to deal with here.*

"Actually, they like Jack. He has charmed them both, but that only makes them resent him the more."

"How can that be?"

"Well, I believe if they felt they could dislike or find fault with him, discover him unworthy of me, then they would be justified in the stance they take and hopeful of winning out in the end."

I nodded. "Of course!" I pulled out my good handkerchief and handed it to the girl. "I am sorry for them, truly I am. But you have your life to live."

"I love Jack so much," she confided in a trembling voice. "I love him in a way I have only dreamed of but never truly believed could come true."

"He is a good lad and a true one," I agreed. "He will take good care of you," I assured her, "never treat you unkindly."

"And he will make every day interesting and full of beauty," she cried, "as he does now."

I am not that much older than this girl, I mused. *It was not so long ago when Eugene and I were miserable and unhappy because we could not yet wed, because we could not spend the days of our life together. Can I tell her, "I know what you are feeling," and will she believe my words?*

"I know you will understand," Aurelia said. "Jack has told me all about you and the other girls and the things that happened in Palmyra before you came here."

There was a warmth in her voice, a respect that touched me.

"He thinks you are quite wonderful, Esther. 'She has never disappointed me, never failed me—never failed any one of us,' he says, 'through the hardest of trials. We know she loves us, we know we can depend on her.'"

My head was swimming. This was high praise that made all my senses go light. "He is mine," I said, "as much as Georgie's. We all belong to one another."

I looked up to see her clear, hopeful eyes watching me. "And now," I continued, "because Jack loves you and because you love Jack, you are part of us, too."

Before I knew it she was in my arms, and I was soothing her, comforting her. She was sparrow-thin and delicate as a china doll to my touch. "I shall find some way, I promise." I kissed her high white forehead, taking in the faint, violet-clean smell of her young skin.

"I remember my mother holding me like this. Such an old, faraway memory."

I fought an urge to cry with her.

"Aurelia. That is a lovely name, and it fits you."

"It was my mother's name, too."

"You wear it well. I am sure your mother is pleased with you; she could not be otherwise."

At last the girl drew back reluctantly, blew her nose once more, smoothed her hair and the bodice of her dress. "Your kindness means everything. I cannot tell you—"

"You do not need to tell me. I understand."

I convinced her to stay for a while, and we spoke of mundane, pleasant matters and were content in each other's company. Half an hour later when Georgie came in we were whispering and giggling, talking a mile a minute, like old friends.

"Well met," she cried. "I am so glad you've come to us, Aurelia."

Georgie, my practical Georgie, I thought with relief, *would think of something to do.* Prompted by emotion I was ready to fly to extremes that would have been far from prudent. As Aurelia took her leave of us I watched after her departing figure. "Surely, a well-formed girl is as much a thing of beauty as a tree in the wind, or columbine against a wall, or a colt running long-legged across the field."

"Surely she is. Surely that one is," Georgie agreed.

Soon, I thought, with a sudden, aching sense of urgency. *We must get these two beautiful young people together soon.*

41

❧

Nathan was ill. He had come in from digging potatoes with a dry, hacking cough. By bedtime he had a fever, and his ears were burning and red. We doused him with a concoction of angelica for his throat, juice of the marigold drunk hot to help sweat out the fever, and insisted he go to bed early. By the morning he was ever so slightly improved.

"Keep him inside and quiet all day," I cautioned Georgie. She nodded solemnly. It is always a hard thing to look after a man who is ill. The state agrees so poorly with the natural, active state of men. Women are accustomed to quiet ways, days full of pain and patience and, like one of Georgie's cats, they usually know instinctively how to take care of themselves. Men, on the other hand, blunder about, awkward, uncomfortable, at wits' end—even frightened, if you ask me, by something they do not understand and cannot fight off with their accustomed weapons.

At the end of the day Nathan was no better than he had been at the beginning; indeed, his fever was rising again. "Get that woman out of here," he moaned in Georgie's ear, "and I shall be well in ten minutes!"

How we longed to accommodate him and do just that!

With a pinched face and a shaky hand Georgie pulled open a door of the big hutch dresser that had been moved into her room. From the depths she drew forth a small drawstring bag and held her hand out to Nathan, with the bag resting against her palm.

"What have you there?" he asked blurrily. "What in the devil!" he exclaimed as he recognized it. "Georgie—"

"I saved some," she said. "I'm sorry. I thought, just in case . . . and now, now it appears that 'just in case' has come." She turned quickly, as though she were afraid she might stop herself. "I'll get one of your pipes."

We helped Nathan sit up in bed, in fine state. Lavinia was asleep in the next room, so we three watched the ritual as Nathan almost caressingly fingered the fine-grained bowl, cleaned and filled it, and lighted the fragrant tobacco. The look on his face as he relaxed into the pleasure of smoking stabbed me with remorse to think that we had denied him. He relaxed back against the pillows and sighed.

"We'll leave you to your pleasures then," Eugene grinned, "and see if we can devise some of our own."

Nathan grinned after us, and I felt somewhat comforted as we went to our own room.

Next morning as I prepared to walk into town, I asked Georgie if she would like to accompany me. She shook her head and lowered her voice. "Nathan is too little improved, and I dare not leave him to Gertie's good offices."

"Shall I pick up a tin of Nathan's favorite tobacco then?"

Georgie made a face and leaned even closer. "Poor lad. After smoking the pipe down to the dregs he confided to me that the tobacco has lost its savor. He could not enjoy the old pleasure, try as he may."

"A blessing in disguise," I ventured.

"I believe so, though I would not have expected it."

"Is he reconciled?"

"Relieved, I would say. He has been nursing a longing for the weed, and the guilt that accompanies the longing. Now he is suddenly, quite unexpectedly, free of both."

"I am glad, Georgie." It made the morning seem even lovelier as I set out toward the markets. I enjoy walking, and Georgie had kept Lavinia with her, so I was free to move with long, relaxed strides and to glance around me, not having to keep my eye steadily on my baby, slowing my step to hers, or carrying her until even my strong arms ached.

Gardeners have to be early risers, and it is also far more pleasant on a summer's day to walk into town in the cool early hours, when the birds are yet loud and unstinted with their morning oblations and the small creatures who frighten and scatter at man's touch are yet about their business and visible to the watchful eye. The dust has not settled, and the heat has not risen to wilt and clog. God is present in the mornings and again in the still twilight hours before night envelops his creations and clothes all his vast existence in rest. I remember well the dark, restless longing that used to trouble my spirit from time to time, as an unanticipated awareness of the magnitude of the universe assailed my being and stretched my powers to comprehend. And I would long to know, to dispel the vagueness which clung to my soul like a soiled, gray garment I was loathe to pull close to me and anxious to shed. Something beyond myself whispered of truths I could not put words

43

to, until Joseph Smith did it for me, until God spoke the answers for all of us through this one man. I was happy with that simple contentment that makes one feel an inexplicable joy and gratitude simply to be alive.

I conducted my errands quickly and decided, on impulse, to visit Eugene for a moment before walking home. He was surprised to see me. I watched pleasure break over his countenance as his eyes recognized me, took in the welcome sight of me, and I knew at that moment what it means to be loved. He sank onto a bench to rest a few moments from his labors, and I brought him a dipper of cool water to drink, then another to bathe his face and hands in. He does not enjoy sweating and straining in manual labor, but I like him like this. There is something satisfying and elemental in working with the hands that becomes somehow obscured when one works solely with the mind and does not appear to get into the thick of it.

As we sat I glanced toward the house entrance a few times, wondering how Emmeline was doing and if I ought to go up. To my astonishment I watched Eden, the eldest Frey girl, mince out with her arm tucked through the arm of a male companion. The sight of them made me go cold.

"Eugene!" I tugged at his sleeve. "That is Jedediah Comstock that Eden is stepping out with."

He nodded, his expression darkening. "Well I know. Andrew's voice is as large as his girth. You should have heard him bellow like a maddened bull this morning when the man came to call."

"Why did he not throw him out of here on his ear?" I demanded hotly. "He is not only a Gentile, but a man with no scruples. I have heard very unpleasant things about him."

"Eden came below stairs when she heard her father and informed him with as much coy smugness as a cat who is licking the last of the cream from her whiskers that he would allow her to keep company with the gentleman, else she would pack her belongings on the instant and go stay with Bertha Walker—who has already offered her the use of a cozy little room above the millinery shop."

I felt sick inside. "Eugene, why? What has attracted her to him?"

"Who can tell, love, who can tell?"

"Does she do it for spite?"

"For adventure, more likely. Some women become enamored of

their own charms and find it is thrilling to test them, to see how far they can go on them."

"All the way to destruction and despair," I cried.

"Esther, Esther!" Eugene kissed my forehead, my lips. Then, savoring the pleasure of it, he kissed me again. "There is no one like you, Esther, when it comes to fretting yourself about the ways and woes of another."

"I cannot help it," I moaned. "It seems I can feel their pain, Eugene, as if it were mine. Their pain, and the pain they inflict so thoughtlessly upon others. Injustice fires up the very depths of me, and I want to put everything right."

"Yes, I know."

His quizzical expression brought a reluctant smile to my lips. I moved to lean against him. "You'll soil your dress," he warned, but I did not care. I wanted the solid touch of him before we took leave of one another. "I like the look of you," I whispered, "in your working smock and leather apron."

The quizzical look returned to his face, but I know my words pleased him. He lifted me from the bench with his hands cupped round my elbows. I wanted him to kiss me again but was too shy to say anything. With reluctance I stepped away, waved, kissed my hand to him, then turned to walk home.

45

But it was enough. Something of his presence remained with me throughout the rest of the day. I was *aware* of him—that was it—as I usually am not during the long working hours. Like a rare, unexpected flower one comes upon and plucks that its fragrance and beauty might stay with him, so were those minutes spent with Eugene—a rare treat that sweetened my spirit for hours before gently dissolving away.

❦

Garrison Woods paid us money, actual coinage! We had not expected it. But he proudly announced one evening that he was working with Brother Brigham, who was building houses all over the valley.

"He trusts that the brethren will pay him, and there are enough with the money who can. So I thought I might spare this from our little store. You folk have been so kind to us."

How much has this funny little Canadian brought with him and clung to, tight and close-mouthed? I wondered.

We had not expected the money, but when it came we four divided it like children who had discovered a hoard of treasure, savoring even the touch and feel of it. And I knew at once what I wanted to do.

When I asked Eugene his face clouded. "Esther, there are so many places, wiser places for the money to go."

"But I have not written once since Phoebe had her baby! I have not even answered Josephine's letter."

"Phoebe knows you love her. In a hundred years of silence she would not doubt it. Has she written to you?"

I scowled back at him. "What difference does that make?"

"We haven't the means any more than she and Simon have." His voice was gentle with compassion. "These are hard times, Esther. There is so much we need. Can you not wait a bit longer? Perhaps there will be more money coming, and if so—"

"If so—the next time—who knows what will happen! You are only putting me off. And I have waited so long already."

"I am sorry, Esther. You know, you must know that I truly am sorry. I'll leave it in your hands." He shrugged with a little-boy gesture that I did my best to ignore. "You know more about these matters than I do anyway. We'll write out an accounting tomorrow, and I'll leave you to make your decision with wisdom and fairness."

That was an unkind thing to do! He knows my conscience; my terrible sense of duty will work against me. Even my pride helped me determine to leave all of the money to him. There was something that stung in asking and being refused. Reason could tell me clearly the strength of his argument, the rightness of his direction. But my heart wanted him to feel my need and indulge me—and then to miraculously make up the difference, somehow.

I said no more about letters or money for stamps, and he did not mention it. And that hurt, too. If I was going to be high-principled and sacrifice myself for the general good, I at least wanted praise. No, not praise, simply tender acknowledgment. But his way, the man's way, was to gratefully avoid the unpleasant, unhappy subjects and leave them to fend for themselves. How I loved him—but how lonely I could feel at such times as these.

Chapter Six

Kirtland: Tuesday, 23 July 1833

I add my prayers to those of every soul here, that the Lord's spirit might attend us, bless this beginning, and magnify our powers to carry the sacred task through to its end. I am overwhelmed and frightened; and yet joy, pure as an elixir, sends light, like a blessing, to surround me, without and within.

On the first day of June, nearly two months ago, the Lord through the means of revelation chastised this Church for failing to keep faith with him and his commandments. Surely he knows our weaknesses, and surely he knows the conditions and trials which we struggle through. To build a house unto God, a temple—we understand nothing at all of such matters, and we have so little means! Yet he said, "If you keep my commandments you shall have power to build it." And he has himself given the pattern, that this holy place be built not after the fashion of man and the world, but according to his will and his design.

There is a work to do, and we must have a temple in order to do it. There are blessings awaiting us, and they can be obtained in no other way, in no other place upon the face of the earth.

Thus stirred to action, Brother Joseph and the brethren selected a spot in the northwest corner of a field of fine wheat, which the Prophet and his brothers had sown the previous fall. They removed the fence, leveled the grain that was standing, and Hyrum—is there anyone in this Church who can match Hyrum Smith for humility and obedience?—Hyrum began at once to dig a trench for the temple wall.

So the ground was broken, and now, today, we gather to lay the cornerstones of the Lord's house. We, his Saints, we few who have gathered to him, heard his voice in our hearts, and felt to rejoice.

Men from among the leading Elders have been selected to lay each of the four stones. Theirs are names that shall go down to posterity because of their part in this momentous event: Joseph and Hyrum Smith; Sidney Rigdon; Newel K. Whitney; Frederick G. Williams; Jared Carter; Orson Hyde; John Samuel; William and Don Carlos Smith; and Father Smith. I like the Smith family. They are men of a unique mold, and there is a look about them that tells of things unspoken yet deeply known. They are strict in their devotion yet humble and friendly and willing to serve. Joseph Smith Sr. deserves well to stand as patriarch to his family, and to this Church. He is a tall man who carries himself with dignity and looks out at the world with calm eyes, guileless as those of an innocent child. He is incapable of even the smallest unkindness, and his patience seems boundless, as does the genuine love we feel whenever he speaks to us, be it from the pulpit or on one of the village streets.

His wife, Lucy, is always solicitous of him, quietly watchful of his comfort and well-being. She, too, is fearless when it comes to defending the truth, yet her home and her heart are always open to the least of us. I feel small and ashamed when I compare my weak efforts with theirs. I am sure they have come to know what it means to love and to give their all. They are worthy of our love and worthy of the emulation they inspire in us.

I look around at the throng of faces, very few familiar to me. Yet all are my brothers and sisters. We come from dozens, even hundreds, of backgrounds, yet the gospel must somehow mesh us all into one. The key is love, of course. Love and faith, both of which engender obedience and therefore create joy.

There is nothing here but a promise in the empty, marked earth before us: waiting and ready, and now consecrated to its high use. And in our lives is a promise sometimes reflected in our countenances but as often not seen, not guessed at, even by ourselves, in our fondest dreams.

So many of those I love are now far from me. Their lives go on, but I am no longer part of them, except in memory. And memories grow dim. Even longings can be dimmed and weakened by the persistent wearing of time. I carry them with me, but where I am, they have not wished to enter; what I feel and comprehend, they do not wish to feel and know.

And thus a part of what I carry with me is sorrow. Sorrow is ever the handmaiden of joy. Joy cannot reach her highest ecstasy without passing through these gates. I know this. I am here today because I wish to learn how to live this and other truths.

I close my eyes and try to picture what this temple Joseph has envisioned will be like. I try to comprehend how it is that I have come to be one of the favored ones. Of all the people who live now, of all the people who ever have lived, I am here at this place, at this moment. A new gospel dispensation is beginning, and after thousands of years a prophet of God is ordained to build a house to the most high God.

These are enlarging thoughts, thoughts that expand my spirit. I attempt to express what I am feeling in words, but it cannot be done. But Eugene understands. Perhaps because he is a lover of words and their meanings and his soul is always in search of a higher expression, he can read in my eyes what words would only demean or confuse.

In only a few minutes the solemn ceremony is over. But the work has not yet even begun. This work will mean sacrifice and a higher and ever higher dedication of self.

49

But Nathan and Eugene are elated. They may not have caught the vision entirely, but they possess enough to go on. They and many others who, as the ceremonies end and talk between them runs down, set their shoulders to the purpose before returning to the tedious perplexities and privation of daily demands.

I am holding onto the words given to Joseph, cupping them in my heart as one would cup a draught of cool, vitalizing water. I am not yet used to such language. I am not yet accustomed to the realization that man can be intimate with God. Of course, it makes sense if one ponders it in earnest. If we are truly his children, then why should he not yearn after us, care for us, talk with us, and teach us? But I was not raised up to even imagine such things. These words to me are sacred and soul-satisfying: "Verily, thus saith the Lord unto you whom I love, and whom I love I also chasten that their sins may be forgiven, for with the chastisement I prepare a way for their deliverance in all things out of temptation, and I have loved you—"

I have loved you . . . This is a thought I must ponder in the quiet of my own soul. I look back at the temple lot, nearly cleared now of people. *Can the very land and the blue sky above it wear an expectant air? Can I hold onto this moment, that its perfection might bless me through hard and good times to come?*

❧

I worry about Peter. I know he is lonely. I know he carries wounds that may take years yet to heal. Now that Jack has Aurelia, I have been praying that the Lord will send someone to stir and lift, yes, and even comfort his heart. I see her. She does not see me, but I know at once, as I look upon her, that she is the one. She has been watching him, following at a discreet distance the two sober young men.

"The aunts would not even allow Aurelia to attend today," Jack was saying as they approached us. "They reason that she is but a child, and a girl at that, and does not require such experiences. Nonsense. They simply don't trust her, don't trust me—don't trust us!"

"How much can flesh and blood bear?" Peter asked him. "Do something about it. Defy them!"

Jack smiled wistfully. "You are a great one to talk."

"We did defy my father in the end—"

"Yes, and it was almost our undoing. *And* we had Georgie and Esther to run to while we licked our wounds."

Their eyes were shining with the memory of their bold deeds. But Jack had always been the more practical of the two. "We have Georgie and Esther still," Peter reminded him.

"It isn't the same, and you know it. We've all grown up and moved on. And besides, if I stole my true love away, what would I do to keep us alive?"

Peter struck his hands together in frustration.

"Something will work out," I told both of them from behind. "I have an idea or two."

They turned. They trust my ideas; childlike still, despite Jack's mature ruminations. The girl had nearly caught up with us. She hesitated, and on impulse I called her over—to her surprise and to mine.

"Are you new to Kirtland?" I asked—always a safe question.

"Yes, we have been here only these four weeks."

"Welcome, then. We are old-timers of nearly five months duration, though Georgie can boast to have been one of the first." I introduced all of us, and we learned that the girl's name was Rose Knapp, and she came from right here in Ohio.

"My family were among the first settlers," she said, "back when Thomas Jefferson opened up the land for colonization in 1788."

"That is impressive. My grandsire was John Swift, the first white man who settled on Iroquois land in what is now Palmyra, New York, in 1789." Peter had spoken up. I considered this a good sign.

"There is more to your story as well," I pressed, sensing it. Peter remained listening, interested. Rose noted this also, I think, as she went on.

"My grandfather was the first attorney general when Ohio was made a state in 1803." She was neither demure nor boastful. I considered this good. Despite his claims to non-partisanship, Peter was impressed or, rather, pleased. It was a point of reference which gave him a sense of having something in common with this girl.

She was not particularly pretty. Her hair was brown, her eyes were brown—but of a rich, shining, fine quality. She had a sprinkling of freckles across the bridge of her nose, reminding me of Phoebe. She was of an ordinary build, an ordinary height, her feet were not particularly small, nor her hands particularly fine, but there was something about her—a vivacity when she moved, even when she stood still to listen; a pleasing sensation, an air of expectation when she talked, as of an underlying strain of merriment about to break forth. I liked her voice. I liked her boldness and her shyness, for her hands, clenched behind her back, were white-knuckled and shaking a bit.

I waited, though Georgie threw me a pointed look and Eugene tugged at my sleeve. I asked the right questions, murmured and nodded at all the right places. As soon as I dared leave them on their own I made sudden excuses, something about getting back to the baby, and we four left in a hurry, so as not to break up the whole party. I glanced back over my shoulder, and they were yet where we left them, heads bent, the conversation still going.

"She seems a nice girl. Very nice," Georgie remarked casually. I thought so, too, but I dared not say out loud what I was thinking, not even to Georgie. For I did not understand it myself.

51

It was all part of some power, perhaps this power of love that moves through us, that creates and re-creates the universe in our eyes, in our little worlds day after day. I knew only what I felt and what experience had shown me. I knew only that Eugene, a boy from Palmyra, had opened up whole new worlds to me, and I had been blessed.

Chapter Seven

Kirtland: August 1833

"Others have done it. Please, Georgie. I cannot live if I don't know what's happening back home."

"You could write once a week," she argued, "and they would know all you are thinking and doing, all that's happening here. But that does not mean they will return your letters. Josephine could, you know. *She* could write once a week and enclose the money for postage, but she does not. Why do you not write to her under condition that she pay to pick up the letter?"

It is a vexing practice of the post that the recipient pay for his own mail. Brother Joseph has dozens of letters sent him: inquiring, threatening, praising. He cannot possibly afford to accept them all. A bit peeved, I responded, "I refuse to operate in that manner. I wish to pay my own way."

"Do you wish to pay your own way, or do you wish to receive and send mail?"

"Georgie!"

"Well, really, which, Esther? Which most?"

"Just agree to make the hats with me. That is what I asked in the beginning."

She acquiesced with a sigh. "You like working with your hands, Esther; I like working with my head."

"I like that, too."

"Yes, your writing and your poetry. But you are skilled at both, you see, and I am not."

Georgie was neither complaining nor seeking sympathy. Practical, straightforward Georgie was simply stating what she felt were the facts.

"But you will attempt it?" I urged.

"I will attempt it for your sake, and for your sake alone."

"Then I get to keep all the profits?"

She took a playful swat at me. But over the next few days we got down to work in earnest. The weather was hot—hot, muggy, and breathless. People would be in need of straw hats for shade and straw fans to cool their flushed faces. We gathered the reeds and palm leaves ourselves along the riverbanks and in low, marshy places. That was by far the worst of the task, fighting mud, mosquitoes, and prickly heat, and hatching a most unwelcome crop of freckles in the encouraging furnace of the mid-summer sun. Catching Sister Frey in a particularly generous mood, we talked her into allowing Emmeline to work afternoons with us the first week until the distasteful task was done. I felt we were taking advantage a bit, but vowed in my mind to make it up to her when the profits started coming in. The girl has turned out to be such an excellent worker after all.

"It is August already," I reminded my somewhat reluctant cohorts. "We must get our wares out and available in order to take advantage of our best market days while they last."

I was determined, and, for their part, they were kind and cooperative. We made encouraging headway.

"Too bad Gertie is not here to help," Georgeanna teased. She had moved out but a few days before we began our project. They had lived with us for seven long weeks and, though it is sad to admit this, there was not one thing about their leaving which caused me the slightest regret. I even felt we had done our very best by them, calling into service patience and charity we did not know we possessed.

"We took their money," Eugene reminded me when I expressed my relief to him.

"They gave what they had to give, as we gave what we had to give," I maintained.

He was as pleased as I to have our home and our lives back again, but it was his way to play devil's advocate with me at times.

"I love to see your eyes flash," he confessed. "You draw yourself up like a queen, beautiful and undefeatable, and you fairly tingle with energy and life."

Strange praise. And such words often made me wonder how I must appear to him. We each carry an image of ourselves with a dark side upon which are recorded all the foibles and sins, all the weaknesses and stupidities of our nature. We carry also a shining side, lit by our fairest hopes, etched with the beauty of the possibilities we feel within ourselves which no other eyes can see. Yet each person who knows us perceives but small bits and snatches of what is truly there. And these are mingled with the viewer's own personality, experience, feelings, and preferences. 'Tis a contemplation that could whirl one's mind into circles if carried on for too long!

❦

The actual weaving of the broad-brimmed hats was less work than pleasure, for we could all sit together and talk, the baby and the kittens playing at our feet, and a cool pitcher of water, or, if we were fortunate, lemonade ready in the kitchen. We wove sweet, mindless patterns while in the world about us dark, sinister patterns were being woven that would entangle our lives.

❦

It was a fortunate turn of events that brought Emmeline back into our lives. Between her commitments to the Freys and time spent with her family, we scarcely saw her at all. She was growing, filling out, and now, every time we saw her, she was actually clean, with combed hair and a frock and apron that did not look as if they had been worked in and slept in for a week.

She still was not very talkative, but she seemed more relaxed and at ease in her movements, and I fancied she was happy enough. But we learned two important things from our conversations during that week.

First, and easier to discern, the girl was making poor progress in her lessons. Georgie had not taken time to catechize and examine her to see if the reading and the ciphering were taking. She had even demurred a time or two when she had gone for that purpose to the rooms above the smithy, because it meant quizzing Emmeline with the rest of the household gazing fixedly on. She realized too late her error. Emmeline had read the books all right—skipping over the difficult words, several in every sentence, which she did not understand. The geography and history were barely touched, and the math sums, nearly all worked correctly, were largely the results of assistance from either Edith or Elinor.

Georgie was a bit discouraged, but being Georgie, she did not show it. Emmeline's wide, miserable gaze, once discovered, was disarming enough as it was.

So we planned a new regimen, much more strict and controlled. But Georgie's main concern was not progress merely for progress' sake. "Do you enjoy what you do understand? Do you like sitting with a book on your lap at the end of a long work day?"

I know she feared that the girl's interest was prompted largely by a desire to please her. She wanted much more than that.

"I like the feel of the pages," Emmeline groped, unsure of herself. "I like the smell of a book. Do you know what I mean?"

"I do."

"It makes me feel . . ." She paused, unable to find words for a thought just forming. "Well, it is as though the people in the book are there, sitting down beside me, as real as anyone else."

"I understand that, too," Georgie replied in the quiet way which means she is very well pleased.

So we have fertile ground to work with, I thought, *just as Georgie believed in the beginning.*

The other matter came up unexpectedly, when we were pushing our sleeves back to wash our scratchy skin, and I noticed ugly red welts along the inside of Emmeline's forearm. I think I gasped a little and spoke without thinking. "Who has done this to you, child?"

She lowered her eyes, and, too late, I bit my lip. "Your father," Georgie said. "What made him do this to you?"

There was no response. I could almost feel the girl trembling. "You must not be made to go back there!" Georgie's vehemence reached out to touch both of us.

Emmeline shook her head. "There's no getting away from him, missus. That's how it is. If I wasn't there when I'm s'posed to be he'd just take it out on the others." A shudder passed over her frame. I wanted to weep. I wanted to snatch her up and cry, "We will save you, we will rescue you! We'll find some way!"

But there are things in life which cannot be attacked bull-like, head-on, which cannot be trammeled down into dust and oblivion where they belong. I was to learn this harsh lesson very powerfully as the next few years etched their unique pattern upon my life.

✿

How to get our really quite superior creations to market? We were tickled with what we had accomplished, but how might we best effect the next step from here?

Brother Whitney agreed to take ten, remarking that they were among the finest he had seen in a long spell. That encouraged us. But there were many Gentile establishments I desired to get into, yet was loathe to approach myself. The lines of demarcation between us and our non-Mormon neighbors were being more firmly drawn every day. The starting of the temple made a difference. They thought us audacious, and they knew that this enterprise meant we intended to stay. As they saw it, the Mormons were squeezing them out already; they would be fools to stand by and watch us grow stronger yet.

"Perhaps Brother Pliny would help," Georgie suggested.

"He is not *Brother* Pliny," I reminded her. "But that is a good idea; I had not thought of him yet."

"He likes you."

"I do not know about that."

"Yes, Esther, he does. Do you not remember when he said you remind him of his daughter who died in childbirth some twenty years ago?"

I had not remembered the conversation. But I liked the old man very much. And I did remember him confiding that both his and his wife's poor health had required that they sell their large farm outside Cleveland. They had moved here to be near their dead daughter's children, but within a year of their coming, his wife passed away. And the young generation seemed to have no time for him, no inclination to make him a part of their lives. He lives alone on a small farm, which must contain little more than sad memories and lonely shadows. He keeps chickens and sells their eggs in town. And he raises squab, which he dresses and sells as something of a delicacy for the tables of the rich. I took some of my herbs to him shortly after we moved here, one day when I learned he was sick. My bit of doctoring and Georgie's warm bread that went along with it must have touched his reticent, long-guarded heart.

We walked to his place the following morning, before the sun got fairly about her day's business. He is a simple soul and moves slowly, as old men tend to do. He wiped his hands along his apron, offered us cups of cool buttermilk, and listened to our plan with interest.

"I can do well for you," he promised, with a slow smile. "I can do very well for you."

"That is grand! We shall work out a percentage of the profit in compensation."

He waved my offer aside. "My pleasure. I'm delivering my eggs already. Won't be any trouble to tote these along." He picked up one of the hats and ran his thumb along the braided brim. "Tell you what I will do. I'll take one of these here in payment."

"Of course. However many you'd like."

"One is all I need." He ruminated a moment longer. "Folks'll like these, no doubt of it." As he walked us to the door he added, "I'm right proud you thought of me, Miss Esther. I'll do the best for you I can."

I am always warmed by any show of kindness from others. But I did not let my hopes for success soar too high. So when the first week's returns came in, I can say I was truly astounded. Altogether we had sold the grand total of seventeen hats and nearly a dozen fans! And I learned that Edward Pliny had set them at what I would consider a rather high price.

"Quality merchandise," he said, when I commented upon it. "Give 'em away and folks won't think they're worth much. How many can you have by next week?"

Suddenly our work was cut out for us. We stayed up till the candles burned down, then we rose with the larks in the morning, our fingers still sore and aching, in order to meet the demand. And . . . to my intense satisfaction, I must admit, we had money in our pockets! At last!

Now the summer days began to run into one another in a shimmer of activity, and Georgie laughed at me, unable to contain her appreciation of the ironies.

"That money is burning a hole in your pocket, Esther, but you are too busy to spend it, too busy earning more to write those letters you've been in such a fever about." And, of course, she was right.

As the month wore itself away our production slowed down to a trickle. But, to our delight, our coffers were full. One hundred fifty hats sold, and six dozen fans, for the grand total of 135 dollars!

"I wish I had known these kinds of earnings were possible before," Georgie said, as she re-counted her portion.

What is more, our husbands thought us the most clever and cunning of creatures; and that did not hurt one bit!

❦

I had not forgotten my promise to Aurelia and Jack. As soon as the Woods quit the premises we let the young couple know, though I was longing for the luxury of using the room myself. Nevertheless, we steeled ourselves for the good of the cause. We even went one step further, coming up with a rather hilarious assortment of needs, excuses, and enticements to draw the aunties away.

First Georgie asked for lessons in tatting, contriving for the four of us to sit round the large kitchen table, where the lighting was good, and practice until we got the hang of it. From Aurelia we learned that Aunt Dorothy's sponge cake was known for the lightness and spring of its texture and the delicacy of its taste. We entreated her for pointers— another kitchen-based activity. In the beginning we gritted our teeth at the ordeal we were setting for ourselves in the service of romance and matrimony. But, to our surprise, we enjoyed the aunts' company and were delighted by the things they were willing to teach us, by their hard-won, practical New England wisdom. We truly benefited from our contrived sessions and began to look forward to them.

❦

Reuben and Claire Lamb run a little bakery together. I had thought all their children were grown until I learned through Peter that their only son had drowned in infancy and their four daughters had all been taken away by diphtheria in a period of three-weeks' time.

One would not know it, watching their gentle, happy countenances. They appear so easily, so simply content. I think of my mother and the bitterness I believe she fosters on purpose, seeming to prefer misery to the peace which could be so easily sought and achieved; her ways are inscrutable to me.

It is good of the Lambs to board Peter and Jack in their attic, and they request the most reasonable of sums in payment, though their own means are modest enough. They have even less room than we do, and nothing like a parlor that either of the boys could use. We are making progress with Jack and Aurelia, but I cannot get that other young girl off my mind.

Eugene chides me, for sometimes I lie awake in bed, my mind in a dither, trying to work all these things out. I do not mean to; I do not consider myself a meddler nor particularly wise or clever, but there are certain things and certain people I simply cannot get off my mind.

I had visited the boys, returning Jack's hat to him, and was actually in the bakery indulging in the purchase of a few sugared cakes to take home as a surprise when a sudden notion came into my mind.

"Have you observed any particular young ladies frequenting your bakery often of late?" I asked Claire Lamb.

She blinked blankly at me, but when she saw I was in earnest she set her mind to thinking. "As a matter of fact—" I felt my heart give a foolish leap. "There is a girl with whom I am not acquainted, a very pleasant young thing, not particularly pretty, but she has a bright, winsome air. She comes quite often, and what I have remarked is that she seems to *linger*. She makes her small purchase but then appears, well, reluctant to leave."

Claire could see at once that her words pleased me, and she was both confused and curious. I drew her aside and confided some of what had happened, even some of what I was feeling, knowing I could trust both her kindness and her integrity. She was, indeed, as they say, all ears.

"Yes . . . yes . . ." She murmured assent half a dozen times as I went on. "Something must be done, some encouragement given." We looked at one another, minds turning slowly, hoping to overturn some little gem of wisdom from the store of jumbled and idle thoughts there.

"Let me sleep on it, dear," she said at last. "Something will present itself, I believe."

I was content with this, but I did not expect such a quick response. The very next afternoon she appeared at our door, her pretty face beaming. She had brought half a dozen warm hot cross buns wrapped in a snowy white napkin, and I noticed that all about her a powdery layer of flour dust clung lightly, softly sifting her gentle features over with white: her hair, the kindly creases in her face, her plump fair hands, her starched clean apron; a more motherly picture I have seldom seen.

I ushered her in to the cool house, but she refused to settle. "I cannot stay long, dear," she said. "But I have found our solution."

I felt as curious as Georgie's kitten, which was curling herself round and round Claire Lamb's feet.

"For these past three months or more Reuben has been after me to slow down a bit, take a little time off for myself." She smiled and smoothed out her apron, which action the little cat took as invitation and promptly jumped into her lap. "Just between you and me, I believe he misses the linsey-woolsey shirts I used to make for him before the bakery got going so good that it became too much for him to handle." She sighed and stroked the cat absently. "Be that as it may, I spoke to my husband, and he agrees that I might take two days a week off and hire this young girl in my place—mornings only, which are our busy time. We can afford to pay her for that time, though not a large sum. But perhaps the young lady . . ."

"Bless you, bless you both!" I clapped my hands together gleefully, and the lines around her small blue eyes crinkled with pleasure.

"It will work splendidly, won't it? That is, if the young girl is interested. I've asked Reuben to make the offer himself next time she comes into the shop. It will appear more natural that way."

"Of course!"

"And he can manage to call Peter in from time to time on the mornings when she is working, to run some errand or lift the heavy pails of cream—he'll think of something."

"I very much believe that he will! I do not know how to thank you."

"Thank us? Nonsense, Esther. It will be a grand adventure for all of us, won't it? What was the young lady's name again?"

"Rose Knapp."

"Rose Knapp. I'll remember that to tell Reuben." She stood, and the cat jumped to his feet to make his purring circuit round her again.

"Fetching kitten, that," she smiled. "You wouldn't be in need of a home for him, would you?"

"We've three others at the moment," I cried, "and the promise of new crops ever recurring, thanks to Georgie."

"You mean, I can take him?"

"Please do."

She made a soft clucking sound far back in her throat, bent over a bit, and held her arms out, and the saucy cat jumped right in. She stroked the mottled gray fur as she swept to the door. "I will bring you a report as soon as things start to happen," she chirped.

"Thank you for the buns and for everything else," I replied, kissing her powdery, sweet-smelling cheek.

I had lit the fire under the pot of chicken on the back of the stove and begun to stir up a batch of dumplings when Georgie came in from the garden, her basket toppling over with tomatoes, little round hubbard squashes, and fine long green beans.

"Oh, you just missed Claire Lamb! I've such a story to tell, and I wish you had been here in time to send some of this produce back with her."

"Actually, we hailed one another as she was leaving, and I talked her into my two largest tomatoes and a very fine squash."

"Oh, good." I stirred the batter contentedly.

"You have been up to your matchmaking then?"

"That's unfair, Georgie. I do not usually do this sort of thing. But this time I have a feeling—something I can't quite explain."

"You've very little to go on besides that. It will be interesting to see what happens."

"A grand adventure for all of us," I repeated. "Oh, you don't mind that she took Miggins, the gray kitten, with her?"

"Heavens, no. You know I like to spread the happiness around, where cats are concerned."

Eugene walked into the kitchen, crossed the room, and came up behind me, kissing the back of my neck, his touch sending a sensation of pleasure all through me.

Spread the happiness around, I thought. I knew I wanted Peter to have someone to love him, to encourage him, to be his helpmeet, as a wise Heavenly Father planned. He has been fighting the noble fight alone for so long. The love of his family, for what it was worth, has been denied him, as though one could cut love out like an offending infection; rid oneself of it, as some folks seemed to think. He must be lonely; he must feel what he is missing, even if he cannot put his need into words. I had seen his eyes these past months, the unspoken longing in them.

It is time that he find the rest of himself in the heart of a woman, I thought, *and find the happiness that only that kind of love can bring.*

Chapter Eight

Kirtland: October 1833

"Esther!" Eugene's voice rang through the house, startling me so that I dropped the cabbage I was cutting and ran to find him, not even bothering to dry my hands before flying off to see what was wrong. Lavinia was right at my heels, but she reached her papa first, and he grabbed her and whirled her high above his head in the air. She giggled with pleasure, begging for more when he at last set her firmly on the ground again.

"What is it, Eugene?" Perhaps I had been wrong to anticipate distress in his wild call, for he was grinning like a boy now, the boy I used to know in Palmyra who would follow the five of us around like a devoted puppy. *He has eyes only for you,* Tillie would smirk; then Phoebe would add gently, *He is sincerely devoted to you, Esther. I know that he is.*

"On the first, unbeknown to the likes of me, Brother Cowdery set out for New York with eight hundred dollars in his pocket and orders to purchase a printing press."

I smiled, controlling my urge to laugh out loud at him. You would have thought the crown jewels or half the treasures of Europe were being brought here for our delight.

"How did you learn this?" I asked. "And is there any chance—"

He drew up my hands in a sort of ecstasy. "Brother Williams, who will head the publishing firm, spoke to me himself of the matter. Said he had heard of the work I did for Grandin in Palmyra and wondered if I would be interested in helping to establish some first-rate publications for the Saints here!"

This *was* good news; it was the sort of miracle for which Eugene had been praying as he trudged back and forth to work at the blacksmith's. I could almost see his fingers twitching, anxious for the sort of action that was life and breath to him.

For days an aura of pleasurable anticipation clung to our

household, enhancing the invigoration of autumn's pungent fragrances and lavish beauties. Autumn is abundance: the harvest, the culmination. I feel intensely alive in autumn, as I do no other time of the year. So we reveled in hope, since autumn is a time for reveling, rejoicing, partaking of the bounties and wonders of life.

As reward for my summer labors I had written lengthy, informative, yearning letters: one to my father and mother; one to my sister, Josephine, and her new husband, Randolph; and one to my dear friend, Phoebe. I had slipped into each the cost of the postage and plead with them to write in return. Mother did not, but my Father penned a short message which he took to Josie, that she might post it along with her own reply. He said little, but there was much behind his words that touched me deeply.

We miss you, daughter. There is nothing to fill the emptiness you left behind. There is no way to smooth it over and pretend we can carry on as usual. I envy the people who get to see you each morning and hear your voice through the day. Give my love to Eugene and little Lavinia, and remember me fondly to Georgeanna and Nathan.

My quiet, patient father. I did not like knowing I caused him suffering. My sister, Josie, wrote:

Myself and this baby do well still. Sometime in November, before the snow flies if I am lucky, he will make his appearance. And this child will live. Randolph says so, and his assurance makes me believe it is possible. He has such power within himself that I think he could will things to be. He keeps me going. He has enough power for both of us.

Nothing of faith, nothing of turning to God for assistance. I began to realize how much Mormonism had changed Eugene and me, Georgie and Nathan. We thought differently, even used different words in writing or speaking. *New creatures.* That is what repentance and baptism can do for one. But I disliked the inescapable and increasing separation between myself and the people I loved.

Sweet Phoebe wrote more cheerfully.

Jonah is a plump, happy baby who thrives on mother's milk and all the love that is lavished upon him here. Esther is devoted to him, as big sisters generally are. She brings me much joy, and, thank heaven,

65

Simon takes great joy in his son. I have noted changes in him since the baby has been here. Perhaps at least some of my prayers will be answered.

I looked at Georgie, and Georgie looked at me. We had raised fervent prayers these past six months on Phoebe's behalf. I could not imagine being isolated the way our friend was, with a husband she had adored since they were children and who yet remained aloof from her in some ways because of the death of his first wife—the girl he had chosen *over our Phoebe,* and now refused to let go of in honor and peace. Simon, whose quiet ways we had all read as gentleness: what were grief and loss doing to him? And there was no help from Phoebe's parents nor the dead Emily's parents, whose daughter Phoebe was raising, the child who had been given my name. Eugene and I had actually come to words upon the subject several times, for Emily was his sister, and their mother in some ways now my mother, too.

"Your mother has been cruel to Phoebe and for no reason. You know this, Eugene."

"She is a woman whose daughter has been taken from her. Every time she sees Phoebe it is a reminder that she is there in Emily's place."

"So Phoebe must suffer for this? Phoebe, who is entirely guiltless and guileless and is raising up your sister's daughter as well as Emily herself could have! Your mother ought to adore and assist this good woman, not make her task more bleak and more miserable."

"'Ought to's' don't count much in life, do they, Esther?"

For some reason, when Eugene waxes philosophical with me it has a maddening effect.

"They can be changed into realities if people care enough, else where is progress, repentance, and change?"

"Repentance and change scarcely show their faces in the history of this old world of ours."

"Eugene!"

"Let go of it, Esther. Your anguish cannot effect these changes you desire. Of what use is your suffering then?"

I did not want his arguments, his logic. I wanted his tenderness and his love. I wanted him to put his arms around me, soothe and kiss the pain away with whisperings of understanding and sympathy. Why could he not see this? Sense it crying out from behind the words I spoke?

This is usually what women want most, at least in matters where the heart is involved, matters of deep feeling. Yet if we begin with reasons and opinions rather than childish anger and tears, men mistake us altogether and seem to feel duty-bound to take the opposing argument and defend that stance till the end.

So our conversations would end in a stalemate, with Eugene weary and frustrated and me hurt, even heartbroken still.

There was also the matter of Phoebe's conversion to the gospel of Jesus Christ. In this, too, she was alone, out of touch with the Saints, unable to grow in experience and understanding, keeping what she knows and feels and is committed to within her own lonely heart.

"Do not dwell upon it overmuch," Georgie warned me, "else you will not be able to bear it."

I blinked back at her. Why, in her own way she was saying precisely what Eugene always said!

"Is that what you do with Emmeline?" I asked. "Put her out of your mind completely when the pain threatens to get too much for you?"

"Esther, you know it is not that simple! But, yes, I have the ability to take a step back from other people's suffering which you do not seem to possess."

Their expressions worry me. I feel vulnerable, even weak and foolish. And, if their descriptions are correct, what can I do about it? How can I make myself different—and do I really want to be different from the way that I am?

I have no answers for questions like these. I pull Lavinia close to me, drawing in the physical nearness of her, the perfection of her young spirit and mind. Her eyes are as green as a troubled sea, her hair like burnished red leaves underneath a hot autumn sun. *She will be a beauty someday,* I think, *and she will have her own mind, and perhaps her own ways. She will see things differently, and do things differently. And she will know pain. And I will have no control over what comes and departs and moves in her life.*

The realization distresses me. I want to protect her as she is, keep her pure and perfect, unflawed and unstained. I know this is not possible. But my mother's heart aches for it and will not be satisfied with what is, and what must come to pass.

67

❦

Aaron Sessions teaches at the modest county school with Nathan. He must be thirty, perhaps older, and his hair has begun balding, moving back from the front of his well-shaped head. It is nice, thick hair of a sandy red shade, and it curls at his neck. He wears a smattering of faint freckles across his nose and forehead, as most red-haired people do. He dresses well; he is clean and intelligent. He has a fine nose and a strong chin, and his quiet ways, his manner of moving and speaking, are not without their own charm. He has never married, and he is madly in love with Eden Frey.

He confessed as much to Nathan. When Nathan reported this information to us, amused and touched, I asked how he had reacted to Brother Sessions.

"Well, I suppose I encouraged him a little. I do not think Aaron would be such a bad catch. His respect for women is tender and sincere; he is a hard worker, intelligent, and skilled with his hands—he has many things to recommend him." Our silent stares were disarming the poor man. "Wouldn't some women find him attractive?" he finished a bit lamely.

"Eden Frey would not. Eden has been keeping company with a man who is not of our persuasion."

"Our persuasion?"

"Esther means that Jedediah Comstock is not one of us, not a Saint."

"Jedediah Comstock. Haven't I heard that name before?"

"I fear you have, dear." Georgie took up the distasteful narration. "He owns several houses in Painsville as well as Kirtland and is a speculator in business, wily and unprincipled."

"And he is a bit of a ladies' man? I think that is the gist of the gossip I have heard."

"He has an ugly air about him. I believe he is capable of cruelty," I added.

"Esther," Eugene admonished me gently.

"You all think I am overdoing it in my usual emotional manner. Well, this time I hope time proves you right and me wrong."

A dampening pall seemed to settle over us after I had spoken. Nathan made one last attempt.

"Perhaps if Aaron pursues Eden it will make a difference, give her a reason to draw away from this character, especially if she has a mind to but doesn't know how to bow out gracefully by herself."

I shook my head. "She is in the process of bowing *into* his life right now, doing her best to convince him that she is as attractive as any of the other women who catch his eye."

"To what purpose? Where is Comstock's charm? If you perceive him as evil, Esther, what can she see in the man?"

"There is a deadly fascination about such characters, or so they say." I shuddered. "And some women like to play with fire. It gives Eden a sense of power, a heightened sense of her own charms."

"Some women thrive on praise, even if it is falsely given," Georgie added. "Eden is the oldest of a large family. Perhaps she feels stifled and unappreciated. Perhaps she is simply eager to try her own wings and entranced by the possibilities he holds out to her when—"

"Enough, ladies, enough!" Eugene waved his arms at us, as if warding off a series of blows. "You'll dissect the poor girl to death if someone doesn't put a stop to this."

Perhaps he was right. I bit my tongue and said nothing. I could not really explain to my husband that we were not being catty, Georgie and I, that I felt deep concern for this girl and her family and the harm that might very well come to her and the consequent shame and suffering to them. But there I was again, getting myself involved in other people's lives. Though Nathan did bring up the subject, he had not expected half an hour's discussion of such terrible intensity to ensue.

I let it pass. Georgie skillfully changed the subject. But the seed of concern had been planted in that dark little garden of woes which thrives in the back of my mind. *Mary, Mary, quite contrary, how does your garden grow?* The old nursery rhyme chanted into my consciousness and left me feeling unsettled and not quite at my ease.

Gertrude Woods came to visit today with a rather strange request. She would like to trade flour freshly milled and cords of cut firewood for some of our potatoes and other produce from our garden. I believe it is an arrangement that could work out well for both of us now, with what is left of my garden, and even next spring and summer when a new abundance begins.

"And I will bring you bread once a week if you will occasionally make me one of your rhubarb or apple or berry pies, Esther."

Her odd request and the courage it must have taken her to make it touched some chord of sympathy within me. "For your bread I shall attempt to exchange evenly, a pie a week," I promised. Gertrude patted her fat sausage rolls into place and beamed at me, and I found myself reaching out and squeezing her hand.

I had not realized how little Georgie and I are in the know nowadays, compared to when Gertie lived here. In a little over an hour we caught up on months' worth of news. One item in particular interested me.

"Your Peter is keeping company with a young lady of his own at last," Gertrude crowed. "I have seen him with her twice this last week."

"Oh? What is the young lady like?" I was curious to hear her opinion.

"Not the comeliest I've seen, but then, a girl needs more than beauty to get along these days." I nodded agreement. "I like her manners, and there is something about her . . ." I nodded again. "She is obviously devoted to him."

"And Peter?"

"Peter is a hard one to read, Esther, do you not think?"

"I do, indeed. But I hope he can return Rosie Knapp's affections, for his sake as well as hers."

All in all I was encouraged. Reuben and Claire were, indeed, working wonders. Now if Peter would just pull through, let himself go a little—which, in his case, means let himself trust a little. I am glad we had opened the door. If Rosie really wants him, I believe she possesses enough stamina to see it through to the end.

The impossible has happened! Jack and Aurelia are engaged to be married in two months' time. The amazing thing about it is the aunts' enthusiasm.

"Many things, all added up, made the difference," Aurelia explained to Georgie and me. "But I think you two were definitely part of it. The aunts came to know you and know they could trust you. I believe they were frightened to death that they would be pushed right out of the picture and forgotten altogether. And, of course, they could not bear that."

Jack enlightened us yet further. "I told them I would be honored if they would come to live with us once we are married."

"Are you certain you mean it?" I asked.

"Here in Kirtland?" He grinned boyishly. "We have few options. Rather the two of them than strangers, trusting the luck of the draw as you had to."

"We did not fare that badly," I said, mildly surprised at my own defense of Gertrude and Garrison.

"Well, to be truthful, in some ways I truly want them. I have come to enjoy their company, and if they can relax about me, I believe I can do the same about them. And Aurelia will have help with the cooking and cleaning." He grinned again. "And, therefore, more leisure to spend with me!"

Suddenly there was much to be done in a few weeks' time. "I wish Phoebe were here," I confided to Georgie, and she ruefully agreed.

But Aurelia had her own friends, women who rallied to help her. Since Jack has no parents here, Georgie and Nathan filled the role in their stead.

"He is so happy," Georgie confided to me one morning when we were separating the cream and getting ready for churning.

"It is gratifying to see him like this, isn't it?" I took a deep breath and added, "Is it difficult, sweetie, to think about your parents? Do you wish they were here?"

Georgie took a while before answering me. "Perhaps my mother—perhaps if things could be as they used to be." Her eyes widened in reaction to her own thoughts. "It is strange, Esther, but I hardly remember what it was like, what they were like, before Mormonism turned our lives topsy-turvy—"

And drove a sharp blade of cruelty and pain between you! I thought to myself.

"And Jack?"

"Jack's all right. He's more reconciled than I am. You know, when

Emmeline died—" Georgie's dark eyes now became narrow slits of pain, and I was drawn at once back to those dark days. "When she died I remember that I cried for my mother. I thought of her first, Esther, before you, before any of the others, even before Nathan."

"That is the way it should be. It was natural, Georgie."

"Perhaps. But it felt very strange to me. I remember thinking: *I have lost my little girl, and my mother has lost her little girl, her only daughter. But is she crying for me? Did she cry that night my father helped burn my house down? Did she watch him write those hateful words to me, and close her soul to the weeping and the pain?*"

"Georgie!"

"Don't cry, Esther. It is all right, really. Just for those few hours, when I was so vulnerable and defenseless, I thought I would die for need of her."

"I understand," I said softly, wiping at the flow of tears that kept coming.

"Of course, you do. It's a bit of the other way 'round, with your father offering more sympathy and your mother determined to be set against you."

"But my mother was always that way—narrow and selfish, refusing to see anything but her own needs and opinions."

"Does knowing that make it easier?"

"Not really, no."

"Well, we have a new chance, you and I, with our children."

"Yes, Georgie, we do."

She looked closely into my face. "I *will* have more children, you know. I have no doubt of that. It may take a while, but they will come, and in plenty. And they will be a blessing in my life."

Suddenly, out of nowhere, I remembered the words the Prophet had spoken—spoken about Georgie and Nathan on that dark, painful night. I reached for her as the remembered glow rushed through me. "How do you *know?*" I asked.

"I have had answers to prayers, experiences, impressions."

I told her about that night, that fearful night when my little brother was dying. And, to my amazement, the exact words the Prophet had spoken came back to me. "Your friends suffer for the truth's sake, and they suffer gladly," he had said. "They will fare well, Esther. Do not worry about them. They will raise a good family, in a home far finer than they have ever hoped for." He spoke the words gently, calmly, but there was a faraway expression in his eyes, and I felt he saw more but was drawn back to the need of the moment, the condition of the dying child.

Georgie's face was glowing. "Do you believe Joseph truly sees the future then—things that will happen, ten years, a hundred years from where we stand?"

"You have read the Book of Mormon," I answered. "From Nephi's earliest visions and experiences we know this to be true."

"I can imagine it with Nephi because he is a faraway figure that I can draw in any manner I like. But Joseph is real. He walks and talks with us of common, everyday matters. I look into his face and try to imagine what wonders his mind and spirit hold." Georgie smiled.

"I do, too. To me it is a comfort."

"To me it is a wonderment."

Chapter Nine

Kirtland: December 1833

Josie's baby is born. A daughter! And both mother and daughter are well! I hold Randolph's letter close to my heart and feel a trembling of gratitude sweep through me. No one but he would think to give me each precious detail: the smallness of her hands, the slender taper of her fingers, the shape of fingernails, toes, and tiny-lobed ears; the way her mouth dimples at the left corner when she smiles, the shape of her eyes, the way she stops crying at once and holds very still to listen when he sings, *My truly, truly fair* against her cheek. He is clearly in love, for the second time in his life—as much with daughter as with mother. And I can only pray that this will please, rather than offend, Josephine.

Josie was the blonde-haired beauty of the family, but Randolph wrote, "I believe Rachel's hair may have red highlights and rich shadings, like yours." I cannot help but be pleased to read this. They are naming her Rachel after our mother. I can picture Mother's enthusiasm and pride, and for her I am glad—for both of them. I pray they will take all the pleasure they can in this miracle child.

"We miss you," Randolph writes.

I miss you. I knew you had been for a long time a strength to me, and a kind, loving guide. But I did not realize how much I depended upon you until you were gone. Half a dozen times a week I think, "I'll take this to Esther, she will know what to do," before remembering that this luxury is no longer mine, that, for all intents and purposes, you are lost to us . . .

Lost to us. What a terrible phrase! These words mean that Josie is still stirring up woes for this young man who loves her, and he is finding it more difficult to direct her life, to make her happy, than he had supposed. Perhaps this child will mature her; perhaps the blessing of her safe birth will occasion a gratitude Josie has not before known.

Randolph tells me of the success they are experiencing at the mills and the different employments and pursuits of their young canal boys— all encouraging, hopeful sorts of things. "Give my special love to Peter," he adds. "Tell him I admire him for what he is doing, though I miss him terribly and at times feel sorry for myself stuck here away from you both—you two, the only ones who kept their faith in me no matter what I did, and whose love pulled me through."

Of course, I could not read his words dry-eyed. As a p.s. he said, "Your sister has tucked in a little missive of her own, so I hope the postage I am enclosing will be sufficient. Write once a week, once a day, Esther. If this is all we shall have of you, then do not deny us . . ."

Bless him! Lulled by his kind words and the generous spirit behind them, I opened my sister's letter with a sense of eagerness. The very first sentence roundly cured me of that!

Esther, why are you not here, here with me and mother—your red-haired daughter here beside mine? It is cruel, too cruel to bear, and I cannot help but blame you. For you chose strangers over your loved ones, and now we are all suffering, and I do not understand why!

Josie, Josie! Please, my heart cried, *have mercy! And think of my pain, too.* "Nothing is simple and good like it used to be," she continued.

Tillie still refuses to talk to me, and it breaks my heart that she will not even come to see my baby and be glad for me, after my years of disappointment and pain. Her own life is far from what she had hoped. Gerard grows more and more cruel and more and more distant, and he has taken over much of the training of young Laurie, who is five years old, if you can believe it. So it appears she is hardening herself against everyone in retribution, when only Gerard is to blame.

I shuddered. My poor Tillie, married off to a man of her father's choosing, doing her duty with innocent and stoic intent—and being thus dealt with! How cruelly the pain and loneliness must eat at her, and I not there to help. On Tuesday afternoons did she ever draw back the curtain in hopes of seeing me walking up to her house? She was locked up in her own hell because in her weakness she had shut everyone out. And the worst of it, the worst of it I knew, would be relinquishing her son to the influence of a father who would systematically train all the kindness and tenderness out of him, while all she could do was sit there and wretchedly watch.

I took pen and paper in hand. I wrote to Josephine:

Dearest Josephine, Can you not see that Tillie is your husband's sister? Can you not remember that she is the bosom friend of your childhood? If she is too unhappy to do what you think she ought to, then do something about it yourself! Can you not go to her and share some of the joy with which you have been so blessed?

I wrote as pointedly to Randolph: "Find some way, I beg of you, to ease Tillie's lot! Make Josephine go to her. Cannot you awaken some mercy in that haughty young breast?" I was trembling as I formed the letters, and the words swam in front of my eyes. Randolph had thought to spare me, my mother had not spared a thought either way for me, and Josephine, as selfish as ever, had taken a warped sort of pleasure in causing me pain.

I felt exhausted as I finished and sealed up my letter. Perhaps I ought not to send it? Yes, I must, I must! I dropped down on the hard floor beside Lavinia who interrupted her game to kiss my cheek, and I spun her little blue top for her half a dozen times before I could muster the determination to scramble up again and get back to my tasks.

Peter came at my summons, and I showed him his brother's letter. He was pleased at the idea of being an uncle, but he said little else.

"Do you ever think it strange the way Randolph is married to Josephine?"

"We always considered her aeons ahead of us—beyond us, rather."

"Well, she is twenty-nine to his twenty-one."

Peter shrugged. "Randolph is ageless, isn't he? And he is man enough to handle her."

I agreed. "What of yourself?" I asked casually; I was not getting far at all in drawing him out. "Would you like to marry, do you think? Do you feel interested, ready?"

"I'm pretty young myself, Esther."

"Not too young, for goodness' sake."

"I feel it."

"You couldn't, not after all you've been through." *I had better drop the subject,* a voice warned. But I went one tiny step further. "I should like to see you settled and happy."

"You're sounding like a mother now, Esther, though I suppose that's all right."

He was relaxing a little. "Are you happy here, Peter?" I asked. "Truly happy. Do you ever regret . . . coming?"

"You mean joining the Church? No. I may not be good at it, this whole business of religion. But I know it is right. I know how much better life is under the principles of Mormonism than the existence I left behind."

I put my arms round him, one quick hug only. But I could not help myself.

"I've missed that," he smiled, and his boyish smile melted me. *You should have a mother hugging you that way every day,* I thought, *or a wife.*

"'Tis a good omen, Esther," Eugene said enthusiastically. "The first number of *The Evening and Morning Star* will be printed before the month's out, before the old year is put behind us."

"I am glad to hear it," I said. He was up to his elbows in printer's ink and loving it.

"We've established a temporary office in John Johnson's inn, though we expect by spring to be able to move up on the hill at that spot near the Methodist meetinghouse."

My husband was elated, and I was grateful, for good Brother Frey had agreed to allow him to work at the smithy however many hours he could manage while he helped with the setting up and getting ready of the new printing press and what is to be printed on it. We needed, after all, a source of income to sustain us; writing and printing could never do that. So Andrew Frey's generosity meant we would not starve to death. And Eugene was happy, happy really for the first time since we came here. And, of course, that happiness spilled over to Lavinia and myself.

❦

The time of Jack and Aurelia's wedding draws near. Aurelia has been here on three separate occasions to copy recipes from us. "The aunts must not do all the cooking! I want to serve Jack myself. How can I please him and win his pleasure if I let them do everything, and I don't learn?"

"Wise child," Georgie muses. "She will make him happy, and he will take good care of her." And I agree.

❦

It was the middle of the night, but I heard the sound at once and sat up in bed to listen. Moonlight poured into the room, and I could see by its dimness that neither Eugene nor Lavinia were disturbed. I slipped out of bed, ignoring the coldness of the floor and the tightness in my muscles that made my neck hurt. *No one should be knocking on my door at this hour.* I knew instinctively that something was very wrong.

Jack's white, hollow-eyed face was the last I wanted to see there! I drew him into the room. "What is it?" I realized I was whispering.

"Is Georgie awake?"

"I do not think so." I rubbed sleep out of my eyes with vigor. I wanted him to relax before my gaze, say something to destroy this pain that was threatening to double me over. I grabbed hold of his arm. "What is it, Jack? You look like the living dead."

"I am. Get Georgie, dress quickly, and come with me. Aurelia is ill, ill to the point of dying."

I did not want to believe him, but I could not stand there gaping. I knew by the look of him that he spoke no exaggeration. I could not summon up any hope inside myself, and that frightened me to death.

It was only a matter of minutes before Georgie and I, white-faced as Jack, were ready to join him. He had brought a light buggy. We left a note for the menfolk and piled in beneath the blankets, which felt stiff and cold against our sleep-warmed skin. Our breath frosted the air, and the horse breathed noisily. I felt that the quiet night resented our intrusion and wished us safe in our beds as much as we wished it ourselves.

In my bones, as in my brain, were stored all the other nights like this one, when life had suddenly become a stranger with a face we couldn't recognize—an essence as slippery as hoarfrost, as intangible as the sunlight that shines or retreats at will—and we stood in awe of what we had been taking for granted.

I had been clenching my muscles so tight that they hurt and, perhaps from the intense cold, my head was beginning to ache. *No, no!* I cried inside. *Do not let this be happening.* I drew a deep shuddering breath and attempted to relax.

It was nearly impossible to talk, but we had need to ask Jack a few questions before we got to the house.

"It was sudden, with no warning," Jack began. "Aunt Helen came herself to fetch me only an hour ago." He swallowed painfully, as if he could not get the words out. "Dorothy says it is a severe case of cholera."

I pressed my hand to my mouth to keep from crying out. I did not ask for the symptoms. I knew them all too well: a pain in the head that wracks the very brain cells, a distress in the limbs that is nearly too much to bear, cramps that tie the body into burning knots of anguish, until everything is weakened, frightened, retreating.

We got out of the buggy reluctantly, yet with an anxiety that drew us relentlessly forward. I avoided Jack's eyes because I had no comfort to give him, and I could not bear his pain. We entered the house. The stillness within had a thick quality to it, and I felt as though I must push my way through it to make any progress at all. Dorothy's face, with its wrinkles that spread in soft white folds, appeared to have crumpled like the icing on a wedding cake left out in the sun. I placed my hand over hers, and she gripped my fingers so tightly that I wanted to cry out.

"May we go to her? May we do anything to help?" I asked.

"The doctor has been and gone and says he will return before morning. He is attending half a dozen such cases," Helen informed us.

I realized that Dorothy was crying softly. *This girl is her life, almost her sole reason for existing,* I thought. *She is frightened at the enormity of what her loss would be.* I wished Dr. Ensworth were here. He has a no-nonsense quality combined with a strong faith that attacks sickness with a vengeance that goes beyond mere treatment and mere hope.

As I hesitated Georgie had walked back to the bedroom. I found

79

her kneeling beside the bed. Aurelia's person was so tiny, so slender that she hardly made an impression beneath the blue and white coverlet. Her dark hair spilled over the pillow, and her face was like a carving in ice.

I knelt beside Georgie and prayed in the darkness, whose smothering weight surrounded us.

When I felt a touch on my shoulder and looked up, I did not know how long it had been. Georgie led me out, and I realized that the sky showing through their small square of window was lightening, the gray washing out to that dull noncolor that precedes the first shadings of dawn.

"The doctor has arrived," Helen explained. I saw only his back as he walked into the room. After a very few moments he called Jack's name. I felt Georgie clench beside me. We four women followed at a distance and stood huddled outside the door.

Aurelia was moaning, then with effort, forming words that dropped upon the ear like hot pebbles. "The pain is bursting my bones apart . . . I cannot . . ."

Jack fell down beside her, his voice as calm and soothing as cool running water. I realized that he had begun to sing to her, his tone low and melodic. I stumbled back into the kitchen. The others followed me. When the doctor came out his face was set in lines of concern that must be permanently etched there. He offered us no false hope.

"Her fever is high, the cramping extreme. This disease has a terrible hold on her."

Silence. I swallowed against the dryness in my throat. "What can we do for her?" I asked.

"Get her to swallow a little water as often as possible." He cleared his throat, the sound dry and raspy. "And pray. Prayer is her only real recourse, I fear."

We left Jack alone with her. We did not speak to each other, for there was nothing to say. Inside my own heart I could not countenance the thought of Aurelia dying. Therefore, I was unable to pray, as I ought to, "*Thy will be done.*" I could only plead, as a child would, in terror and need.

It was only a matter of hours, but I felt as though I had been sitting in that hard ladder-back chair for half a lifetime. When Jack called out suddenly for the aunts, we all knew. I rose slowly and came at a distance, watching the others as though we all moved through a dream. But there was room at her bedside, and I stood close enough to look down at her drawn face: brow and eyes, nose and mouth and cheekbones as perfectly formed as the hand of the most skilled sculpture could have made them. So slight, so weak—yet so beautifully real and alive!

"I do not mind going. Please do not weep for me. Jack—" She attempted to lift her head but could achieve no movement at all. "Dear, dear ones. I will wait . . . I will be happy . . ." A strange expression, a sensation of light passed over her features. "Do not . . . forget me . . ."

Her hand holding Jack's relaxed, and the gentle features went limp. Jack buried his head against her bosom. Dorothy began to weep loudly. Helen turned, taut as a sail when the wind holds it, and walked from the room, from the house. I put my arm around Georgie and lead her back into the kitchen.

The winter day dawned as gentle and gray as a dove's breast, with tendrils of rose at its wings. I could not weep. I felt I could hardly draw breath beneath the weight of sadness that sat on my heart. The blessed numbness of grief covered me like a shroud. And beneath the bitter shroud my torn spirit piteously, silently wept.

❧

Over the next two days people come forward to help, and there is not enough for me to do. I take care of Lavinia, plague her really, with my attentions. And in a frenzy of energy I scrub floors and walls, clean candle wax from pewter, and wash every streaked chimney lamp in the house. Work is the only comfort such times as these afford.

Jack is magnificent. I know the Spirit is blessing and sustaining him, and my heart aches to see the nobility etched upon his features that was not visible before.

I am concerned about Peter. He is angry and depressed for his friend's sake and will not be reconciled.

"Others have risen from sick beds as severe," he has been protesting endlessly. "She was sweet and innocent, as pure as a young girl could be. It makes no sense that God allowed her to be taken."

"The 'sense' you speak of exists nowhere in the earthly experience," I chastise him. "You ought to remember that. Such is not the purpose of our being here."

"Well, I see no purpose whatsoever to how the whole thing is arranged. The good suffer, and the wicked prosper. And the better you are, the worse it is for you."

I say no more. He is beyond counsel or comfort and will be until this bitterness and pain run their course through him.

We busy ourselves preparing—not for the last minute details of a joyful, beautiful wedding—but for the somber burial of the expectant bride.

The day comes, despite our dread, despite the piteousness of our loss. It is Georgie and I who have dressed the slim body in the gown which had been lovingly, hopefully created for such a different purpose. Some think it cruel to see this maiden laid out in her wedding attire. But perhaps it is as it should be. She returns to her God as the bride of the man who still loves her, whose love will not dim, though time robs him of the object, the reality. If anything at all as we know it persists, it is love. Love lives on.

"Remember me." Aurelia's last painful words lurk like haunting shadows at the edge of my mind. But there is also a comfort cupped within them, this assurance that all will be well as long as love is remembered and honored.

The aunts lean on Jack's arms. They look shrunken, broken, as if the vitality within them snapped when Aurelia's spirit, pouring the warmth of her affection and support into them, ceased to be. It is all I can do to turn my eyes on Aurelia—frozen in beauty, beyond help, beyond blessing, beyond joy.

Jack is the only one who does not shed a tear, whose features reflect that peace which is beyond comprehension. I know the source, and I stand a bit in awe of his power to call down and contain this peace.

It is Aurelia's influence, a voice within me whispers. *Her spirit remains with him still and will succor and uphold him until he no longer requires it.*

I am drained, as weak as a kitten. as I walk away from that place. Such sorrow hallows human suffering, lifts it to a level that even the weakest among us can feel. We cannot expect to understand with our limited vision. I know this is true. I know, but like Peter, I am not entirely reconciled. Yet I find, at the end of this endless day, that I go down on my knees gladly, that I am hungry for the opportunity to lay my heart open to God. I am childlike still; I know he has power to push back the dark void and send rays of sunlight to pierce the blackness. Without this assurance, without him to turn to, what would I do? It is with deep gratitude that I lift my thoughts and my desires to him.

❦

December is a month for looking inward, as even the celebration of Christ's birth, itself, is. In a December which is beginning to seem far away, my sister, Josephine, married Alexander Hall. In December Jonah Sinclair brought Peter's brother, Randolph, to me, cut up and hurt terribly in a canal-side brawl. In December of the next year, after he had run away in despair, he was brought back to me again. In the same December Latisha's daughter, Sarah, was born. Come another December Jane Foster, the beloved midwife who had served others while pain was eating up her own life died. And the last December before I left home Josephine, newly widowed, married young Randolph Swift, who was willing to give his life over in service to her. All this in the matter of a little over five years.

Now I am a grown woman. I have met life and merged with it and must recognize the good in it and find value in the bad of it if I am to go on.

An ending, a beginning. A constant rebirth and renewal. In this December of the year 1833, on Wednesday, the 18th day, the Elders assembled at the John Johnson Inn to dedicate the new printing office. My Eugene was there, glowing, grateful, and hopeful. During this same meeting Joseph the Prophet called and ordained his father as patriarch to the Church. A holy calling—to be the mouthpiece of God in pronouncing blessings upon his children. A restoration in this dispensation of a most priceless gift! And if any man is capable, worthy, pliable in the hands of Deity, that man is Father Smith.

Blessings were bestowed in that very meeting; first, as a type and example, by the Prophet himself. I think with timid exaltation that there is a blessing for me! Words and counsel, love and encouragement from Heavenly Father meant for my heart and my life alone. At this moment I crave the love and reassurance such a blessing would bring. Such an experience seems nearly too good to be true. When the time comes Eugene and I will go to the patriarch together, and perhaps Georgie and Nathan will go with us. I should like to bring Jack along. And Peter. Peter is in greater need of a blessing right now, I fear, than perhaps any of us.

We go on. Aurelia's influence, like the influence of an angel, goes with us still. And we have much to which we look forward, in faith.

Chapter Ten

Kirtland: February 1834

A letter arrives. I open it eagerly, with no presentiments. And my father, in his small, cramped writing, informs me that my mother is dead.

I care nothing for the details; it is days before I pick up the letter again to read them. I know only that she who gave me life is no longer among the living. I cannot go, fly to comfort and be comforted. I walk to the window and gaze out upon the frost-hardened trees, the snow-swept fields, and the frozen river. I have not the means to make such a journey. And Nature, with a power that cannot be questioned, also prohibits it. All the money in Kirtland could not make my odyssey possible.

I return from the window and stare into the fire. I had expected to have my mother here for years to come yet. I had expected—what had I expected, secretly hoped for? For years her heart had been hardened to me. She had her son, her last child, to hug to her, and Josephine remained daughter enough for her need. She had been willing, and would have been willing, to spend the days of her life without me. I do not understand. Now her sudden death unlocks the rusty gates that have enclosed my pain, my longings, my need of her! Since I have become a mother I believe I have resented her coldness more. How could a mother's heart reject what is so really and truly a part of her? How could she not have been drawn toward me, as I—despite all disappointments and differences—was drawn toward her?

For a few moments I feel entirely a prisoner; all joy choked off and denied me. Then my own little daughter comes into the room. Even the weak winter sun picks up the glowing highlights in her red hair. She smiles at me. I feel her love mingle with my love as it goes out toward her. I hold out my arms, and she comes eagerly to me, tucks her bright head under my chin. I know I am grieving for what my mother has lost in withholding her love from me, as much or more than I am grieving for myself.

᪣

Eugene was busy doing what he loves best. But he was fair in dividing his time between working for Brother Frey—which assured us an income—and the work which I consider for the Church *and* himself.

"My hands are black with soot from the smithy or ink from the printing press," he would laugh. "One or the other, day in, day out, so I'd best resign myself to it."

We both were more than resigned. We felt fortunate that he had work, and work in plenty, and that part of that work could feed the mind and spirit, as well as merely physical needs.

He was more tender than I thought he would be when I told him the news of my mother. "She dies leaving you both unfulfilled," he said, "with things between you unsettled, and I know how hard that is for you, Esther."

For once he instinctively knew what I needed most. He enfolded me in his arms and let me weep against his strong shoulder. And for that night, and many following, he held me tenderly, too, just letting me feel his nearness, the reassuring touch of him. Once or twice the thought came unbidden: *What would I do if Eugene died?* At such moments I would cling to him, though he knew not the reason. Only a blind darkness would answer the unwanted question. And during those days my life became gentler, as I recognized the worth of each moment, held it in my hands like the fleeting treasure it truly was.

᪣

Georgie had a bee in her bonnet. "There is suffering enough in the world," she said, storming about the kitchen with a pent-up energy uncommon to her, "but I can do something about this, and I have not. And that is a crime."

I was not certain what she meant. She has begun taking pupils: any size, any age, any variety, we all have teased. She now tutors them here or in their own houses; she is not fussy. None of us knows exactly what she is charging or where the money will go.

"Poor dear, she asked me the other day if I thought it fair if she turns over half of what she earns to me for household needs and expenses and keeps the remainder," Nathan confided to us. "This is something very important to her, but she will not say what it is."

"Not yet," she insisted, when I questioned her following our conversation with Nathan. "After I know for sure."

And there is no way any of us can get anything further from her.

❦

Jack is adjusting. He still seems at peace within himself. But this day he had come to me to confide a concern we both shared. Georgie was in the small parlor with one of her pupils. I took him back into the kitchen and gave him something to drink.

"Peter is angry with God, I believe," he started, mincing no words. "I think Aurelia's death frightened him, and he has somehow retreated within himself."

"Odd," I mused, "that this should happen to him, as though in your place."

"I have had the same thought myself. I asked him last week if he would come with me to work on the temple, but he simply stared at me. When I persisted he said, 'You hope for great blessings from this temple. But there is no happiness in this life. What makes you think it will come in the next?'

"I tried to push, to get him to tell me what he meant by that, but he closed up tight as a clam."

I sighed. "I fear for him, Jack. I think the heart has been taken out of him, and he is weary of suffering."

"And he no longer has faith."

"Why should he? Look at the pattern of his own life and the lives of the people he loves. He is young and not securely rooted nor able to reason as deeply as you do." I glanced at him sharply and decided to hazard the question that I had been itching to ask for these past weeks. "Why is it you are so strong?" I did not know how else to put it. But a gray shadow passed over his face before he answered.

"Through the grace of God, Esther. I knew from the beginning when I watched Aurelia slip away and leave me that I could not possibly bear this loss of her without help."

I nodded. I had stirred up the ashes of his suffering so that a few embers were glowing into life, hot and scathing.

"Even then, there have been times—" He stood, turned, and walked away from me, and I sorely regretted that I had been foolish and selfish enough to question him on the matter.

"Another time, Esther. There is more I should like to tell you, but not now."

"I understand, Jack! Please forgive me, I meant—"

He smiled wanly. "There is nothing to forgive, Esther."

We talked for a few more minutes before he went on his way. I still felt miserable after I watched the door close upon him. And my folly had prevented the asking of another question: What of Rose Knapp? Was Peter still being seen with her? How was all this affecting the way Peter was treating this girl?

I had my own doubts and fears that were gnawing painfully. *I shall have to go to the Lambs,* I resolved, *and discover something of what's going on.*

What better time than the present? I asked Georgie, still at work with her pupil, if she would keep an ear open for Lavinia, who was napping upstairs. *I can walk the distance to the corner of Palmyra and Chillicothe Road where the little bakery sits in no time at all.*

There was a brisk wind outdoors, scurrying about its own business, but it was pushing in my direction, so the going was pleasant enough. It seemed I could taste the water of Lake Erie on that wet wind, and for a moment I wished it could lift me up and blow me away . . . back home to Palmyra, where I had as many old problems waiting as I had new problems here. For the moment, my heartstrings were not tugged in that direction. Perhaps I wished to go to some faraway place where fear and heartache had never existed and where the spirit could be fed—if only for a short while—on beauty and peace.

Though I walked with swift, purposeful strides, my heart remained aloof and wistful, listening to the muted voices of the wise, well-traveled, vagabond wind. And so intent was I that I literally bumped into the young woman who was leaving the shop just as I approached. Chagrined, I took a step back as I muttered an apology, feeling my cheeks go red.

"Sister Thorn! You are an answer to my prayers."

"Whatever do you mean, child?" I looked into Rose Knapp's bright face and felt my heart give a leap.

"If I had left ten minutes ago, as I intended, well, I would have missed you. But Claire asked me to take her hot buns from the oven while she waited on a customer, so here we both are."

"Indeed!" I returned her smile, still very puzzled. She drew me by the arm further away from the shop door. "Could you spare me a moment or two, please, before you go in?"

I nearly laughed. I almost confessed that I had walked this distance solely for the purpose of obtaining information concerning Peter and *her!* "Gladly," I replied, "for I have been worried about you."

"About me?" Her nose crinkled in what I think was a pleased surprise, and the faint freckles danced across it. "You think of me, Sister Thorn?"

"Esther, to my friends. Yes, I think of you often. I . . . I . . ." *How could I frame this?* "I am aware of your affections for Peter. I respect whatever it is that has drawn you to him, and I am concerned for your happiness—especially these past weeks since Aurelia died."

The words were a shiver in my mouth, and suddenly the wind seemed to go through me, and I drew my knitted shawl close. The girl was watching me, and I tried to read the flickers of expression as they passed through her dark, thoughtful eyes.

"You do care for me, not just Peter. I can see that you do."

"I hope you never doubt it, my dear." Pleasure lit her gaze and relaxed the lines of her face. "These have been difficult weeks, have they not?"

"Yes!" She reached out, and her small fingers groped for my hand. "You are cold," she cried, "and I am keeping you standing here! Do you think we dare go into the shop?"

"I believe so. Claire Lamb shares more or less our sympathies and our knowledge of what is going on here."

Rose laughed—the fresh, open laugh of a young girl. It warmed my heart. "What is going on here? I wish *I* knew what is going on here, indeed I do, ma'am!"

The warmth of the fragrant, cozy bakery was most welcome. Claire found chairs for us to sit on and, though the place was at present empty, we sat close and spoke in guarded whispers.

"Tell me about Peter," Rose asked at once, "all you can about his past life before he came here."

"My dear, I cannot do that in minutes, even in hours. But I will make a beginning which we can build upon later." I gave her a sketchy background of the Swift family, of my friendship with Theodora, of Mr. Swift's haughty pride, which has brought such unhappiness to them all. I drew rough pictures of Peter's life as a canal boy, and of Randolph's troubles and the cruelty of Tillie's husband when Peter worked under him at his father's bank.

The more I revealed, the larger and more mournful her eyes grew; the brown shades darkened, and the lights were all but snuffed out.

"I understand. I couldn't before, you see . . ." Rose's voice was low, the words hard to catch, and her eyes were flooding over with tears. This time I reached for her hand and held it between mine, smoothing and warming the soft skin with my fingers.

"I believe our poor lad is afraid to love," I said, "harsh as that might sound." She swallowed her tears and nodded. "For more reasons than I have yet begun to explain, and for others which I am sure neither one of us knows."

"If I felt that he cared for me, I could go on. I could be patient, I could take anything—but he shows no sign!"

"How has he behaved since, since—"

We skipped over the hard words as she took my meaning. "He is usually quiet, sometimes bitter and angry, but mostly he refuses to discuss what has happened. He refuses to talk about anything that has any real meaning."

"But he continues to see you?" I asked.

"Every day."

"And what do you do?"

"Sometimes I sit with him over supper, and it ends up that I eat Claire's good cooking with him or leftovers from the day's baking. Sometimes we help do the dishes, or he brings in a stack of wood. We take walks when the weather is fine enough. One evening I helped him mend a harness, another he helped me wind wool. Little things, and we do not talk much. It is just—being together."

I smiled in relief. "That is your sign, sweet girl. *He needs you*—already. And though his pain and fear may push him away from you, he has not the heart to go."

My simple words opened her eyes. "I had not thought . . . of course!" Happiness laughed in her voice and lit the candles behind her eyes again.

"I know him well," I reaffirmed. "You can be certain of what I say."

She sank back in her chair a little as her thoughts took her forward. "But what beyond that?"

"Patience," I said bluntly. "Patience for the moment, and no guarantees for where the moment might lead."

She drew her face up into a grimace that made her appear little-girlish, even impish. "Sounds like a dose of medicine."

"'Tis," I replied. "Some of life's bitter dregs."

"But," she said softly, "I have not yet tasted the wine."

"That is where faith must come in, dear," I said carefully. "Faith, which goes far beyond patience. Faith and one more thing."

"Love?"

"Yes." I drew a deep breath. "Heaven knows why some people are drawn to each other, why you should feel something for this young stranger . . ." I smiled woefully. "You must try to decide if you love him and if what you feel is the right kind of love—deep enough, strong enough—"

She nodded. "If so, it will be able to pull me through . . ."

"And if not, you must be on your way again, no matter how cruel that seems."

She sighed, and for a moment closed her eyes, as if to shut out my words. "You are already weary," I said softly. "I know. Would to heaven it were different. But the order of things is ancient, and not of my doing, though if I could I would help. I would—"

"You have helped already." Rose leaned forward swiftly and planted a small kiss on my cheek. "I must be off . . ." she hesitated, "I should be worried over if I am late, and I would not want that."

In a scoot and a scurry she was off, the door pulled shut behind

91

her, and I had not even had time to urge her to come to me anytime she thought I might be of help. And I realized that though I had now answered many questions she had concerning Peter's life, I knew very little of her.

I called out a farewell to Claire and slipped back outside again, anxious to share with Georgie all that had happened, and see what she had to say!

I found Georgie with her tin of savings poured out on the kitchen table, so intent on counting that she scarcely heard me enter. After a few moments I ventured to address her. "Enough yet?" I asked.

"Nearly," she replied, without thinking, then looked up and tried to glare at me. "I am securing more and more pupils," she said, "and they keep me very busy. And you have been quite unwell—"

"A little unwell this winter," I admitted, confused entirely.

"You have the baby to care for, and your husband, for all intents and purposes, is working two separate jobs and is gone constantly."

"Not constantly, though a great deal of the time."

"We could use someone to help us. That makes sense, doesn't it, Esther?"

"Yes, I believe that it does." She was going somewhere; I could see it in her face. But I could not yet begin to follow.

Perspiration was standing out in tiny beads on her forehead as she began her next sentence. "If Emmeline worked for us on her weekends, and more money went to her father—if we could convince him that she is worth more to him here than she is worth to him at home—"

Oh, Georgie! I blinked back tears that I knew would undo her. "Yes, that makes sense enough. And I believe it may very well work."

"I have money. I saved most of what we made from the straw hats. And since then I have earned—" She picked up a little pile from the table and let the coins run through her fingers. "I have enough to keep her with us for a few months right now—without earning more. That is, if her father does not prove too greedy."

I stifled an urge to rise and hug this dear woman to me! "Have you thought who would be best to approach him, to do the asking or bargaining?"

"I have, but I cannot decide."

"Have you spoken about this to Nathan yet?"

"Last night. It is easier for me to talk in the darkness, where he cannot see my face. He listens more carefully, too, since there is nothing else to distract him."

"And—"

"He really understands, Esther. He will support me, stand beside me whatever I decide."

"Of course he will! Nathan is one of the best of men."

We laughed together then and hugged one another, and I told her of my conversation with Rosie, and suddenly we felt hopeful and happy as girls again.

That evening we were so high-spirited that our husbands shook their heads and called us silly. But we knew they were pleased. Life must sometimes draw back from the shadows and suffering and assert itself. Hope must have its day, and the spirit must believe in its own power to reach upward and triumph and experience its own share of joy.

Chapter Eleven

When the Prophet Joseph dedicated the printing press in December he asked God "to establish it forever, and cause that His word may speedily go forth to the nations of the earth, to the accomplishing of His great work in bringing about the restoration of the house of Israel."

Eugene has since learned of the powerful forces in opposition to our work and the necessity of calling upon God every step of the way. Persecution directed toward the brethren is particularly severe, and they must sleep with firearms to protect themselves and with a twenty-four hour watch on their homes and their persons. Anyone involved in publishing Mormon "heresies," in strengthening the Latter-day Saints, or in building the temple is under suspicion or surveillance, if not yet open attack.

Many Gentiles refuse to trade with us; in some areas our women are not safe to walk alone on the streets. The spirit of justification spreads like wildfire, and we are caught in the midst of it, like an island at sea. But we carry on. With trouble on every hand and nightmare conditions in Missouri, our missionaries are still being sent forth. A few months ago the Kirtland Stake of Zion was officially organized, and on May 3, at a conference of the Elders, it was determined that the official name of the Church will hereafter be The Church of the Latter-day Saints. Perhaps now people will desist from calling us Mormonites.

As this spring month began Brother Joseph led a company of men to assist the Saints in Missouri, who have been suffering cruelly under the hands of crazed and cruel men. We women have been in a frenzy, preparing clothing and other necessities to take to the brethren and sisters who have been robbed of their all. When the Prophet heard news of the families being driven from their homes and farms in Jackson County, he burst into tears. I believe he would fly to the aid of any one of his people, bear our burdens for us, if he might. I believe he has mercy like unto the mercy of the Savior.

So they are gone. Gone on a dangerous—and what some consider foolhardy—mission. We who remain behind, safe in our houses and positions for the time being, pray daily for this little group of brethren, marching solemnly into the very jaws of the lion . . .

I look about me at faces of strangers and nonmembers. I try to imagine what they would be like hardened into lines of anger and hate. How much would it take to light such a spark of destruction in Kirtland? *But surely not here!* The Lord has asked us to build a temple—a place of beauty, a place of worship, a permanent place, designed by his hand. Surely that must mean we are to stay here and do his work as he has ordained.

And, in the midst of all this, my father has written with an amazing request. He wants me to come and take my young brother, Jonathan, to live with me and to raise him up as my own.

I am stunned; I would never in my life have expected this. The first thought that leaps unbidden to my mind is *How angry my mother would be if she could see this turn of events coming to pass.* It is surely an answer to *my* prayers. Jonathan, from the beginning, has been an exceptionally gentle and goodly child. To know that the blessings of the gospel will be coming to him is a happiness I had never expected to know.

Eugene approaches the situation with more prudence and discretion than I. "Why has your father chosen you over Josephine as a guardian? It makes little sense. Your sister has the means to raise a child, and she lives nearby, which means your father would still have an influence in his son's life."

"It does seem strange," I admitted.

"And you shall have the dickens to pay where Josie is concerned; you know that."

"I do, indeed!" I shivered at the very prospect of confronting my sister.

"Whether she wants him or not, she will be offended that he is given to you. And you must go there and face her wrath and be dragged back into all the old problems, just to—"

"Do you want Jonathan to be with us, Eugene?" I had not thought to ask him directly, but now I realized that I must. "It will be an extra expense, an extra responsibility."

Eugene seldom demurs or dissembles. He looked me straight in the eye while his mind mulled over the matter. "I can think of no reason why it would not be good for us to take him, Esther. It appears to me that the Lord has brought this unexpected decision about. The boy will, I suspect, prove to be a help to me. And I know you love him dearly." He reached out a work-calloused finger to brush a tear from my cheek. "God willing, I will do my best by him, Esther. I just do not want you to go!"

My heart softened. *He is worried about me. It is concern for my safety and well-being, it is the prospect of being without me that has rendered him a bit ill-tempered.*

"I will be very careful," I promised. "And I will come back as soon as I can."

Thus it has been decided, the funds got together, the preparations made. And an added blessing has come about because of it: We have yet another legitimate reason to require Emmeline's services, and her father agrees that she can come to stay and work for us at the week's end, between her everyday schedule of work at the Frey's.

Georgie herself approached the old brute. I do not know what she told him, what demeanor she adopted, but she secured what she went for, and I shrink to ask at what price—not only in dollars and cents but in what it must have cost her in mind and courage and sheer will!

The week before I was scheduled to leave, Emmeline appeared at our door bright and early on Saturday morning. She is such a sprite of a girl. I forget during the periods when I do not see her often. Her demeanor has improved since she has been a part of the Frey house-hold, but she still holds herself in an attitude of cautious expectation, almost uncertainty, that tugs at the heart. I do not wish to think of how often her father hits or in other ways abuses her. We have her, for the time being, out of his clutches; and with God's help we shall keep it that way.

She is a bit timid around me still, but she is not shy with Georgie.

A sweetness comes over her face when Georgie walks into the room, and she is entirely pliable to Georgie's will.

I do not know for certain what my good friend has in mind for the aid and education of our Emmeline, but I have implicit confidence in her. As I watch Emmy trot after Georgie, cheerful and trusting, it makes my heart glad. We *have* discovered that the girl's frail arms can lift and wield an iron with incredibly fine results. She works hard, and I believe she is also well organized; perhaps some of this will rub off! It is pleasant to have her about the house. Her spirit is like sunshine, and she has a willingness to co-operate, serve, and help. She speaks little, though. She is still very cautious when it comes to expressing herself. And I wonder what goes on inside that small, quiet head.

It is time to leave. I am, of course, taking Lavinia with me. The only other time I have been separated from Eugene since our marriage is when I went from Palmyra to Kirtland; now I am returning the opposite way. I am not anxious to leave. Oh, what strange creatures we humans are! I indulge in pity for myself that I am torn from my friends back home and can no longer attend their daily lives and associate with them. When the opportunity comes to me, I shy from it, go on my way with reluctance and backward glances. Am I ever to be content?

I do not relish the trip on the canal boat either, but I make a brave face of it. I shall have company this time, at least. Lavinia will keep me busy, that is for certain, and the hours ought to pass more quickly that way.

Eugene kisses me before we leave the house and again before we board the boat. I kiss my hand to him from the deck. Lavinia waves. My eyes meet his and hold for one long moment before he at last turns away. I turn, too, willing myself not to look backward, but set my face resolutely ahead.

The days on the water pass with no mishap, no tragedy; I am grateful for that. The food, the sleeping conditions, the care I must take to protect my toddling child while we are on deck are all challenges to both my patience and my ingenuity. By and large, people are kind. A woman alone with a baby occasions some little deference, at least from most. But I discover the first morning when we rise and the motion of the boat nearly bowls me over, and then again a bit later when I try to keep down my breakfast, that I am most surely with child. I thought as much before I left, but I was not certain. Now I am stranded alone, a stranger among strangers, when my woman's heart longs for the comforting arms of my husband, his protection and care. If I had confessed my suspicions before, he would have forbidden the journey. Would that have been right? I do not know! I have prayed and prayed about this and received no warning, no dark feelings against it. Jonathan must have his chance. That alone is worthy enough cause for my going, for my troubling Eugene with my absence.

There is one thing that happens on board which disturbs me considerably. Two days out I see a rather florid, well-dressed man walking toward me, with a woman as primped up and proud as can be mincing along at his arm. I do not know the female, but I recognize her companion: Jedediah Comstock. He leans close to whisper something intimate to her, and his lips brush her cheek. I think of Eden, vain and foolish, and I want to go over, take him by both his shoulders, and shake him until I rattle some decency into his head. He would disdain and mock me, nothing better. I know that such behavior cannot really be indulged in, but how satisfying the thought of it is!

Why is it nearly impossible for most of us to learn from the wisdom or experience of others? I agonize over this question, as I have many times before. Wickedness has so many cunning disguises, and it is the most innocent and guileless who often fall prey—though I fear Mistress Eden is seeking dark waters for some thrill of her own. Yet in her ignorance and willfulness, she is innocent still and can be as easily scarred or ruined for the rest of her life.

Over the past few days I have seen Mr. Comstock enough times that I believe he has come to recognize me, at least in a vague sense that makes him uneasy. He gives me a wide berth whenever he can comfortably do so. And this morning when Lavinia slipped on a wet board and fell, skinning her knees and the tender palms of her hands, he walked right past the distressed child, without sparing even a glance for her as he went on his way.

Palmyra *is* home. I had forgotten—how could I have forgotten? My father's was the first face I saw. I reached out for him, mindless of all the others, needing his arms around me and the sound of his voice. Over a year had passed since I had seen him, but he had aged more than that. The death of my mother—I would not have thought it to affect him so strongly. In so many ways she was a trial for his gentle nature. But then, she was his wife, the wife of his youth, the girl whose promise and beauties he had recognized and responded to.

Lavinia went to him freely, which both pleased and surprised me. Jonathan came up shyly beside me and slipped his hand into mine. I held it tight and kept him with me as I greeted the dear friends who had come to meet me, one by one. Theodora was missing from the group; I had expected as much, but it hurt just the same. To my disappointment, Phoebe had sent word that her baby was ill and she must wait a few days to see me. Latisha, Tillie's little sister who so surprisingly attached herself to me in the early days, came forward and kissed me heartily—she, with her substantial, trustworthy husband, Jonah Sinclair, smiling and kindly as ever.

As I may have expected, Josephine hung back. And Randolph, aware of every underlying current, remained at her side. But how the sight of them both filled my heart! I pushed my way through to them and embraced my sister. Then Randolph drew me into his arms.

"Do not sniffle so, Esther," Josephine scolded me. "You will make me cry, too."

She was always like our mother, I thought. *Now will she fall into the role more entirely and be the matriarch to whom all must answer and around whom all must mince carefully?*

We drove through town, and my eyes ached with the looking from spot to spot and from side to side. My own dear little house, where I began my married life, was occupied now by another; I did not wish to see that. But when we approached the house of my birth, the house of my childhood, tucked into the quiet fields my father had worked since before I could remember, the tears flowed in earnest.

We came into the city when the last rays of sun slanted long and cool across its quieted streets. Randolph, wise, as always, beyond his years, forbade any celebration until the morrow. So my father drove us back to the silent homestead in peace. Lavinia's head drooped on my shoulder, and my own eyes grew heavy, my muscles stiff with fatigue.

We were shown into my own room, recently cleaned, and with

every little comfort contained therein. Even the sheets and coverlets of the bed were turned back to receive us. In no time at all we were undressed, unlaced, Lavinia settled into her trundle, and myself drinking hot milk sweetened with honey and nutmeg. A few luscious sips before I slid under the covers, closed my eyes upon the luxury of the sweet familiarity and comforting darkness, and slept.

Chapter Twelve

"She does look like me!" I was delighted at this diminutive person who opened her arms at my beckoning. "Rachel!" She looked up at the sound of her name and smiled at me—with Randolph's eyes.

Josephine reconciled herself. She was truly delighted to have me home. The first few days passed in a whirlwind of visits, and Josie always accompanied me or escorted me in her own fine carriage. The luxury, I will readily admit, suited me well. The little ones, if they grew fractious, were left behind with one of Josie's boys, or a neighboring girl, or at times even with Jonathan, who volunteered to see to their care.

"It will not always be thus," I promised him in a whisper one morning when Josie was determined to get us out of there at once, though both children were howling for their mothers and making a terrible noise. "I shall not expect you to see to such unpleasant tasks so frequently. In fact, Eugene is looking forward to having another man around to even things up."

He smiled at me through the most patient eyes. "I know, Esther," he said. "I am not worried about what you will do."

For the first time I wondered if this decision regarding the boy's future had been partly his own. I never once thought that Jonathan, himself, might entertain desires and preferences. I kissed his cheek before stumbling after Josephine, still in a fervor to be on her way.

But there were a few ticklish situations in which I had to come right out and forbid Josephine to come with me. Of course, she did not understand.

"Tillie, perhaps," she stewed when I told her. "She has been so rude to me, and neither one of us could abide the other's presence for very long. But Phoebe! For heaven's sake, Esther. I've a right to see Phoebe with you."

"It has nothing to do with rights," I explained patiently. "I have my own reasons, and I will not give way."

"You have changed, Esther." My sister inclined her pretty golden head and regarded me with narrowed, appraising blue eyes.

"Life has not been easy since I became a Mormon." I would not hedge with her, as I always had when we were girls. "I have been an observer and participant in much suffering, Josie, and in much joy. And both have enlarged my capacity to—"

"Oh, stop it!" She put her hands up to her ears. "Do not go on so, the way you always used to. We have suffered here, too, you know."

"Yes, I know." My pulse was beating with anger and disappointment, and later that evening when I found myself alone with Randolph, I could not hold my tongue.

"She grows worse," I told him, "and that means you have spoiled her terribly, which is not a good thing for either of you."

He had come to borrow some eggs for the boys' breakfast the next morning. But I think the errand was largely a pretext: it was necessary for the two of us to have a long visit alone.

"She grows secure, which, in her life, means complacent," Randolph said.

"But complacency in Josephine breeds this sharpness of manner and tongue." I leaned forward and lowered my voice. "She grows more like my mother each day."

"As is the natural process with most daughters."

"Why are you so calm and resigned?" I laughed. "You must love her to distraction!"

"I'm afraid that I do." He picked up the old cat, who curled into his lap with accustomed pleasure. "And I have been counting my blessings these past months."

"I know." I proceeded to tell him the sad details of Aurelia's dying, Jack's courage, and Peter's unexpected despair.

"He was pushed into growing up too quickly and in the wrong way," Randolph said. "You and I both know that better than anyone, Esther."

"Indeed." I nodded my head. "What can I do for him, Randolph?"

"Give him time for the principles of your religion to work upon him. And love him as you are waiting—which I know you will."

"That is an odd thing for you to recommend."

"No, Esther. Do not turn those burning eyes on me and get any mistaken thoughts in your head."

"Why not? If Peter could recognize—"

"Peter had a great need; he still has."

"And your needs are all tidily boxed up and taken care of?"

"Not hardly, as well you know."

I sighed. One tends to love those one has served a little more deeply. Randolph and I are bound by such ties.

"I want no part in religion right now, especially the type that would make demands and require a constant dedication. Can you imagine your Josie as a Mormon?"

I had to smile with him then. But he knows me well enough to realize why it was that I could not help hoping and yearning after him. "Esther, have you any regrets?"

"No, I have not. This life is very trying and challenging, as I think you have also discerned. But the rewards . . ." I paused. "I cannot make you understand what it means to live with spiritual knowledge, spiritual guidance."

"I am glad you will take Jonathan with you, then. I had worried a bit."

"I do not blame you."

"There is danger in being a Mormon. You will possibly be placing his life in real danger."

"Along with our own."

"Precisely. Have you thought about that?"

"Thought and prayed."

"I worry for you sometimes, Esther. I cannot bear to think of you suffering, being in real distress."

"I know, Randolph."

"Will you promise to let me help—no matter what—if ever you need me? I want a true, solemn promise, little sister."

I took his hand and pressed it with mine. "I give you my word."

"And you will remember, even if years and distance might separate us?"

The very thought chilled me, but I gave my promise again.

"Why do you suppose my father has chosen to give Jonathan to me?" I could ask Randolph this, where I never could Josephine.

"Ah, your father has always had a soft spot in his heart for you. And not merely in compensation of your mother's sometime neglect, Esther: he knows your worth."

A warmth rushed through me at his generous, tender words. I lowered my eyes, lest he see the flood of emotion there. "Will you write to your brother now and again?" I asked.

"I am not much for putting words on paper, Esther."

"But this is important."

"I'll try then. Now, I want to hear somthing of what you all have been doing before I must depart."

There was more news of this nature to share with him than I had thought there was! He was interested in everything Georgie and I were doing: in our adventures, our enterprises, our friends, even our follies. We laughed over Garrison and Gertie Woods and discussed the dubious merits of newspaper work as a means of making a living!

In this very kitchen, I remembered, *Randolph struggled through the blackest depths of despair, never dreaming of the riches life had in store for him, if he would but lift his head.*

"I know what you are thinking," he startled me. "And, of course, you are entirely right. I tremble to think how close my desperation brought me to giving up altogether. How different my life would have been."

"But you didn't, and it wasn't, and you have won your place in life nobly and well."

"God be praised!" he said under his breath, and I pretended I did not hear.

❦

Jonathan's seventh birthday came on the 11th of June, and we celebrated all together upon the occasion, trying not to think of the fact that it might be for the last time. Although mornings had become a faint, queasy time for me, I kept a cup of chamomile tea at hand and baked a sponge cake, Jonathan's favorite, lavished with nine eggs and two cups of sugar. I had found Mother's six-pound sugar cone still hanging from the dark ceiling of the pie cupboard. Strange to touch it and think of those fingers that had touched it last! As I chipped away at the crusted surface, then pounded and rolled the hard bits into fine, separated grains, I thought of her, of the hours we had all spent in this kitchen together, of her hopes and her fears.

The night of the twins' birth was still vivid in my memory. How frightened we were! How determined Dr. Ensworth and I had been that she and her babies should pull through this time. But what a struggle it had been, and we nearly lost all of them, not only one. *Only one. Nathaniel's tiny body lying on the hillside graveyard these many years. Now she is there with him—*

My musings caught me up short. *Where is my mother?* I wondered. *Will she be any happier in heaven than she was in this place? Does she know regret, bitter regret, over her faults and failings? Or does she justify all things, as was her custom down here?*

Such questions disturb me; they always have. Yet now I am learning some answers. *Light and intelligence.* No words more perfectly describe this restoration of the gospel through Joseph Smith. I am content, though curious and impatient still. After all, I have trouble enough keeping up with what has already been given and making it become a real part of my life.

We invited all our friends to the party: mine and my parents and children Jonathan's age. I was reminded of the old May Day celebrations and wished fleetingly that we five girls could dress up in frocks as sweet and enchanting as we used to. I was grateful that so many came, and I was able to spend a few moments greeting folk who for years had been dear to me. Just a smile, a word, a warm handshake: how much they can mean.

Eugene's parents were very pleased to see their granddaughter and made me promise a visit to their house before I left. I suspect they in some way blamed me for their son's involvement in Mormonism; though, ironically, Eugene was the first to read the Book of Mormon, the first to be converted. But they saw what they chose to see, as is well proved in the case of Simon and Phoebe. Perhaps Mrs. Thorn knew, or strongly suspected, that I did not particularly like or approve of her since those days. Eugene's father was kind but did not talk overmuch, and neither really asked any questions concerning how their son was getting on in our new life in Kirtland or what things in our home there were like.

Do they, too, expect us to give up at some stage and come running back—hopefully with our tails between our legs, as they all hold we should do? I wondered.

Tillie did not come. Had I expected her to? I know I had hoped and prayed she might, thinking a large gathering would make it easier for her than an intimate confrontation, as she might view it. I sent an invitation by messenger, ensuring that she would receive it. But she did not come. And I felt the emptiness of her absence most bitterly.

❦

I was sitting with Phoebe, sipping rosehip tea and admiring the children: my namesake, who is now quite a big girl; and the new son and heir, who is as pretty a child as his sister. Phoebe was telling me that she had become reconciled to what life requires of her.

"Do you read your Book of Mormon?" I pressed at first.

"Every night, either before or after our prayer time." Her full lips parted in a smile. "And in the mornings, too, after Simon goes off, if the baby still needs nursing."

"But, my dear, that is not enough. You need—"

"What do I need, Esther? I've asked the question hundreds of times. I need to stay with my husband; I need to raise up my children and do my duty the best I know how."

You need happiness, I wanted to say. *You need something to be easy for once. You deserve an opportunity to soar.*

"Do not worry about me, Esther," she chided gently. "I am all right. I have much to be thankful for. I will not lose the faith."

"I know *that,* dear, dear Phoebe," I soothed. "I have every hope that—"

A scream, piercing as a bevy of screeching owls, crowed suddenly above us, freezing my voice in mid-sentence. Little Esther moaned and scampered over to stand beside her mother and grab a handful of her skirt. The scream came again, accompanied by the sound of footsteps, the front door opening with a slam as it hit against the far wall.

I rose, because something in the scream burrowed below my consciousness, traveling along old, scarred causeways of pain. "Josephine!"

She sank to her knees and wrapped her arms around me. "They have taken my boys!" Her sobs came in gulps and shivers. *Do I understand what she is saying?* "Esther! They have taken my boys!"

After we had coaxed her to a chair and made her take a few swallows of tea, we got the whole story from her. But she was still wild and distraught.

"William and Joshua. They have been with us only a few weeks. But they have made such progress, Esther, and I had such high hopes!"

"What has happened?"

"They stole leather and some change from the shoemaker's till."

"Are you certain?"

"Yes, they were caught red-handed. But I know what made them give in to the temptation—" Josie groaned, and her shrill voice rose into a sort of wail. "I told them only last week that new shoes would be too much of a strain on the budget, at least for the present." She leaned close, her long fingers reaching for me frantically. "I did not know that they were cutting cardboard to patch up the holes, Esther. They did this to spare me!"

"Oh, Josie! Surely you will be able to explain that!"

She gulped and shook her head. "The judge has taken them into custody." She clasped her hands before her in a dramatic gesture, as she used to do when she was a child. She had every appearance of the golden-haired princess in distress.

"But judges are human beings; they are open to reason," I tried.

Her face went white, chalk white, and her bright eyes narrowed, almost in fear. "Gerard Whittier is not human. And he has sworn that if he catches just one of my boys getting into the least bit of trouble, he'll get rid of the lot of them."

It was as though someone had thrown ice water over me. I could feel myself cringe and shiver.

"He has said this?"

"Many a time."

"Why, Josephine?"

My sister dissolved into loud, wet tears.

"It is as though he has marked us," Phoebe said quietly, "each one of us who used to be Tillie's friends." For once I was speechless. I stared at her, feeling some of Josephine's wildness creep into me. "Then there is Randolph, too," she continued. "Whittier despises the lad. And the more successful Randolph becomes, the more it sticks in his craw."

Josie stared up at me with little girl eyes, almost demanding my sympathy. But my thoughts were no longer of her. I could see Theodora's face, young and tense, staring back at me. I could hear her saying: "It is Father's choice . . . Oh, it shall come to pass, dear Esther. I have nothing to say in the matter . . ."

Nothing to say in the matter! Tillie, my dear Tillie! That she should be married to a man such as this. I shivered because I also remembered the last time I had looked on her face. I remembered the cold emptiness that had shrouded her eyes when she stared back at me. "It is wicked. Anything that parts families is wicked," she had said. "I shall forget you, Esther, and I shall forget Peter, too."

"Esther!"

Phoebe's voice startled me. Both she and Josephine were staring at me. Josie wailed, "Well, tell me, Esther, what shall I do?" *The same little-girl plea, the same petulant demanding, though she is the older sister, and I the younger,* I thought.

Phoebe lowered her voice to a murmur. "Do not think about *her now,* Esther. Do not torture yourself."

Dear Phoebe! Like Georgie, she could read my mind. I rose reluctantly. My knees felt shaky. "Where is Randolph?" I asked.

"He has gone to try to reason with them! Oh, Esther, I am so frightened!"

I was frightened myself, but I would not admit it to Josephine. Phoebe knew. She insisted on keeping Lavinia with her while we went to find out just what was happening. She kissed my cheek as I started off with Josie. "I will say a little prayer as soon as you leave," she promised. And for the first time since I heard my sister scream I felt an inkling of hope.

The prospects were dark. We learned this from Randolph, who met us at the mill house, this lovely spot that originally belonged to Josie's first husband, Alexander Hall.

"They offer us no choices," he attempted to explain, while Josephine paced back and forth, back and forth, her hands clasped behind her. "They want to dissolve our unofficial charitable institution—which they consider a danger to the community—and send all the boys back canal side, where they say they belong."

Josie sat, her hands clasped now in her lap. She looked up at her young husband entreatingly. "Can they do this?" she asked.

"They have power in their hands. There is no law or protection we can call upon, but they will use statutes against public disturbance, public menace—they do not need much, Josie, to manipulate the whole thing their way."

"They cannot go back. What would become of them?"

I had never before heard so much pain in my sister's voice. Randolph looked long at me, his face weary with discouragement. "I can think of nothing further, Esther, that we can do."

"Will they need a writ? Something official?"

He shrugged his shoulders. "If so, I am sure they will provide it."

"Do we simply wait? Perhaps their resolve will weaken after a good night's sleep on it."

"Perhaps." Randolph rose to his feet and went to stand beside Josephine. He dropped his hand onto her shoulder, and she reached up to grasp it for dear life, as a child would. "The boys are waiting. We must tell them something." His very indecisiveness was a pain to him. "Ought we to frighten them at this point by telling them all?"

I could not advise him. "You know them best," I said finally.

He nodded slowly. "Yes. I will think of something." He extricated his hand gently from Josephine's and walked out of the room. She and I sat miserably staring at floor or ceiling—anywhere but each other's eyes.

An hour passed. We assumed Randolph was out with the boys, explaining. We heard a light wagon enter the yard. I knew it would be Phoebe, as it proved to be, bringing us food to eat and our babies to put to bed for the night.

She helped, quiet and calm, demanding nothing of us, certainly not polite conversation at such a time. She agreed to take word to my father that I would spend the night here with my sister.

When at length she left us, a gloom settled over the house. I felt lonely and found myself longing for my husband to be there. The realization came over me that I could not kneel and pray with these two people, so dear to me. *If Georgie were here. If Josephine could be like . . .* Foolish, unprofitable thoughts!

Randolph came back but said nothing. I was relieved to excuse myself and go up to my room. The night was heavy but not too hot. I prayed so long that my knees cricked when I rose. After getting into bed I lay and listened to the cicadas and crickets, and their chorus seemed somehow comforting. *The night would be so still without them. Too still, too lonely.* I closed my eyes and drew deep breaths of air scented with the honeysuckle vine that grew beneath the window. I listened and tried not to think about home, about Josie and her boys, about anything at all.

I thought it was night still. But it was actually very early in the morning. I sat up and listened, but the silence was deep around me. What had made me awaken then?

I fell back upon my pillows and pulled the coverlet under my chin. But sleep would not return. *There is something . . .* I got out of bed and dressed quickly, and my fingers were shaking before I was through. Going downstairs it appeared that the house was deserted; no one stirred about. *Have I been foolish?* I thought.

I walked through the empty rooms. When I reached the generally unused parlor I saw a light coming beneath the closed door. Without even thinking I put my hand on the latch and pushed the door wide. Randolph was sitting in Alexander's huge wingback chair, his chin resting on his folded hands. He looked very young. We forget how young he really is and expect so much of it. Inadvertently I thought, *Randolph is no more than twenty-three, and Joseph Smith was only twenty-four when the Church was organized, twenty-five when he moved his people to Kirtland and began to build up a whole community of Latter-day Saints.*

"They are gone, Esther."

I blinked, uncomprehending for a moment. "An hour ago, just past first light. A posse of men came, headed by the sheriff and—"

"Not Gerard Whittier?"

"Who else? He was mightily pleased with himself. I believe Danny would have knocked him down where he stood if I had not stopped him."

Danny, the first of the canal lads who had ever come to them, had outgrown his old status both in years and position, and was virtually part of the family now. "And Josephine?"

"She does not know yet. She remained asleep, like yourself."

I sat down beside him. After a few moments I asked timidly, "What are we to do?"

"Carry on, Esther. Haven't we always?"

That would be reasonable enough to attempt, I thought a bit grimly, *if we did not have Josephine to reckon with, too.*

Chapter Thirteen

Palmyra: July 1834

Tansy had been a wedding gift from my father; she was my horse
as long as I could remember. When we went away I left her with
Josephine for safekeeping, not having the heart to sell her. As soon as
the roads dried out in the spring, Jonathan had taken to riding her,
and it pleased me to see how fond the boy and horse were of one
another. And I liked to think of her being both loved and useful
again.

"I still feed and board your little beast," Josie pointed out, by way of
mild complaint.

"That is as it should be, since you can afford to and Father cannot,"
I reminded her.

She merely smiled, a bit insipidly. But I could not fault her, especially now after what had just happened with her beloved boys. When
Randolph first broke the news, when she realized that what she loved
best had been snatched away from her, she had dissolved into weak,
horrified tears. But after the first onslaught, a dry, angry resolve replaced
the temporary helplessness. Josephine is accustomed to controlling and
manipulating everything that touches or involves her, and when anyone attempts to tell her what she may or may not do, they have a real
fight on their hands. Alexander Hall began late, but his quiet tenacity
helped him come off victor a crucial time or two. Randolph has been
lucky. His easygoing ways serve as the velvet glove under which the
firm hand exercises as much influence as it feels necessary. He loves
Josie too well. But she loves him, too, as she has never loved another,
and there is some little salvation in that!

Friends in high places have advised them to lie low until the
excitement dies down a bit. I believe this is sound advice. But Josephine
chafes at this sharp-edged bit she must so unwillingly clamp her mouth
upon while she remains quiet and still. Even her attempts to see the

boys—marching down to the canal side, making demands with her hands on her hips, her voice and manner strident—have met with defeat. She is passing the stage of pity and anguish for what her young charges are suffering, to pity and fury for what she is suffering on account of blind, wicked men.

❧

"Have I not done this community—this state—a humane service?" Josie demanded hotly.

"No one sees it that way," I pointed out patiently. "They consider those boys just fine where they are."

"Being worked like beasts! Fed poorly! Brutalized by the riverside rabble!"

I placed my hand on her arm. "They care not a bit for those things, as long as the scuffles and trouble are contained and controlled by canal authority."

"Someday these boys will grow up, take a place in society. If they are taught no morals nor any decent way of making a living, they will prove a liability wherever they go!"

Randolph, getting in on the discussion, shrugged. "People do not think that far. Nor have they much faith in the notions of reform."

"Despite what we have shown them?" Josephine was breathless in her indignation.

"We haven't been at it long enough, nor have we had all successes." Randolph spoke gently, but Josie's eyes blazed still.

"These people you despise would love to see you this way," I interjected, a bit sternly. "Do not allow them this power over you."

"What power?" she screamed.

"The power to make you unhappy, even to the point of illness. The power to take peace from your life, muddle your thoughts, and—"

"Esther! I am sorry I asked!"

I stopped speaking, her unkind words acted like a cork popped over the neck of a jar, bottling all that remained inside. I was not used to her sharp retorts anymore, I realized. And it hurt me more than it should have.

Randolph understood, but he did not attempt to apologize for her.

113

He merely increased his own watchfulness and tenderness. But I was relieved to get back to my father's house. My father had never raised his voice or his hand to me, nor to anyone else that I know of. He was lonely, and I knew he must be thinking of what it would be like when I walked out of his life again and took his young son with me. He would be left then with only his memories. *Are memories, even when one grows older, enough?* I wondered, but I knew he would never talk about it and never, never complain.

⁂

I am in the midst of all this, and I wish it had not happened during my stay here. There are loose threads I must secure before I can go home again, and the most difficult and painful things I have put off. I must tackle one this evening after the hot sun retreats in the heavens and the softer hues of twilight blow in on the breath of evening.

I am not well. But I have said nothing yet to my family about my condition. Things have been too hectic and disorganized; there have been too many diversions, too many demands. I might have confessed to Phoebe if Josie's overriding crisis had not come upon us!

I am contented to be alone. I ride Tansy sidesaddle and we go slow and easy through the wide streets of the town until we reach the intersection of Main and Church Streets, where the four solid churches which support this community sit in emphatic, informal indifference. What in this world could possibly dislodge them? Certainly not that young upstart Joseph Smith and his rabble! They've taken care of that lot—sent them scampering heaven knows where, and good riddance!

I dismount and tie Tansy to a post, then take my time walking up the hill to the old burying ground. Mother, I am told, lies near the others; the babies and children she lost during a lifetime of child bearing. I find the location with ease. The shadows spread kind gray fingers to soften the still unhealed scar, the digging and disturbing upon the great breast of the earth to place one more of her children at rest. Such a narrow indentation, really, for a mortal receptacle flattened by the absence of breath, blood, and spirit!

I read her name carved on the headstone.

RIP

Rachel, Beloved Wife of Jonah S. Parke

My eyes skip over the dates to the words my father has had inscribed there:

Rest well-deserved until the trump of God shall call his children home.

What do they mean, these words of comfort; what do they mean to my father? Are they words of faith to him, too? Does he truly believe them in a literal sense? Or are they merely to chase the shades away, the shadows so crowded with dark misgivings?

When I told my father that I had read Joseph Smith's book and believed it to be true, he stared at me for a long, long minute before he replied, "I have always trusted your powers of reason and discernment, Esther. If you have found something there you cannot leave alone, so be it."

But I remember thinking, *My father is being kind to me, but his eyes are so sad.*

A few days later I had returned and added reluctantly, "You realize what this means, Father?"

"It means you have chosen a different path for yourself."

"Yes. It means I will be baptized."

"You were baptized as an infant."

"This time it will be after the pattern the Savior set and with the proper authority."

"If you say so."

If you say so! What had he meant with those words? He would not criticize, nor would he question or search for himself. I could neither beseech nor condemn him, because I did not know how.

I touch the rough stone with my fingertips, warm yet from the sun. "You would not kiss me good-bye!" I choke back the tears. "Why wouldn't you kiss me, Mother?" I drop down onto my knees and sit hunched, like a child. I had not seen my mother for over a year, and I could no longer color in all the shades and details of her features; my remembrance failed me and blurred, just as the painful tears blurred my eyes.

My legs cramp, and my back begins hurting. I grasp the stone and lean heavily against it to help me rise. Tears can be cleansing, but these are not. Too many unanswered questions, too many unhealed scars block the sense of peace my heart longs for.

I read the carved, somewhat faded names of the others: Jonah and Jacob, who died the same week of scarlet fever; Edith, who was taken by influenza when she was just six weeks old; two infants, both given the name of Eliza, who had expired within hours of their coming, scarcely time for the bright meadow lark, herald of the morning, to trill out a welcome. Four-year-old Thomas I remember. I remember his limp, wet body when they carried him home. I remember my mother's eyes. For years the remembrance of the look in them haunted me.

Suddenly other memories, bright as new pennies, glitter before me. How white my mother's skin was, how girlish her laughter, how blue her eyes—how fearful and childlike the timid soul who looked out from them.

"She hollers to scare the shadows away." That is what my father used to say of her. "She doesn't mean half of what she says when she is like that. You just pay her no mind."

And love her, I thought, as he always had! The weakness of sorrow swept through me, and I felt all trembly and shaken. *Thin wisp of a girl, as pretty and pert as her daughter, Josephine. How she loved pretty things. And praise. And good company. And beauty.*

I took a few uncertain steps to where the infant brother I had nurtured rested his small, solemn head.

Nathaniel Parke

Purity requireth no testing

We had sung "Rock of Ages" when we buried him. I sang it under my breath now, every verse all the way to the end, until the comfort I sought came. And I thought in my heart that perhaps for the first time, my mother truly was happy in a way she had neither sought nor imagined during this life.

I walked then to that other grave where the eldest Smith boy was buried: Alvin, who died because of a tragic error in the medication administered. Alvin, considered the best and the noblest, even by Joseph himself.

"You are proud of your brother, of that I am certain," I said out loud. "He has been faithful to his trust, though the powers of evil have gathered in dark strength against him." I settled onto a soft mound of grass where the sun's warmth lingered pleasantly and continued my somewhat foolish reverie. But it helped, somehow, to think, to speak to the silence of such matters.

"Yes, I am one of the foolhardy who followed him, though it took not a little persuasion." I laughed softly. "Really, especially now, being able to see a contrast, I cannot believe how fortunate Eugene and I are."

The peace stayed with me. As I walked back past my mother's grave, I paused and, bending low, whispered, "I am with child again, Mother. Perhaps this will be a boy, a little playmate for our Jonathan." I drew a deep breath. "Do not be vexed with me, Mother, for taking your last child away. I will do well by him, and you can trust Eugene to be fair with him." I kissed my fingers to her. "Give Nathaniel a special hug for me—" I wanted to add, *Pray for me, Mother!* But I could not quite do it.

I took the slope carefully, and I had the strange sensation that someone from behind was watching me. I paused, but I did not turn round. There was no need to. The feeling was one of love, a tenderness reaching out to me that was almost palpable. I paused again and stood quietly, simply to draw the sweet spirit in, as one pauses before the glory and wonder of a sunset, filling one's soul with the sight. Then slowly I took the rough path down to where Tansy waited.

117

❦

Randolph gave me the money for postage that I might send a letter to Eugene! I could not disguise my delight. I hugged him, and I hugged Josephine, who smiled wanly and then straightened her rumpled collar. "Really, Esther, this is not like you," she said.

"Esther misses her husband, as perhaps you would not," he teased. But she paid him no mind.

"When are you leaving?" he asked.

"Do not bring up the matter!" Josephine cried. "It is wicked of you to make Esther think of it, Randolph! We do not want her to ever leave."

He walked me out-of-doors and handed me into my sister's carriage. "Still one of the finest conveyances in town," I remarked, raising an eyebrow.

He hunched his shoulders, boy-like, and winced in mock pain. "Do not scold me, Esther. It is not an easy thing to deny her."

"Yes," I mused. "I ought to remember that." I leaned forward a bit, my hand still on his outstretched arm. "Why does she claim to want my presence so passionately, Randolph, when she seems to take no pleasure in it?"

This time he winced in earnest. "It is her way; it has always been her way. Do not ask me to explain."

I acquiesced. "You are right. Will we see you tomorrow—for dinner?"

"I do not want you to overdo, Esther." His fine brow furrowed into the lines of concern that well become him.

"What do you mean?"

"I think you know what I mean. Will you tell Eugene in your letter or wait until you get home?"

"Home . . ." I mused at the word. "It is strange. It was coming home to return here. Not until I left it—and left what I love best waiting there for me—did I truly consider Kirtland as home."

"'Tis natural enough. But you are evading my question, Esther."

Suddenly his meaning was clear to me, and I felt the color rise to my cheeks. "You know? You have guessed? How, Randolph?"

"I am observant, my dear, that is all. I know you well enough that when I see you constantly weary, rubbing that spot in the small of your back, sitting down to rest, looking pale, refusing food—all things not common to your behavior—"

I held up a hand in protest. "All right, all right!"

"You forget," he continued quite soberly. "That I have been more than once a runaway and a fugitive. Such wretched states train men to a finely-tuned degree of watchfulness. It is an old, deeply bred habit that I have not yet shed."

I understood. I kissed his cheek, and he clucked to the horses. And I was driven safely and comfortably back to my father's place.

Susan Evans McCloud

It took days of praying and preparing my thoughts to get up the courage for it. But at last I sent word to Randolph—by letter, which Jonathan was more than happy to take—that I should appreciate the use of my sister's carriage the following morning.

I arose and dressed carefully but found my stomach too delicate for food, due more to nervous excitement than anything, so I took only a little milk and plain bread. Randolph had sent Danny to drive me, and I must admit that his dependable presence lent me a feeling of added support.

The hour was early, and Lavinia dozed in my arms. The new day was uncommonly fine, with mist clinging to the hedgerows and the wrens and wild plovers dressing the still morning air with their unstinted praises. But fear kept me from enjoying it entirely.

As the landau drew up before Theodora's house I was struck with the size and splendor of it and wondered fleetingly at the contentment Georgie and I managed to feel in our inadequate, cramped abode. *If Tillie could see us!* I shuddered at the mere idea.

Danny walked me all the way to the front steps and stood off a little distance, waiting. He seemed to know (perhaps Randolph had primed him) that I would want him close by until I saw what might happen. A maidservant opened the door.

"Is Mrs. Whittier at home?" How strange this formal manner felt here!

"Madam does not generally accept visitors at this hour. Who may I say is calling?" The saucy girl glanced over the baby in my arms with clear disapproval. I wanted to scold her roundly, push her aside, and rush back to find Tillie. *Has she been given instructions?* I wondered.

"If you would tell your mistress that Esther Parke is most anxious to—"

"Oh, no!" A resolute expression came over the youthful face to render it most unpleasant. "I am sorry, ma'am, but by no means are you to be—"

"Nonsense!" Lavinia stirred and lifted her head to look round and see where her mama had taken her. "I will have none of this. I will not be threatened nor sent away—nor even driven away!" I could feel my insides churning, but I ignored the uncomfortable sensation and blustered on. "You tell Mrs.—you tell Tillie that I *will* see her! I love her as I have always loved her, and I will not be denied!"

Taking advantage of the maid's shocked confusion, I pushed past her imposing presence and began to make my way down the long hall.

"You come right back here this moment!" The girl had regained her wits. She was at my elbow, grabbing hold of it. I felt Lavinia lean away from her touch. "I'll call Master's man, I will, and he is one to be reckoned with. I'll see to it—"

"That will not be necessary, Mary Anne."

I could not tell where the commanding voice came from, but my first impression was *Tillie's mother! What is she doing here at this house?* Then I looked up and saw the altered, though still dear, features of my childhood friend.

We stared at one another. Some compartment of my mind was taking everything in: the slender, silk-covered slippers, the silken morning gown dripping with fine lace—lace has always been Tillie's passion— her hair, still thin and flyaway. One graceful hand—her hands are Tillie's most beautiful feature—pressed to her throat, the slender fingers overwhelmed with the weight and size of the gems and jeweled rings that encrusted them. I must have sucked in my breath.

"Esther, you wear your emotions on your sleeve. You always have, my dear."

Did I discern a little warmth in the careful, emotionless voice? I set Lavinia down on the ground and reached my arms out in a wide gesture of welcome. "Good. Then you will know how much I love you, how truly happy—" My voice broke, and I swallowed. "How happy I am to see you."

I do not really know what happened. I think Tillie's first steps were slow and uncertain. Then she was in motion, running toward me, drawing me into her arms, pressing her wet cheek against my cheek, trembling, as I was.

When we drew apart my heart was beating wildly and my head was beginning to ache.

"In here!" Tillie breathed, pulling me after her. "Where we will not be disturbed."

She closed the door behind her and relaxed her long frame against it. "You are more elegant than ever," I said, unable to help myself.

A hint of merriment moved across her face and played at the corners of her stern mouth. "Appearances. Oh yes, I have mastered appearances. But you—" She flung one arm out in an almost grandiose gesture. "You, Esther, remain unchanged."

"Unchanged!" I was truly taken aback. So much has happened to me. I feel older, wiser, even weary; I feel altered entirely, from the inside out.

"You are still fresh and idealistic and looking for beauty wherever your eyes happen to light."

"No!" I shook my head at her. "No, I am no longer a girl, Tillie. I have been through too much. I have—"

"Haven't we all, my dear?" The frosty edge was back in her voice. "Try to deny what I say if it makes you feel better. But I know you too well, and you have only grown better, Esther, as I always knew that you would."

I could say nothing. My mouth was trembling, pulled at the corners with the terrible threat of tears, and I dared not trust my voice. I sank into a chair. Tillie's girl must have been hovering outside the closed door, for in what felt no more than a moment, a glass of chilled lemonade was placed in my hand and Lavinia was being hugged and admired and offered an enchanting array of cakes and cookies off a silver-tiered tray.

"Bring in the children!" Tillie cried, and Mary Anne scurried to obey her. Children bridge so many gaps and fill up tense, awkward silences. May, four years old now, flitted like a butterfly to hover beside me, asking question after question, her eyes bright and curious. I answered with pleasure until I realized no end was in sight; then I laughed and drew her into my arms. "Enough, enough of this! I need a kiss, lovely May. I have come a long, long way to get your kiss and your hug."

She complied with gleeful grace, fidgeting with sheer energy in my arms. But Edward Lawrence, whom we had always called Laurie, stood at a distance with his hands clasped in front of him, watching with Tillie's veiled eyes.

"Are you still called Laurie, young man," I asked, "or have you graduated to your full name?"

"Do you know how old I am?" he asked unexpectedly.

"Let me see. I was here when you were born, on a lovely day in September nearly . . . goodness, nearly six years ago! You have grown into quite the young man."

He glowed, despite himself. "Mother still calls me Laurie," he confessed. "But my father and his friends call me Edward."

"As they should," I conceded. "Man to man; I understand that."

He took a few steps forward. "Leave the lady alone, May," he scolded. "She is enough to wear a soul out, isn't she?"

He must have heard that phrase many times. "Indeed she is. But I love it!" I hugged the lithe, wiggly body to me before reluctantly setting her down. "I should like you to meet my little girl," I said to both of them. "This is Lavinia, whose hair curls like her father's, but you see she has my green eyes."

Laurie laughed. "How old is she?"

"Just three years." Hearing herself discussed, Lavinia held up three pudgy fingers, and added, "I am as pretty as Mommy. Daddy says so."

Tillie's mouth softened a bit at this. "What does your mommy say?" she asked.

Lavinia did not seem to hesitate. "She says that I am as smart as my daddy and that I can only keep one of Aunt Georgie's kittens, no matter how many beautiful ones there are."

"You may have a kitten," May responded impulsively, "but I have a big brother."

"And a very fortunate girl you are to have him," I assured her. "I always wanted a brother when I was your age." My eyes lifted to Tillie's face. "None of us had big brothers," I went on. "When we were Laurie's age—"

Tillie put her lovely hands up to her cheeks. "Don't!" she entreated. "I forbid you to talk about it."

"You are right," I agreed. "It is too painful for me as well."

So we skirted all the real issues: all that was unresolved, all that was painful, all that we could not agree upon, all that we suffered, all that we longed for; all that tore at our hearts.

An hour passed quickly. When Mary Anne appeared and asked about the luncheon meal, I rose reluctantly. "I really must go, Tillie, before—"

"Gerard never comes home for the midday meal as he used to."
She gave a short laugh. "Indeed, he seldom comes home at all." My
heart felt as though a great weight had been bound to it, and
my tongue felt thick in my mouth. "Did you not expect as much?"
Tillie continued relentlessly. "If things do not get better, then they get
worse, Esther. You know that."

"I do, though I am not reconciled to it!" I could not drain the acid
bitterness out of my voice.

"I am reconciled," Tillie said.

"And that means?" I held my breath, awaiting her answer.

"That means no expectations, no intimacies, no dashed hopes, no
complicated deceptions."

I dropped my gaze, afraid to meet the cold light in her eyes. "Was
that the only way?"

"You knew Gerard, Esther. What would you say?" My silence was
acquiescence. "There will be no guests for luncheon," Tillie said, turning to her waiting maid. "Take the children away with you. I will eat
my meal alone in my room, when I send for it."

The spell had been broken. I stood in the big room, with the two
beautiful children staring up at me, feeling suddenly awkward and out
of place.

"Mary Anne!" The children gave the maidservant their hands and
followed her silently, without once looking back.

"I am not helpless, Esther, as you fancy," Tillie said, watching me
closely. "Nor am I altogether unhappy."

I knew that this was a lie, a lie she had told herself so often, for such
a long time, that it had become a halfhearted truth, a substitution for
the precious real thing which was lacking. I nodded my head. "I know
what you mean."

"No, you do not. Compromise is not in your nature. That is why
you went away from us. That is why you have grown, despite everything, while I have—" She stopped herself cold.

"We can change some things," I said, almost timidly. "And some
things will never change."

"Whatever do you mean?"

I had turned the anguished moment away from her. Now I needed to muster the courage to press on. "We can still share so much, be part of each other's lives despite all that separates us."

She was shaking her head. "Such a change is not possible."

"It is because of the other, the thing that will never change: *our love for one another.*"

"For heaven's sake, Esther!"

"I mean it. You know I mean it, Tillie."

"Of course you do—"

"I want to know your children. I want to be part of their lives—"

"You mean you want to be there when their world falls apart on them. You should have thought of that, Esther, before."

We were going from bad to worse. I crossed the space between us, standing so close to her that I could see the fine etching of worry lines forming around her long, almond-shaped eyes. I leaned over and kissed her cheek.

"I did not wish this to happen, Tillie. It is bitterly cruel that I have been forced to choose!"

"Would you choose differently now, a year later?" There was a mockery in her tone that pierced through me.

"Would to God I could—but I do not think I would do differently, if it all happened over again."

"Well, then—" Tillie shrugged her thin shoulders beneath the light, shimmering fabric.

"You have the chance to choose again, Tillie," I said, shaken by my own boldness.

"Choose pain over resignation? You do not know what you are talking about, Esther."

"Pain *and joy*—over emptiness, my dear one. And emptiness can be one of the worst forms of pain."

She turned her scathing eyes upon my face; the anguished intensity of her gaze made my soul shrivel. "I should not have let you in!"

She walked away from me, toward the closed door. I followed, dragging a tired, half-frightened Lavinia along with me. I did not know I was crying until Tillie turned to dismiss me.

"Esther!" Her whole face melted, and the black pain flowed out of it. "My dear Esther, my only true friend!"

There came the sound of voices from the other end of the

corridor. Tillie glanced round in panic. "Do you wish to undo me altogether? Go quickly—go! If you have any mercy at all!"

Was it Mary Anne at my elbow? I was at the door, which someone was opening for me. Danny stepped forward out of nowhere—had he been standing, poised, at the edge of the long porch all this time?

I was in the carriage. I could feel the movement, and I leaned back against the seat because my head was spinning. I was dimly aware of cradling Lavinia in my arms and murmuring snatches of melody until she relaxed into sleep. It could not have been long, but I felt I had spent hours within the dark, stifling cavern of that carriage.

When Danny lifted me out I had to lean on his arm because I had not the strength to walk by myself. He told me later that I was crying softly still, but I do not remember. Nor do I remember someone—was it my father?—gently helping me into my bed. I closed my eyes in exhaustion, and sleep was the mercy provided to snuff out the pain.

Chapter Fourteen

I am ready to go home. I have been ready for weeks, but circumstances keep intervening.

The morning spent with Tillie must have drained me, or been what they call the final straw, forcing me to succumb to the demands of both body and spirit. For two long, luxurious days I rested, staying in my room or puttering about my father's house with nothing in the world to do, no demands or responsibilities crowding and pushing.

Somehow, between them, my father and Jonathan saw to Lavinia and kept her contented and occupied. My father has planted a rather sizeable garden, though he apologizes for it. "It isn't pretty as yours always was, Esther, and I can't seem to manage those herbs and things you know all about. Far as I'm concerned they grow just like weeds and crowd out the other vegetables, even the flowers."

I know what he means. But remnants of my mint, the worst of the offenders, still flourished. And to my surprise, my father brought tea and hot cereal into my room each morning and found other little dainties to tempt my palate, serving them up with a touch any woman would have been proud to own.

"Where did you gain such skills?" I asked him one afternoon.

"Skills? Of what sort?"

"I don't know. Serving, fetching, and carrying, nursing others." As I said the last two words, I suddenly knew. "'Twas Jane Foster, was it not?"

My father nodded. "I guess a few things rubbed off on me."

"You miss her, I suppose."

"I must admit that I do. Those months I drove her round from call to call, need to need, whatever the hour; well, I guess I felt I was involved in something important."

"Something essential," I thought out loud. "Of course you would feel that way. All the clutter of life we generally concern ourselves with falls away then and what is really important to us is given the chance to shine through."

"You put things well, Esther. Always have." My father's voice and face were softened by a tenderness that brought tears to my eyes.

"You have always served others, though," I said, "in one way or another. I remember many times throughout the course of my life."

"Course of your life, indeed!" He gave a little laugh, stood, and stretched. "You are but a lass still, Esther, scarcely a woman full grown."

I like it when he teases me, I thought. I smiled up into his lean, time-gentled face, trying to memorize every line and feature about it, that the precious sight of this moment would never grow dim.

As I first stepped back into the land of the living I continued to take it easy. And I must admit that I avoided Josephine altogether, at least for a few days. I went the rounds again, visiting those most dear to me and those to whom I felt most obligated. Now that my secret was out I was met with a bit more kindness and deference than I otherwise might have been. I did not attempt to contact Georgie's parents, even her mother. I feared her father. If he could do what he did to his own daughter, what might he be capable of doing to me? I had heard things about him since my arrival, new tales of cruelty and bigotry, so I knew I must leave him to the ragings of his own spirit and the dark way he had chosen. Georgie would hope for, and I had desperately wanted, some little crumb to bring back to her; but it was not to be so.

Two mornings in a row I spent with Phoebe. The first day we brought our children and spread out a picnic in a shady spot beside the river. I told her about every possible scrap of life in Kirtland, every detail I could think of. She drank it up, as a thirsty tree would. I thought: *She does not show her parched state any more than the solid, healthy trunk of a tree does. Only her highest leaves, pushing for their share of moisture and sunlight, droop and pale with the strain of what they are doing without.*

The second day we spent alone. For one precious hour, ah, more—perhaps two or three altogether—we read passages from the Book of Mormon, sharing our favorites, discussing their meaning, and the beauty of the very words themselves. There were moments when I felt heaven near us—an engulfing light and warmth that floods suddenly through one's whole being with such an exhilarating effect that you know of a certainty forces from a higher world are touching you, loving you, whispering strength and comfort and wisdom to your soul.

There were many, too many, and one passage led to another, until we found ourselves at the end, the very last page of the volume, marking a verse we both loved well:

"Yea, come unto Christ, and be perfected in him, and deny yourselves of all ungodliness; and if ye shall deny yourselves of all ungodliness, and love God with all your might, mind and strength, then is his grace sufficient for you, that by his grace ye may be perfect in Christ; and if by the grace of God ye are perfect in Christ, ye can in nowise deny the power of God.

"And again, if ye by the grace of God are perfect in Christ, and deny not his power, then are ye sanctified in Christ by the grace of God, through the shedding of the blood of Christ, which is in the covenant of the Father unto the remission of your sins, that ye become holy, without spot."

"You see, Esther," Phoebe said, as we closed the cover on the book, "I trust in Christ to make up the difference I am lacking. He is able to do so, you know."

"Yes, dear one. I see before me the results of it." She pushed my words away, for praise has always discomfited her. So instead I told her of my baptism on that chilly May morning.

"May Day," she mused. "If someone had told us, five years ago, three years ago, would we have ever believed that such things could happen?"

We marveled together. "We were just girls then, with all our hopes new and shining, unmarred by reality . . ."

"Esther! The imperfection is part of the beauty. You must embrace all of it! All that happens, good and bad, makes up the sum of you, and you would not trade what you have learned from life, would you?"

"No, no."

"Dear Esther, you suffer as much for each of us as we suffer for ourselves."

"I do not know how to do otherwise!"

128

She smiled, and I think I have never looked upon a more beautiful face.

Before we left I read Phoebe some of the revelations that have come to the Prophet, those that had been printed in Missouri, and told her how the priesthood brethren, my zealous Eugene included, would be printing more and more of them, now that a press was set up in Kirtland.

Oh, a spiritual sharing such as we experienced is a rare thing in everyday life! It filled and renewed us, pushing out the stale breath within us, purifying our thoughts and desires, reinforcing our strengths.

One of the last things Phoebe said as I left her I shall never forget. "He was a stranger among us, young Joseph. Do you remember him as a boy, Esther?"

"Very well; yes, I do."

"We liked him, we were drawn to his goodly qualities, but we could not see into his heart."

"'Tis a strange idea to think upon."

"Yes. Great forces working through one solitary person can change the very course of things, alter hundreds of lives."

"Thousands and more, Phoebe, if you think upon it. Joseph says the gospel will spread to every land and nation on the face of the earth."

"I cannot understand it; the concept is too vast for me."

I agreed.

"But," she added, "we are among the few God has chosen to bless and lift from the beginning. When I am unhappy or discouraged, I have only to think upon that."

I remembered her words. They remained with me for days, just at the edge of my consciousness, like a small, glowing light. I was to recall them later, at a time when I very much needed them, needed the strength of her testimony and spirit to help me go on.

129

❦

"Esther! Esther!"

I opened my eyes. Had I really heard someone calling me? There came a faint scratching at my window. "Esther!" The same voice again.

But the thick darkness muffled all my senses, and I could not tell who my urgent night visitor was.

I struggled out of bed and wrapped my mother's long shawl around me before padding over to the window. "Who is there?" My voice was husky with urgency and the caution I could not dismiss.

"Jonah Sinclair, missus. Would you like me to come round to the door?"

I walked through the dim rooms, still knowing by sixth sense how to find a sure path. *Jonah Sinclair.* He had come to me on midnight errands before and always with ill results. I released the lock and pulled the door open. "Haven't we met before like this?" he grinned.

I opened my arms to him. The most unlikely friendship of my life was this with he and his wife, Latisha, whom I had looked at through the years as no more than the spoiled, scatterbrained little sister of Tillie. Now life had repositioned us all to her pleasure, and the rich girl had become a very sensible, devoted wife to a man who—on the social scale that was religion to her father—stood many rungs below her. They had come to me hungry for friendship and acceptance and thought well enough of me that they assumed I would show them kindness; which, in my astonishment, I had done. All to *my* benefit, for they had proved true and stalwart through many a twist and trial. And now here was Jonah at my doorstep in the middle of the night.

"I missed you at the picnic." I said.

"I have been off checking locks up and down the canal and Latisha with me."

"That is nice for you both."

"It was, but we did not intend to miss so much of your visit—"

"Yes, I have not even seen your new baby yet," I said.

"She's pretty as her sister. Tisha dotes on her."

"I am glad to hear it," I sighed. "But you have not come about that."

"No, ma'am." He took his hat off, as though remembering, and twirled it in both his hands. I had forgotten how much hair this short little man had growing in the oddest places on his head and his face. Such a picture! Yet he was tender, even gallant, with his young wife, and he had a good head on those broad rounded shoulders. "Randolph asked me to come."

"Has it to do with Josephine?" I felt my heart begin to pound.

"Not directly. Has to do with her boys, which is just as bad."

He knows my sister well, I remembered. *He has helped out at the mill and about the place in half a dozen different ways, and Tisha has been teaching at Josephine's school.* I recalled then someone saying that Jonah Sinclair, engineer and towpath walker on the Erie, had used what influence he could to ease things for Josie Swift's orphans, thrown back on their own resources among strangers who cared not a whit whether they made their way or not.

"Two of 'em got into a scuffle. Both were hurt, one badly. He's up at the doctor's place now."

Sadness, much like a great weariness, came over me. "However did Randolph find out?"

"He and I have our spies there—pay 'em well. One of the lads hightailed it all the way out to his place soon as the fighting begun."

"Thank heaven! But they were still too late. By the time they returned—"

"On the contrary, Miss Esther. Randolph got there in time to save an all-out slaughter; I can assure you of that."

A shudder ran over me.

Jonah continued, "They're a rough lot, as you know, they that keep and run the canal. They resent these pampered boys who've been thrown back amongst them; natural it should come to blows in the end."

"Is there no help for them?"

"They need a powerful friend. I did my best, but I'm nobody. If a person of influence took their part and urged mercy, I b'lieve they would possess a very good chance."

I felt suddenly faint and light-headed and made my way to a chair.

"I'm sorry! I knew this would not be easy for you. But Randolph thinks you should come."

"Of course. Can you give me a few minutes to dress?"

"Don't hurry yourself. I'll wait as long as it takes, ma'am."

I walked back through the shadows and dressed without light. I felt through the blankets until I found Lavinia's cheek and pressed a long kiss there. I did not like the idea of being gone when my daughter

131

would wake. I left a note for Jonathan and my father propped against my mother's cruet set, then followed Jonah out into the night.

He handed me into Josephine's carriage. "Is she hysterical?" I asked, once we were on our way.

"You can bet she is! Poor thing don't know to act any better when she's that afraid."

I sat in silence, grateful for the darkness that enclosed us. I was humbled by his simple, matter-of-fact wisdom, and his obvious understanding of my sister made me feel somehow ashamed.

When we reached the old house, I steeled myself for the ordeal I would be facing. Here, on the edge of the woods, night had settled in pockets of dense darkness. The shadows were deeper, and the silence was eerie. I took Jonah's hand and let him guide me to the front steps and the safety and light of the house.

When Josephine saw me she turned her eyes, then her face away. "Who asked you to come?" It was the petulant voice she had used since we were children. But it brought tears to my eyes.

"Sit here, Esther." Randolph regarded me with concern, his own eyes narrowed, tucked among lines of anxiety etched like deep grooves in his face.

"This matter is of no concern to you, Esther, not really; in a few days you will be on your way. What happens here you will neither know nor care about."

I knew my sister was using me as a scapegoat, since she could not rant and rail at the men whose stony-heartedness had thrown her boys into harm's way. She could not pummel the chests of the villains who had hurt them with her own fists and expel on the just objects the hatred and pain she was suffering. I knew all this—and I knew also that there was truth in the unkind words she had thrown at me. I *would* be leaving, walking out, as she saw it, and for reasons she could not hope to understand. She would be unable to turn to me, and I would be unable to help her; and that was that.

Latisha entered the room from some other part of the house. When she caught sight of me her face brightened. "Esther!" She ran, bent over, and hugged me. "You look as lovely as I remember you. But pale. Have you been unwell?"

"I am a bit . . ."

"Nothing that six more months won't cure." Josephine threw me a dark glance as she took up her pacing again.

But Latisha clapped her hands in pleasure. "Another baby, is it? Good. I am enjoying my second more than my first, though I did not think that was possible." As she spoke she drew up a small stool and sat companionably close to me. "And I've just settled the two of them into bed."

I smiled, though my mouth and facial muscles felt stiff with my efforts to control them. "Sarah and Susan. Those are nice names," I said. "You have become a good little mother, I understand; even Tillie says so."

"You saw Tillie?" Tisha's eyes widened but with a delighted surprise. "That was a miracle of sorts."

"Yes." I leaned close and, lowering my voice, told her a little of what had passed between us. Not the worst but enough that her brow clouded and she grew thoughtful.

"My poor Tillie," she murmured. "For the obedience and respect she showed our father, this nightmare has been her reward. While I, the independent and imprudent one have been blessed so abundantly!" Her eyes sought her husband, as if in reaffirmation.

I had never heard her talk like this before, had never thought much about what sort of a relationship might exist between the two sisters now that the family had become reconciled to Tisha's choice and they were both grown women with children.

"Do you see her often, Latisha? Go on outings with your little ones?"

"That is how it should be, but it isn't." She glanced around. "Might be if Jonah and I did not work here and associate with—"

"With your own brother, for the love of heaven! And with a girl who used to be one of her very best friends."

"Precisely."

I sunk back into my chair, feeling entirely exhausted.

"Do not take it too hard, Esther. We have tried, time and again. And we will not give up on her."

"She has no one. She will not even allow herself to take much pleasure in her children."

"And she refuses to have more—well, I mean—she and Gerard have little to do with each other."

I put my hand to my head; I think I wanted to shut everything out. But Randolph must have been listening to our conversation, and he came and stood over me. "You are unwell. It was thoughtless of me to think of awakening you in the middle of the night this way. Let me have Danny take you back home."

He looked harried and unhappy. I put my hand out. "This should not all be on your shoulders, my dear boy. If my being here helps *you* and no one else, it will be worth it to me."

Even as I spoke, the big front door rattled open and we heard footsteps and muffled voices out in the hall. Josephine screamed dramatically and put her hand to her throat. Danny entered the room with the doctor at his heels, not old Dr. Ensworth but a younger man I had no knowledge of.

Randolph rose heavily and went to them. I saw the doctor glance uneasily at the circle of faces staring up at him.

"Young Harry is going to pull through, though he will need a good deal of care yet. But we have lost Albert. He sustained some severe blows to the head; I fear he never regained consciousness."

It was as though his words had sucked all the air from the room. I began to feel uncomfortably warm and leaned on Latisha's strong arm to help me rise to my feet.

I walked slowly toward the empty space where my sister stood, stunned by her grief. She looked toward me in horror. "Do not touch me, Esther! I want no comfort from you."

For a moment, as I blinked back at her, it was my mother I saw standing there, tossing her pain at me, like handfuls of sharp pebbles, to bruise and sting. "Never anyone but yourself," I said, "just like Mother."

Josie gasped and began to sputter, but I paid her no heed. "You know how we felt when we were girls and she treated us this way. But now you behave just like her and punish others because you are unhappy!" I believe my voice was rising to an unseemly pitch, but I did not care. "I would ease your pain, lend you my strength, as would Randolph and all the others who love you. But you would rather dump your sufferings over our heads like scalding water and leave us entirely miserable all together. And to no purpose—no good purpose at all."

I drew a deep ragged breath. "I am going home. Randolph—"

He was at my side in a moment. "I will drive you myself," he said.

I took no farewells and did not once look behind me as I followed him out of that dreadful, oppressive room.

I did go home. The following day I secured passage for myself, Lavinia, and Jonathan on the steamboat *Walk-in-the-Water*. The Erie Canal, hooking up with the Ohio, would take us all the way we needed to go.

Sometimes it is not wise to say good-bye too many times—nor to attempt to go back to times and places that no longer exist as they used to, save in the mind.

We had three days in which to pack and make ready. On the morning of our final day Randolph rode into the yard. I was out in the garden with Father, and he walked over to us with long, purposeful strides and such an expression of relief and gladness on his face that I found myself feeling hopeful as I rose to greet him.

"I am driving out with Dan this afternoon to collect the boys," he announced, tickled at being able to shock us.

"Bring them back?" I was dumbfounded. "What has happened?"

"You would not guess, not in a million years."

There was a vulnerable boyishness to his manner that I found very touching. "Tell quickly," I cried.

"It was the honorable Lawrence Swift himself who spoke to the city council and demanded, not requested, that the boys be returned. My own father!"

When he said the words *my father,* my heart leapt with a sensation both of joy and of pain.

"He pointed out that it was only wisdom to place these orphaned children into a safe environment where they would be taught skills enabling them to enter society as responsible, contributing citizens— you know the sort of thing." He waved his hand in a motion of excitement. "Of course, his opponents sat there and seethed. But they knew they were beaten once he placed his power on the side of the table that favored returning the boys."

"Why did he do this?"

The muscles in Randolph's face twitched a bit, but he held his ground admirably. "Certainly not for our sake; heaven knows if he even

135

spared me a thought." I gulped down a sensation of keen resentment, bitter as bile; for I remembered Lawrence Swift well. "It was a power struggle, really, between himself and the son-in-law he has come to loathe," Randolph continued. "I think he has just had enough and saw this as an opportunity to thwart Gerard, to dig the knife in and twist it a little."

I nodded miserably. "Well, if good ends can be served by their enmity—"

"Exactly what I thought."

We indulged in a few more moments of reveling before he withdrew reluctantly. "I shall be there to see you off tomorrow, Esther," he said as he mounted his horse.

"I am glad of it."

"Let me know if there is anything you need in the meantime, anything at all—send the boy over for it."

"Thank you!" I waved my hand after him, struggling to keep my feelings from being grateful and relieved, disappointed and weary, all at once.

"I was beastly with Josephine," I said, not looking at him. "I have never acted in quite that manner before. "

"It wounded her less than it wounded you, Ester." His voice was kindly and patient. "You forgive others their weaknesses and excesses. Forgive your self this time as well."

❦

I had done this before. The memory mingles painfully with the moment. Randolph pressed something into my hand. "God bless and keep you!" I murmured, kissing his cheek.

"We will do well. Do not worry about us, Esther. Think of yourself and be happy."

Think of yourself and be happy. What a wonderful thing for him to say! I looked at my father's face. He seemed to have aged ten years since morning. He knew that this was the end. And he was willing to trust me still, love me still, after sacrificing everything. *Oh, this is torment I cannot bear! This loving and parting!*

It was cooler down by the water. I took Jonathan's hand. The small fingers were cold as ice and clammy as they closed around mine.

My heart was heavy with all it carried away with me, all it must retain and somehow keep bright and alive. We were suddenly moving. My father kissed his hand to me. If Jonathan had not been beside me I think I would have cried like a child.

I stood on the deck a long time. Jonathan waited patiently, with Lavinia beside him. There was nothing more to see, and my eyes were aching. The familiar scenes had all slid by. There was nothing but brown water now with green fields stretching on either side of us and a blue cloudless sky overhead.

"She is heavy for you; let me take her." I turned to Jonathan at last and held out my arms. He came to me, baby and all, and I enfolded them both against me, as tight as I could. And in the fierce aching of that moment my first flicker of comfort came.

137

Chapter Fifteen

---❧---

Kirtland: September 1834

"Brother Joseph is back! The Prophet is back!" I had only been home a few days when that cry rang through the streets. The terrible journey of mercy and death was over, and the men of Zion's Camp had come back—weary and disheartened, weakened from the terrible effects of the cholera which had swept through their ranks. But, oh, to have the Prophet to preach to us once again! To feel the warmth of his countenance, the security that his presence inspired!

To me all seemed well. I, too, was safe home with my precious cargo, reunited with my sweetheart again. Georgie was well; Nathan and Eugene happily about their work. Yes, we were very poor; I had forgotten how poor. But everyone shared the same challenges, so somehow it did not matter. But my husband saw things in a different way.

"Joseph has come home only to be drug through the mud, tormented, and slandered again," he complained.

"He will always have enemies; it is the nature of his work. I think he understands that."

"Understanding makes it all right?"

"I did not say that, Eugene."

"But, my dear, not all the Saints are hailing Joseph's return. Some are crying 'tyrant, false prophet, usurper and user of men.'" The strident words chilled me. Our enemies were one thing, but betrayal within the ranks had a different sting.

And Eugene was right about the seriousness of our troubles, for Joseph Smith had held a council of all high priests and elders on the 11th of August in which he addressed the jealous slanders of men like Brother Sylvester Smith, who were maligning him boldly. He tediously answered and addressed many of the accusations being made against him until the offenders agreed to publish a confession and retraction in the pages of the *Star*.

"It's beneath Brother Joseph to have to deal in such petty matters," my husband fumed. "They eat away at his time and energies, Esther; you should see the great weariness that is sometimes upon his face."

I was grateful I did not have to. But I tried my best to ease the lives and circumstances upon which I exerted control. Eugene was doubly tense these days because he and his friends at the printing house were working long, difficult hours to get the first edition of the *Messenger and Advocate* to press.

"There is nothing more powerful than the printed word," he said night after night, as he came home weary and ink-stained and nodded over a late, cold dinner I had saved for him, often too scanty to satisfy the hunger of hours on end without food. "This is one of the few ways we have to fight back and to get our views and the rich matter of the gospel before the people."

Thus, during this time, everything seemed to require great effort to bring to pass. And we felt the exhausting effort of moving through deep water, against the press of opposition, every step of the way.

Jonathan eased into our household with no trouble whatsoever, seeming almost to anticipate our patterns and ways. He was delighted by the kittens; Georgie had a new half-grown litter, of course. Watching him play with them, I was reminded of how fussy my mother had been when Josie and I brought home a kitten to give to Jonathan when he was about Lavinia's age. He had, thankfully, survived those accident, illness-prone years and become a fine, responsible lad.

The first thing I noticed was an obvious lightening of my work-load. *How can one little boy make such a difference?* I wondered time and again.

"He has taken over half your chores and half mine," Georgie reminded me. "Not to speak of the hours he spends minding Lavinia."

Lavinia! There, too, a great difference could be seen. This quiet boy seemed to possess endless patience, and I believe he sincerely enjoyed being around the child.

"He has not been raised in the company of other children," Georgie reminded me. "And—" she hesitated ever so slightly, "he grew accustomed to dealing with your mother and handling her, I am sure, in his own way."

I had to smile at the idea of that. I had told Georgie every detail of my days in Palmyra; for a good week after my return we spent every spare hour together, and our husbands could not tear us apart. Of course, at length I had to get round to the hard parts: my failure to make contact with her parents; the dreadful morning with Tillie; the final scene with Josephine. But as I scattered the days all out before me like so many of a child's wooden blocks and began fitting them into shape and sequence, I realized how many good and gratifying things had happened. The pattern before me held much more of beauty than of discord and pain.

I remember one day shortly after my return to Kirtland. The exhaustion of the trip and the late nights I had kept, either with Eugene or Georgie, were beginning to catch up to me. I slept very late because no one disturbed nor came in to wake me. I was aware of nothing until notes of music began to sift into my consciousness—a mere suggestion of melody that grew and built until I opened my eyes and ears to it, and it seemed as I lay there and listened that the music came through the pores of my whole body right into my soul.

> Are you going to Scarborough Fair?
> Sing parsley, sage, rosemary and thyme.
> Remember me to one who lives there,
> For she once was a true love of mine.

A clear, sweet voice, unadorned, sang the simple words that floated up to me:

> Tell her to make me a cambric shirt,
> Parsley, sage, rosemary and thyme,
> Without a seam or fine needlework,
> And she shall be a true love of mine.

I lay back to listen, spreading my hair over the pillow. The haunting cadence of the song made me feel young and lithe again, and I was assailed with a wistful inclination to close my eyes and dream a maiden's long, tender dream.

I held my breath, but the music neither ceased nor faded. I dressed to the strains and combed out and braided my hair.

> Alas, my love, you do me wrong
> to cast me off discourteously . . .
> And I have loved you oh so long . . .

I hooked the last button on my shoe and stood up with a sigh. As I descended the stairs the unwavering cadences wrapped their golden threads round me and I came face to face with the songbird herself. We both blinked at each other; then I drew up her hands in delight.

"Emmeline, bless you! You have the voice of an angel, child! Who taught you to sing that way?"

Pleasure colored her cheeks, but she dropped her gaze before an enthusiasm to which she was not accustomed.

"No one, ma'am. My ma says I was born singing, and she's never figured out how to shut me up since."

"Shut you up?" I gave her shoulders a brief hug before releasing her. "We do not want to do that!"

"She has a gift, hasn't she?" came Georgie's low, husky voice.

"Indeed she has. And we are the lucky recipients."

I fear we pestered the girl all day, urging her from one song to another. I felt I could not have enough. Now and again we found ourselves joining her for a few phrases or a chorus, and there was nothing more conducive to delight and goodwill than singing together.

❦

So the days slipped past. Georgie was still teaching, Emmeline still coming weekends. I threw myself into the work of harvesting and preserving the remains of the garden I had planted and left. I did not realize how long a time had passed since we had seen either of the boys until Jack appeared one Saturday morning with Emmeline riding behind him, hanging on tight.

"This is only the second time Emmy's been on a horse in her life," he said, helping her down. She looked the truth of it—pale, with her muscles all tensed into knots. "Here are some cookies warm from the oven, compliments of Claire."

I snatched at them eagerly. "I shall go thank her for them myself," I said.

"Good idea. You can check up on Peter while you are at it."

"Check up? Is something the matter?"

"You might say that." He leaned against the post, and when I motioned toward the house shook his head. "I really haven't time. I promised Brother Thompson I'd drive his wagon out to the quarry this morning since he and his two sons are ill."

"How many days a week do you work on the temple?" I asked.

"Never the same," he hedged. "I suppose at least one day in seven, as the Prophet asked."

At least. I knew for a fact that it was more like two for starters; Jack didn't seem aware of the zeal he exhibited, though we all thought we understood why.

"Since the first of the month Brother Joseph has been working almost daily at the quarry himself. Do you know what a joy it is just to be near him?"

Jack's eyes were shining. This activity was the best substitute for Aurelia we could think of, and we were all grateful. *But what of Peter?* "So what is Peter up to?" I asked.

"He's taken a piece of work for a man out of Fairport Harbor."

"That isn't more than twenty miles from here."

"True, but he stays over during the week and comes back only on the weekends."

"And? Tell all—I can see behind your eyes, Jack."

A slow smile came over his features, then a sad, grave expression as he began to speak. "He is working for a ship builder, carving, staining wood pieces; he likes the work, and he likes being near the water; perhaps a holdover from his days on the canal. But he comes home altered, somehow, more turned within himself, and tired. Sometimes it seems all he does for those two days is sleep."

"What about meetings on the Sabbath?"

Jack shook his head, shamefaced for having told me, as though the confession were his.

"I see."

"I am sorry to bring this to you, Esther. But I thought you and Georgie ought to know"

"You did right, of course. Who else can help him?"

"Don't frown so, Esther."

"I was just thinking. What about Rosie? Does he—"

"I am afraid he does his best to avoid her, poor girl. Though thus far she remains persistent."

"Just what Peter needs. But it is not being fair to her." I was distressed, more than I wanted Jack to see. "Have you any ideas, anything you think might work?"

"Not yet."

"What if we had you two over to eat on Sundays? He would come, surely."

"I believe so."

"Well, at least we'll try that."

"Do not invite Rose. At least not at the beginning."

"I should like to. But no, you are right." *Patience. Why does everything in life require patience?*

"You're beginning to bloom a bit, Esther." Jack mounted and tipped his hat to me. "You look lovely, your cheeks all rosy and that sort of light in your eyes."

"Off with you." I felt the color begin rising in my cheeks. "I'll have none of your sweet talk, young man!"

I watched him ride off, wondering why life is so difficult, so full of trouble and loss. *Do we truly need the bushelfuls that seem to be constantly dumped on us? Are we such pathetic creatures that we cannot be trusted in a state of happiness for very long at a time?*

143

❧

"Freys' cat was crushed at the smithy this morning," Georgie announced, coming out with the breakfast leavings to throw into the garden compost. I followed after her. "How awful. Did Emmeline tell you?"

"Yes, and they'd like another."

"Well, that is not a problem for us, is it?"

She ignored me as usual. "Shall we pick out a kitten and take it over this afternoon? Lavinia could come along with us. Are you up to the walk?"

"In this sweet, bracing air? I think that would be splendid."

We were not able to slip away until mid-afternoon, and Lavinia had fallen asleep, so we left her for the young ones to watch. A bit of a blustery wind was puffing its cheeks out in an attempt to get going, but I did not mind. I like to drink the musky chill of autumn deep into my lungs; I think it clears out the cobwebs. Georgie does not agree. "It fills your head with all sorts of fancies and wild longings, especially when the wind blows." And, in truth, she knows me too well.

We made it to the Freys' in no time, blown along as we were. Janet loved the white kitten and praised our choice, and we sat for just a few minutes to talk over the news of the past week, as women do, and to discuss the various merits of our young protégée. Elinor, playing on the floor with the kitten, listening, I am sure, with one ear, blurted out, "Emmy sleeps with Edith now, and I have Eden's room all to myself."

Georgie and I exchanged glances with each other, and I said, rather too quickly, "Strange how Emmeline's name fits in with yours, beginning with *E* like the rest." And Georgie, going yet further, stated, "You'd best give that cat a bit of an egg now and then to make her coat shine. She is used to it." And the awkward moment was past.

But my heart went out to the pale-eyed woman who sat through it all, tight-lipped and uncomfortable. I wanted to wrap my arms around her and tell her I understood what she was suffering. When I said as much to Georgie out in the yard, she wagged her head at me.

"I am glad you desisted, Esther. You would have only made her cry."

"I suppose you are right, but—"

"But you want to set all things in order because you cannot bear to watch people suffering. I know, I know."

We had not walked far when the wind, filled up with all its sails flapping, struck us fair in the face and nearly blew us a few paces backward. I clutched the tails of my long shawl, wrapped them at my waist and tied them. "We'd best make haste, Georgie."

We bent our heads to the gale, which seemed to grow colder and colder the longer it blew. We had already left the streets of shops and houses behind and were out on the open road. When we rounded a bend only to have a handful of brittle rain spat at us, I felt a twinge of dismay. The bluff lay ahead and a stretch of hard uphill walking. "We may have to stop, Georgie," I called, tugging at her sleeve. "Is there a house nearby?"

"Over there." I looked where she pointed to see a tiny bit of a log structure that seemed to grow out of the brown mossy hill that hung over it. It appeared no larger than a child's playhouse and far less secure. I hesitated. We would have to walk a short distance off the main road to get to it. Perhaps we ought to just push on.

"I don't know of another for quite a distance yet. Shall we risk it, Esther? At least *you* ought to have shelter, especially if this storm breaks fair."

She grabbed hold of my hand, and we ran as the rain pelted down like so many black whiptails lashing through the darkening sky. I saw the house and the muddy yard only through watery streaks and smudges as the rain blurred my sight.

Georgie knocked boldly. When at first nobody answered she set the flimsy wooden planks to rattling. Then, in desperation, she turned the handle herself, and the door pushed inward with a loud creak of protest.

"Rose?—is that you?" The voice startled us. It was a man's voice, thin and largely colorless but with a bitter edging of hope.

Rose? I thought, as Georgie pushed me gently forward. *There must be many Roses in Kirtland. Surely not—the name had merely startled me, called out like that—*

Georgie was in the midst of explaining to our startled host who we were and what we were doing bursting in on him so. When I looked over I saw a man as thin, as dusty-hued as a scarecrow. He sat hunched over atop a high stool, which had a curved wooden back for support. On either side of him were tables, one piled with long wooden handles, uneven of shape and roughly hewn; the other quite covered with dried rushes and grasses from which emanated a mingling of fresh, pleasant scents.

The stranger returned my stare. His expression was sullen, his eyes too big in his pale face, with the whites showing all round the irises. I glanced away. "Nothing for you here," he said, drawing the last word out on a sort of whine.

Georgie rubbed her cold hands together and looked about in her usual cheery manner. "Well, we won't bother you long, just until the wind and rain die down a little." She sighed and hummed a little under her breath as she walked over to the one small window and peered out. "Those are fine brooms you are making. Do you live here alone?"

The man's shoulders twitched as he turned reluctantly to answer her. "Makin' brooms for folk ain't what I'd like to be doing. And I'm not grateful for it, as Rosie b'lieves I should be."

"Rosie?"

"Aye, Rosie takes care of me." The words were a petulant boast, a crying out of some sort that made me feel colder than when I had first stepped inside.

"Well, they are extremely well crafted and fine looking, whether you enjoy the making of them or not." I smiled to myself at Georgie's energetic, no-nonsense attitude. *The teacher in her,* I thought, *coming out.*

I wanted nothing more than to walk out as quickly as I had come in! I glanced at Georgie and cleared my throat rather loudly. "Well, look who is out there!" she cried. "Dear old Brother Pliny!" She was as anxious, then, as I was to be out of this place. "He's got his wagon with a little umbrella top fixed over it." She fairly bounced across the small room to me. "I think he must have seen us come in here!" She took hold of my arm and began to move toward the door. "Thank you so much, Mr.—" The stranger glowered and said nothing. "Well, thank you very much just the same, sir."

Robert Pliny *was* waiting for us. He helped us up to the high board seat, where we all huddled close together, sharing the bit of protection the wide tattered umbrella provided. And, by some mercy, the wind had died down. "'Tis the lull before the real storm hits," he assured us as he clucked to his old mare and urged her to a good lively pace.

"When I saw you two being blown every-which-way comin' up to the hill, I thought, *Those are my girls. I'd bet my best socks on it.*"

I hugged the thin, gnarled arm that held the reins. "Bless you for rescuing us!"

"Are you acquainted with yonder fellow?"

"No, we stumbled upon the place," Georgie replied and then described for him what we had seen there.

"I know the man's a cripple but little more. Did you notice that?"

"We did, without realizing it—is that why the high stool and the twisted sort of way he sat?"

Mr. Pliny nodded. "'Tis a sad state to come to for one not yet old."

I took a deep breath. "He mentioned someone named Rose. Do you know anything about her?"

"I cannot help you there. Could be his wife or his mother; I told you I don't know much about them that lives there at all."

In a few minutes we found ourselves safely deposited directly in front of our own house, and we scurried inside like little mice, wetted and frightened and anxious for our own cozy hearth.

While we sipped hot ginger tea and warmed our feet by the fire we plied Emmeline with the questions our visit to the Freys' had stirred.

"Yes, Miss Eden's moved out—these three weeks since. Lives above the dress shop, or hat shop, or whatever."

"With her parents' approval?" Georgie scowled, her eyes bright.

"They fought something fierce about it, I know that much, and poor Mrs. Frey cried her eyes out for days."

"What about Eden's gentlemen?" I used the word in the plural tense, not wanting to be too pointed or come anywhere near naming names.

"The nasty fellow whom her father calls 'that despicable Gentile'—and sometimes worse—we hain't seen hide nor hair of him since she went away."

Georgie rolled her eyes. She had been trying and trying to improve Emmeline's speech, but she bit her tongue now, so as not to disrupt the flow of pertinent conversation.

"But that other one, he comes every day or so, moonin' about the place. Last week he had a long talk with Mr. Frey, and the master came in a-beamin,' and he and the missus cried a bit together before he went back to the forge."

"I see . . ." But I did not, not a bit of it. I would have to ascertain what further information I might get out of Eugene.

We thanked Emmy and sent her back to the kitchen. Once we were alone, Georgie wiggled her toes as close to the fire as she dared and whispered, "The girl sings like an angel but spoils the effect when she talks, Esther."

147

"She is not as bad as you think; you are just anxious for her to meet with your high standards."

I had something else I wanted to bring up, but my heart began to pound when I thought of it. "That place, Georgie—" I began. "There was something strange and pathetic about it."

"I know . . ." Her voice was filled with concern. "Who on earth could he be?"

"And who," I breathed, "is Rose?"

The misery in my voice alerted her. "Rose—Surely, Esther, you do not think—no, it simply could not be."

"That's what I thought. And yet . . . it *could* be that . . ."

"It could not."

"I have a feeling, Georgie—"

"You have a fear, Esther. And that is not the same thing."

I sighed, acquiescing for the moment, but her words did not entirely comfort me nor put my ill feelings to rest. Later that night, when I was alone with Eugene, I asked him about this other suitor who had been paying his attentions to Eden Frey.

"Ah, Esther, it is a sad case. Aaron Sessions. Do you know him?"

"Of course I remember him. He must be persistent. Does he know of—"

"Of Eden's Gentile admirer? Yes. And the nature of man Comstock is? Yes again."

"He *is* smitten then. But has she the slightest bit of interest in him, or could she have?"

"Who can guess that? You are the woman, Esther; would you dare risk it?"

His tone had become playful. I smiled and kissed his cheek, liking the subtle smell of his skin freshened by the tangy lime scent of the shaving soap he uses. "It's a pity," I mused. "Aaron could make her happy, whereas this Comstock fellow . . ." I told him my experience of seeing the man on the boat accompanied by a woman of questionable repute.

"It is clear as glass to anyone who will see and blindness to anyone who won't. Simple in theory but invariably entangled when it actually comes to application in human affairs," Eugene said.

I agreed. "Do not be so glum," he urged. "Come, sit here, and let me rub your cold little feet, Esther." He settled me on the bed, with all the pillows propping me, and I gave way to the soothing luxuriousness of his ministrations. "You must take better care in the future, you know, Esther, seeing that you carry my son."

"Your son, is it? You are certain of that?"

He paused. "Not certain but I have a feeling."

"Well, well!"

I had no feelings myself, only gratitude that I had weathered the difficult months in Palmyra so happily as I had. I wanted the baby to be strong and healthy; that was all I asked. To be honest, I cringed at the prospect of undergoing the birth process again. *Had I been only fortunate the first time? Dare I hope for as successful a conclusion this second time round?*

The following morning the powers that be in this household— namely Eugene and Georgie—deemed it wise and kind to allow me to sleep until I awakened naturally—a luxury to which one could grow all-too-easily accustomed! The sun was high in the sky when my eyes opened, even then with reluctance. The house was still. I dressed and ate in the blessed peace of solitude. But by the time I heard the steps and voices of my family I was more than ready for the pleasure of their company again.

149

As my little Lavinia came sleepily into my arms I noticed that Emmeline was wearing the Sunday dress that Georgie had managed somehow to make for the girl in her spare time.

"How was meeting?" I asked. "Did I miss the Prophet or Brother Brigham?"

"You did miss a good sermon," Eugene admitted and commenced to tell me all he could remember. But it did not slip my notice that Georgie was carefully avoiding meeting my eyes.

"So you all went together," I said at length. "Did you enjoy the preaching, Emmy?"

"Very much, missus." She, too, dropped her gaze and fidgeted beneath my questioning.

"I am glad you did," I said sincerely. There was no reason to fault her, and heaven knows, the child deserved every exposure to truth, every opportunity.

It was Georgie I scolded later when I got her alone. "You may bring about more harm than good if her father finds out what you are doing." It was a cautioning more than a scolding.

"I am not daft, Esther. I know this. I have thought long about it and prayed and have decided it is worth the risk."

"The risk to whom?" I pressed. "You and I would not suffer as the child would be made to."

"How well I know!"

Her subdued, almost despondent tone went straight to my heart. "I'm sorry, dearie. I meant to help but have only made it worse."

What a sticky business life is! I thought with vexation. *Never a dull moment, as the old saying goes. Never a moment when we are not in need of help and strength from the Lord.*

Chapter Sixteen

Kirtland: December 1834

Where have these last months gone? Can it really be December and the end of another year? The days may pass slowly, but where do the weeks go? The fact that Eugene has been busy helping to write and print the first issues of the *Messenger and Advocate* makes a difference. In fact, last month they moved into their own new building, to be shared with the Prophet's school, but with room enough for their needs, and the added attraction of being their own—free from constraint or restrictions those of not our faith would impose.

I, too, have been busy harvesting my produce. Thank heaven for Jonathan's help! With only two months left until the birth of this child, I find it difficult to squat or bend over my garden, not to speak of standing long hours in a hot kitchen drying and preserving the beans, squash, and crisp, sweet fall apples. Always more and ever more work to do.

Very little of my days belong to myself, so that I begin to treasure more and more my quiet evening hours, especially that time when Georgie and I kneel in prayer, uniting our voices with the voice of a loved one so far away. It is not difficult for me to picture Phoebe kneeling on the pretty blue-shaded rug she wove with her own hands—perhaps alone, perhaps with her children gathered for a moment beside her. There have been times when my mind is empty of what to say and, as I appeal to the Father, thoughts and concerns come as if from nowhere, and I know the rightness of them and am given the words and the understanding and even the faith I need.

We pray much in our household, I suppose. Georgie's family and mine pray together in the evenings, and then Eugene and I hold a separate family prayer of our own both morning and night. In the beginning Jonathan was very uneasy kneeling with us; he had never done such a thing before. But I do not think he minds now. In fact, once or twice he has reminded me, "Don't forget Lavinia's cough," . . . "Don't forget the cat's hurt paw," . . . and once, "Don't forget Father, Josie, and the rest back in Palmyra."

What would I be without prayer? Especially since I am so impatient! And though I do not show it, I become easily discouraged inside.

For instance, I cannot get Peter to come to Sunday dinner! I must send word to him by Jack, for I never know when he is home and am not in a state to go trotting into town in continual search of him! But even when I have written special notes for Jack to give to him, I have heard nothing at all in return.

"He is not eager to face you, Esther."

"He knows I would be ever kind to him, Jack!"

"Dear Esther, it is not that at all. His own shame would make him uncomfortable in your presence, and a few concentrated hours of eating and talking and probably answering questions would be daunting. My guess is that he cannot face even the idea of it."

"But it would not be as he imagines, and it is not like him to run away."

"Not really, but people change. He has changed a little . . . since Aurelia died."

I was stunned to hear Jack say this and did not know what to say in return.

Jack has come occasionally, but each time he has thrown himself into such a frenzy of work that I believe he virtually collapses on the Sabbath. I have worried more and more as the anniversary of Aurelia's death approaches. Everyone is concerned, even Eugene.

"I saw Jack before dawn Tuesday morning when I got up to set type, Esther," he said at Saturday's breakfast table. "And I saw him coming home near midnight on Thursday when I'd gone to help Andrew fix the draw on his chimney."

"Perhaps it is like yourself," I suggested, "an unusual happenstance that he should be out and about at all hours."

"I do not think so. He's into the fields early as possible; too early, really, so that he's drenched in the cold dews all morning. Then he goes directly to the hardware store or to some building site or another, and from there to the quarry or the temple lot. I don't know when he eats or sleeps, Esther."

I did not want to hear this. Especially as my own time was

approaching, I wanted to feel that all things were in order—tight and tidy and provided for. But that was in no way the case. "Go talk to him," I urged. "He may listen to you."

"I doubt it."

So like a man! "It's worth trying, Eugene! If you are that worried about him."

But, of course, he did not follow my counsel, and Jack did not let up on his own punishing routine.

❦

Then there is Rose. Through great effort I have found out a few things. I know that she works days in the Whitney store and as a maid two nights a week at the Johnson Inn. A great deal of work for a young woman—especially a young woman of means and good family. I cannot just go up to her and demand to know where she lives and what her circumstances are. Twice I have sent word to the store that I should like her to come to visit us, come to Sunday supper, but she always declines. Once Eugene ran across her by the Methodist church in town. Thank goodness he had enough sense to stop and talk to her. After pleasant greetings she asked him how Peter was doing, and he had to say, "We know little about him, save what we learn from Jack now and again. Yes, he still lives above the bakery, though he is seldom there these days."

She had known of his work in Fairport Harbor, so perhaps she had been speaking to Jack as well. Eugene said it was pathetic how she affected cheerfulness on his account. "It was her eyes," he told me. "Such a sadness in them, so close to crying she was, right there in the street."

So I worry and fume and fume and worry.

153

❦

We all work on the temple. Eugene gives Thursdays; Nathan Saturdays, though now with cold weather setting in the work is much hampered and may have to be discontinued altogether for the space of these worse bitter winter months. Georgie and I sew shirts for the men and help provide food for the workers every other Monday. It is not easy. Most of the time we find ourselves doing without that we might provide what is required. But we are no different from others doing the same thing. Indeed, we are more favorably situated than many, and for that I am more grateful than I can say. I do not like suffering and doing without; it frightens me, even now. I grew used to my father's provident ways: our larder was never empty, our means never depleted, though we lived modestly.

Now it is Christmastime, and I want to rejoice and give gifts, not practice frugality to the point of deprivation. A woman's heart delights in beauty, and the humdrum of existence can wear down her spirit if she is not careful.

And another problem has arisen: Emmeline's parents want her to come home. I cannot be entirely heartless; whatever else they may be, they are the girl's father and mother. But she is so happy in her joint life, moving between us and the Freys' house, being loved and taught and respected. It is weekends only they require; they will not give up her entire salary. But this means *we* are the losers—Georgie in particular. And what if the man takes to mistreating her once again? These past several months, a day here and a day there spent in their company has always seemed to suffice. Perhaps the holiday spirit has hold of them, and they'll think better of it in a few days' time. We can only hope and pray. Georgie is not reconciled; I am not either. I do not know what Emmeline thinks. I am tempted to ask her outright but cannot quite bring myself to that point.

❧

A letter arrived with a Palmyra postmark and Randolph's characteristic writing. I tore at it with a mixture of eagerness and apprehension. A generous amount of money was enclosed, enough to cover postal costs several times over, bless his heart. He had written all the good news first: my father is well, so is Phoebe. Latisha and her babe thrive, and she is busy again teaching the canal boys, and their little kingdom has settled down to a lovely order—save for one thing. My sister, Josephine, suffered a miscarriage in October.

"She was not far advanced," he explained.

Thank heaven. But it was still a most unpleasant and frightening thing. She had her lads back to fuss over her, and that was, as you can imagine, a boon—not only for her but for me. I waited a time and asked if she would like to write to you herself, but she refused. Now at my second request, she is still unwilling. I wish she were different; you know how much I wish this and lament the current state of things, my dear Esther.

I knew. I knew this and all that he demurred from saying, all that crowded, unspoken, but so strongly felt, between the lines. *She will not yet forgive me for the necessity of living my own life,* I lamented. *Indeed, I would not be surprised if she actually blames me for the loss of this child.*

Randolph continued: "There has been much to upset and trauma-tize her in the past months, mainly, of course, the traumatic loss of her boys and the death of one of them."

What does he want? I thought. *What is he leading up to requiring at my hands?*

155

Perhaps your kindness and understanding, even your forgiveness, would do much to help. Oh, Esther, I know how much I am asking of you!

I threw the letter on the table and rose to walk, agitated, back and forth across the small room. *Always me, always, always!* I fumed. *First Mother sheltered her from facing life straight on, from being responsible for her own actions, then Alexander took up the coveted role. And now Randolph. She is lucky and cursed, both at the same time.*

Jonathan came into the room with Lavinia. I swallowed my bitter ire and read him the pleasant parts of the letter, wishing I knew what he was thinking. This would be his first Christmas away from home, from his own father. I tried to read his face, even the expression in his eyes but could not.

"You may answer the letter, if you'd like," I said. "Your uncle sent a generous sum for postage. And you may put in something for Father." His eyes lit at the word. "Would you like that?"

"Yes! If you're sure."

"I'm sure." Poor boy. I may love him and try my best: tuck him in at night, hold him close to me, even sing to him as I do to Lavinia. But I am not his mother, and Eugene is certainly not the father he left behind.

This thought jumped me to another, unexpected one. *If this child I carry is a boy, what kind of father will Eugene be to him?* I tried to guess or imagine, but even with my knowledge of my young husband, I could not. And our lives—would they leave much room in them for the quiet day-to-day training up of a child? A chill settled upon my spirit when I thought of this, and I pushed it aside. I would not mar the spirit of the season by giving way to such fears and gloom. I would make something special, something warm, even something holy of these most memorable days of the year.

✤

Robert Pliny is becoming frail; this winter has taken its toll of him. I do not know how old he is. But surely his heart has grown while his limbs have shrunk and diminished. Two days ago he showed up at our door with an odd-shaped packet tucked under his arm.

"What have you there?" Georgie asked, wiping her hands along her apron and taking the welcome interruption to sit down and rest.

He motioned toward the children, and we contrived some errand that would take them out of the room. Then he carefully folded back the cloth that covered his burden and revealed a miniature wooden horse he had carved and painted—every aspect so perfectly framed, so fluid in line, so true in detail that I had to reach out and touch it to make certain it was not real.

"For the lad," he said. "And look here—" He unveiled a small wooden peg doll with a round cherub face, green eyes that seemed somehow to sparkle and a crown of hair painted a deep honey red. I put my hand up to my mouth to suppress a cry of delight.

"They are dear, too dear! Too delightful. How can we ever, ever thank you?" I reached out my arms to him, and a slow, thin smile transformed his lined face into a thing of beauty.

"Your gratitude is enough and more. Not to speak of your praises."

"Would you come Christmas morning and give them to the children yourself?" I cried.

"And spoil the magic? Not I." His eyes widened in his efforts to say the next words. "But I will come, if you truly don't mind, to watch!"

Then we both had to hug him and fuss over him a little before he went on his way.

"There are so many to whom I want to give some small remembrance!" I moaned to Georgie.

"I know, dear," she commiserated. "We shall have to find something easy and inexpensive to do."

Time and energy, as well as money, were hard to come by. But we did concoct a small plan. For the children on our list we salvaged snips and squares of working cotton and fashioned handkerchief dolls. For the women we used the scraps in our workbaskets to crochet brightly colored hot pads; there is not a kitchen ever lived and worked in that does not have a constant need for more. The men? Much more difficult. Neither one of us especially enjoys sewing, so we made our own pattern and cut out huge, rounded, jaunty gingerbread men, sprinkled them lavishly with sugar, and used our precious raisins to make buttons and eyes. It was something, if not what we wanted. But one cannot truly celebrate such a holiday as Christmas if one cannot give! As a true labor of love we cut out and sewed a soft, large-sleeved work shirt for old Mr. Pliny, with which to surprise him on Christmas day!

I had something for Rose, something a little extra special. But I felt guilty in wanting to give it to her because my intentions were not entirely pure. I *did* wish to please her, lift her spirits a little, and let her know we still cared. But I also wanted, very badly, to find out about her—to learn where she lives and if my sad, fearful premonition were true.

No one knew; no one could tell me anything. She slips in and out of work, quiet and efficient as a shadow. Oh, friendly enough when need be, but closemouthed about herself. Even Claire Lamb at the bakery, who has chatted and visited with the girl more than most, had no enlightenment to share, until at last she said thoughtfully, "When she comes to meetings, she comes alone."

"Are you quite certain?" *Why had I not thought of that?*

157

"Not entirely. She usually sits with a group of young people and ofttimes walks off with them before they part ways. But come to think of it, I have never seen her with either father or mother or with what might be brothers and sisters. No, not once all this time."

I felt a tightening in the pit of my stomach as I thanked her. There was only one thing to do. But it took me three whole days to talk Eugene into it.

When at last he agreed I took up my wrapped parcel, and he handed me, somewhat reluctantly, into Brother Frey's borrowed carriage. Then we drove the short distance to the little knoll that swells up before the line of bluff begins to rise. We turned off onto the unlit, largely untraveled dirt path that leads to the small house that grows out of the cliff. Eugene made a clucking sound of disapproval when he first saw it, and his sense of uneasiness grew. "What are we to do now?"

"You know what we are to do now; we've gone over and over it. Pull off the roadside and wait."

"This is madness, Esther!"

"No, it is not. I should call it necessity; and, if unpleasant, I am sorry enough for that."

We sat in silence, which made the minutes seem longer. I was aware of an ache in my back and an itch just below my left shoulder blade where I could not reach. *Please come!* I half begged, half prayed. *It is dark now; we cannot have much longer to wait.*

Eugene heard her first. She made little noise in her passing, one lone girl walking the shadowy road by herself. I sucked in my breath when I saw her pass within feet of our hiding place. But she looked neither left nor right, and the lines of her body betrayed the fatigue she was feeling.

"It is her, our Rosie!" I whispered, clutching Eugene's arm.

"Esther, she is not our Rose." His voice was tender, despite his impatience. "What do you wish to do now?"

I was uncertain. We could wait a few moments, then turn around and go back and carry on as though this had not happened, as though I knew nothing of her poverty and troubles. But the little present so carefully and lovingly prepared for her sat like a weight in my lap. And sometime, somehow, we must break through her reserve and whatever it was she was hiding. We could not go on forever like this.

"Wait a few more minutes; then drive me up to the door," I told Eugene. "I will take the gift in myself."

He did not protest. But, oh, when he stopped beside that low doorway my heart went faint within me, and I doubted if I had courage to follow my noble purposes through. I stepped out, drew a deep breath of the cold winter air, and uttered a prayer; then I rapped emphatically upon the wood with my knuckles. No sound came from within. I tried once more. I could feel myself trembling as my muscles tensed. Someone was at the lock now. I drew another deep breath and tried to form the lines of my face purposefully into a smile.

She stood framed in the dim light, looking small and uncertain, as she peered out into the night.

"Rose," I said, "it is only me, don't be frightened. It's Esther Parke—"

"Esther!" She gasped and nearly choked on the word. Instinctively I put my hand out to steady her.

"I have come with a little gift for you, my dear. You see, we've missed you these long months while Peter has been wandering where he ought not to and frightening us all."

She did not speak nor even move.

"Rose?"

"How did you know I live here?"

I had not thought of her asking this question, and I hesitated.

"Oh well, that makes no difference, does it?" she said. "Not now. Will you step inside?"

I hesitated again. What if the man inside recognized me and grew belligerent and embarrassed her? "I honestly haven't the time, Rose."

"I understand." Her countenance fell, and I instantly felt stupid and little.

"This is for you, my dear." I held the gift out to her, and it seemed to take the longest time for her to reach and take it from me.

"Thank you. You shouldn't have . . . thank you, Esther."

"I mean it when I say we miss you, Rose. Will you not come to the house and spend some time with us?"

"I will think about it," she said. "But to what purpose?"

The last words were no more than a haunting echo of the pain that was burning in both our hearts.

"That is for God to determine. We must have faith, Rose! I believe something good and true will come of this, at length. For some reason which I cannot explain. I have believed so all along."

I could not see her face very well, with the inadequate light coming from behind. But I boldly put my arms round her and gave her soft cheek a kiss. "God bless you!" I murmured as I turned and walked back to the carriage. She did not call after me, but I could feel her eyes following me. And when I glanced quickly, as Eugene maneuvered the horse round in the narrow space, she was standing there still, a slight, dark outline against the greater darkness.

"You are crying, Esther."

"Am I?" My cold hand found Eugene's, and I clung to it in silence as we drove the short distance home.

❦

As the ill-fated anniversary of Jack and Aurelia's hoped-for wedding came nearer, Jack became more and more distant and withdrawn. He did not respond to the messages I left at the bakery; he did not come to the house.

"Let the lad weather it in his own way," Eugene advised me. "You fret far too much."

"He may be in need of us!"

"That is neither here nor there, my love. You cannot force him to turn to you just because it may be good for him. Pray that he is turning to God."

I felt the right in what my husband said and began to concentrate my energies to praying all the more fervently for Jack's well-being, praying that the Lord would ease his pain and enlighten him.

The day came marked on the calendar as the very day one year ago when Jack and Aurelia were to have been united as man and wife. It was a clear day with a cold slate-blue sky, stretched high and closed and indifferent above our heads.

From the moment I awoke on that morning I had an uneasy feeling.

Both Georgie and Jonathan were suffering terrible colds, but baby and I were still well. Eugene was working late at the printing office, and Nathan was at a special school meeting. There was still nearly an hour until dinnertime, and I had a chicken stew on the back of the stove. I glanced about me. It was a silly notion, really. But it might put my troubled mind to rest.

I told Jonathan I was going for a walk and asked him to listen for Lavinia; I would not be long. I drew my heavy woolen cape around my shoulders, the one that used to belong to my mother. I believe it still carries a lingering trace of her fragrance, the clean, rose-sweet scent of her skin and hair. I thought of life and death and dying as I crossed lots from my place on Joseph Street the two longs blocks to where the cemetery nestles behind the Methodist church, there on the west side of Chillicothe Road. The temple lot is but a few feet away, at the corner of Chillicothe and Maple—perhaps too close to this meetinghouse of another, unsympathetic, faith.

It was the hour of twilight, when it seems for a few brief moments that two worlds merge, as the heavens open to draw up the day to their bosom and the light goes out with a showering of red and gold. The colors build to a brilliance that seems to come from everywhere, not only the high heavens but the hidden core of the earth itself. Then the colors fade to a dozen intermingling shades of rose, mauve, cobalt, and gray. This in-between time can be startling and lonely, yet comforting, too. The whole universe seems to be holding its breath, and I sometimes feel that those of the other world move softly among us, unheard and unseen.

As I approached the burial ground I walked more slowly, and my thoughts grew heavier. I seemed to feel, like a weight, the loss of each man, woman, and child who slept in this place. The shadows of night were beginning to form here, like pockets of sleep. I wove my way among the skeletal-gray gravestones, keeping out of their way. And I saw the dark form of the man, his body curved in an agonizing shape, over a grave that I knew.

I approached him timidly. I do not think he heard me but felt me. As he lifted his eyes I dropped down beside him and drew his cold hand into mine. But before I could speak even his name, he said, "Esther, I have been with her."

A thrill of amazement and incomprehension swept through me. "Jack, what do you mean?"

"I have been desperate these last days," he confessed. "The more I tried to forget Aurelia, to push my anguish away from me, the more it seemed to overpower me. I could not eat or sleep; I could not think or converse or work; I was like a man in a dream."

I could say nothing, but no words were needed. He drew a breath and went on.

"I came here at first light, hoping for comfort to make it through the remainder of this interminable day." I felt a shudder pass from his hand into mine. "But no comfort came. Nor later when I returned. My nerves were so fraught I could not eat. I came again, an hour ago, when the sun still lay golden across the yellowed grasses. And this time I prayed."

A softness came over his expression. "I humbled myself before God. I confessed my weaknesses and entreated his aid. It was then that I saw her, Esther, standing right there." He indicated a spot a little to the left of where I was kneeling.

"In the air?"

"Just a little above the ground. It was only a moment. She smiled at me—oh, that smile, coming alive in my heart again!" There was a sort of sob in his voice, though his eyes were shining with joy. "She did not speak, but I could hear her just the same saying, 'All is well with me, Jack. I will be here when you come. But now you must be valiant and faithful for the rest of your life.'"

I wiped stinging tears from the corners of my eyes where they were gathering.

"I gazed into her eyes, and we sent our love to one another. And nothing stood between us. Not distance or time or pain or even the space of a heartbeat. And then she was gone."

I must have leaned against his arm; I don't remember. But I believe that a long time passed unheeded before we rose to our feet and reluctantly broke the hallowed spell that encircled us. Now I truly understand that spiritual light is a very real force, that it can cleanse, nourish, renew, enlighten, and cause the whole soul to rejoice.

❧

She stood at my door with a look on her face I will always remember, as hesitant and fearful as I had been on that dark night when I had taken my present to her. I drew her in—into the warm room, into my arms, into my affections. "Dear Rosie," I said. "I am so glad you have come."

I sat her down by the fire with a hot drink to warm her and sent Jonathan upstairs with Lavinia. "Tell me all," I urged, feeling that this was why she had come.

"I do not know where to start or how to explain . . ."

"First tell me who the crippled man is."

Her eyes darkened. "He is my brother." I tried to conceal my deep sigh of relief. "My older brother."

"Has he always been—"

"No. That is part of the story, alas."

"But your parents. Is it true that—"

"Yes, all is true which I told you that first time we met. My family is prominent and wealthy. But my brother, Thaddeus, and his wife, Jane, were part of Sidney Rigdon's congregation, who nearly all joined the Church. They both were converted, and my father disowned them."

I nodded solemnly. *So often, too often, the story unfolds this way! Oh, why are the disciples of Christ scourged and hounded and punished only because they have discovered the truth?*

"Then this terrible accident took place. The horses bolted, and my brother tried to stop them and save his wife, but she was thrown from the wagon and he pinned under it. She died the next day, and he was left as you saw him—" She drew her apron up and hid her face in it. I did not know what to say.

"Were there children?" She shook her head. "How did you come to be with them?"

"He had taught me the gospel, he and Janie—as sweet a woman as ever drew breath. When my father learned of this he was furious. He behaved . . ." She lowered the apron slowly to show me her pale, tear-stained face. "He frightened me; I did not recognize him, the way he ranted and raved." Her little chin quivered, but she went on bravely.

163

"He told us both he never wanted to see us or hear our names spoken again. My brother had no one to care for him, no way of making a living, so we came here together."

"And you have watched over him and served him."

"I do not mind, Esther—you must believe me! Only . . . only, I cannot bear to see him so changed."

"He has grown bitter at what he has suffered, nearly mad with hopelessness," I murmured.

Her brown eyes widened. "Yes, you describe his state well."

"And the glad tidings of the gospel are of no use to him, as he chooses suffering instead."

At my words the poor girl buried her face in her hands and began to cry. "Don't, Rose, I cannot bear your tears!" I put my arm around her, and she buried her head in my shoulder. And for a moment she became everyone all together: my mother and Josephine and poor, poor Tillie and my brave little Phoebe and Georgeanna when she had lost her child. All the tenderness of womankind trembled between us, and I felt the strength of him who loves beyond our understanding flow into my heart.

"We will find a way," I whispered. "We will find a way to reach and help him and to lighten your burdens as well."

I spoke the words, but I had no idea how to fulfill them, and deep within my own heart I feared. Only that love, too real and sweet to ignore, gave me the strength to dare to believe.

Chapter Seventeen

※

Kirtland: February 1835

For the second time in my life I experienced a miracle of the most intimate kind; a miracle so impossible of comprehension that one can only look on with amazement and awe. For the second time I came through the valley of shadows—battered, exhausted—but unharmed and bearing a child in my arms. And the child is a son, as my husband predicted. I named the child Nathaniel, after my infant brother who died in my arms.

"I shall be his godfather, no gainsaying me!" Nathan proclaimed, lifting the tiny boy up in his arms. I looked on, exhausted but dazed by my own happiness.

It is too early to tell what he looks like, this one. "He is his own self," Eugene decided. "Lavinia is very much a miniature of her mother"—that is how he wants it!—"but my son may well be his own man."

I lay back and listened and my happiness turned inward. I was content.

Later in the evening, after the others had worn themselves down and the baby was sleeping, I called Jonathan to me and told him about his twin brother, who had died shortly after their birth. He listened intently. "Did you know any of this?" I asked him at length.

He shook his head. "Only that you loved him. Father always said, 'That child may as well have been Esther's own, the way they took to one another. I've never seen such grief as hers when he slipped away.'"

Tears choked my throat. *My father!* I felt a sudden rush of longing for him. His tenderness reached across the years and embraced me again. "I miss him, too," Jonathan, who had been watching me, said. I pulled him down beside me on the bed, and we talked for a long time, until my eyes became too heavy with sleep to keep open. Then he kissed my cheek and tiptoed away, and I felt my baby breathing gently in my arms as I slept.

✤

It was not an easy birth for me, and Georgie was ill with the first stages of pregnancy—a very important pregnancy, for she must at last have another live, healthy child! Everyone has come; everyone has offered to help. And Georgie, ingenious Georgie, has contrived— without outright fibbing—to let Emmeline's parents believe that there is a great need for her in our house. There *is* a great need, but it is as much spiritual as material. A week before the child was born Emmeline came to us, and Sister Frey gave us leave to keep her until after I am up on my feet again.

So I am pampered in a way I have never known before. Rosie has come often, too. She and I—*what is it that draws certain souls to each other? I cannot say.* We have made poor progress thus far with her brother, though he has agreed to let Brother Pliny sell his brooms and other wares to the local merchants, and he is making considerably more money now, though at times he cannot keep up with the demands of the work. And on his own initiative, Jonathan volunteered to help him, and now he goes to the small cottage two days each week. *If anything can break through his shell of pain,* I keep telling myself, *this child can accomplish it, in an innocent way of his own.* For the man's nastiness and ill temper has not seemed to touch my young brother. The tongue-lashings, the sarcastic criticisms, the unreasonable demands—Jonathan takes it all in stride. And he can talk to Thaddeus, where none of the rest of us can. I suspect that when they are alone, the unhappy man relaxes his tight rein and reveals just a little of the person he has shut up inside.

So I am encouraged, and so is Rose. We are determined to exercise patience and not expect too much at once. Georgie tells me, "If that girl can teach you such a lesson, 'twill be the first time." I do not mind her teasing me; there is so much love in it, and this has been her way since long ago when we were just little girls.

Jack is changed. Others note it but cannot account for it; perhaps only I know the cause, the powerful motives that fuel his determination and forbearance, the spirit of hopefulness he carries with him wherever he goes.

❦

We had not seen Peter these many months, but with the new baby's appearance, he could not resist it. Out of nowhere he appeared at our door. And as the kindness of heaven would have it, Rosie was here helping me.

She looked her prettiest, too, in a blue frock that sat well with her coloring and enhanced the fine line of her brow and the warmth of her brown, gold-flecked eyes. She did not demur; I do not believe she knows how to. But she approached the young man with dignity and held out her dainty hand. He took it gingerly, as though he was afraid he might break it. But I saw the look on his face when he touched her.

"I have missed you, Peter," she said. "It is very good to have you here again. Come meet Nathaniel."

She led him back to where I lay on a trundle in the kitchen. Chairs were brought, and we all began talking, as though no time had passed and no strain existed. If we got tears in our eyes now and then—myself and Rose and Georgie—we brushed them quickly aside. Nathan came home from school, and we cut into the brown sugar pie Claire Lamb had sent over, and there was an air of festivity in the small, crowded room. And Peter lingered. I exchanged glances with Rosie, and we both held our breaths.

As the dinner hour approached I insisted they both stay. We had plenty of food, and there was still much to say. He agreed, and so there was a great scurry of preparation. I whispered to Jonathan—bless him!—and the boy invited Peter to go out to the lean-to barn we share with the Cutlers and two other families to look at the little chair he'd been carving for Nathaniel.

Peter could not help but smile at the gesture. He put his arm affectionately on Jonathan's shoulder and said cheerfully, "Lead the way."

We worked all the faster. So when the boys returned, the meal was spread out on the table and waiting. But there were not enough places to sit. We had worked it out and subtly contrived to put Rose and Peter in the parlor together, with only Nathan to accompany them, and he was to pick up the latest number of the *Messenger and Advocate* and become at once engrossed.

I kept a covert eye on them and was encouraged that something was happening, for they sat with their heads close together, their food scarcely touched. I had been praying silently inside myself ever since he arrived. But oh, I was on pins and needles as the evening wore on! When at length Peter rose and stretched and began to speak about leaving, I tried to catch Rose's eye, but she had turned away, and Peter was alone beside me. "Thank you, Esther," he said. "You have been so good to me. Now, as always."

"I love you now, as always."

"I know."

"You will come back soon? It is not right for you to neglect us."

"I don't like to. But it is not easy. My work is so far away, and the nature of it such that I cannot always walk away from it until a project is done."

"And you still are content there?"

"Yes."

My heart was caving inward, deflated. "But you will not, you must not, wait so long the next time."

"I promise." He kissed my cheek. I put my arms around him for only a moment. *How thin he has become; how well toned his muscles are.*

Rose did not walk out with him. He turned his head round to cast a farewell glance at her, but this was all. When he was fairly gone, I nodded to her, and we walked off together. But all she said was, "He spoke much of his work and his love for the water and the waves and the seagoing vessels."

"Did he ask concerning your life while he has been absent?"

"Not really. But I did work up the courage to ask him if he has been going to meetings even occasionally. And he said, 'Not to speak of.'"

"Did he say anything kind to you? That he missed you, at least?"

Rose smiled faintly at the intensity that flashed in my voice and in my eyes, despite my efforts to control it. "He said, 'you are as pretty as I remember, Rose, perhaps prettier. And you are a great deal too good for me.'"

I kicked at the wood pile and stubbed my toe. "It is all right," Rose soothed. "I did not expect even this much. At least I know now that he cares. With that knowledge I can wait as long as it takes."

I was not so reconciled; I feared my Georgie was right. Patience and reasonable expectation are not in my nature. Besides, I know life too well. Anything could happen; Peter could ruin his life in half a dozen ways, any of which would ring the death knell to Rose's hopes and dreams. He was in harm's way, and I prayed that this girl's love might have some power to protect him, along with our prayers and our faith.

Chapter Eighteen

Kirtland: July 1835

Our men have been going out in every direction; the field is indeed ripe for the harvest of the souls of good men and women. There have been converts in Indiana and Illinois—literally hundreds. In fact, a conference was held in Illinois in April at which eight different branches were represented, all with new members declaring themselves firm in the faith. It was inevitable that this work, in due time, would touch our lives as well.

In March, Nathan was called to preach in Maine and the tiny Fox Islands off the coast of her. He was to leave as soon as all could be made ready for his departure. We were surprised; I could safely say stunned. Georgie said little at the time about what she was thinking, but she must have been afraid, especially with this new child growing within her.

Eugene and I drew back, gave them as much time alone as they needed, and kept our own thoughts to ourselves. But how foolish and unschooled we are in the things of the Spirit! Nathan was thrilled, deeply honored that he had been thought worthy to serve. He gave Georgie a special blessing before he left her. Listening, I felt particularly ashamed. *After all the tender, loving experiences my Heavenly Father has given me, why am I still so weak in faith?*

The same month Nathan left, a special meeting was held to give blessings to those who had worked on the temple. In the morning the Prophet Joseph spoke to the Church as a whole and reminded us of the importance of purifying our lives and purifying the kingdom. Then the blessings were given, under direction of President Rigdon. Our Jack was aglow, and I felt humble and terribly worldly beside him. The work marches on. Brother Joseph received a grand revelation on the priesthood, how it should be organized and administered. He and the Twelve went forth on missions to seek out those who are ready to hear and receive the truth. I forget sometimes what our real purpose is here in Kirtland. The responsibilities of everyday life are demanding and crowd out the higher purpose that brought us here. And I have begun to wonder of late how much I do for the kingdom and what in ignorance I may be neglecting from day to day.

My Eugene is involved in the publication of *The Northern Times,* a political paper, which draws him to issues of social order and government and the affairs of man. At the same time the revelations the Prophet has been receiving are being readied for publication in book form. There is nothing more sacred than this work. I am amazed to even contemplate God speaking through Joseph, speaking to him, *speaking to us.* I can tell the difference; I can guess with amazing accuracy whether Eugene has been working on the doctrinal writings or on political issues. I can tell by his mood, his countenance, the things he chooses to talk about around the fire at home.

The temple steeple is now erected, and work on the interior plastering has begun! Work will progress more quickly now, and I think the reality is sinking into me that this building and its purposes are real and will come to pass.

My Lavinia is a big girl of four. On her birthday in April she received a new doll—her counterpart of Mama's baby. Emmeline dressed her for the child, who could not be more delighted. Together each morning we bathe and feed our little ones and sing them to sleep. She could not be a more conscientious mother. Sometimes my heart aches when I watch her and think how quickly the time will pass and she will in truth be a mother with her own beautiful children. But where will I be? I cannot imagine myself growing older, giving way to a new generation. I still feel very young, very little changed from when I was a girl.

Emmeline—who has fit back into her end-of-the-week routine with us—has also taught my Vinnie to sing. Her repertoire includes a full dozen songs by now, and she holds forth at the top of her high little voice, often startling her baby brother into tears! At such times Jonathan takes her out of doors, where she sings for Georgie's kittens or our cow, hobbled to graze at the end of the lane, or any stray chickens or birds she can find. Her favorite is "Oh, Dear, What Can the Matter Be?" and she gets the words helplessly tangled up. But when she triumphantly finishes with "a bunch of blue ribbons to tie up my bonnie brown hair," I look at her red-gold curls and long to see them festooned with bright ribbons and wish in my heart that Phoebe were here to fashion frocks for my daughter and hers, the way she sewed for us when we were young.

But that is like me: always wishing, lamenting, looking back. Those who live for the day perhaps possess more wisdom. Worry never changed yesterday nor altered the pattern of tomorrow. I have to remember to keep telling myself that!

It is July. Nathan should be home in less than two months, and I am glad. The doctor has told us that he can hear two heartbeats, and Georgie can expect to have twins. *Twins!* "Two for the price of one," Georgie quips to me. But it is not really so. They are taking a great toll on her strength. She droops in this hot weather, and so does my little son. He is not unwell exactly but what some folk would call "delicate," and I find myself watching him closely. My Lavinia has become such a strong, strapping girl. Perhaps Nathaniel, too, will in time grow into the strength he will need to meet the world as a man.

Last week a letter arrived from my sister—oh, bittersweet, bittersweet! She has humbled herself enough to beg a boon of me, which I am forced to deny! She is expecting another baby and wishes me to come out and stay with her. But there is no way on earth that I can! I dare not expose Nathaniel to the heat and the rigors of travel, and I dare not leave Georgie alone—not to speak of coming up with the money, though I know Randolph would provide that, if asked. I am in a quandary and fuss and fret about how to manage it, seeing really no way at all. If I refuse!—I dare not think of Josie's wrath and disappointment. And one thought keeps teasing my brain: *What if things go wrong? What if something happens to her? What if I should never see her again?*

Eugene has been preoccupied, but at last when he saw how distressed I was, he made a rather startling suggestion. "Ask Josephine to come visit you here. At least that will be better than an outright refusal."

"She will laugh."

"Of course, but she may well take you up on it, if the notion strikes her fancy."

I consulted with Georgie. "I do not think she will come, Esther, but if she did we could manage it. And write to Phoebe as well. Perhaps if Phoebe *offers* to help, Josie will not refuse her."

I took their good counsel and felt much better after sending off my two letters.

Last night when we knelt down to pray, Jonathan asked, "May I say the prayer, Eugene?"

"Of course." Eugene smiled at me. "That would please your sister and me well."

And how he spoke! With no hesitation, no awkwardness. I thought, *He has been praying much by himself.* And he remembered things and people I seldom think of, including Rose's brother, Thaddeus, who had become a very real part of his life. Last month was Jonathan's birthday, and he is now eight years old. I must remember this and treat him accordingly. He gets lost in all the confusion, I fear.

Earlier this month Aurelia's aunts were both sick with summer fevers. I took them a bowl of Georgie's lemon jelly, a decoction of angelica root for the fever and rosemary for a sweet, soothing bath.

They have aged much since Aurelia's death, especially Dorothy. During my visit I sensed that they were doing little more than going through the motions of living—because they must. A twinge of guilt assailed me, for we have neglected them terribly this past year! So I stayed a bit longer than I had intended and encouraged them to ramble on a bit, since I was there to listen. And in the course of conversation, I heard half a dozen times, "When Jack was here last week he brought . . ." "Well, Jack is always saying . . ." "What a dear Jack has been these past days! . . ."

I learned there is scarcely a day that passes without him coming to check on them and perform some little service or bring some little treat.

"Last winter right before—well, you know—there was a rough spell."

"Yes, I remember. It was only to be expected."

They both nodded in response. *So he is taking care of them,* I think, *without saying a word to any of us.* I should have expected as much. The best people of the earth operate in such a manner.

After I left the aunts' house I took a short detour to check on Claire Lamb at the bakery. I was also anxious for one of her sweet sugared donuts. They count many Gentiles among their customers and are therefore able to purchase the flour and sugar and other ingredients they need to concoct their fine wares. I did not expect to find Peter sitting on a high stool behind the counter, helping Reuben frost little cakes.

"What are you doing here?" I said before I could bite the words back.

"Lending Reuben a hand, as you can see."

"Do not be fresh with me, Peter." I was hurt and fuming inside, and my words had a sting to them which I did not intend.

"The lad has been ill and took a few days off from the heavy work he's been doing," Reuben said.

I peered at Peter again. *Does he look pale? He is even thinner these days than he used to be.* "Why have you not come to see us?" I asked.

"I did not wish to fret you."

"Or get mine or anyone else's hopes up! Peter!" I wished he could feel my longing, know the pain he was causing. "What has happened to you?" I blurted out.

"I do not know what you mean."

"You know precisely what I mean. You took this job away from Kirtland, away from all of us. You no longer come to meetings, or associate with the Saints, or read your scriptures—"

"You do not understand, Esther."

"No, my dear boy, I do not."

I was scolding him, but he made no move to stop me. Perhaps he *could* feel my pain. *At least he knows how much I truly care about him,* I thought. "I cannot help trying to help you," I said. "You ought to realize that, to remember—"

"I do." He rose and came round the counter to stand beside me. "Esther, I'm sorry I've hurt you. And I'm sorry I'm hurting Rosie. Tell her—" His face was pale, and there was a misery in his eyes that I could not bear. "Tell her she deserves someone who can make her happy."

"You are willing to lose her then, Peter? Lose the best thing that's come into your life?"

"Now or later, what difference does it make, Esther? Besides, I could not make her happy."

"You have convinced yourself that you can't!"

"Look around. How many people are truly happy, Esther? How many have you known in your life?"

"Peter, for goodness' sake! You would be happy with Rosie, and she wants no one but you."

He shook his head. "I believe I would make her unhappy and spoil her hopes. Or else other things would happen to separate us."

I reached for his arm, but he moved away from me and returned to his post. Dear Brother Lamb had retreated discreetly back to his ovens. "Peter, please do not let your fears ruin everything. You have seen the results of that, too."

He said nothing. He would no longer look up at me. If Georgie had been there she would have said, "Leave him alone, Esther. There is nothing at all you can do."

In fact, that is precisely what she did say when I told her about it later.

"It is because of you that he joined the Church," I reminded her tartly. "You brought him here. Now you are willing to let him flounder and make no move to help him?"

She raised up from the bread she was kneading and rested her hands flat on the table. "I cannot live his life for him, sweetie, the way you wish to do. He is not ready for help—you saw him yourself. There is no way he can take it until he is ready. It is only sorrow, even poison to him now."

I slumped into a chair. This mortal state does not agree with me! "Let go, Esther," Georgie said gently, bending back to her work.

"And accept his misery?"

"Yes. That is a very real part of it."

"I do not like how things are!"

"You never have, my dear. That is why you suffer so."

I knew that Georgie was right. Through the exertion of a supreme, exhausting effort I *can* do as the others *seem* to do with ease. But I do it with pain. And age and experience and what ought to be maturing, seem to have made no difference at all.

❦

Something extraordinary has appeared in our city that has made quite a stir. Early in this month a gentleman by the name of Michael Chandler arrived with a story of wonder, which he brought to the Prophet's ear. It seemed he had been willed seven Egyptian mummies and the contents of their cases by an Italian uncle who dealt in artifacts and secured the treasures before his death. It is the papyrus scrolls wrapped in linen which he brought to Kirtland in hopes that Joseph Smith might translate them, for various authorities in the East have advised him to bring them here. Curious, indeed! Everyone in the city is talking about it, and some gentlemen not connected with the Church have contributed to purchasing the scrolls and making the Prophet a gift of them.

That was but weeks ago. Joseph Smith has begun translating the ancient markings enough to know that one of the rolls contains the writings of Joseph of Egypt! I try to imagine how he must feel with such a treasure in his possession and the power to penetrate and reveal its great wealth. Surely these things came not by accident into his hands. What will we learn through this gift God has brought to his servant?

All are eager to know. A sense of excited enthusiasm has touched our hearts anew. Joseph Smith has given over his life to the service of the Lord. I cannot understand this. I am grateful, but I am not really able to comprehend. Yet look how we have been blessed, not only Georgie but our whole household while Nathan is serving this mission. Surely the blessings to the Prophet and his family will prove rich and abundant.

While such men as Joseph go forth, others flounder and fail and choose darkness and death rather than light. Eden Frey has run away with that libertine Jedediah Comstock. Her parents found out today. They are sick with regret and fear for her. They do not know where she has gone. Eugene says she will return because Comstock never keeps to the company of any one woman for long. But what will become of her—as a person, inside herself? This is the horror that haunts our hearts. Aaron Sessions has gathered a party to go in search of her, but if they find her, what then? Does he like the idea of winning her back from danger, stalwart and true as the ancient knights were? Would he still want her if she came back?

Such are the questions that pester our peace and form the burden of our prayers. And I have not heard from my sister, Josephine, though there has been time for reply. So it is with us, at present. And so we move forward, one day at a time.

Chapter Nineteen

---❦---

Kirtland: December 1835

Nathan came home safe and sound and glowing from the successes he had had. He was here when the babies decided to come, three weeks early. With the power of the work he had been engaged in still upon him, he blessed his wife and the new lives that were struggling to be born. I felt a peace, remembering what the Prophet Joseph had said about the future happiness and success of my friends.

How tiny those little forms were as they lay side by side together—not much longer than their father's outstretched hand. Georgie was exhausted and weak, but there were no complications. Emmeline stayed with us around the clock. And Rosie came often to spell the girl, that she might sleep now and then.

There was no doubt, no discord as to what Nathan and Georgie would name their children: Joseph, for the prophet, and Lucy, in honor of the Prophet's mother. I liked to look into my dear friend's eyes and see the absolute contentment that pulsed there.

Georgie did not have enough milk to feed the two of them, so we found a wet nurse for Joseph, whose demands were lustier, and Georgie fed her daughter herself. I was reminded often of those other twins, born nearly nine years ago. One day I pulled Jonathan aside.

"You are here because of the Prophet Joseph," I said. And I told him the story again, lest he forget it and the significance of it as he grew into his life.

Josephine's baby came, too, in good time and good order, which proves prayers are answered, indeed! And our Father in Heaven is merciful to all his children. Josie bore her husband a son, and Randolph named the boy Alexander, after that good man who had been his friend, whose death had, in truth, made the existence of this little one possible. There is no better man than our Randolph! I have for a long time known that.

Josie did not write; he did. But I penned a long, happy letter back to her. Randolph said Phoebe had come time and time again, persistently, and had at last been admitted to help near the end. All Josephine really needs, as I well know, is attention, someone seeing to her needs and fussing over her; and Phoebe is much better at such things than I. I was happy for both of them, relieved and pleased at what I hope to be a reemergence of an old friendship too long neglected and laid aside. And oh, a son!—for Randolph and for my father in his frail old age.

My father is failing; both Phoebe and Randolph have said so. Perhaps this child will revive his waning interest in life. He has done his work now; perhaps he feels no reason to linger, to go on performing the simple functions that take him from day to day. I wish I knew what was in his thoughts, in his heart as he comes to the running down of his life. I wish—but no matter.

On the 2nd of November the School of the Prophets started up again. Hebrew is being offered this term, and Nathan is eager as a boy at the prospect. Georgie says his days as a missionary have changed him, and she would gladly send him out again every year or two, just to keep him in shape.

"Brush off the old coat," she said, "give it a fresh lining, and it will be better than new."

She made light of it, which is her way. But I knew what it meant to her; and I, too, have seen the changes, the refinement of the inner man, and the increased closeness between them, as a result.

179

⁂

The year is beginning to round itself off and make way for another, yet some things have made no progress yet, no progress at all. Peter came when the twins were born; again I think he could not help himself. At such times he feels the strong pull of old ties, old loyalties, old affections.

He did not see Rosie this time. Georgie says that may be good rather than bad, but I do not agree. He did not look well, and he did not look happy. He is not taking care of himself. The holidays are coming, and he will be alone and lonely. And I know he is frightened. Fear plays a big part in his life. I have asked Jack to speak to him, but he has made the attempt so often that now Peter has taken to avoiding him as well. Nor does he keep the old quarters above the bakery, but lives week-round by the lakeside and takes only an occasional room at the inn for a night or two when he is in town.

Rosie says little. She is still working at the inn two evenings a week but spends her days helping Widow Godfrey at the dairy. Work so far is her remedy, though Eugene says there is a young man who has been paying his attentions to our Rosie of late.

"If it is meant to work out between her and Peter, it will work out, Esther," Georgie reminds me often, "no matter how things seem."

Sometimes I feel guilty, encouraging her feelings for the boy when perhaps I ought to do my best to help her unknot the invisible strings that tie her to him and let her be on her way. Between the ghost of Peter and the specter of her brother, she has little enjoyment and little peace. Yet she does not discourage easily, and that sparkle is often in her eyes.

Thaddeus is a moody brute at best. He has drawn nearly entirely within himself and will not come out save for Rosie—upon whom he depends entirely—and our Jonathan. The two have worked out a pattern, a rhythm of getting things done, and orders for brooms and brushes keep coming in. Rosie has fixed the place up some: we helped her braid a new rug for the main room, which makes ever so much of a difference. But the best thing is that after Nathan returned, he and Eugene built a small lean-to, attached to the house, which Thaddeus might use as a shop. Now there is a loft overhead for Rosie to sleep in and a house that is not littered with straws and shavings! She purchased a settle bed from Sister Godfrey which the men set up in one corner and whereon Thaddeus sleeps. There is a proper kitchen table now for preparing and eating meals and a comfortable chair by the fire and a kitten, of course. A soft gray female, one of the prettiest, from last summer's litter. And as the cold weather came on, I hounded Eugene until he and Nathan came over and stopped up the chinks in the walls—as many as they could. And they spread a new layer of tar on the roof to keep it from leaking. So this winter has been far cozier than last winter was.

Jonathan has discovered that Thaddeus is more skilled with his hands than the making of brooms would reveal. He came in one day unannounced and found him working on a fine cherry wood clock case, which he at once hid beneath a cloth on the lower bench.

"He growled at me the rest of the morning," Jonathan confided. "But I knew what was bothering him, so I didn't much mind."

We must find a way now to draw him out into the open, but that is not a simple matter. There are times when the blackness assails him and holds him in its grip so tightly that he cannot manage at all. On such a morning he will shout at Jonathan and order him to go home, and if the boy does not mind him, he will pick up something, anything, and throw it at him with a vengeance. Eugene and I have warned him that he must not wait 'til this happens, for he could be hurt very badly if the tool or stretch of wood happened to hit him.

We have invited the poor man to go places with us—not meetings, not yet. But even for the prospect of a picnic along the river where no one can see him, he will not leave the house.

"He is living only because he must," Rose has confided to me. "Some days I come home and he has not eaten at all. He sees no use in his existence and the prolonging of his suffering. And I believe he thinks I should hate him because I am so cruelly tied to him."

I praise her patience and try not to worry about how dismal her young life must be.

181

In September the edition of the Doctrine and Covenants was bound and finished! The revelations are a great comfort to me. They speak in a different voice—a voice directed to us, naming many places and people we know. I love the simple words of counsel, the times the Savior seems to yearn over us and understand what we are going through. Such as this, given to Joseph and Oliver Cowdery at Harmony six years ago: "Therefore, fear not, little flock; do good; let earth and hell combine against you, for if ye are built upon my rock, they cannot prevail. . . . Look unto me in every thought; doubt not, fear not."

If I could only emblazon such a message on Peter's mind!

We read at least a few passages aloud every evening, and Jonathan loves to take his turn. He does very well—Georgeanna sees to that!

Indeed, if the truth be known, Jonathan and Emmy are far beyond others their same ages.

Though just yesterday I heard Georgie asking Emmy how old she would be on her next birthday. "Seventeen," she replied.

"No, surely not," we both exclaimed. "You look no more than a fledgling; twelve or thirteen."

But time has slipped away from us, in this, as in all things. The twins love Emmeline well and will go to her sometimes before they will go to their mother. And they both mind her well. She has become quite proficient at all the housewifery skills, right here under our eyes.

Now and again in a drunken blindness her father finds his way to us. But it is really money he wants. In fact, we have taken to hiding a small amount, no matter how tight things are, in a tin in the kitchen cupboard. A few coins will usually placate him and get him to amble away. We never mention it afterward, and Emmeline says nothing about it, but we have found out that she gives part of her earnings to her mother, not her father, so that the rest of the children might eat and have fuel for the fire of a winter night and clothes on their backs.

Just last week Robert Pliny drove over with a pile of wood in his wagon. "For those youngsters of Emmy's," he said. He is a remarkable man. He does not seem to get older, though he has looked bent and frail ever since we have known him, and I am afraid to ask what age he is!

Emmeline is so quiet, so even-tempered. But last week she blew in like a little storm cloud the wind had carried. "Do you know what I have just heard?"

We shook our heads and hastened her on in the telling. "Millie Johnson—she is such a flirt, and she has not a thought in that head of hers. She was mincing about and bragging that our Jack had said she was pretty, and she expected any day now he would come courting her!" We laughed out loud at the mere thought. "There are others," Emmy persisted. "How dare they make such presumptions!"

"It is nothing to Jack nor to us," we assured her. "Such silly girls have always existed and always will."

But the incident made me wonder whether Jack will ever marry or if the promise Aurelia gave is enough and will be for the remainder of a long, solitary life.

❧

It is a bitter December. There have been many ill with bad colds and coughs that go into the quick consumption. The frost is deep in the ground, and the winds off the lake are wet and heavy with unshed snow. As the saying goes, "The weather's always ill when the wind's not still."

It was the evening of Thursday, December 10. How could I ever forget? We banked and covered the coals carefully before going to bed and checked to see that the children were well covered. And as my cold feet slid between the cold sheets, I hoped Rose's little house would not prove too drafty on such a night.

That was all. The cold settled in, and the darkness surrounded us. It was Jonathan who heard one of the twins moving about restlessly in his sleep. But should so little have awakened him? Nevertheless, he sat upright in bed.

"I knew something was wrong," he told me later, "so I went to the window and looked outside. I could see the flames like red streaks that kept moving and growing."

He woke Eugene and Nathan, who scarcely could credit his story until they saw the murky red sky for themselves. "Must be the wood kiln," Nathan guessed. "It's caught on fire before."

They dressed with haste and perhaps not as warmly as they ought to have. By the time they reached the kiln, perhaps fifty other brethren were already there. They were positioned into lines, handed heavy buckets to haul from one man to the other, and in the matter of a few moments they were engulfed in an inferno of acrid smoke that burned their lungs more than the cold air that the relentless wind churned round with it.

I do not know how Jonathan survived. None of the men seemed to take notice of the fact that he was only a boy. How did his hands maintain the strength to close round that cold handle, his thin arms to heft the cruel load? He maintained his place in the line for nearly three-quarters of an hour, when suddenly he slumped to the ground. Strong arms lifted him and carried him out of harm's way, and from somewhere a blanket was provided to cover him as they laid him out on the ground.

By this time close to two hundred of the brethren had gathered, and the flames were nearly extinguished and in control. So Eugene carried the lad home again, and he and Nathan washed him down and re-dressed him before they came upstairs to wake me.

I cannot describe my feelings as I fled down to stand over him, shivering in the freezing kitchen. But as Nathan and Eugene told the story of what had happened, Jonathan grinned up at me. He was pleased as punch with himself.

"You'll be too sore in the morning to move a muscle," the men warned him. But he paid them no mind.

"He's the one who woke us, and he held his own bravely." Eugene was warm in his praise. "Those first few minutes were crucial, and I believe our being there made a difference. We saved less than half of the lumber, but that is better than losing all."

Losing all. I had lost nothing dear to me in the night's adventure. Thank heaven for that.

We let Georgie sleep, though she scolded us roundly in the morning. And for the next few days Jonathan could barely hobble about. I know it hurt him to lift or bend, but he saw to most of his usual chores and duties without complaint. I was so terribly proud of him, but something kept me from saying so. He had acted the part of a man. Holding his own and keeping his place, even now in the aftermath, meant more to him that the coddling and praising of all the women alive!

184

❧

I do not get around enough in this weather, especially with a baby still nursing. I did not know Jack was ill, not until Claire Lamb appeared at my door, just two days after the fire.

"He needs someone to help him," she said, before I had even poured her a cup.

"Quick consumption?"

"If it is not, then it will be. But he will have nothing of my help."

"All right. I shall have the men bring him here."

Jack protested weakly, but there was not much oomph left in him. We put him on a bed in the kitchen and kept the fire blazing so that the rest of us were uncommonly warm. His cough was terrible, and sometimes would go on for minutes before giving him a chance to draw breath. I treated him with every remedy I knew of, but the disease had already taken a tenacious hold. He sank rapidly during that first week. At last Nathan and Eugene gave him a priesthood blessing, and this seemed to rouse him, to wrench him back into a semblance of life.

Slowly he progressed and was able to speak again, a sound faint as a reed the wind moves through. And he was able to open his eyes for more and more minutes at a time before the weakening fatigue overtook him and made the thin eyelids too heavy again. Nothing seemed to give him any rest or comfort until one day when Emmeline, working in the kitchen, forgot herself and started to sing. Georgie and I heard her and rushed in, fearing the sound, however pleasant, would cause his head to start aching and put his exhausted nerves on edge. But as we hushed her with whispers and signs, we heard Jack from his cot, mutter weakly, "Please let her go on."

Holding our breaths, we sat her down a short distance away from him and bade the girl sing, every sweet, tender song she had ever learned. In a matter of minutes, he slept. That night he woke in a fever and called for her, but she had gone back to the Freys'. So we sent for her the following morning and prepared a bed in the parlor.

How willingly she placed herself at Jack's beck and call! He had but to moan or utter a sigh, and she was beside him, brushing his hair back from his fevered forehead, cooling his skin with her breath, drawing the distress and pain out of him with the powerful magic of song.

Life went on about him; there was no way we could avoid it, especially with three babies in the place. Christmas came and departed before he really began to get better.

The year is now at an end. Jack can lift his head from off the pillow. He can smile at Emmeline and laugh at Lavinia's antics. He is beginning to look truly alive again.

This time last year he nearly lost his life when his heart and spirit failed him. This year he nearly lost his life when his body was assailed by disease. Strange indeed, the ways of the world. I do not understand them. I can only watch and be grateful and try to leave the rest in God's hands. "Look unto me in every thought; doubt not, fear not." It is my sincerest desire to learn how to live by those words.

185

Chapter Twenty

Kirtland: March 1836

In January in the upper loft of the Lord's house, the Prophet blessed the priesthood quorums, cleansing and empowering them for the challenges of the work yet ahead. At this time Roger Orton saw a mighty angel riding upon a horse of fire. He carried a flaming sword in his hand. Five other riders followed the angel, and together they circled the house, protecting the Saints, the Lord's anointed, from the power of Satan, and those evil spirits who, with him, desired to destroy the Saints.

Joseph promised that if we purified ourselves before God, when this temple was finished, there would be a great outpouring of blessings upon our heads. He called it a Pentecost, as the ancient Apostles partook of—a time to rejoice. We, his people, believe him. We have gone to bed hungry many nights since the new year began that there might be food for the laborers, so that the work might go on. Money is needed—perhaps above everything. Jack sold his gold watch, the one his father gave him many years ago, probably his last connection to home. I sold the necklace that had been my mother's; I have the memory to keep. And Eugene goes with stockings worn threadbare and shoes stuffed with newspapers to keep out the water. I never would have believed that so many people could do so much on so little. It is a marvel to see. We are like watchmen set on a tower, a tower raised in the midst of our enemies. We cannot be hid. But we are constantly reminded that our God is with us. And when the God of hosts stands as our shield and our protector, what heart can fear?

For in our poverty and beneath the hand of persecution have we gone forth. None has been spared entirely, but the bulk of the burden has been Brother Joseph's to bear. Day and night the Elders have had to keep watch to protect and preserve him. On every side he is troubled. On every side calumny and deceit raise their heads. I wonder at Emma and the Prophet's aging mother, at what their feelings might be. *Doubt not, fear not.* Surely the Lord has shown us his miracles day after day. And now the heavens shall overflow for us, manifesting his acceptance and love.

At this sacred time, within these sacred portals, the Prophet saw the glory of the celestial kingdom, entered by a gate like circling flames of fire, with streets that had the appearance of gold. There he saw Father Adam, Abraham, and other prophets. He also saw his brother Alvin, who died before the Restoration, and was given to know that they who die without a knowledge of the gospel but would have received it will still be heirs to this kingdom of glory. And little children who have died before the age of accountability are heirs to celestial glory! He saw with his own eyes and had the understanding of the vision revealed to his heart.

I see my brother Nathaniel and the faces of the other children my mother lost, Josie's babe who lived but a few hours, and so many more. I have a picture of them in my mind, gathering around Alvin Smith and watching what we are doing here. And there must be others—more than we can count, down through the ages, who have waited for this day to come. Surely they will care for us, and we will feel their love as part of the joy of this day—we who are somehow privileged to stand in this moment of time and see in the flesh wonders that the righteous have prayed for and will hail with thanksgiving and praise.

❦

It is the Sabbath, March 27. I cannot sleep and arise earlier than I had intended. I wash and dress, grateful for the silence around me. I kneel to pray, but ordinary words will not serve to express my thoughts and my hopes. *This day, this day of days . . .* I stay on my knees until I feel the Spirit as literally as I feel the floorboards I kneel on. I pray until I forget myself and begin to open up my heart to God.

There will not be room within the temple walls to hold all the people. Emmeline, unwilling to stir her father's wrath and knowing our need, has agreed to tend our children and the children of several others so that their parents are free to go. We are very close to the temple; I can see it from my front door and from the small attic window.

When Emmeline arrives I am too excited to give her instructions.

I kiss her cheek, kiss my children and Georgie's, and take Eugene's arm. We all walk together: Eugene and me, Nathan and Georgie, Jack and the aunts, Rosie and Jonathan. I feel the strength of family, like a warm mantle draped over us. But I sense the loss of those who are missing, like an old aching grief.

We do not walk far before the whole way is clogged with people, and it is but seven o'clock. Yet there is no sense of hurry, no tension, no self-concern. We wait patiently and converse in quiet tones with those who are near us. Someone starts up a hymn, and the morning sunlight floods through the greening branches of the trees overhead. I think: *I am in the one place on the whole face of this earth where I most desire to be.*

When the doors are opened at eight o'clock, nearly a thousand people flood inside the main hall. Those who are turned away gather in the schoolhouse, as Brother Joseph has instructed, or remain outside, close to the doors and open windows, that they might hear. Jack's eyes are filled with tears, but his countenance is beaming. He has earned his blessing; far more, I feel, than I have. While we wait I hold Eugene's hand. We have taken many walks together since our childhood and will take many more. But none will be more important than this short walk to the house of the Lord.

It is a beautiful room in which we are sitting. There are two large meeting rooms, one above the other, both drawing light from a magnificent, single arched window. The ceiling, too, is arched, and the room is divided by two rows of square columns, flanked by rows and rows of boxed pews. And three levels of triple pulpits rise at each end of the room, with a delicacy of carving and a symmetry that makes my heart soar. But I believe this beauty also reflects the many spirits whose efforts have gone into its making, whose sacrifices are felt by him who alone can look into the human heart.

The meeting begins with prayers and singing. Then President Rigdon speaks. He is eloquent and powerful, but he is not Joseph. He speaks too long. But he strikes deep chords with his recital of all we have been through, the toils and anxieties of those who have wet the walls of this house with their tears. Many have tears in their eyes as they listen. We raise our hands to the square to sustain Joseph Smith as prophet and seer, and the conviction of that calling runs like fire through my bones! We stand to sing one of my favorite hymns of Zion:

"Now let us rejoice in the day of salvation, no longer as strangers on earth need we roam." There is one voice, one harmony, one joy in the words.

The first part of the service ends, but we stay in our seats for the brief interlude between the two sessions. My heart is too full for speech. At last the Prophet dedicates the building with words that have been revealed to him, praying that this temple might be "a house of prayer, a house of fasting, a house of faith, a house of learning, a house of glory, a house of order, a house of God . . ." There is poetry in the words as well as power. When he is done the choir sings a new song by Brother Phelps. In his words the whole essence and glory of what we are experiencing is contained:

> The Spirit of God like a fire is burning,
> The latter-day glory begins to come forth;
> The visions and blessings of old are returning,
> The angels are coming to visit the earth . . .
> We'll sing and we'll shout with the armies of heaven—
> Hosanna, hosanna to God and the Lamb!
> Let glory to them in the highest be given,
> Henceforth and forever: amen and amen.

How can I explain what it was like? How can I possibly put such things into words?

The sacrament is passed to every one of us in that large congregation—imagine! And there *are* children present, but they do not fuss or stir. Even babes in arms look out with an intelligence in their gaze that seems lent them for the occasion. Testimonies are borne, and Hyrum Smith speaks for a few moments. I imagine Alvin to have been much like Hyrum in temperament, in gentleness of spirit.

Now with one cry we raise up in the Hosanna Shout. Three times the magnificent words are repeated and thrill through the air, as though all the voices of heaven have joined with ours. The power which Joseph must be sustained with daily flows through us all. Brigham Young arises and speaks in tongues, and Brother Patten is able to interpret. Strange and marvelous things. There is a reluctance to end, to speak the last word, to get up and walk away from this place.

It is four o'clock when we file silently out, which means it has

189

been eight hours since we first stepped inside. I blink my eyes and struggle to bring my surroundings into focus. I feel weak and yet strengthened. Eternity clings to me like a light, fluid, and I am careful not to brush it aside. I know I have seen and heard things beyond my present comprehension, and I am thrilled to the depths of my soul.

❧

We walk home in a comradeship that would be marred by words spoken. We find all at home ordered and peaceful. I lift my baby into my arms and croon to him wordlessly. My world seems altered and hallowed by what has just come to pass. We eat a simple meal, and I look into each face in turn, but I cannot tell what their thoughts are.

In the evening the men return for a priesthood meeting. We clear up the dirty dishes and put the children to bed. I hum that new song without knowing it, then realize that Georgie is humming it, too. Emmeline and Rose remain with us, and after the children are settled we kneel down to pray, pouring out our hearts in gratitude to our maker. *I do not want to forget!* I do not want one moment of this blessed experience to dim into the ordinary and leave me as I had been before.

In the stillness following our prayer, Emmeline is the first to hear a great rushing sound, as of a mighty wind singing all round our heads. We hurry outdoors, and for a moment my heart fails within me, for it appears as though the temple is being consumed by flame. A light more bright than any I have ever seen before rests upon the building, so glorious that I cannot believe my eyes.

Rosie cries out and points—our eyes follow. And there on the roof of the temple are the figures of personages standing, moving together! And from them arises music so pure I think the beauty of it will melt my very bones within me.

Emmeline clasps my arm. I can almost hear her heart beating. "What is it? Have you ever heard anything to compare with it?"

I have not. We stand with our arms about one another and listen and watch. All is glory, and there is no way of doubting whose power this is, for there is nothing of fear or strangeness about it—only joy and light. We stand for a long time, caught up in the wonders before our eyes.

Later, when the men return, they tell of yet further wonders: visions and prophesying and angels within their midst. Every man there received his own manifestation of God's power so that he could no longer doubt. Every man knows that this work he is involved in is sacred and true.

☙

I cannot sleep, though the hour is very late and I am exhausted in body and mind. Eugene sleeps the peaceful sleep of an innocent baby. But I have written and written so that I might remember! My hand aches and my eyes burn with fatigue. Before he went home, I saw Jack take Emmeline aside and speak to her privately—earnestly. His whole countenance reflected that light which he had been cleansed in, immersed in, for hours.

She listened intently, only nodding her head every now and again. He must have been explaining to her a little more of what had just happened. He is patient, but he is also passionate. I wonder what the girl thinks. It is like Jack to be aware of such things; a quiet little person and her need—even now, when his thoughts must be drawn to Aurelia, his desires, his love.

But there is enough love and to spare. I realize that as my head nods and my tired eyes blur. That is the core my mind has been trying to get at all day. The power which has swirled and swelled around us in majesty and glory is the *power of love.* God is love, the scriptures say. And the Lord has told Joseph: "I will call you friends, for you are my friends, and ye shall have an inheritance with me."

Love. Like a light within that keeps building until it blesses all it may touch. Love—beyond my comprehension—extended to me.

I snuff out the stub of candle with the tips of my fingers and crawl into bed. Eugene does not stir, but I lie very close beside his warm, sleeping body and, at last, close my eyes.

Chapter Twenty-One

Kirtland: October 1836

On Monday nights in the temple a singing school is held under direction of a committee appointed by the Prophet himself. And Jack, bless his heart, has made arrangements for Emmeline to attend!

I learned this at last Thursday's prayer meeting, in conversation with Claire Lamb. We have become a most organized group of people since the Lord's house has been finished; I do not believe it sits idle for ten hours during a week. The high priests quorum also meets on Mondays, the seventies on Tuesdays, the quorum of Elders on Wednesday nights. On Thursdays prayer meetings are held in the evening; at times a fast and testimony meeting under the direction of Father Smith, the patriarch, is also held, and this lasts for most of the day. The "Kirtland High School" has been given permission to meet in the attic of the house during the week. Our Nathan is employed in the school, though he and Eugene have also become more actively involved this year in the growing and selling of corn.

Emmeline is not a baptized member of the Church; she could not be without her parents' consent. But at the beginning of the new year, she began studying the Book of Mormon with Jonathan. They take turns reading the verses and pages out loud. When a question arises they ask whoever is nearby and keep asking until they receive what they consider a satisfactory answer. Like as not, this comes from Nathan, who during his mission, developed a familiarity with the scriptures the rest of us do not have. Eugene reads for employment, and his interest these past few years in reading at home has waned. Not so for me. I will take every book I can get my hands on, and Georgie and I still read poetry aloud to each other while we work in the kitchen or sit by the fire to sew.

Emmeline is overcome by this opportunity to attend the singing school. Jack assures her that she will feel comfortable with the other musicians and singers who have gathered.

"You can hold your own among them," he has assured her. "And you will enjoy it, if you can force yourself to relax."

She believes him; she accepts his words and opinions without question. She looks to him with a quiet faith, which is touching to see.

Jack has begun a new business himself. Back in Palmyra his and Georgie's father ran a successful hardware store. He is following that same pattern here and with immediate success, for there is such a need for every basic commodity as Kirtland grows.

I asked him outright, the last time he was here visiting, where the money came from which enabled him to buy stock, rent a building, and outfit himself properly.

"I have been putting aside this while," he replied.

"You have partners, for you would need more money than you could save."

"Indeed, you guess right, Esther. And yes, I will satisfy your curiosity. Peter has invested his money in me and my enterprise and therefore owns part interest in it."

193

Peter is prospering exceedingly well. We do not see him above once in a three-month's time, and then he is silent and nervous, a bit shallow-eyed, reminding me of what Randolph was like during those terrible days when he was in trouble and did not know how to get out. He spends all his time and attentions upon matters of commerce and profit and has probably inherited business and money skills from his father, and his father's father, on back through that distinguished line. More's the pity. And I am afraid Jack is not as concerned as I am.

"Leave him alone, Esther. He is what he is for the time being, and Peter is still a good lad who indulges in no vices. You ought to be grateful for that," Peter has told me.

"I am. But I see things you are not mindful of."

"You see young men courting your Rosie." It is amazing how tender Jack can be with me. It almost brings tears to my eyes. "That, too, must work itself out as it is meant to."

"He loves her, Jack, I know he does. And as for Rose—"

"Now, Esther, you cannot second guess the Lord. You ought to know that by now."

Jack can calm me where even Eugene cannot. But then, Eugene is my husband, and there is much more between us that can sometimes get in the way.

Rose is not happy, though. Only another woman can know this, in the way women know. I do not give her advice anymore; I simply love and support her. But I have my own hopes; despite the suitability of some of the men who come round to court her, I have my hopes.

Speaking of Rose, a terrible thing happened directly after the temple dedication. The outpouring of the Spirit and those miracles which attended it did not cease after the first few glorious days. For weeks on end in every meeting, every gathering, wonderful things came forth. There was much faith demonstrated and, therefore, much healing of the sick, the sightless, the lame. We did not know what was in Rose's heart nor that she had fasted for days before coming to Nathan and Eugene with her request.

"I want you to administer a blessing on the head of my brother," she told them, "and heal his legs. If he can walk again, he will have a new chance for happiness."

When they did little more than blink back at her, she told them firmly, "I have fasted and prayed. I have the faith that is necessary if you will use your priesthood for me."

The men also prepared themselves for this arduous challenge before they ventured forth. And though the three knelt in prayer yet again before leaving, Thaddeus would not admit them at all. He must have sensed the probable purpose for their showing up on his doorstep. When he pressed them and they began to explain, he burst forth in a diatribe of anger and accusation, reducing Rose to heart-broken tears.

"I want no part of you!" he shouted. "Mormonism has already ruined me. How dare you think I would admit you after what has happened to me."

Eugene attempted to explain, to make him see Rose's faith and her longings, but he would not listen at all. Her faith was sufficient, I am sure. But it was he who needed the blessing, who needed to open his heart before any light could be admitted.

It was a bitter disappointment for her. Nothing new for Rose, after what she has been through. Her patience in trial encourages me, shames me even at times. I am reminded of our Phoebe; there are many similar traits between them. And both have been called upon to endure more than most.

We are still doing what we can for her brother. Last summer Georgie and I were too busy with babies to bother, but we set up the hat business again under the direction of Thaddeus himself, though he grumbled something awful, of course. Emmy and Jonathan were his helpers, and Brother Pliny agreed to assist them with the marketing again. Though he looks frail as a reed in autumn, he seems strong and fit enough and as kindly a soul as ever.

So much has been happening these last months! It seems that everywhere things blossom and grow. The hands of the Saints are at last being prospered, and there is a love and a harmony which one can feel in the air.

Eugene is working less and less for Brother Frey, who is busier than ever and who has taken on two new apprentices. So we have made an arrangement with him. Three days a week Jonathan works at the blacksmith shop, assisting the others and performing the simplest of tasks: cleaning hardware and harness, caring for tools, learning the rudiments of working with punch and adze. He is learning and earning a few coins of his own, and he enjoys the independence so much. I have written to my father to tell him how his son is progressing. I do hope to hear from him soon. I can go days and days without thinking of him, and then suddenly a loneliness will well up, a desire to hear his voice once again, see his eyes crinkling into a kindly smile, feel his strong, unquestioning arm supporting me. He knows less and less about his daughter as the years pass and the gospel molds and changes my life. He no longer knows his own son, and his grandchildren would not recognize him if they passed on the street.

But "that is mortality for you!" as Georgie is wont to quip. Very, very seldom does she ever speak of her own family, so entirely lost to her now. But then, she has Jack, and he is both strength and comfort. And I have my little Jonathan, who will very soon mature into a man. And it brings me pleasure to see him growing and learning, becoming more like his gentle father with each passing day.

❧

The harvest this year was more plentiful than usual, and Georgie and I have amassed a few luxuries, such as new feather ticks for our beds, a cow all our own, and fabric for a new frock each, and whatever hat we choose to go with it. Eugene is talking of building a house. I should like a home all to myself, with space for a proper garden and room for the children to grow. There is talk, there is always talk, about the Saints going to Zion. Some have picked up and moved already, but conditions in Missouri have never been right, never been stable. And it is so far away! Here, if the need is strong enough, I can still get back to my family or they to me. That is a comfort. But Missouri would sever all ties between us, and I would be cast afloat in the big world. I pale at the thought. Kirtland is fine for me; I am becoming contented here.

❧

Brother Frey gave Jonathan a horse to ride! An old pony, really, with a few careful years left in him and which Andrew hadn't the heart to sell. The boy was beside himself. "It makes me miss Tansy something awful," he told me the first day he rode her. "Me too," I confessed. "But it is good to be riding again, isn't it?" He came racing up last evening as if the very winds were chasing him. When he burst in the door his eyes were bright with more than the exercise of riding and fresh air.

"Eden Frey has come home."

"Are you sure?"

"I saw her, saw her myself this morning. She brought her father's dinner in to him. She looked awfully thin and dull, Esther. And she didn't smile."

For a boy not quite ten, Jonathan can be very discerning. "Poor girl," I muttered. "Was her father kind to her?"

"Oh, very. You could tell he was pleased to have her there."

"I am glad to hear it." But I could not help wondering what would become of her now. And did she run home because she had no other place to go, or was she glad to escape and return to a nurturing environment?

Emmeline still spends part of her days there, so the next time I saw her, I asked what she knew.

"Eden has returned, it is true. But she keeps much to herself, Esther. I believe she's been ill."

"The rest of the family—are they treating her kindly?"

"Oh yes, from what I can see."

"Has she taken her old room back?"

"Yes, and she seldom comes out of it."

"Well, I am sure it will take her a while. Perhaps you and Rose ought to find some little way in which you could make her feel welcome."

"She always frightened me, ma'am, and she frightens me still."

Emmeline still slips now and again and calls Georgie or me "ma'am." I let it go by, so as not to embarrass her. She really is growing up. Her skinny limbs have filled out, and her light hair has more of a deep, burnished shade to it and falls in thick, shiny waves that want to escape, even when she ties them severely back. Her eyes are expressive and soulful, unable to disguise the things she is feeling the way they did when she was a child. Sometimes I look at her and am struck by her beauty and wonder if others react to her this way, too. Georgie has taught her to speak well, to have impeccable manners, and to walk like a lady walks, with a slow, measured step. *What shall become of her?* I sometimes wonder. She is still reading the Book of Mormon with Jonathan; they are nearly through the book of Alma. What if she were to develop a testimony and wish to become a Mormon? What on earth would her parents do then?

197

❧

"Prosperity is indeed paying us a visit, and I hope she extends it for a good long while."

They were strange words to hear Jack speak, but the men were huddled together talking, over plates of apple pie and mugs of fresh cider, which Gertrude Woods had brewed and brought over last week.

"So, what do you think of the Kirtland Safety Society Bank?" Nathan asked between bites. "Even Joseph himself is behind it, I hear."

"Yes, that is right. They are selling their first stock right now."

"Do you intend to buy into it?" Eugene *would* hazard such a pointed inquiry!

"I believe I will watch it for a while first, but it is tempting. And I see no reason at all why it should not succeed."

They talked on, and I listened with one ear while I got Lavinia and Nathaniel ready for bed.

"I have come tonight to discuss a business matter of another sort," Jack said quite suddenly. And he glanced very pointedly my way. "Where is Georgeanna? Do you think she would come in for a minute?"

I called Jonathan to watch the children and went to fetch her myself. "What does he want with us?" she wondered aloud. We had no idea what it might be.

"I am expanding my business," he explained, "and I need to hire new people. And frankly, I have been thinking of both Emmy and Rose."

Our amazement was evident. But it seemed to have no effect upon him. He went on to explain.

"They are both hard workers, and they both possess excellent natures and excellent manners."

"And each would profit by the opportunity," Eugene put in.

"Yes, that is one of my purposes. Look at Rose, doing menial labor day and night. This would be a step up for her, fewer hours, less strenuous work, and more money."

"And you can afford to work it that way?"

"Afford to pay them well and be fair with them? Yes."

"And what of Emmeline?" Georgie asked, her safety defenses on the girl's behalf going up automatically.

"Emmeline needs exposure to life; she needs to learn how to get on with people. Think what she has known so far: the bleak existence with her parents and the shameless way you and the Freys have pampered her!"

Georgie raised a warning eyebrow, though she knew her brother was teasing us.

"She would shine, and you know it," he pressed. "And you do want what is best for her."

So with an ease that surprised me, it was all arranged. Jack even spoke to her father. "I want to be completely above board here," he explained. Money spoke loud enough to get Jack the conditions he wanted. And when I saw how happy the girls were in their anticipation, I became more excited myself.

Georgie and I were the losers in the bargain, bereft of Emmeline's company as well as her invaluable help. Jack realized this and made every compensation within his power, even arranging her schedule so that she could be with us at the few times we needed her most.

We shall see what happens and how things develop. I feel very hopeful myself. They are both in Jack's safekeeping, and we do not have to worry. That is a marvelous boon in itself.

Aaron Sessions has begun to court Eden Frey again. This is the news Jonathan brings back. Aaron has called on her several times at her home already, and they went out riding last Sunday evening, when the autumn colors were deep and brilliant beneath a wet sky. I hope the tongues do not wag.

"Good for him," I said when we heard. But Eugene scowled.

"She'll break his heart again, if he is not careful."

"That is not a kind thing to say."

"But a true one."

"Perhaps she has learned her lesson."

"Perhaps. But can she unlearn the wiles and deceits to which she has been party? Can she fit into a mold she had outgrown over a year ago?"

I hate it when Eugene asks questions like that! He does not mean to sound calloused and unfeeling, but he does. It is the logical side in the male way of thinking coming out in him, perhaps the reporter as well. But it makes me uneasy. I remembered Eden's eyes the last time I saw her. I remembered Jedediah Comstock on the riverboat. I hoped Aaron Sessions could heal her wounds and, in the process, find some of the happiness he had waited so long for.

❧

There is one lad who is far more persistent than the others; I have seen him at work. He is after Rose with a vengeance, and I fear he may get her. Just last week I was coming out of the temple and I saw them walking together. He had his arm round her waist. His head was bent low as he spoke earnestly to her. They made a handsome pair, so handsome that I felt my heart turn within me. *Who am I to stand in her way?*

Then two days ago Jack came to me with a story that would have been encouraging some months ago but now just leaves me feeling hopeless. Rose was working at one of the counters when, unannounced, Peter walked in. He was in town for the day and had just stopped by to see how things were coming. Jack, busy with a customer, said, "Rosie will show you around."

And he let her. They walked round the whole store together, and Jack, keeping an eye out, said she answered a full dozen questions or more. The longer he stayed, the more he seemed to linger; the longer they talked, the more reluctant he was to go. So Jack waxed bold and asked him to stay on for lunch, and the three walked to Johnson's Inn and shared a meal together.

"He was more than civil," Jack told me. "His eyes melted when he looked at her. And he even asked her questions about herself and how she was doing. When we parted he said, 'I am glad to find you here, Rose, under Jack's protection. Thank you for seeing me again.'"

Poor wretch! My heart goes out to both of them. For, at closing time, when Rose's new beau came in and asked if he might walk her home and spend a few minutes, she told him she was too tired—could he make it another night?

But the exchange between them has set Jack to thinking. He went right out and found a modest house Rose and her brother could rent, situated on one of the streets right in town. Clean and airy and close to everything. He *says* the rent would be only nominally higher, but I am sure he intends to pay a portion himself.

No matter. Thaddeus has dug his heels in. He refuses to move. "I couldn't stand to be that close to you Mormons," he taunted. "The stench is bad enough way out here."

He is vulgar and rude on purpose; we have learned to pay him no mind. But he is more cruel than I had already known to keep Rose cooped up in that place! He is afraid. He does not want people to see him or mock him. But he does not mind what humiliations and privations she suffers on his account.

It is nearly too much for me. Jack assures me he will keep on trying, but I believe he is wasting his time.

❦

Jack! He has come up with one surprise after another. *He* has been reading the scriptures with Emmeline—after hours or during their noon mealtime. He says she is an adept student and asks thoughtful questions. He says her spirit has already been awakened to truth.

"She is ready; she has been ready for a long time, Esther. We have been denying her blessings she has a right to enjoy."

"Meaning?" *I could not keep up with him!*

"Meaning I intend to baptize Emmy myself within the next month!"

Chapter Twenty-Two

Jack was right. Why is he always right, in his quiet way? He pronounced Emmeline ready; and if he believes she is ready, she must truly be so. Permission to baptize her? He obtained that from her parents somehow. The girl is eighteen and of an age; she had her birthday in February, but I cannot come to see her as such. *Eighteen? Impossible! Where has the time gone?* I am certain, nevertheless, that Jack sweetened the proposal sufficiently to make it palatable for Emmy's father. Be that as it may, the baptism was a lovely occasion, at which a choir made up from the singing school students, Emmeline included, performed several hymns. Music makes all the difference at such times. It has power to open the heavens, as well as our hearts. The Spirit comes naturally through the medium of music, with no restraints.

This was a day I had never thought to look upon. How little faith I possess! If Jack had not been mindful of this girl, taken it upon himself to assist her—well, I do not like to think. Georgeanna is too pleased for expression. She has had faith: in God's timing, in Emmeline, in her brother. But it seems especially fitting that Jack was the one to bring Emmy full circle and into the fold.

Our little Jonathan asked to be baptized at the same time as his friend and companion, and we all thought that fitting and well. I wonder if he resents Jack's involvement, even a little. He certainly has seen less of Emmeline, who quickly progressed far ahead of him with Jack's help. But perhaps not; he is only a child yet, and she continues kindly and thoughtful with him. He is sure of his place in her affections, and that is enough.

Nearly four years ago Eugene and I were baptized at this very spot. So much has happened in four years, so very much, and yet I do not feel changed or even older. I can feel tired and world-weary and even disheartened—but not older. That is a singular thing! I have to remind myself sometimes that I am not of an age with Rosie and the other young girls who are just starting out their own lives.

Rose attended the baptism. She has been very kind to Emmeline and eased her into association with some of her friends. Rosie is Peter's age nearly to the month, and he will be twenty-four come June. Jack is a year older. They would be considered adults now, I suppose. Georgie turns thirty this summer, and I but a year behind her! So the facts read, but they mean very little to me.

"You will always be young," Eugene often tells me. "It is that confounded idealism of yours." He says this with frustration in his voice, and I know it is real. But there is a tender pride in his eyes that lends me the assurance I need.

Jack invited Peter to come to the baptism, but he would not commit himself. Yet he did arrive—when the ceremony was nearly over. And he did speak to Rosie, alone, screened by the thick-branched chestnuts. This store of Jack's is what has made the difference. Peter can make occasion to see Rose without seeming too obvious; he has a ruse to hide behind, to use for excuse and protection. I still feel anger when I think of it—that frustrated sort of anger that has nowhere to go and no means of alleviation or retribution. But we must be content with small things when we cannot get what we truly want, I suppose.

Rose's beaus have begun to tire and fall off one by one in discouragement. I have begun to feel that we are being unfair to her, all of us who have encouraged her feelings for Peter—myself foremost. But now it is done, and she makes her own choices, and she has not tired yet. I believe she exerts the same sort of patience with Peter as she does with her brother. Is that good, or is it detrimental to any relationship they might have? Such questions go round and round in my brain and torment me, especially when I see them together.

But this is a day for joy and celebration, and I would not spoil it one bit. We have invited friends; as many as we can think of. We have good food prepared and waiting, and Emmeline has promised to sing. We shall make music, and we shall make merry, and we shall rejoice.

❦

Only days following the baptism, Eden Frey was joined in marriage to Aaron Sessions. When I first heard, I could not believe she had said yes to his proposal and consented to be his wife. I have watched her closely these past months—perhaps because of Eugene's gloomy predictions. And I fear that he may be right. She seems quieter and more pliable, but she does not seem gentle or meek. Or repentant. And I do not mean this in a bad way, that she ought to flagellate herself in humility and self-recrimination. I suppose the best way to express it is that I do not see joy in her countenance. I do not see the light of the gospel shining out of her eyes.

"That will take time," Georgie has assured me. She wore her scolding scowl when she said it. And perhaps she was right. "This marriage, this good man, could be the salvation she requires."

It could be. I sincerely hope that it is.

�֎

Thaddeus has been an absolute terror of late. It is as though he slid down a steep toboggan hill, landed in a drift head-first, and arose roaring like a lion, with his nose—his whole face—out of whack. Is that unkind to say of him? I feel all the progress we have made with him has been purposefully discarded—as though he took it off like an old coat, rolled it up into a bundle, and threw it away. I am impatient with him, at least in my feelings and, therefore, probably in my behavior as well.

"I believe he misses Jonathan," Georgeanna suggested. "Think how little they see one another now that Jonathan is working with Brother Frey."

"Of course!" How thoughtless of me. The man must be terribly frustrated and lonely. "But he seems to almost enjoy being miserable," I pondered aloud. "He refused a decent place to live in; he refused a blessing which might have healed him, he—"

"It's a vicious circle, I suppose. His misery makes him behave in a malicious and irrational manner, and then he becomes more miserable yet."

I tried to pray for him, with sincere intent, three nights in a row. The fourth day was a Saturday, and I awoke with the impression that I ought to send Jonathan over to see if Thaddeus needed anything. It was the first day the boy had been home all week, and I had a list of chores and errands I needed done very badly, but I put them aside. Part of me was frustrated at this silly impulse to fly out and "do good." I wanted my own affairs taken care of and neatly seen to before the Sabbath. A part of me wished the impression had not come.

We had baked that morning, so I sent along a cobbler and a loaf of warm bread. "Don't dally," I instructed. "And do not stay if, well, you know . . . if there is really nothing to do."

Jonathan understood me, and I knew I could trust him. He rode off, and I turned back a bit grimly to the extra work that awaited me.

Time got away from me. Nearly four hours passed before I glanced at a clock. "Have you seen Jonathan?" I asked Georgie.

"I do not believe he has returned yet."

"But I told him to hurry."

"Do you suppose that something is wrong?"

I knew that Rose would be working for Jack at the store today. "Perhaps we ought to check," I told Georgie, though I hated the idea. Just then Jonathan rode into view. I called out to him, "Come see me as soon as you've taken care of the pony." He nodded and waved.

When at last he walked in, Georgie and I were right there beside him. He took a step back, probably a bit overwhelmed by us. "What happened?" I asked. "You are later than I expected."

"Did you know?" he replied.

"Whatever do you mean? Know what, Jonathan?"

He dropped into a chair, but Georgie and I remained standing. "It was a strange thing, really. He was black as a cloud when I entered, sitting all hunched over and glowering—the way he used to—" We nodded. "But when I brought out the things and told him you'd sent them, his face kind of crumpled, and he got tears in his eyes."

"What did you say?" Georgie asked.

"I don't exactly remember."

"Well, try to think."

"I must have said, 'My sister said she'd been thinking of you, and she told me to bring these things to you and see how you are faring.' Something close to that. And then he said, 'I wonder if Rosie told her.'"

"Told me? Rosie has told me nothing."

"Well, he thought she had. He said, 'Yesterday, four years ago my wife was killed, and I was left worse than dead.' I did not know what to say back to him! And before I could think of anything, he put his face in his hands and just sat there and cried like a baby. It was awful."

Jonathan stood up again and began to pace the perimeter of the small room. "I did not know what to do. After a little while he began to calm down, so I brought him a glass of water, and then he began to talk about her."

"Oh, Jonathan! I scarcely believe it."

"He told me what it was like when he had courted her. That she was the prettiest thing in the county and she sang like an angel and there were two other men who were courting her, but she picked him."

I looked at Georgie and closed my lips against the trembling that was coming over them. "I had no idea. Was it awful, Johnny?"

"Not really. I think it made him happy in a way to talk about her. After a little while he stopped and rubbed his eyes. Then he said he had a chair he needed help with and would I stay for a while."

"Did he seem to enjoy working with you?"

"Oh, sure. It was just like old times. He said he'd missed me, and he asked right kindly how I had been doing, so I told him about the activities at the forge and some of the fellows I work with."

"Did he seem interested?"

"Yes."

"Well," I sighed. I did not know what to make of this. I did not want to think about what might have happened if I had kept Jonathan at home.

"We must find ways for you to spend more time with him again, Jonathan," I decided. "Would you mind?"

"No, long as I get to work at the smithy still."

"Of course. We'll work something out."

"Let us have a prayer for him right now," Georgie suggested. "It's nearly our prayer time anyway."

We took off our aprons, made sure the children were safe and out of trouble for a few minutes, then knelt down together, we three. Georgie was voice for us, and I am glad of it, for I do not believe I could have made it through. *How kind you are to us, Father,* I marveled. *Through the mists of my preoccupation and self-interest, you were generous*

enough to direct me and speak to my heart. Thank you for helping me to lis-
ten! What if I had not listened?

I had almost entirely forgotten that this is one of the purposes we
are here for: to feed his sheep; to care for the halt, the lame, and the
needy; to do as the Master himself would do. God had allowed me to
give a little and then be blessed abundantly. Is that not always his way?

※

"I have bought Brother Johnson's shares in the bank," Eugene
announced at the supper table a couple of months ago, not long after
the new year began.

"You already own stock," I said. "Why do you think you need
more?"

My husband smiled indulgently. "Nathan and I sold a portion of
that land we bought together last autumn. I thought it was a good place
for some of the profits to go."

Eugene has done well these past nine months or so, riding on the
tide of prosperity, learning a little of the tricks of commerce, and enjoying a little good luck as well. It has caused him to behave now and then
in a smug, self-satisfied manner that I find very repugnant.

"What about the fact that it is now the antibanking company?" I
asked. "Does that make a difference?"

"It is our enemies playing games with us again," he explained.
"Brother Joseph did everything properly, and we had every right to
open our doors for commerce. But our charter was denied for no better reason than because we are Mormons, and they will not give us an
inch if they can help it."

"Yes, but how will the antibank work?"

"In simple terms, the title indicates that we do not have a bank
charter from the state. But this is not unusual; there are several other
such organizations in Ohio right now as we speak."

I nodded. *Whatever you say,* I thought. "Are you sure the risk is not
too great, Eugene?"

"The best men in the kingdom are behind this, Esther. That ought
to say something."

Perhaps it ought to. But I have noticed that Nathan has not

207

involved himself. I wonder if Jack has. I shall have to remember to ask him about it. Nathan does not seem as concerned about making money and getting ahead as Eugene does. But then, he is by nature a teacher, not a man of business. He is content in his own pursuits, and I can understand why.

❦

Phoebe gave birth to another son this spring. All is well, and I am happy for her, though this means she will have her hands full. Georgie and I had been hoping against hope that we might talk her into coming out here, just for a visit. But a new baby makes that impossible. She did not tell us until two months before the child was due. But then, we do not write often, not often enough for my liking. I asked Eugene if he thought we might finance her journey, now that we actually possessed a little money, but he did not much like the idea. I have noticed a tendency in him to be selfish now that he has some means, where he was not in the least bit before. I do not like this; but then, there is much about human nature to which I am not reconciled!

Now, 'tis a moot point, is it not? We cannot go; Phoebe cannot come—I so much wanted her to see Kirtland! To enjoy the fellowship of the Saints, even for a brief time. I am still concerned about her. Perhaps because I do not trust myself to be able to do what she is doing; I do not believe my resolve and my dedication would last. She and Josie are still seeing a lot of one another, and I am most grateful for that. They will profit mutually, in different ways, from the association. Randolph writes:

> The boys are getting on splendidly, doing us proud as they go out into the community. Two have married and settled here. New ones keep coming, and the more the merrier as far as Josephine is concerned. Latisha makes herself invaluable, and Jonah has been promoted somewhere in the hierarchy of canal management, which is all a bit vague to me. The mill is more profitable than ever—and your niece may soon rival you for beauty, Esther. I wish you could see her—and I dearly wish she could know you.

Eugene does not like it when I cry over these letters. He understands, but he does not like it. I think my tears make him feel inadequate and in some way powerless. But I cannot help that. I am such a baby. I am such a homebody.

"You want to have your cake and to eat it, too," Georgie consoles me. "I wish I could arrange it for you."

Randolph is the only one who will truly tell me everything, and he also writes:

> Gerard Whittier has taken a mistress, and he is not being discreet about it; I fear the whole town knows. No one says anything, and Theodora is seldom around—servants deliver and pick up her children wherever they go. I know her nature, and I fear for her, Esther. I do not believe she is capable of taking much more. I should like to confront the black-guard myself and have it out with him, but he is already an enemy, and would I do anyone any good by it? Regretfully, no! And I could cause harm to so many, Tillie not the least of them. I have no access to her or her children, though I have made countless attempts. My father is becoming a faded shadow of what he once was and all because of that man . . .

209

"His father," I told Georgie hotly, "is merely getting his just desserts." But we are sick with concern for our friend. We pray for her every night when we kneel to pray for Phoebe. Now we shall redouble our efforts. "Is there nothing else we can do?" I cried out the words to Georgie, and the anguish of that cry, trapped inside me, haunted and weakened my waking hours—because I do not know how to let go of such things! Prayer, prayer only is my salvation, but it requires such energy to make it work to the degree that it can truly lift my burdens and bring me a state of peace. I keep trying. I will not give up! What other course is open to me, except to persist and persist and continue to persist.

❦

There is no peace for us. The Prophet is hounded with lawsuits over this banking business—which is just one more ruse, one more excuse for getting him into his enemies' clutches. I cannot bear to hear of it or watch it happen. It makes my whole soul sick. We cannot pros-per amongst such severe jealousies and animosities. The other night I asked Eugene what he thought would happen, and he surprised me by saying, "I think we will win out in the end. There are too many of us, and we are both wiser and stronger than they are."

But Nathan maintains that we, the Saints, have weakened ourselves by speculation and debt and an almost feverish seeking after the things of this world; and I fear he is right. Prices are climbing sky-high, yet non-Mormon banks and businesses are refusing to honor our currency. Many fear we are in for a fall. But Eugene remains hopeful. And I cannot say whether this is a good thing or a bad.

❦

Peter came, out of the clear blue. I opened my door to see him standing there, shifting from foot to foot uncomfortably. I urged him to come in. "Have you been to see Jack at the store?" I asked.

"No, I came here directly." He is still awkward in my presence, and that breaks my heart. I placed my hand on his arm. "Peter, what is it? What have you come for?"

He still demurred. "Not much, really. Seems a bit silly, now that I'm here."

"Well, there is nothing for it, you know." I made my voice cheerful. "What is it, then?"

"I have truck with the Gentiles, as you call them, and I've friends among them, as you must know, Esther."

"Yes." I tightened my hands at my sides, struggling for equanimity.

"I am here to warn you; I suppose I cannot say it differently. I have heard things—" He hesitated, running his fingers distractedly through his hair. "There is more mischief afoot than you would want to believe and more *danger*—" He spoke the last word slowly, with emphasis.

"And where do you stand in it all?"

He had not expected my blunt question nor had I. We stared at one another.

"I mean it, Peter. We've been through rough times together and made it because we stood by one another. Will you stand by the Church now? Do you count yourself as one of us?" He did not reply. How young and vulnerable he looked and how handsome, in a lean, brooding way. "You are not happy." Some imp inside seemed to be driving me. "It is not hard to see that. You are making money. What else in your life is as you would have it?"

I did not care a twig if I was making him angry. Something would not let me stop. "It will come to choosing sides in the end, and you know it, Peter. Then what will you do?"

"I suppose I shall face that when it comes."

What a piteous response! "I expected more from you than that." The bite in my own voice surprised me.

"Haven't you learned yet not to expect things of me?"

It was an unkind question; it seemed to open a floodgate through which all the misery of the last months came pouring over me like icy water, chilling me to the bone. There was not just Jack and Aurelia, himself and Rosie; there was his brother, Randolph, and his sister, Latisha. "Do you ever hear from your family?" I asked, annoyed that my voice was shaking.

He shook his head.

"Do you ever write to them?"

"Course I don't."

"*Course you don't!* Why—because it is difficult and unpleasant for you?" I did not attempt to hold back my disdain. "It appears you have made many of your choices, Peter, and I wish you joy in them."

I turned my back on him and busied my hands rearranging the jars and crocks on the drain board in an attempt to collect myself. He stood there a moment, shuffled his feet a bit, then said under his breath, "I suppose I'll be going now."

"I suppose you will. I'll not try once more to stop you."

"Esther—"

I waved him away. I did not realize I was crying until he was gone, until I heard the door close softly behind him. Then I burst into tears and did not even try to stop when Lavinia came up and put her head in my lap. Not until Georgie brought me a cold cloth for my forehead was I able to gulp the sobs back.

It never rains but it pours. The following Sunday when Rose came to dinner, she drew me out into the yard alone. "I must talk with you."

Her tone was so earnest, her brow so creased, that I felt myself frown in response.

"I saw Peter in town yesterday."

I nodded, as my throat tightened in fearful anticipation.

"He was with Eden Frey, Esther. They were sharing a drink together—and it was not sarsaparilla."

"No. I do not want to hear this." My hands felt cold and clammy as I wiped them along the front of my apron. "Please, Rosie, this cannot be true. Where was . . . was Eden's husband with them?"

"Aaron? I did not see him. I am afraid he was nowhere around."

"How was she behaving?"

"Flirtatious and giddy."

"And Peter?" I knew this was as painful for Rose as it was for me, perhaps more so.

"It is hard to say, Esther. He was responding to her. He seemed relaxed, at ease."

"Perhaps it is not quite as it looks—at least on his part."

"That may well be so. Men are blind as bats when it comes to such matters; I well know that."

I smiled ruefully at her dour worldly wisdom.

"But nevertheless—"

"Yes, nevertheless . . . did you talk to him, Rosie?"

"Not then." She swallowed painfully, still solemn as a judge. "Later he came into the shop."

"Did he know you had seen him?"

She shook her head. "But he behaved in much the same manner to me—gay and light, as though nothing at all really matters. Something within me snapped, and I said, 'Do you still care for me, Peter?'"

I put my hand to my throat, where I could feel my pulse beating.

"He did not want to make a reply. After a few awkward minutes, when he realized that he had to, he said lamely, 'I cannot answer that.'

"I said, 'Well, when you know what it is you want in life, you can come back, if you've a mind. Until then, I do not want to see you, not ever again.'

"I think I was crying, Esther, though I was trying so hard not to!

He went so white I thought he might faint, but he just turned and walked out of the store, without even a backward glance at me."

She was blanch-faced herself in the telling. I drew her small hand into mine. "Rose, Rose," I crooned, "I am so very sorry."

"I shall be all right," she said slowly, as if from a great distance. "I think I shall give Hiram Morley permission to begin paying his attentions; I believe I must."

"Yes." *How stoic we were both being about it.* "Yes, I think that would be the best thing."

A pall hung over us for the remainder of the day. Rosie carried it home with her—a vague, gray essence as heavy as coal, as devoid of hope as the grave. I felt it too, a pressing weight on my spirit that I could not dislodge even when Eugene wrapped his arms round me and held me close.

All's well that ends well—is that how the saying goes? Our Jack has proposed to Emmeline. I could not believe it was true. I found Georgie and asked if she had expected this, but she was in the same state as I. Eugene laughed at us. "You were both blind as bats," he told us. "And could that have been on purpose?"

On purpose! I do not believe so. When Jack came we two cornered him. "Do you love her?" we demanded, and we might as well have been glaring at him with our hands on our hips.

He smiled. "I do indeed. I have loved Emmy for a long time."

"But I do not understand."

"She is only a child, Jack."

He was calm in the face of our shock, which came close to expressing disapproval. "You ought to trust me by now, certainly. Both of you. I know what I am doing, and so does she."

"She is but eighteen, Jack. You are a good six years older."

"Yes, and is that so unusual? You are grasping at straws, my dear."

Why had Georgie and I not seen this? I thought. "What about her father and mother?"

Georgie was eyeing him sharply. "Jack, did you buy them off?"

"You might put it that way." He was grinning like a boy, almost enjoying our discomfort. "It has worked out as I'd hoped, even better. Now, can you two be happy?" He took up our hands and drew us near to him. "I need you. What would I be without you?" He looked into our eyes. "Can you accept it, accept us being together? Even the aunts have softened and opened their hearts to her."

"Of course we can!" After a bit of the shock wore off, the beauty of some of the possibilities began to break through. *Of course Jack would think of the aunts and make room for them in his happiness.*

"Give us a few hours to think about it, and we may well be ecstatic!" Georgie glanced over and winked at me. Her brother laughed out loud, swept her into his arms, and trotted with her through the room. His joy was becoming our delight. We found ourselves laughing with him, though there were tears in our eyes.

Who would have thought—whoever would have dreamed this could happen? Life is a strange thing indeed, with its impossible twisting and turning and its love of surprise.

"We marry next week," Jack announced.

"So soon?"

"It must be. There is no reason at all to delay."

Remembering other times and circumstances, we gave him our wholehearted assent.

"There will be good times now," I told Georgie, after he was gone, "and happy things in the planning."

"Yes," she agreed, "and we have all earned them."

I could not argue with that. Yet there were those among us who had earned them a dozen times over and still lived in sorrow and pain, still went on in hopelessness and deprivation.

"Esther—" Georgie's voice was gentle. "Don't think about it, sweetheart. There is not a thing you can do. This is Jack's moment and Emmeline's. We must not cheat them of one bit of it—nor ourselves, either. *That* alone would be foolish and wicked."

"Dear Georgie, I know you are right. Forgive me."

"Esther, do not be a ninny. There is nothing to forgive." She leaned over and planted a little kiss on my cheek. "With you, my dearest friend, there is never anything to forgive."

Chapter Twenty-Three

Our world is falling apart, bit by bit, all around us. In March a banking panic struck the whole nation, beginning in New York, spreading within days to our little part of Ohio. The Kirtland Safety Society Bank had to suspend payment in specie, as other institutions were doing. But of course many shareholders withdrew their support. Eugene did not because the Prophet was encouraging members to invest and to accept the banks notes, else its failure would be inevitable.

That was in April. By June Joseph had resigned himself to the failure, though he had done the best that he could, even using money which he had borrowed personally to attempt to keep it afloat. His financial losses were much greater than those of the other investors, which should not have been so! For what time has the Prophet to see after the affairs of making a living when he gives all his time to the Church? He has resigned his office and interest and urged others to do likewise, though the institution hobbles along under new management.

Meanwhile, prices rise monthly, weekly—sometimes daily. It is a financial panic of sorts, felt very strongly here and influencing the money market as far away as England. But there is no comfort in that. I have urged Eugene to withdraw his stock; but either way we are ruined. There is no value in the stock, no recouping of investment, much less hope of profit. We, like many others, are left suddenly with nothing. Money is only a concept, I have decided: pieces of printed paper circulate and have value as long as men say they do. When that is altered, they become instantly worthless, and everything slides back to the starting point, and the game begins all over again.

Last month Nathan and Eugene sold another parcel of land at a ridiculous sum because land prices had nearly doubled in just a week's time. So we had means for a while, but food has become so expensive that we need to exercise caution in every move. Thank heaven for my gardens and the potato fields in which the men still have an interest. This should keep us from starving at least.

Yet speculation and borrowing are still running rampant, even among the Saints. Jack has seen no decrease in his sales at the hardware store; there is yet building and buying and an attempt to ignore the stark realities and go on. Eugene wrote a scathing article about these issues in the *Messenger and Advocate,* and that very evening someone threw a bevy of rotten eggs at our house, staining the door and breaking one of the windows. Georgie and I were relieved that the children were already in bed. We waited until late and then helped the men clean up the mess by lantern light so there were no traces left in the morning for the curious eye to take note of or to confuse and frighten the little ones.

"We will not be building a new house now, will we?" I asked Eugene the following evening as we were getting ready for bed.

"Perhaps. It depends very much upon whether—"

"Eugene, please. I know this is as hard for you as it is for me, just in different ways. This is not the time; it would be madness to begin such an enterprise. Perhaps this is not even the place."

"We can weather this storm. It is not restricted alone to Mormons. The whole country—"

"I know, I know. But our enemies see the advantage this gives them. Surely, you ought to know this more than I, Eugene!"

"You are frightened."

"And *you* are not?"

"No. I am watchful and even angry. But there is a difference." *Yes,* I thought. *One has to be humble to be frightened.* "It is a matter of faith, Esther."

"Is it? Then we will tighten our belts more and share with those in need of our generosity because they have next to nothing themselves. We will not make worldly plans but spiritual plans."

"Esther!"

"What am I saying that disturbs you, Eugene? What am I saying that is wrong?"

"I do not think even Brother Joseph expects us to sit on our hands and wait for ruin to overtake us."

"That is not what I suggested, and you know it." I do not like to

216

bicker. I turned away and said no more. We were not agreeing, even on essential issues, and that frightened me. I try to understand the needs of a man, which are so different from the needs of a woman, but it is not easy to do. The general failure of things in the world in which he labors makes Eugene somehow feel like a failure himself. Men partake of the coloring and texture of the world of commerce and wear it home with them like a coat. Women are insulated; the walls of their homes insulate them, though those walls be of the most flimsy and modest construction. And we work daily for people who love us; people we love. When I take time to think of this, my heart goes out to the brethren, and I can exercise more patience toward them and count my own blessings for the role in life that I play.

So the summer has seemed tedious, with this pall of uncertainty and confusion swirling round our feet like dust devils, rising up now and then to obscure our vision and choke the clean air. Family is our mainstay, and the temple. Prayers rise daily from the temple, and in them we find strength and a remembered purpose. There is much murmuring against our commitment as Saints; there is much murmuring against the Prophet. Every night I pray that this spirit will not creep into my life unawares.

Gertrude Woods came by last Monday morning to borrow eggs.

"You have a cow of your own," she observed, "and a good number of laying hens."

I offered her a round pat of newly made butter to go along with the eggs and tried to redirect the conversation, but she would not be put off.

"We left a good situation to come here. I remember all the glowing promises, not a fig of truth in the lot of them." She sniffed and scratched with a long finger at the intricate lacing of her hair.

"Is that why you came?" I asked. "Because of the promises of prosperity?"

"We came to make a home for ourselves here!" she retorted. "But there is no hope of that, is there, missy? If our enemies have their way with us, we'll lose what little we've got."

Her words haunted me for days afterward. *Why did you come here? No hope of prosperity . . . We'll lose what little we've got . . .*

Why did I come here? I have asked myself over and over again. Did I understand what I was doing? Were my motives at all clear, much less pure? I wanted the truth in my life, I remember that much. And I wanted it for my children. But did it go beyond that? It seemed appealing and heartwarming to live as the Saints lived. But was I ready to be a Saint? And what does it mean to be a follower of the Savior?

I asked myself another hard question: *What is it, as a Latter-day Saint, that I have?* A plot of earth, half a house, a cow and some chickens. Beds and furniture and a hearth at which to warm myself. And in essence, does my poor Tillie, with her big house and expensive furnishings, have more? Beyond the necessities of life, her existence, compared to mine, is a desert—a dried-out desert, scorched with pain. I cannot put my finger on what it is the gospel gives me. I do not always have peace, and I have not learned how to live without fear. Trials come despite the truth—many times because of it! And prayer does not turn away the arrow of the destroyer or the sharper arrows of thwarted hopes and disappointments that pierce the heart.

So what is truth? Is it, in part, a state of being? knowledge which serves as a light to our pathway? a purpose that works its way into the sinews and cells of our souls?

This was my answer: at the end of the long dark passageway, *light*. In a very real sense, as Joseph experienced it in the grove. Man's might is puny compared to the Lord's and is but for a moment. Truth is light, and light is the power of the universe, the power of joy. When I remember, when I fan the embers of my convictions into bright flames again, I am all right. Poor Gertie, with her grumbling and complaints, served to strengthen and bless me, though she knew it not.

❦

Thaddeus is ill. He had no more than a cold, Rosie thought. But soon after she went off to work he slipped from his high stool and injured his arm in falling, and he could not raise himself up again. She found him lying there several hours later, burning up with fever. She called the doctor in, and we have been taking turns caring for him, but he does not rally at all. Even Jonathan can get no more than a weak smile from him. And his fever remains high, no matter what we do.

I was there two evenings ago, spelling Rose, who had gone to a dance with Hiram Morley. But I tried not to think about that. I was alone, and the house was quiet. I believe I was humming some pretty melody under my breath. Thaddeus started, opened his eyes, so sore and red, and just stared at me. He was breathing heavily, and I could see that he was excited or in some kind of pain.

"What is it?" I asked.

When he heard me speak he shuddered and seemed to sink back down within himself, and a dullness clouded his gaze.

"He thought you were his wife," Rose explained, when I told her what had happened. "She used to sing to him. It was his greatest pleasure. She had a beautiful voice."

I knew at once—before she was even through speaking. "We will ask Emmeline to come and sing for him!" I whispered.

"Do you think she would do it?"

"Of course. I will get Eugene to take me to their house to ask her this very night."

It still feels strange to walk into the pretty little house where Emmeline and Jack live together. It still does not seem quite real, and I have to keep myself from laughing nervously or from asking foolish questions just to cover my sense of embarrassment.

Emmy keeps a good house. She has a feel for what is lovely and how things should go together. She has created a sense of harmony and a beauty that is subtle, more felt than seen. And there is the beauty of her person. She has bloomed in the warmth of Jack's love, flowering, discovering her strengths and her powers. It is a wondrous thing to behold, to see the emergence of a rare human being whose soul may very well have lain dormant without this love to awaken it into life.

Age, I remind myself, *is a reckoning of this earth only. In the long, long view it makes little difference at all.* Emmeline is as fine and prudent a homemaker as any I have encountered, and she takes great pleasure in it. And is that not wise?

She listened carefully while I explained my special errand, nodding now and again.

"I will be glad to help him," she said, rising as she spoke. "Would you like me to go with you right now?"

"Heavens no, dear. Morning will do just fine, I am sure."

I walked home with Eugene. The night was mild, and I felt well satisfied and pleasantly tired from the long day's exertions. We went to bed a bit earlier than usual, and I fell into a deep, restful sleep.

I did not know that Emmeline awoke in the middle of the night, of a sudden, and sat straight up in her bed. "He needs me right now," she said, shaking Jack into waking. "Hurry. We must go to Rosie's right now."

Once fully awake, Jack was not one to question such an impression of the Spirit. Within minutes they were standing in the murky darkness outside Rose's cottage, knocking tentatively on the door.

Rose opened at once, and when she saw them, her eyes filled with tears. "I have been frantic with worry. He is restless with the fever, thrashing about, and I cannot hold him. And he keeps calling for her."

Emmeline walked past them and in to the sick man. She placed her hand on his head. "Hush," she said softly. Then she started to sing to him. After a few minutes Jack brought in a chair. Half an hour later he brought in a glass of water to cool her throat and a quilt to cover her knees.

"From the moment she opened her voice," Jack told me later, "Thaddeus stopped thrashing and moaning. In fact, he became so calm and still that we wondered for a moment if we had lost him." The picture he drew was so pitiable.

"She sang for over an hour," he continued. "Then I made her rest for a while. But he opened his eyes and asked for her, and his expression was so haunted, so wild—"

This must be painful for Jack, too, I was thinking. *Bringing back terrible memories and a need as consuming and vain as this man's.*

"The doctor came near morning, but I had thought to give him a blessing by then, and he slept peacefully. The doctor said the fever had broken and he would soon be on the mend. I had to talk firmly to get Emmeline to come home with me, but she is back with him now."

There was a quiet pride in Jack's voice as he spoke of her. And suddenly I was so thankful that he had found this sweet girl to love, that this love had lifted both of them out of a state of loneliness to an existence where joy was the breath of life that moved through them.

I reached for Jack's hand. "We have been blessed—despite everything, we have been richly blessed."

He put his arm round me, and I hugged him almost fiercely. And he did not mind my weak, tender tears.

*

My father is gone. Randolph wrote to tell me, but I think I know when he went: I remember the day, if not the hour. I recall what was happening, and what I felt. I was gathering the pretty, daisylike feverfew to prepare a treatment for the aunts' arthritis and also as a wash for the insect bites Lavinia had been complaining of; though, in truth, it works well for headaches and fevers and half a dozen other complaints.

I was alone, enjoying the quiet morning hours in my solitary garden, humming under my breath. Suddenly a thought came to me, light as the gentle breeze on my face. *My father is walking in my garden, and he is at peace.*

So strong it was that I glanced about me, half-expecting to see him. But of course it would be in my garden at home that he walks. Yet I seemed to feel his love beaming on me, warmer than the sun. I closed my eyes and drew in the peaceful sensation before I returned to my tasks.

So when Randolph's letter came and told me the day of my father's passing, I knew he had, indeed, been with me, somehow, for those brief moments before leaving this sphere. And though my heart cried out to him, I felt no black sorrow, only the same sense of peace that had surrounded me that morning in the garden. *Stay near me, Father,* I prayed. *Do not leave me without the comfort of your presence in these most difficult days.*

I believe my Heavenly Father, in his graciousness, heard and answered my prayer.

Chapter Twenty-Four

Kirtland: August 1837

The Kirtland Safety Society Bank has formally closed its doors. Ironic name: "Safety Society." Considerable sums have been lost, and small families such as us are the hardest hit, for all our savings—which amount sometimes to a year's or more income—simply exist no more. Many are in a state of near destitution, and we are not far behind.

"This is a time of winnowing," Nathan says. But it is already being referred to as a great apostasy, for so many Saints are partaking of the darkness around them and turning their backs on the Church. And when they do that the spirit of hatred possesses them, misery compounds upon misery, and they seem almost to become obsessed.

Eugene is distraught. He had such high hopes, whereas Nathan was always more temperate and realistic. They were worldly hopes, but I cannot entirely fault him, being human myself. However, I hate to see him unhappy and angry, especially now, when I need his strength and support more than ever.

He came in raving the other day. "That Jacob Bump is a mean, distempered rascal! He has called in half a dozen mortgages held by good men, Esther—men who gave freely of their means that the temple might be built—and then, again, that the bank might not break. Now he has no compunction in ruining every last one of them!"

"What will they do?" I asked. His words seemed like a nightmare which could not be true!

"Do? Why, they will do nothing, Esther. They will suffer and go without; that is the only course open to them."

Every day brings new tragedies. We awake in the morning and steel ourselves, tensing when we see anyone approach our door, for fear of what news they might bring. Gertrude Woods came by a few days ago with a story to tell. Brother Barrett, the gentle shoemaker, has been ludicrously charged with stitching upturned nails and bits of sharp glass into the soles of the shoes he sells to non-Mormon customers. The accusation is being seriously entertained!

"He will be driven from town or forced to pay a large fee or both!" Gertrude bristled. "This is no place for any sane-thinking person to be."

"You are thinking of leaving then?"

"Garrison is making plans for us to return to Canada." She drew herself up a bit, her massive hair waving. "And none too soon."

"What of Brother Brigham? Have you told him you are going?"

"We would not dare!"

I laughed out loud at this. "Yes, Brigham Young would talk you into remaining with the Saints, if anyone could, Gertrude. Or give you a proper Scotch blessing for running away!"

She scowled at my dubious attempt at humor. But I felt sad and deflated and would have urged her to reconsider, if I'd had the heart.

Brigham Young is one of the prophet's loudest supporters, and he is hated for it. How awful that sounds—*hated for it!* And yet, it is true. Those who desire to ruin this people and literally destroy the Prophet want no one as powerful and determined as Brigham to stand in their way.

223

Many of Brother Joseph's most trusted friends have turned against him. Eugene came home to tell us that Warren Parrish has drawn a group of supporters around him who call themselves the "Parrish Party." Others have formed what they call "The Independent Church." And to what end?

I asked Eugene this, and he said, "To the end of their own power and glory. But why, I do not understand."

He is weary; he works too hard and gets nowhere—and every day we have less and less.

Sometimes I am concerned that the worry and distraction have penetrated more deeply than he or I realize. In the mornings, for instance, when we gather for prayer, he refuses to take his place acting as mouthpiece. He will not pray aloud. Last night I asked him why, and he said, "I cannot tell you that, Esther. I do not understand it myself."

"But you need the strength of prayer now more than ever!" I protested. He shook his head. "I mean it, Eugene. We will not pull through this without God's help."

"Pull through it—what does that mean to you, Esther? What do you see our future to be?"

He stared at me, his eyes cool and demanding. I had no answers, not really. "We must not lose the faith or turn away as others are doing," I began. "We must stand by the Prophet and the truth we've embraced."

"To stand by the Prophet, what will that mean to us, Esther?"

"I do not know, but God does. He will not fail us, Eugene, and he will take us where he wants us to go." I could say no more, for my throat was choking with tears, and I did not want him to see. Nor would he comfort me by telling me what he was thinking, what was going on in his mind.

Georgie and I work furiously, obtaining and preserving food, cutting down old frocks and shirts for the little ones, doing all in our power to scrimp and save and to make ends meet. Every day I look at my children and wonder what will become of them. Lavinia is now six years old. She can read and do simple sums, and she can hemstitch hankies better than I could at twice her age. She knows what are vegetables and what are weeds, and she can recognize most of my herbs now and even tell me their use. She is bright, and she is feisty, but she is also gentle and sweet, and I thank heaven for that. I fear from time to time that she might turn out like my mother and sister—does this seem a cruel thing to say? I want her to be kindly, to enjoy the fruits of a good life. Selfishness can be such a tyrant, especially in a vain woman's life. I want much more for her than that. She is very pretty, but I hope she may not be a beauty; rather, attractive enough to get by, aided by a fine personality and a sensitive spirit.

"You do not want much," Georgie says, with raised eyebrows. "Only the perfect ideal."

I cannot help it. 'Tis a natural motherly feeling. But for the moment, I find all these concerns pushed aside. I am dealing with the essentials of life: protection and sustenance. I am fighting for each tomorrow and struggling just to keep my little ones unharmed and safe.

We try to have a good time with the children as often as possible so there is some semblance of normalcy. We gather berries or windfall apples from the big, ancient tree near here. The first real winds of autumn shook the horse chestnuts into tumbles of spiked-green casings in which nestled shiny smooth nuts of variegated brown. We took deep baskets and gathered up as many as we were able, though there was not much we could do with them but appreciate their beauty and string the smaller ones for rough, imperfect necklaces to adorn little necks and bracelets to adorn little wrists.

Jonathan is a great help. He possesses the steady nature of my father, and I do not think he is ever really afraid. Because he is much with Thaddeus, he has occasion to be of assistance to Rosie, and this is a good thing. He is getting big enough to do the heavy work she cannot manage and to keep her company now and then. I am sure she finds it difficult to be alone in such an isolated setting. She still works for Jack, though not so many hours. His patronage has fallen, but his goods are too superior, his prices too fair for the Gentiles to be able to wean themselves from his store altogether. There are always rumors afoot of atrocities practiced against the Mormons: houses ransacked or set afire, stock killed, men walking right into a house and stealing whatever they see.

It frightens me, too. I cannot help but remember Palmyra and the frenzy of the people who were determined to hurt Joseph Smith for what he had done. I remember the alarm being sounded when Georgie's house was set to the flame. I remember the thick, burning smoke, the terrible damage, the sense of futility and outrage—of being violated and set up for public ridicule.

Now the same things are happening here. But much worse, and there are more of us to cause offense, more of us to terrorize and despoil. Thus it has been in Missouri, yet the Saints in this city are still planning to go there. Of course, where else have we on God's earth to go?

Someone set fire to Brother Frey's smithy, scattering the forge fires about, smashing and breaking tools. It happened midday, when Andrew and Janet were at the temple. One of the girls, as they came screaming down from the rooms above-stairs, recognized Jedediah Comstock. But who would believe what they say? And what justice would be attempted on their part?

Elinor said that when he saw their shocked and stunned faces he laughed out loud. Eden said nothing because the same day this happened, she miscarried her child—near term, so near term that the tiny infant breathed and lived for a few moments before slipping out of its diminutive body of clay.

My heart aches thinking of it. *Why Eden? Why now, at this precarious time?*

At length she began to ask the same questions. Emmeline came for a few moments after singing practice to tell me she had seen Sister Frey.

"She has aged ten years," Emmeline sighed, picking nervously at her thumbnail. "I hated to see her that way."

"What did she tell you, dear? Your eyes are as big as new saucers."

"Ill news, all ill news. Eden refused to let her mother and sisters in when they went to assist her. 'Why are you so blind and foolish?' she shouted at them. 'Why did you teach us such pitiful lies? Your God did not save your shop from harm, Father, though you were in his house, praying to him! Nor did he preserve my poor baby, though I swallowed my pride and came back to him.'"

I shuddered. "Oh, Emmy, oh, Emmy." We sat and just stared at each other until Georgie came in and we were forced to go through the painful recital all over again.

"Poor Aaron," she murmured. "I fear she will not stay with him."

"Georgie!" we cried together.

"Well, I truly fear it," she said.

They did not hold a service for the infant but buried it privately. So we paid our respects to Janet and Andrew. We wept and then prayed with our friends. Two days later Helen Willis died of pneumonia; we did not even know she was ill. Dorothy, the fragile one, is left to wonder why she is still living and what living in this place, in these strained conditions, is even about.

❧

We bury Helen in the late afternoon, when the shadows are long on the ground. It is an Indian-summer day, with the lazy crows circling and piercing the still air with their quavering, questioning cries. I feel lonely and hold to Lavinia's hand tightly. Dorothy leans upon Jack, and with her free hand she gropes to find Emmy's thin wrist and close her trembling fingers round it.

"She will come to live with us now," Emmeline told me this morning. "Jack would not take no for an answer."

That is as it should be, and Emmy will rise to the challenge, as she seems so consistently able to do. I wonder if she remembers the time when Jack was preparing to marry Aurelia. I wonder what he has shared with her and what the child thinks. I should like to ask him but have not yet worked up the courage to do so. Helen lies near to the slender grave where her niece has been sleeping. But where will Dorothy, or any of the remainder of us, be laid to our rest?

I was tired when we returned to the house. Funerals always exhaust me, weigh down my spirits till I am able to shake them loose. This was no exception. I stretched out on the horsehair sofa, and Jonathan brought a cover to warm my legs and feet. It seemed a very real possibility to me suddenly that any of us might be the next one to die. There is nothing but this uncertainty and danger assured us from day to day. I closed my eyes, but the throbbing in my temples did not lessen. I felt someone shaking me, with a gentle hand on my arm.

"Esther, I must go back and take my shift first, but Jack will come to spell me in time for supper."

My eyes flew open. "Jonathan, what are you talking about?"

"I thought you knew." He could tell from my expression and the tone of my voice that I didn't. "I thought Jack had told you or even Eugene."

"No one told me anything."

"Well, I'm going back to the cemetery for a bit—to keep my eye on the grave."

A repulsive awareness began to penetrate me with the shock of cold rain. "Do you think it necessary?"

"Jack and the others do. There were two graves robbed just last week—one only three days ago, both of them newly dug. Esther, I'll be all right!"

I saw such concern in his eyes that I attempted to smile, but my mouth only crumpled the more. "Oh, Johnny, how awful!" I moaned. "Why must such things have to happen?" To think of students from the nearby medical college at Willoughby stealing bodies to use for experimentation and boasting in their youthful ignorance that it is no sacrilege to dissect a Mormon, dead or alive!

He shrugged his thin boyish shoulders. "Don't worry about it, please, Esther. We've got it all in hand."

How solemn his expression behind the reassuring words he spoke to me. He looked far beyond his meager ten and a half years.

"All right." I nodded. "Watch yourself, and be careful coming back. We'll keep supper for you."

⁂

Why, I thought angrily, as I lifted myself from the pillows, *have they given the lad a turn?* When I found Nathan and asked him, he said plainly, "It will do him good, Esther. He thinks of himself as one of the men now, and who knows what he may be called on to do." I swallowed and nodded miserably. "Twilight will linger for a while yet, and Jack will be sure to get there before real darkness sets in."

I must be content with this! I thought as I stumbled back to the kitchen and prepared to nurse Nathaniel. He can wail like a banshee until he gets what he wants. I was determined to keep my fears to myself, but I prayed mightily as the slow minutes that finally marked an hour moved on. Just as we were setting the last hot bowl on the table, I heard his voice and had to clench my hands into fists to keep from running to him.

"You are just in time," Nathan boomed out. "And we've plenty this night to fill your belly. Have you worked up a good appetite?"

Jonathan grinned and took his place at the table. My own stomach began to settle itself again, and I thought that perhaps I, too, might be able to eat. I heard an owl hoot. He sounded terribly near, and the hollow sound startled me. My eyes sought Eugene's face, and he seemed to feel my impoverishment, for he looked up and met my gaze. All my need, mingled with a terrible tenderness, went out to him. I felt the force of his love come back to me. The corners of his mouth lifted a little.

"Pass that platter of chicken to Esther first, little brother," he said to Jonathan. "I want her to be able to pick the best piece."

⁂

Georgie was right. Aaron came to Jack early this morning, his eyes red-rimmed from crying and wild with a pain he had not thought possible. "Eden has left me," he said. "She is distraught and does not know what she is doing. Will you help me to find her, Jack—please!"

Poor man. Jack set him down and gently but firmly said, "It is futile, Aaron. Eden knows what she has done, and she has done what she wants."

"No, no! You are mistaken!"

"Dear friend, I wish I were. Stay here as long as you'd like; I do not want you to go home alone yet. Emmy will bring you a warm drink."

He went off in search of Emmeline, and together they calmed the poor man a little and fed comfort into the cavern of his terrible pain.

"She will return, she did before," Aaron kept saying.

"She will not return this time. Heaven help both of you, Aaron. It is not to be so."

What heroism exists in the most common of us! This thin, freckled, slightly balding man had loved the errant girl to distraction, given over his life to her purposes and her needs. Now there was nothing but the most bitter of disappointments and useless hopes.

"You must rally," Jack told him, and he bravely struggled to. "You gave your best; you gave several times over what most men would have given, Aaron. You must let that knowledge reconcile and support you."

In his helplessness he accepted his friend's terms, his friend's advice. "I loved her," he said. "You must know I still love her, Jack."

"I have no doubt of it, Aaron. I believe you always will love her; you are that kind of man."

"I cannot go on." How his pain must have seared through Jack's remembrance!

"You can go on; I assure you." Aaron felt those words tear through him, and he recognized from whence they came. How could he cry out to this steady, calm-eyed man that he did not understand?

"But the healing is another matter," Jack continued. "The healing will take a long time and perhaps never be completed entirely while in this life."

Emmeline heard these words, too. And, in hearing, she opened her heart to them and received into her being all they might mean. And, in doing so, she won Jack's love and devotion entirely—she bound herself to him with cords of faith and affection stronger than steel. As she confided this thing to Georgie, when he found her crying that night he gathered her into his arms, thinking that the passion and truth of what he had spoken before her had been too much to bear.

229

"I am sorry, Emmeline," he crooned, "sorry to have hurt and stung you, my darling."

"No, Jack, you do not understand." She struggled in his suddenly confining embrace. "I have been thinking of all Aaron and Eden have suffered, all you and Aurelia suffered, and I am afraid at how happy and blessed I am."

"Dear little one!" He mingled his tears with hers. "It is I who am the most fortunate of men, Emmeline, and I pray I may never forget."

He will not, I trust; his happiness has been too dearly paid for, his devotion too firmly fixed. He has trusted in that Being whose love and power has brought him safe through—to the point where this joyous fulfillment could flood through his existence like light.

❧

"We have lost our cow."

"Do not frighten me, Georgie. I am sure she has just wandered off a ways."

"The rope is cut clean through, not frayed, Esther: someone has taken her."

"Oh, Georgie, what are we to do?" I plunked myself down and sat with my head in my hands, as Lavinia does when she is peeved or unhappy. I felt very little more than a child: angry, misused, frustrated, and at my wit's end.

"As Eugene always says, 'What will we do? We will do nothing; for no course is left open to us.'"

"Georgie, please!"

"I am sorry, love." She was distraught herself and trying hard to conceal it, even from my eyes. "I shall go myself to ask the Cutlers if they will not share with us once more. We still possess a half-interest in Melinda, though we have left her entirely to their use these many months."

It was true. We had deemed the good relations worth the sacrifice: when we obtained our own milk cow, one hundred percent of her, we left the Cutlers to enjoy Melinda. Yet I was glad Georgie had offered to approach them and did not expect me to.

It was of no use. Patience sent Georgie packing without so much as a friendly word. "We'll lose the cow ourselves if we have to do with you folks. We're being watched, you know, and dare not show kindness to Mormons. Now, be on your way."

This and no more. It was really insufferable. But even Jack advised prudence.

"She may have used the truth for an excuse, Esther, but it *was* the truth she spoke."

It was all well and good to say so, but in actuality our provisions were shrinking at an alarming rate. Within the space of two weeks the price of meat and that of eggs had nearly doubled. We have our own laying hens, true. But we must protect them now, as we have learned to our great loss.

"We have been watching over our graves for more than two weeks, and you tell me we must continue. You mean that someone with a gun must also now guard our poultry, as well as our horses, both day and night?"

"That would be advisable."

"Jack, really! Advisable but far from practical."

"A nuisance," he conceded. "But I know not what else to do, dear."

231

❧

It is November, the year's on the wane, and the old days drag wearily toward their end. I am not happy to part with them, for I fear what will come after; I fear it, indeed. All Kirtland is in turmoil, and all the powers of darkness fight against us—some boldly attired, some in crafty and subtle disguise. We are in danger because we are different. We are despised because we are loyal and faithful to what we know to be true.

Christmas is nearly upon us, and we have nothing with which to mark the occasion and make merry. Eugene still works, but there is no money with which to pay him. Nathan teaches but only the children of the Saints, and the Saints have no money at all. We walk by faith because we must! Yet it still lightens our burdens and empowers us with the strength to go on.

Chapter Twenty-Five

Kirtland: January 1838

"It would be to your advantage, madam, and such a little matter for you to see to."

I was not acquainted with this man who addressed me, but I could not call him a gentleman by any stretch of the term. He knocked on my door and entered my house unbidden, he and three other men who stood close together in a dark silent arc, looking with curiosity around the room. My skin crawled, and I thought of how in the world I should get rid of them before Georgie returned from Rose's house and brought the little ones home.

I wanted to defy them and their unsavory suggestion and shout out my principles, chasing them away with my tongue. But I dared not. I knew it, and they knew that I knew.

"What you ask is impossible," I said. I chose my words carefully. "I have no access to my husband's papers; in fact, he seldom brings them home with him, and I know very little of what they contain."

"We have told you." There was impatience in the man's tone now—impatience and an icy disdain. "You can find ways, my dear. It will be worth it—for your sake and the sake of your children."

He was offering me protection—or, rather, in veiled terms he was threatening me. My blood ran colder than his voice.

"I dare not offer you false hope; I know my husband, and I know how little my chances are to leave my home at an odd hour, unobserved and unaccompanied, to obtain access to the printing offices and perform such a task."

"A little is all we ask, all we require. Some proof that Joe Smith perjured himself in the manner in which he disposed of his bank stock, that he dealt dishonestly with even one of his creditors, some little figure that we can use—"

Flesh and blood has only so much strength to endure! "That will be all, gentlemen." I moved to the door and opened it wide. "I can be of no use to you." I stood aside for them; my stance was painfully clear. I was certain that they could hear the wild pounding of my heart as they filed past.

"You are determined?" the spokesman asked.

Surely he can see me trembling! I thought. "I am perfectly sure."

He bowed himself out with an oily smirk that nauseated me. After he was gone, I dropped into a heap on the floor and sat hugging my knees and crying in dry, wracking sobs.

Georgie found me there, and I tried to rouse myself for the children's sake and force a weak smile as I wiped a smear of tears away and listened to their excited babbling. Their mere presence was a comfort to me, and I wanted to gather them all to me, Georgie's as well as my own, and be strengthened by the tangible, pulsing feel of their arms about my neck and their cheeks against mine.

Later I told her what had happened, and a scowl, like a little dark storm cloud, played over her forehead. "You did the right thing," she said. "But we must still be ready for repercussions."

Terrible repercussions were implied in her tone. With an entrapped feeling of guilt I shrank from them. But I know that she meant what she said to me and would have behaved in the same way herself.

Eugene went pale when he heard. He is a man; he would have liked to confront these vulgar ruffians himself and make them pay for the effrontery of entering into the sanctity of his home, threatening his wife, and tempting her to betray him.

"We should not be called upon to endure this!" he fumed. "There ought to be some means at our disposal to combat them."

He is neglecting his prayers still, and words like these make me worry, worry terribly. Nathan has done his best to encourage me.

"When a man works his heart out and still cannot feed his family, it knocks the slats out from under him, Esther. He'll regain his footing by and by."

By and by. As if there is leisure for such indecisiveness! I need my husband's strength and comfort right now!

233

⁂

We are awakened in the night by an alarm that sears through my consciousness: *Fire! Fire!* The words have power to send hot fear racing through me. *Where?* I shake Eugene until his eyes open; then I run to the window. The ground outside is light as day, but the light is lurid and tinged with an awful yellow. And the sky, in contrast, is an ugly, swirling black.

"It is the printing office!" Georgie called up.

Eugene was on his feet. *Dear heaven!* I paused to murmur a prayer, most heartfelt. *If our enemies cannot obtain what they want, they will destroy.* My mind reeled. There is always destruction, and the very real power of fear.

We are but a block away, more or less, from the printing office—and the temple, which stands nearby. Eugene had gone out, still pulling his shirt over his back. I stood at the open door and watched the tall flames, beautiful in their power, lick skyward, fueled by such precious substance! I stood for a long time and watched the red cinders spray and the flame spread outward. The men arrived too late. They had already lost the battle, but they kept fighting on. Georgie folded a warm shawl around my shoulders and brought me a cup of ginger root tea. My eyes were burning, but I could not make myself turn away from the lurid scene before me.

"I am hungry," I said, idly. Georgie brought me a stale piece of bread, and I dipped it into the hot liquid, then sucked on it.

"Will the temple catch fire—can you tell from here?" Georgie asked. For the first time I roused myself and thought of that very real possibility. I took a few steps forward and stood on tiptoe. "The wind is favorable, turning the flames away from it, I believe."

"Come inside, Esther," Georgie urged. "We can do nothing here."

It was hours before the men returned, Jonathan trailing behind them, almost too tired to move his smoke-blackened legs and place one foot in front of another. "Lost just about everything," he told me. "Saved a few books—most of them badly scorched."

Eugene's hands were badly blistered; he must have been one of the foolhardy who attempted to rescue books and papers. I got some salve to smear over them and tore up a clean rag for bandages.

"I'll be all right," he muttered.

"Yes, but this will help them stop hurting."

He suffered my ministrations, his face as black as the soot that had peppered his hair. "They get what they want, one way or another."

234

There was such discouragement in his words that I wanted to cry out. I placed my hand on his forehead and drew him carefully back to lean against me, his body trembling with exhaustion and rage.

There was such a solemn feeling in our little room that it choked all conversation. We sat stunned and, for the moment, defeated. But there was a further sensation, a grave sense of affirmation that could not be denied. I perceived there may very well have been others with us whom we could not see. I closed my eyes and let this solemnity move through me, cleansing me as it did.

❧

Lavinia saw them first—my innocent little Lavinia. She screamed and screamed, as though a dozen snakes had bitten her all at once. She would not stop. I raced to her, my heart a tight fist within me. She was standing on the small porch and pointing, with her hand crammed into a fist at her mouth.

I looked and gasped. I think a short, terrible scream escaped me, too. All four of Georgie's cats had been strung up on a length of clothesline stretched along the line of our roof. They had been horribly mutilated. I grabbed Lavinia and turned swiftly away. Georgie, right behind me, looked before I could prevent her. She sank onto her knees and just kept staring. I called for Jonathan and told him to take Lavinia away.

In a glance he saw what had happened. "You go upstairs with Vinnie," he said. "I'll see to Georgie and—the rest of this."

I felt no inclination to argue with him, since I was faint and nearly ready to vomit. I rounded up the other children, and we all traipsed upstairs. Bless them for their innocent, pliable spirits! They were soon occupied, one way or another. Then I drew my daughter onto my lap.

"I am sorry you had to see the kitties like that," I whispered. She is nearly seven years old and was thinking very hard about this.

"Did some mean people kill them?"

"They did."

"Well, I feel sorry for them! Heavenly Father will be angry with them, and how will they explain?"

Her bottom lip was quivering. I knew she did not want to cry. I brushed her hair back from her forehead. "You are very brave," I told her. A sudden thought came to me. "Would you like to help Jonathan bury them? I think the cats would appreciate your helping to care for them."

"*And* Heavenly Father would."

"Yes. Let me go and see how he is coming. I shall call you down in a bit."

I was crying inside. That is the very worst kind of grieving. I felt a bit light-headed still and was sick to my stomach. When I got outside I walked round to the rear and away from the house a distance to where Jonathan was digging the last hole in the unyielding winter ground. Three stiff little bodies lay beside the narrow graves, waiting. Georgie came back with the last—her favorite tortoise-shell tabby, whose thick long fur was matted and dull, dark with blood.

Tears were running down her cheeks, but she disregarded them. I stepped close and in low tones told them what I had promised Lavinia. "Let us place them in first," Georgie said. "Then you may call her."

There was no way for me to escape altogether. Lavinia, once summoned, felt the somberness of the occasion and behaved accordingly. "They need proper markers!" she cried suddenly. "Don't put that dirt in, Johnny; we'll lose track of who is who."

We paused while Jonathan located a thin plank of wood and cut and trimmed it into four rough, uneven sections. Then, with a stump of charcoal, he scratched out the four names, and Lavinia herself placed them with tender ceremony at the heads of the graves.

"We must sing a hymn now," she announced, "and then have a proper prayer, Aunt Georgie."

We steeled ourselves for it and got through one verse of "Rock of Ages." Georgie and I were both crying, but the others did not seem to mind.

"I am the only male representative at this gathering," Jonathan told her, "and I will offer the prayer."

And a very good prayer it was; thorough and to the purpose, remembering every sufferer, not leaving one important point out. *He is coming along,* I thought. *My father would be very proud of him.*

We opened our eyes, and the service was officially ended. I gave my brother a quick hug before I took Lavinia's hand and stumbled back into the house. Georgie did not follow us. I glanced back to see her sitting cross-legged on the cold ground, her arms folded, her eyes fixed upon the new graves.

❧

Nothing stops. Nothing becomes any easier. The killing of the cats oppresses our spirits, as it was intended to do. We begin to reconcile ourselves to the fact that we must make plans to leave Kirtland, as everyone else we know seems determined to do. I refuse to let myself think about it, lest it entirely overwhelm me. But Eugene broods darkly upon the daily injustices until it begins to twist and rankle his heart.

❧

Hiram Morley has asked Rose to marry him. She has not given him an answer yet, but I believe she will say yes. And why should she not? What reason has she to keep yearning after old ghosts, after a long-lost cause?

As if thinking about him had the power to make him materialize, Peter appeared at my door. I had not seen him for months, and he was a sight for sore eyes: browned with working out of doors, lean still, and well dressed; his thick hair worn long, nearly touching his shoulders.

He greeted me briefly, then said, "Hold the door open, Esther. I will be right back."

He was driving a wagon, from which he began to unload three large boxes, which he carried all together into the house. The boxes were loaded with grocery items, commodities we were direly in need of: flour, oats, cornmeal, salt, dried apples, a cheese, a large haunch of ham. I began to shake my head.

"It is not all my money," he said imperturbably. "Some comes from Jack's store. But—as you well know—no one will sell goods like these to Mormons."

"Is Jack still making money?"

"A bit. I have let it be known, as widely as possible, that I am partner in the business. Therefore, my friends still patronize and leave it—in other ways—untouched."

"You do not need to quibble terms with me, Peter!" Watching him, I felt a bit ill.

"Be as angry as you'd like. I do not blame you for being angry."

"How can you call such low, loathsome creatures your friends?"

He did not answer but continued unloading the food until he was through. "I'll be back," he informed me. I opened my mouth to snap back at him, but just then he turned to face me. I looked into his eyes and saw a terrible longing there that caught me quite off guard. "How is Rosie faring?"

The question was so gently, so quietly put that for a moment, I was not certain I actually heard it.

"Rosie? She gets by no better than the rest of us. I have not seen her for days."

"She has moved into town, hasn't she?"

"No, she intended to. But Thaddeus will not budge, and she refuses to leave him."

I shrugged, but his face grew livid. "You must insist, Esther! Get Nathan and Eugene to go for her. She is too isolated to be safe."

"There is not much to attract robbers and marauders to her little cottage," I responded. "And, you know Rose, she will not be led, and she will not be frightened."

He was beside himself, and his concern began to alarm me. "Do you know something we do not know? Are you aware of—"

"Hush, Esther. Keep your voice down; those who would harm you may be lurking nearby."

"Peter!"

"Please, Esther. Make Rose come here with you."

"I shall do my best."

My tone lacked the conviction he desired, and he fumed a bit longer. "I shall speak to Jack. Jack will help me." He was distracted, as though he were talking to himself now and scarcely mindful of me.

He moved to the still-open door, his eyes searching the horizon. "I must away, Esther. I have stayed too long already." He bent over, placed his hands on my shoulders for a moment, and kissed the top of my head. "Give my love to the others," he said. "God keep you, Esther."

He was outside, jumping onto the wagon even as he clucked to the horses, in motion before I could gather my stunned senses and call out to him. I watched him move on down the road, turn a corner, then disappear behind a large stand of trees. I leaned against the doorframe, feeling a bit weak, feeling apprehensive though I could not say exactly why.

As soon as Eugene comes home, I told myself, *I shall make him take me over to Rose's, and I shall see what I can do.*

Chapter Twenty-Six

Kirtland: March 1838

Everyone is going! So many of our friends have already packed up, leaving their homes and properties behind them, and are now on their way. Brigham Young was forced to flee the city before the old year ended because of his fearless defense of the Prophet. His calm assurance maddens the dissenters, and for this there are many livid with anger, clamoring against him, determined to take his life. Joseph's name has become a hiss and a byword, which is painful to see. Those who love him defend him, but they do so at their own peril. And to our great sorrow, it is often difficult to determine the faithful from the turncoats and apostates, whose venom and bitterness know no bounds.

As of a few weeks ago, Joseph himself is with us no more. He has eluded his enemies, at least for the time being. But he is a wanderer abroad: torn from his family, torn from the comforting association of his people, torn and severed from all but his God. His words haunt me. "We have waded through affliction and sorrow thus far for the will of God, that language is inadequate to describe," he wrote to the brethren in Missouri. "Pray ye therefore with more earnestness for our redemption."

We do, indeed, need all the prayers we can get.

Phoebe has written, begging us to come home to Palmyra. *Phoebe!* I would never have expected such unfeeling counsel from her.

"She is afraid for us and cannot see beyond that!" Georgie scolded me. "You are too harsh in your surmisings, Esther. She does not understand what is happening here nor what is required of us."

"She ought to be coming with us!"

"She ought to be, but how can she, given her present circumstances?"

"I do not wish to be so far separated from her!"

"I know, Esther, I know."

Randolph is appalled. "I will come for you." His manner was more one of command than entreaty; he, too, was afraid. "You must return! I will do anything in my power to help you!"

I thought this pain was too much for me. Then I read:

Tillie has gone, Esther. I may as well be brave and tell you. We believe she is some place in New York, lost in the city, living in a house Father has provided there. Of course the children are with her, and Gerard is free to do as he likes. There is no longer any pretense of goodwill between him and my father. And though my father is known for a hard man, general opinion is on his side.

And Tillie's? Suddenly so many memories flooded over me: our May Day picnics when we were girls; that day when she told us her father had betrothed her to a stranger and she must comply to his will; her honeymoon homecoming, when she put on such a brave face; the day her first baby was born and Gerard coldly told her what the boy was to be called and showed no tenderness, no interest in her. I could go on and on; I cannot shut out the memories!

"You torment yourself needlessly. Suffering for her sake will not change things for Tillie nor bring her back." Georgie is never one to mince words with me.

"We shall never see her again."

"Most probably not. Not in this life."

"Can you reconcile yourself to that fact?"

"And many others." Georgie's tone was gentler than the relentless words; she was trying to talk some sense into my head. I love her for it. I love her for the kindness and faith in her nature. I do not know how I should go on without her.

241

❧

I am with child. And, as Jack tells us, so is Emmy. I fear for the girl. So young, facing such an uncertain future. It should not be happening this way.

Jack is more hopeful—as usual. "God will take care of her," he has assured me. "And, with a little help from us, and a little clever conniving, he shall also provide."

He would say no more. "He is selling the store," Eugene guessed, "and using the money to outfit us all."

"We cannot let him do that," Nathan said.

Men! "We cannot refuse him," I countered firmly. "Or we would be breaking his heart."

We are striving to be ready to leave by May. Reuben and Claire Lamb will travel with us. She confided last prayer meeting that she has been receiving clandestine assistance from Peter, too.

"We would not survive without him," she confessed. "The mob took over our bakery, as you know. And Reuben has no way of making a living. Even the garden was trampled, and if we stayed, they would never allow us to plant it."

"What of your interest in the property? I happen to know you nearly own the bakery outright."

"It will all go by the wayside, my dear."

I am put to shame daily by the patience and forbearance of the Saints here, by their cheerful, never faltering faith. Rose among them. She will not hear of leaving Thaddeus, even less of forcing him to move. "You may as well kill him," she says. I have talked her into a night or two now and then, spent with us or with Emmy. But at such times we send Jonathan to watch out for Thaddeus in her stead.

I find it a bit strange that Peter has not asked concerning Rose and her safety again; but he has not mentioned her name one time since that first visit. He knows we are going away. I made bold to ask him what he intended to do with his own life, but in this, as in all things, he will not give a direct answer.

"I have hopes," he said once. "I have tentative plans of my own that I am mulling over."

And that is the closest he came.

I could not find Jonathan anywhere, and I was at once concerned for his safety. Georgie had thought he was in the house. But we looked everywhere we could think of and found not a trace of him.

"Do you suppose he has gone to see Thaddeus and forgotten to tell us?" Georgie asked.

"Perhaps." I wanted to believe so, but something prevented me. I found myself pacing the floor, the hours dragging like Indian rattle gourds behind me. It was all I could do to concentrate sufficiently to prepare the children for bed, listen to their prayers, and tuck them in with a lullaby.

When I heard the men enter the house, all my senses were strained to listen. Instinctively, before I untangled the voices and identified the footsteps, I knew that Jonathan was not with them. I flew down the stairs. Both Nathan and Eugene were concerned when I told them how long it had been since we were aware he was missing.

"I'll ride over to Thaddeus's right now," Eugene offered.

"Sit down and eat your supper first," I advised, though the patient words clogged in my throat.

Just then I heard something, a common enough sound, but it arrested me. I drew the front door open a crack, cautiously. I listened and heard it again.

"Is that a cow?" Georgie asked, nearly ready to laugh.

"Yes, I think so. And it seems to be coming from the direction of the shed."

243

We had not a proper barn but a small building that had adequately housed our cow and the few hens and hogs we kept. I could feel my heart beating in my throat. I called out, "Jonathan! Jonathan!" until my voice was hoarse and would not carry at all.

Eugene pushed back his chair and, stuffing a piece of bread into his mouth, came to join me. "I'll go out and see, Esther," he offered. "It could be anything; you're so on edge."

I saw him then—his face white and ghostlike in the shadows. He swayed as he came into the range of light that the open door threw. Eugene ran forward, Nathan right behind him, and they caught him before he had time to fall. He moaned as they carried him through the door and into the kitchen, and he slumped in his chair, as though he had not the strength to sit upright.

"Johnny, what has happened to you?" I was staring at his face, criss-crossed with bruises and scratches. There was a large lump forming under one eye, forcing the swollen eyelid nearly shut.

"Someone go secure Missy," he mumbled. "I'd hate to lose hold of her now."

Nathan went quickly, but Eugene stayed to hear the story, for Jonathan was waving his hand. "Pliny—" It seemed painful for him to get the word out. "They beat us up awful bad. Left him for dead. I couldn't move him, so I took the cow and came along home."

What incredible outrage was this? Georgie held a cup to his lips, and he swallowed. "You must tell us what happened," I said.

"Old Pliny came here. Said he knew who had taken our cow off, and if I'd go along with him he thought we could get her back."

"And you believed him and went—without telling anyone?"

He mustered enough strength to grin sheepishly before he went on. "They're a big, rough family live further down the road from Pliny, and the lot of them gets dead drunk every Saturday night. Soon as dusk fell we worked our way up to the barnyard. Sure enough, our Missy was tethered with half a dozen others. We had no trouble at all getting her loose and leading her along with us.

"Old Pliny laughed and said, 'They won't know the difference 'til Monday night, when the drink wears off.' "

"What happened then?" Georgie asked.

"It was not them but a bunch of bullies looking for trouble, pretty drunk themselves. They didn't know who we were, and they didn't care. 'Long as we were Mormons, they thought they'd rough us up a bit. I told them that wasn't so, but they weren't of a mind to do any listening."

He sighed and moved the muscles of his cut face gingerly. I had the ointment ready and was beginning to spread it carefully with the tips of my fingers. But still he winced at each touch, and tears gathered behind his eyes.

"We weren't no match for 'em, a kid and an old man. Once Pliny fell they kicked him around pretty bad. I cried out at them, and someone coming along heard and halloed back at me, and that made them scatter."

The telling was getting harder and harder, as Jonathan was forced to relive those moments. I saw the fear and pain in his gaze and had to turn my own away from it.

"I couldn't move him, so I came along with Missy. He might—I'm afraid—"

Eugene had long ago nodded to me and gone outdoors to fetch Nathan and retrace the unlit path to see what they could find.

We made the boy sip a bit of broth and drink a bit of cumin and ginger tea to calm the nerves after a shock; but we did not get much down him. At length we heard the men's voices outside.

I knew as soon as I looked into their faces. I held my arms out to Jonathan, but he rose shakily and stared right past me. "Is he out there? Will you take me to him?"

Eugene held out his arm, and Jonathan leaned upon it. "It looks like a blow to the head is what killed him," Nathan was saying. "We'll have the doctor by in the morning to check."

Of course, the doctor. Of course, the death of an old man whom no one cared much about. I took a few steps out-of-doors, and the great darkness seemed to swallow me. I heard Jonathan crying softly, and the noise sounded muffled and far away. Nothing seemed real, and nothing seemed to matter, nothing in all the wide world.

We buried Robert Pliny on the following Wednesday, after making several efforts to locate his children. I hated to think of him going down to his grave unremembered and unmourned. I was taken by surprise, therefore, to see how many attended the quiet services that marked the end of his life.

245

"We are not the only ones he took under his wing and befriended," Georgie surmised.

I was cheered to know it. Many I recognized as Gentile neighbors, but most of them were people I had never seen before nor knew at all.

Not much was explained about the manner of his dying; that determination was the doctor's, and I was grateful he took it into his hands. "The least told, the better, on all counts," was his succinct decision. No one questioned the possibility that the old gentleman, frail these past years, might have fallen and hit his head. The bruises and cuts were carefully camouflaged and covered, and his frozen face looked out upon the world with the same serenity it always had shown.

At first I worried much about Jonathan. "Give him time; give him time, Esther," Georgie urged. I said special prayers for him when I went to the temple and did my best to be patient. The evening of the burial he came to me, his face puffy from crying.

"I think he would want it this way," he said.

"What way?" I wiped my hands along the towel that hung at my waist and sat down. My young brother moved to stand close to me, his hands clasped at his back.

"Well, you know, doing something, being of service to somebody—he worried a lot about that."

"Yes, he often said he did not want to outlive his usefulness."

"That's what I mean! And he would not want me to make myself sick over his going."

"No." I lowered my head because fresh tears were threatening. "He would want us to let him go with dignity—and to carry on in the same way."

The tension eased out of Jonathan's features, and I felt myself smile. *Good lives touch others long after the spirit departs,* I thought. *And the nobility of some souls is a power that lingers to bless every life they have touched.*

I watched Jonathan walk out into the cold sunshine and went back to my work.

⁂

I was at Jack's house, bringing Emmeline some raspberry leaf tea for her queasy stomach; I was there to see for myself. Her father entered without even knocking, and her mother followed. I had not set eyes upon them for years. The man was much ruined with drink—his flesh loose and of a dull, pasty color; his eyes puffy and rimmed. His hair was thinning at the back of his head, and he had put on more weight. I turned my gaze to the quiet woman and in her saw some traces of the beauty she had bequeathed to her daughter; but she, too, was wasted and lackluster.

I glanced quickly at Emmeline. She did not appear frightened or even disturbed. But for my own part, I wished that Jack was with us. I watched her movements covertly: she walked to his desk, rummaged among the papers and ledgers neatly stacked there, then took a chair near where I was seated, and suggested that her parents sit too.

"We come to see if what we hear is true, missy. Are you leaving us, then? Running out on your father and mother?"

"Jack and I will be going to Missouri within three months," she replied.

"Just like that! Not so much as a 'by your leave,' missy!"

I was shocked to hear the woman's voice, whiny and cloyed with self-pity. I watched Emmy's face blanch.

"I am a married woman now, Mama, you know that. My husband has—"

"Your husband! What does he intend to do for us now?"

I rose to my feet, wanting them to at least be mindful of me, to perhaps blunt the edge of their malice. I was certain that this distasteful scene had been played out many times before. It was part of the price Emmeline paid for her freedom; part of the price Jack paid for the woman he loved.

The front door opened and shut decisively. Jack stood staring down at us, his arms folded in a tight line in front of him, as if to ward off all opposition.

"How are we to live," the father began, "with you runnin' off this way? 'Tis disgrace enough havin' a girl who's turned Mormon and shamed us. Folks think—"

"Mormon money has not shamed you, though, has it? You have cared naught what folks say about that."

Jack took a few long strides forward. His presence seemed to dwarf them; I could almost see them shudder and cow. "You will have what you need. Have I failed you yet?"

"Now, Jack, we didn't mean nothin' . . . " The big man had risen, but he stood hunch-shouldered, uncertain.

"Now get out of my house!"

As the big man began to move, Jack walked closer, not stopping until their shoulders were almost touching. He grabbed hold of the fellow by the scruff of his shirt. "You listen to me very carefully. If any harm comes to me or mine—to this house—to Emmeline in particular—you will see all you own, all you are, come down around your heads. And you will never get another penny out of me. Do I make myself clear?"

Emmeline's father cleared his throat and nodded. Jack fixed him once more with his burning gaze, then turned his eye on the mother. "Can you make certain that he does nothing foolish, madam?" She whined and mumbled something. "Well, see that you do."

He walked them out, a hand on each of their shoulders. Emmy sank into her seat with a sigh.

247

"I am so grateful Jack happened to come just at that moment," I breathed. "What good fortune for us."

"It was not good fortune but good planning, Esther. There is a button in his desk that is wired to a bell in the store and also to the warehouse. If he is at either place he will hear it and know that I need him at once."

"You have thoroughly astounded me!" I acknowledged. "What a canny brute that husband of yours is." We laughed together in relief. By the time Jack turned back to us we were both ready to throw ourselves into his arms, to make much of him.

"You see how well cared for I am!" Emmeline crooned. She moved to stand beside him, and he tenderly pulled her close.

"You are a most fortunate woman, and I am happy for you," I cried, "with all of my heart."

Jack grinned a bit sheepishly.

"Yes, you are clever indeed," I admitted. "And I shall know better in future than to lose any sleep over you two."

I drank in the sweet power of their happiness, like a pure elixir: kith and kin to the power of love. *Sacred and wonderful and beyond our understanding,* I mused as I walked back to my house.

Chapter Twenty-Seven

Kirtland: Late May 1838

We have done well in this matter of gathering supplies for our leaving because we have had help. If Jack were not of our party, for instance, I do not know what we should have done. There is a goodly number of us: Widow Godfrey, who keeps the dairy; Reuben and Claire; Aunt Dorothy; Jack and Emmy; our two families; and, I dearly hope, Rose.

She has told Hiram Morley that she will marry him but will not set the date until after we are settled in Missouri. Yet she hedges in coming.

"A large group will be leaving later in the summer," she told me. "I think I should wait here. The Morleys will be among them, and I shall be well looked after."

"Thaddeus will not come any more easily for them than he will for us."

"He will not come at all if he has his way. Oh, Esther!"

I seldom see her distraught, but her eyes were pools of misery.

"He must know you cannot stay here."

"'Leave me!' is all he will say. I believe he sincerely expects me to do so and to let him grovel out his life in this place."

How complicated human nature is! How intricate and unassailable. We sigh; we encourage one another, but we really get nowhere at all.

When Eugene came home tonight he said he thought the Freys might come with us.

"The entire family?"

"Yes, minus Eden."

We have seen her now and then about town. Sometimes on the arm of Jedediah Comstock, sometimes with another gentleman— using the term loosely. I do not try to avoid her, but she will not look up if we pass. She is always dressed well and carries herself haughtily, but that means nothing at all. I fear she is miserable inside and dares not admit it.

"It is difficult for you to conceive of people being drastically different from yourself," Eugene reminded me. "She may truly have chosen what she wants, though the thought of it is appalling to you." He leaned over to kiss me, then added, "If the Freys join us, Aaron will come along with them."

"Good." I could not bear the idea of the man being alone. He is so quiet, so uncomplaining. "Perhaps he is simply boring," Georgie says, but I think not. He has a quick wit, and at times I have seen him smile much and engage in lively conversation. And I know he loves reading and the higher things of the Spirit.

"They were not well matched," Georgie has concluded. "'Tis a pity he loved her."

I wonder, for the hundredth time, how love can be so unwise, so indiscriminate. Surely the heart should know its own and should not feel at ease with a spirit whose essence is largely unlike it. Yet life proves just the opposite, time and again, to be true.

❧

"There are men at Rose's place," Jonathan told us one day, when he came home from visiting Thaddeus.

"Two of them, young men, sort of loitering about the place. I've seen them before."

"In full view? Just doing nothing? That makes no sense."

"They disappear if they think I've spotted them, and they always keep a good distance and don't seem to want to do harm."

I told Eugene what the had boy said. "Do you think he knows what he is talking about?"

"I don't know, love. It's hard to tell."

"Should I mention something to Rose?"

"By all means, no. Tell Johnny to keep his eyes open, but don't get Rosie upset and frightened. For now I would leave things alone."

Eugene comes home dead-tired every night. He is doing something that holds no appeal for him: preparing and planting the rich wheat fields of another. But at least he has something to do. There are a few Saints who plan to stay through next winter. Perhaps they are deceiving themselves. But perhaps they are right, and the troubles will die down with most of the Mormons gone, and they will be able to hang onto the extra lands and properties they are buying up quietly for less than a tenth of their worth.

But I would not wish to be here. Joseph is gone and Brigham Young and most of the brethren. The spirit of the work is no longer here. I go to the temple at least twice a week, for one purpose or another; I see it standing graceful and comely every time I look out my door. God is in his temple as long as there are those willing to worship and honor him. But his prophet has gone where the Lord, himself, instructed him and the rest of his people to go. That leaves no room for hedging or contending or coming up with countersolutions, as far as I am concerned.

It is not easy. I see Mother Smith coming and going. She is regal in her own quiet way and reveals none of the concern she must be feeling for her sons right now and for the future welfare of her family as well as the Church. She was present at one Sabbath day meeting in the temple I attended when a number of the most bitter apostates forced their way in, armed with daggers and a loud, murderous spirit. Some of the women, seeing the commotion, screamed, and the sound grated against the mind like a blow. Fainthearted men actually ran in confusion and jumped out of the windows, in fear for their lives.

It was heartrending to witness such scenes enacted in this holy place. Darkness has no compunction and recognizes no bounds. I cringed to to recall the meeting in which Warren Parrish attempted to drag Father Smith from the stand, and when his son William defended him, the dissenters surrounded him and held a sword at his breast. People are terrified, naturally, by such proceedings. The very next day a writ was sworn against Joseph Smith Sr. for rioting in the temple. It is nearly enough to laugh at, if tears did not so easily rise.

Those who have denied the faith are eager to defame and discredit that which is sacred. This, more than anything else, incenses my heart. I am ready to leave them behind without a backward glance. Yet I know well that many of these weak, despicable characters have banded and gone to Missouri to try to wield their influence there. This alone has the power to truly discourage me.

"I need you with me at the temple more often," I have pleaded with Eugene.

"I know—I have been remiss." He stroked his long mustache fretfully. "I have been out of tune."

I must be content with this, and it does mark a progression of sorts. But I need so much more and resent a bit the fact that I find myself turning to Georgie for counsel or strength or comfort when I long to turn to my husband instead.

❦

There is work and more work, constant and never-ending. Georgie spares me as much as she can, Jonathan is a tireless worker, and even Lavinia has become a great help. She sings as she works, thanks to Emmeline, and sometimes I get the delightful feeling that there is a little bird flitting happily about my poor house. I am not ill with this pregnancy, but I feel constantly tired, and often my nerves are on end. Emmeline does well, I believe. But she is so closemouthed and patient that it is not easy to tell.

I try not to worry about the ordeal of a journey nor what we will find when we get to Far West.

"We will find the place in turmoil," Eugene glumly predicts. "The Saints have too many enemies there."

"Brother Joseph has just this month surveyed a new community there," Nathan counters. "It is about twenty, twenty-five miles south of Far West. Adam-ondi-Ahman, it is to be called."

"I know. I wrote a piece in the paper about it. It is the spot where Adam is said to have blessed his posterity and where he will visit his people again. We could establish a city a month and that would not keep us from harm's way, and the Prophet knows it better than the rest of us."

We are not often alone, Eugene and I, but we were enjoying a stretch of fine weather, so the following evening I coaxed him into taking a walk with me.

"We have seldom been to Lake Erie," I said, by way of conversation. "I wish now that we had taken the children there at least once to see the boats and play in the water."

"We have been too busy establishing a home and making ends meet. We thought there would always be time."

"Yes." I drew a deep breath for courage. "Why are you going to Missouri, Eugene?"

"That is a strange question to ask."

"Have you ever thought of going back to Palmyra instead?"

"It is not often that a man can go back. We have cut all ties there and would not be looked upon kindly, still being of the same odd persuasion."

"So we go on to Missouri because there is no place better we know of to go."

"Esther, what has gotten into you?"

"I need to know where your heart is—where your convictions lie. These past months I feel I have been largely without you, Eugene, and I do not like it that way."

"I've done my best, but I've had a hard struggle with some things, Esther."

"I know. But you have held it in to yourself, and it has forced us to go separate ways."

"I have been ashamed, and that is the truth of it." His voice was nearly too soft to hear. I leaned closer, and he placed his hand on my shoulder. "Can you understand that?"

"I can. I have had my own fears."

"But never doubts."

"Never doubts, Eugene, though I cannot really say why."

"You're a better person than I am, plain and simple. You always were a far sight too good for me—"

"Then why did you suppose you might win me?"

"Oh, I never supposed, not for a minute. I only hoped." A tender banter had crept into his tone. He leaned back, remembering. "I never believed you'd say yes. That is why I was so wretched when you put our wedding day off." His eyes were moist, and for the first time in months I could see something behind them. "I remember waking up every morning and thinking, 'If I can have Esther for my own, I shall be happy for the rest of my life.'"

He realized too late what he had said. He raised his eyes to mine. The tenderness in his face gave him a boyish air that tugged at my heartstrings. "You look ten years younger suddenly," I murmured. "It must be the light."

"It is the light, all right, the light of your spirit, which I have not been able to quench."

"Eugene—"

"Please. I never deserved you less than I do at this minute."

What to do? What to say to him?

"I am not worthy of you."

"The adversary would have you think so. Do not speak that way, Eugene! Are we not worth some struggle, some price?"

I knew his answer. He did not have to put words to it. He drew me into his arms. "Do not give up on me, not yet," he pleaded, his lips covering mine. I thrilled to the touch of him, and I felt the years fall away from us: the babies, the hardships, the struggles and disappointments. They had no place in this moment that drew us together again, held by that pure love which had at first united us but had been tarnished and corroded by the heat of the day. I rested against him and marveled at the hope that love brings—like no other hope in the world.

254

༉

We cannot find Peter! Even Jack has sent for him half a dozen odd times. I cannot leave this place without seeing him! I will not! Palmyra seems like a dream; I can do nothing about the people I love in Palmyra. But I cannot leave Peter in this emptiness, this unresolved void.

We are nearly ready. It is down to a matter of days now, each one more wrenching, more difficult than the last.

༉

It is night. No, the sky outside my window says that morning is beginning to come; the gray dove of morning spreading her wings over the darkness, making way for the sun. I sit up in bed, rub my eyes, and wonder what has awakened me. Then I hear Georgie call to me. I turn my head and see that Eugene's side of the bed is empty and his clothes are no longer draped over the ladder-back chair.

I pull a shawl over my long gown; that should be sufficient. My stomach feels sick because it is empty. I press my hand over it and take the steep steps with care. Georgie is watching me impatiently. "Hurry, we have Rosie in the kitchen."

"She has been hurt." I knew it at once.

"But not badly. I thought you ought to dress the wounds."

Rose was so pale that her freckles stood out and looked three times their normal size. She showed me the scratches and shallow cuts along her right arm.

"Tell me what happened." I reached for the tin of salves and the crock filled with linen packets of herbs, thumbing through them, instinctively pulling out the ones that would do the best service.

"It was late and we had just put the lamps out when I heard a great noise in the yard. Horses and men—it sounded as if there could be a dozen or more. I froze, Esther! But Thaddeus said, 'Come, dear, do what Jack has told you to do.'"

"Jack has told you—what do you mean, Rose?"

"These past nights he had daily sent a saddled horse and kept it tethered in that little rock hollow a few yards behind the house. He told me to take the low door that leads to the cellar, then slip outside, find the horse, and ride at once to your house—without looking back. I had to feel for my way and slid on some sharp stones into a thorny bush of some kind. That is how I cut myself up."

I was dumbfounded. She winced as I drew the skin tight around the worst cut.

"Nathan was awake and saw me coming," she continued, "so he and Eugene were nearly ready to ride off as I pulled up to the house."

I felt a constriction in my chest, but my fingers kept working. "The men—did you recognize any of them?"

"I did not go out that way, remember—or even peek through the window. But I did hear one of them say, 'It will serve him right; he thinks he can keep the upper hand on us'—something like that."

The words made me shudder. They seemed to embody some evil portent I could not understand. The kettle was singing, and Georgie rose to pour cups for the three of us. I sank gratefully into a chair.

"Thaddeus—do you think our men got there in time?"

"Thaddeus had a gun," Rose said.

"A gun! Why do I know so little of what is going on here!"

Rose grimaced. "I think because Jack organized it that way. He did not want to worry you," she added when she saw the look on my face.

"It was not the kindest thing," Georgie mused, "but no doubt the wisest." She glanced up. "Could the men be returning already?" Even as she spoke the door burst open with a gust of cool air and the murmur of voices. "We are here in the kitchen," Georgie called out.

Jack entered the room with Nathan and Eugene. They all wore an exultant air. "Tell us what happened!" I demanded breathlessly.

Eugene began. "It all worked out as planned. Our boys heard the men ride up, and Gilbert went to warn Jack, while David entered through the cellar to stand in defense with Thaddeus!"

"What in heaven's name are you talking about?" I was not amused now but quickly growing angry. Then all at once, my memory dragged out a faint, half-buried fact. "There were two men skulking round Rose's place! Jonathan told us, but we never found out who they were." I swung round to face my husband. "You told me it was best to forget them, and let sleeping dogs lie."

"And so it was." Jack moved forward and walked over to stand beside me. "I am sorry, Esther, but it was an ingenious plan, and it depended upon secrecy and the element of surprise to make it effective—and if it failed to be effective, Rose might well have lost her life."

"You all knew of it, and Rose—of course, Rose had to." I was thinking out loud. "No wonder Thaddeus urged you to leave so calmly; he knew he would not be alone."

"I am sorry." Rose lowered her eyes. "I did not think it would hurt you."

I could not say why it did, why I wished so strongly that they had taken me into their confidence. "Is Thaddeus all right?"

"Unhurt, though well shaken."

I could perceive that the men still considered this, at least in some part, a pleasant lark. I should have realized the exultation they were feeling to have in any way triumphed over their foes. The constant brutalities, the humiliations we have been forced to patiently swallow chafe against the male pride. I try to think of these things and not make myself appear petty before them.

"Rose needs some rest," Georgie said. "Can she stay here for the rest of the night?" She looked to Jack for an answer.

"Thaddeus has company," he said, "and I'll stop in on my way back to let him know she's all right."

This is just like Jack, I thought, remembering how he prides himself on his cleverness. "You contrived this plan yourself, then?" I said, "just like the buzzer in the desk drawer?"

"Ingenious, isn't it?" He grinned and kissed my cheek before pulling on his coat and making ready to leave.

It was not until later I realized that his answer was evasive: he never truly *said* it was his plan. Why does that little fact bother me?

⚜

We leave tomorrow. I have said too many good-byes already. I have burned my eyes with looking, looking—trying to imprint on my memory every precious place, every beautiful spot I shall be leaving behind.

I thought Rose would be staying behind, until this morning when Jonathan came skipping into the house. "Thaddeus is all right. He'll be coming."

"What? Jonathan, say that again for me."

"Jack came this morning and gave him a blessing. He read the scripture, and I said the prayer."

I still was at a loss! He had to explain more slowly and in much greater detail.

"Jack has been telling Thaddeus that it is imperative that Rose come with us and not wait for the others, and Thaddeus believes Jack." *How interesting, when he would never give the rest of us the time of day!* " 'You have to decide now,' Jack told him last week. 'You must come with her, or you must stay behind. Rose comes with us, if I have to bind and carry her.' "

"Why would Jack talk like that?"

"I don't know. But I think the scriptures have been helping."

"What scriptures?"

"I've been going through the Book of Mormon with Thaddeus for quite a few weeks now. We take turns reading out loud. He has a fine expression, Esther, and he says the words with real feeling."

"I do not believe you."

"Well, you must, 'cause it's true."

"And he let Jack give him a priesthood blessing?"

"He did."

"I guess that should shame me for my lack of faith," I muttered. And I meant it. So many things had been happening lately, right under my nose. I had been preoccupied with the care of the children and the preparations for leaving. Yet I cannot get over the feeling that I am missing out on some very meaningful things.

Eugene had, too, become suddenly eager to shake the dust of this place from his feet. "You are right, Esther. Everything that had life in it went when the Prophet was forced from here. Only the dregs are left. There will still be work for me to do where we are going."

This night I went for the last time to the temple. I watched Emmeline sing with the others. She sounded like an angel, and her whole countenance was shining. Tears rolled down my face. For a long time after the others left and the quiet had once again settled, I stood in the shadows and just looked up at that building, which is more than a building. The solid stone walls, so smoothly covered with plaster, the dormer windows, the gabled roof and bell tower, the delicate arches of the windows, top and bottom, set in the long, graceful sides—all reflect more than the architectural genius that conceived them: they speak with a voice that is almost audible of the men and women and children whose faith and sacrifice caused this building to rise. I could feel the imprint of so many spirits, almost as though they stood with me in reverent awe and rejoicing, filling their eyes and their souls with this glorious sight one more time.

My view blurred and dimmed because the tears kept coming. It was a calm, peaceful night; not even a ruffle of wind disturbed the stillness, and the stars burned like little spiked fires set along the spine of the ebony sky. I closed my eyes and talked with One I had also been neglecting during these last busy days. I spoke haltingly at first, until I began to forget myself, and the feelings and the words to express them started to pour from my heart.

And it was this, in the end, that gave me the power to walk away.

Chapter Twenty-Eight

Portage Bank, Ohio—Erie Canal: June 1838

We left Kirtland before the city was up and people could gawk at our going; Jack insisted on that, and we were all in agreement. There were twenty-five of us altogether, counting the children; nine from our household, seven from the Freys'. Then our number included Aunt Dorothy, old Brother Barrett, Aaron Sessions, Reuben and Claire Lamb, Jack and Emmeline, Thaddeus and Rose.

Dorothy, frail as old lace, rides in the wagon, of course; Thaddeus must, too. He set his lips in a grim line and said nothing when the men carried him in. They have set him on a chair where his legs will have room to stretch without cramping, and yet he has a view out the back of the wagon. He did not thank them; but neither did he speak one word of complaint.

We will hire wagons to use between water transport, and in that Jack has not indulged us, allowing only the necessities of bed and clothing, tents, tools, cooking utensils, and food and but few of those items which are suddenly termed luxuries: a rocking chair, a clock, Nathan's mother's old dresser, paintings to hang on the walls of wherever it is we will live.

I try not to think about that. I must take this one day at a time . . . one hour . . . one turn of the wheels. We will travel five days a week, using Saturdays to rest the animals, bake, hunt, and do our necessary washing. We intend to honor the Sabbath day, even aboard vessels— hold our own modest meetings, sing hymns, and pray. Our company is not too large or cumbersome, so we ought to make good progress. Our route lies along the Ohio–Erie Canal to the Mississippi, which will eventually run to the Missouri, which will carry us most of the way across the state of Missouri. Jack figures, if there are no major setbacks, we ought to complete the journey in eight weeks or less.

Eight weeks. I will be full into this pregnancy by that time! Already my condition shows more than Emmeline's does, being the young skinny thing that she is. I do not mind. I just worry about the well-being of this child growing within me. It will be born in a strange place, a place that is not yet home to us—no matter how many Saints are there. But as long as all is well, as long as all is well, I will try very hard not to complain.

Who can say what each one of us is suffering—the many anguishes which the heart supports and the eye cannot see? Jack took Aunt Dorothy to visit Aurelia's grave and the grave of her sister, Helen, one last time. She longs to remain here and be buried with her loved ones, but such a thing is not possible. Her feelings—Jack's feelings—I can only imagine them. I heard him telling Eugene that some of the graves had been disturbed, and he feared dear Brother Pliny's might be one of them; but I will not tell the others that, not even Georgie. We do not know for certain if it is so, anyway.

Eden had promised her folks that she would come by the last evening to bid them farewell, but she did not keep her word. Brother Frey saddled a horse and rode all over Kirtland looking for her but came home tired, wet, and disappointed. He had hoped against hope that she might be there in the morning. When he had to ride off without seeing his eldest daughter, kissing her, blessing her, it was nearly too much for him to bear. He waited with his hand over his eyes, gazing into the darkness, tears rolling shamelessly down his cheeks. I stood and cried with him, for Peter did not show himself either, and I knew, at least in part, how he felt. I noticed that Rose, although she said nothing, was weeping too.

We have been a somber group, actually, if I think of it. It has been raining all day today. The children are wet and cross, having been largely confined to the wagons and unable to stretch their legs. Little Esther Frey brought her cat along, a descendant of one of Georgie's kittens, and how could any of us say no to that? But how shall we keep track of the little beast during all our comings and goings? Aaron promised he would build an acceptable cage in which to keep it safe while we travel the waterways.

We are camped along the banks of the canal and will take passage tomorrow morning. Then there is really and truly no turning back.

I see the rider approaching but do not recognize him—even when he pulls up and slides to the ground—short-legged and barrel-chested and a bit stouter than the last time I saw him.

Jack cried, "Jonah, you have come to bail me out again! Bless you!" and they wrap their arms round one another.

"Not I, lad, not I! 'Tis a great thing to set eyes on you, lad."

We all crowded close to him then, and he opened his bags and pulled out letters and other small treasures to put into the children's hands. We had a fire going and food left. After he had eaten one plate and then another, he explained his errand—and I learned once more of Jack's ingenuity, his scheming for the good of us all.

"Randolph received your letter and thought it a good idea, a solid plan."

"Not solid," Jack protested. "But a possibility which may in time yield return."

"Be that as it may, have you the deeds to your properties? I am empowered to accept them and give you this in return." He pulled out a thick wallet and began to count bills out. Brother Frey began to bluster, and Claire Lamb turned as white as her sweet dusting flour. Little Jonah Sinclair, amazing Jonah Sinclair, waved away their protests. "Just a little advance against the sales, to keep you going."

I sought out Georgie to talk the matter over.

"So many of our members have had to turn the key and walk away from their homes and properties with no compensation at all." It was a fact of which she did not need to remind me. "Jack's plan is that we sign over our deeds to Randolph. When he comes in as a disinterested, non-Mormon owner, he will be accepted and dealt with fairly. They even hope he can rent out the bakery and the smithy and begin to bring in some profits."

"It sounds—"

"Yes, it sounds too good to be true. But there is nothing to really prevent it from working. And he has put the matter in good hands, using Jonah as his agent."

With that I was certainly quick to agree. I held my breath, trying

261

not to count and figure and project into the future. A little money at a time like this means the difference between starvation and survival, between a hovel and a house, between existing from hand to mouth or really getting by. I was weakened almost to the point of tears by the relief I felt. Only then did I realize how fearful and worried I really had been.

The men were engaged in quiet conversation as we women began to put the children to sleep. There had been much excitement the last few hours, coming at the end of a long day for such little ones. Yet they were restless, unable to understand why they could not go to their own little beds in their own dear, familiar houses.

Emmeline walked from wagon to wagon and sang lullabies to the children. Even my little Nathaniel settled down at the sound of her voice. I had letters in my hand I was eager to read, but I paused for a moment and closed my eyes so that the sweet melody might penetrate my weariness and the tender words lift my heart.

Rosie came to sit beside me; as she leaned against my leg I reached out and placed my hand on her head. So I was there to see it all from the beginning; to see the tall, narrow shadow approach and slowly materialize into a man; to feel Rosie start and lean forward; to hear a strained voice cry, "Rosie! Thank God you are here and all right!" I watched her stumble to her feet and go into the arms that were held out to her. I heard, from my veiled place, a young man and a young woman weep together for joy.

I kept my place for many long minutes, marveling, wondering. When the two let go of one another, with some reluctance, Peter came toward me and dropped down at my feet, wiping a smear of tears from his cheek.

"I have much to explain to you," he said. "I only hope you can forgive me and understand."

I was stupefied. "Where is Georgie?" I said.

"Here I am."

"Good," Peter said, "for you must hear me out, too."

Then came such a tale, such a tale as we could never imagine!

"In the beginning, when I first took the job in Fairport Harbor, I was disaffected. I was afraid of loving, afraid of love's power to hurt. I was confused by the hardships which even the very elect had to suffer—" He grinned lopsidedly. "In short, I was running away."

I realized I was holding my breath. I let it out slowly. "Something changed that?"

"Don't jump ahead!" Georgie scolded.

Peter smiled and went on. "I *did* make the acquaintance of many Mormon haters and apostates. They tried to draw me into their group. *They* made the difference and affected me in precisely the opposite manner from what they had hoped. I found them weak, ill-tempered, and disgusting. They had nothing to recommend them, and their pride and lust for power soon became repulsive to me.

"One night as they were railing against Joseph Smith, such a feeling came over me: an anguish yet accompanied by a tingling throughout my whole body, a sensation almost of joy, and I knew—I knew beyond any doubting, Esther, that he was a prophet of God.

"I stood and denounced the lot and said that if I never laid eyes on them in this life or the next, that would suit my mind well. I thought I could simply walk out and that would be that. I could not have been more mistaken."

He looked down at his hands that were clenched into fists and flexed them out again. I felt a shiver run over me and wondered if the fire had burned low.

"Three of them followed me back to my room and gave me such a beating as I have never had in my life."

I gasped and clenched my lips tight lest I cry out.

"They named off everyone I know, everyone I care for and promised me that if I turned against them they would begin to pick my friends off, one by one. 'Slow and painful,' one of them grinned. 'We'll make 'em suffer if you do even one small thing to hurt us and our cause.'

"I could not protest, I could not beg, I could not reason. They just kept repeating, 'it's too bad for you, boy. You know too much; it's too bad for you.'

"I don't think I slept for three nights. I was incensed, and I was frightened. At length the anger won out. I wanted to get word to Jack but couldn't figure out how best to do it. At length, in desperation, I decided to pray. The very next day he came, on some pretext, to visit me, and I told him all."

He grinned unexpectedly. "I hear you have come to appreciate

Jack's cleverness and his boldness." I rolled my eyes. "We discussed it a time or two and prayed on it before he came up with a plan."

Jack came up behind us. "Nothing clever about it and requiring boldness only on Peter's part." I could hear the lilt, almost of pleasure, in his voice. "We merely determined to serve the blackguards right by making Peter a turncoat or in other words, a spy."

"In the beginning it seemed to make sense. We even decided that if it got too hot for me, I would take off for Missouri and wait for the rest of you there. That way I could tell you what was going on—I could tell Rosie—"

I could imagine too well the existence he was beginning to describe to us; I felt myself recoil from it in pity and horror.

"But the deeper I got into their organization, the more I found out. Week after week, month after month I was able to warn people, save property, save lives. It seemed cruel and selfish to stop, so I kept putting it off . . . and putting it off . . ."

"I can understand all of it," I said, "except Rosie. What you did to her was so cruel. Was there no way you could tell her, even an inkling?"

"And risk her life more!"

There was an anguish in his voice that brought a hush over the assembly. Rose covered her face with her hands.

"They knew what would hurt the most, and they threatened her especially. Now and again, when they suspected me of weakening, they would give me little warnings. It was their men who killed Pliny." He spoke the words with such bitter self-accusation that I put a hand out to steady him. "And there was a time or two—do you remember being followed, Rose?"

"Yes, once in particular." Her tone was carefully expressionless.

"We posted men to watch her and the place on the hill day and night." Jack wanted to hurry the painful telling. "*Boys,* actually, most of the time. Cost us a pretty sum!" He chuckled under his breath, and I tried to smile in response. "Well, anyway, we can sort out the particulars later—take them to pieces and marvel over them. Suffice it to say, we got Peter away with one last ruse, and he did not dare join us until the very last minute, for his safety and ours. Yes, Peter played his part nobly through to the end, with one tiny exception." The amused laugh came again.

Georgie's quick mind was with them. "He could not let Rosie

marry Hiram Morley. And there was no way he could leave her behind, without Jack's protection."

"That's right. Jack talked her into putting Hiram off until we all got to Missouri. But especially since Thaddeus wouldn't budge, she refused to come. That is part of what was explained to the both of them the evening before we left."

That is why she went into his arms with such an aching cry of longing! The realization shuddered through me. I could picture Peter waiting, watching from the shadows, his melancholy spirit drawn out by her music, by the sound of her voice. *He has paid a high price for her. He has paid with his heart's blood and won her fairly. He is worth yearning over. He is worth believing in.*

❦

Exhaustion! Eugene materialized from somewhere and gave me his arm to help me rise. All my limbs were stiff and achy. "I will rub your back to help you relax," he said, planting a kiss, in the darkness, somewhere between my cheek and my chin. Peter and Rosie had melted into the soft darkness somewhere. As Jack walked by I reached for his arm and detained him a moment. I was almost asleep on my feet, but I managed to say, "I am proud of you, Jack. God bless you for your goodness—and for your cleverness, too." I could feel his grin, though I could not see it. A fleeting image of his weak, lackluster mother and his cruel father flashed before me, and I blinked it away. "Aurelia is well pleased with you—I know she is."

Even my voice was sleepy. He leaned close and whispered, "Bless you, Esther. You have always stood by me and understood."

❦

I want to weep. So many emotions are struggling through me, and I want to weep every one away and be a clean, empty vessel, not over-crowded with complexities as I now am. I tuck my letters into my bosom—they will have to wait until morning—and lean on Eugene's arm heavily as he helps me into the wagon, where a bed is waiting for me.

❦

Yesterday's rain has cooled things, and the morning is fresh and inviting. The water is churning, the boat is poised for her journey, and hope as exhilarating as excitement beats in my veins. Randolph has written:

> You cannot go so far as to escape us! Our love will follow you, and there will not be a day the sun sets on that we do not think of you.

Georgie was right! Our sweet Phoebe writes:

> Go with my blessing. Someday I will follow you, or so the Spirit seems to whisper. I will not lose faith, not if you remember your prayers for me, not if you continue to love me.

Somehow a sense of completeness, of rightness has come at last. I feel better this morning and stronger. I draw the clean air into my lungs. My baby boy cuddles his head beneath my chin; I can feel his breath rise and fall with mine. I am where I want to be. I have so much that I love within the reach of my eye. My life has been filled with blessings enough to overwhelm me—and there is so much yet to come.

I wrote down these words the Prophet Joseph said and have committed them to memory. I say them over in my mind as I watch Eugene and Lavinia playing and Rosie and Peter walking hand in hand onto the boat.

"And I know that the cloud will burst, and Satan's kingdom be laid in ruins, with all his black designs; and that the Saints will come forth like gold seven times tried in the fire, being made perfect through sufferings and temptations, and that the blessings of heaven and earth will be multiplied upon their heads."

He once spoke much the same words to me, concerning Georgie and Nathan. I will be happy to see Brother Joseph again. I am happy—filled with happiness this minute—to be part of the Father's design, even a little thread in the beautiful, many-colored fabric of this glorious kingdom which he is allowing us, his children, to help create.

266